Drowned
by Deceit

Drowned by Deceit

The innocent victims of atrocious crimes

SARAH LYSAGHT

Elusive Spirit Publishing

Disclaimer: Drowned by Deceit / Born to Deceive is a work of fiction loosely based on historical events. All the characters are fictitious and exist only in the imagination of the author. Any resemblance to actual persons, living or dead, is purely coincidental.

Warning: This book contains passages some readers may find distressing including sexual violence, child abuse, alcohol abuse, suicide and murder.

First published in the United Kingdom in 2021 by
Elusive Spirit Publishing

Produced by The Choir Press

ISBN 978-0-9571850-3-6

Dedication

For my indulgent husband, Tony

and our children
who never complained when Covid struck,
tolerated three national lockdowns,
accepted they must wear face masks and endure numerous
restrictions,
hardly complained when they were forced to miss out on significant
birthday celebrations,
vital educational opportunities and visiting family and friends
yet
when I shared with them my ideas for two new novels
behaved as if the world was about to end.

I love you all dearly.

Acknowledgements

Mum, thank you so much. You were there for me again, for the endless proof reading at the early stages and handing out helpful advice.

Many thanks to Den, without your positive support I may never have written the sequel to this story. You encouraged me out of my comfort zone to explore my darker side.

While writing this novel, I continued to research my own genealogy and discovered I had family in Norway, also with a keen interest in family history. My sincere thanks to Linda Augland and Karina Huseby, for all your kind words of encouragement throughout. You can finally read the books you have so patiently waited for me to finish.

My sincere thanks to Tessa and Gary for giving me a bed for a couple of nights while researching in Portsmouth.

My appreciation must go to the many services who have assisted in the research for this book.
Flintshire Records Office
Kent and Medway History Centre and Archives
Surrey History Centre
Hampshire Archives and Local Studies
Portsmouth History Centre
The British Library APAC Reference Service
RAPC Regimental Association
Prudential Archives
Specialists who helped me to understand the characteristics and mannerisms of my main characters.

Finally, a huge thank you again to Miles, Naomi, Adrian and Rachel from Choir Press for getting my books to fruition. As always, your suggestions and advice are invaluable.

Selina

⎯⎯◁◦▷⎯⎯

Selina had lived in Calcutta all her life. She was a woman with British citizenship who felt at home in India, possibly more than the natives did at this time. Her home was comfortable, close to the local amenities, and it was where she had brought up her five children.

"I just wish he would hurry up and die," Selina sobbed. "For all our sake."

"I completely agree, Selina. No man should have to go through what he is. It's such a terrible illness. It takes away a man's dignity," observed Frank.

**

Selina was well known and highly regarded in the town. She had trained as a nurse and had lost count as to the number of people she had helped nurse back to health over the years. She appeared to know everyone in Calcutta and always had a story to tell about the families she had come into contact with. She never forgot a name or a face, and this only made her more amenable to the people she looked after.

Selina adored Calcutta, with its vibrant, busy markets which sold an array of fruit and vegetables, displayed at ground level for all to see. An abundance of herbs and spices resting in large jars—rich in colour, smell and taste—were readily available at these marketplaces, which were always so busy. The people were just as colourful as the food, with their mix of religions, cultures and skin colour. It was normal to see goats wandering freely through the dusty streets in search of anything to eat, and occasionally one might see an elephant being led through the town. India's festivals and celebrations were exciting to observe. Selina would always stop what she was doing to stand and watch the exuberant displays of music and dance.

Selina's husband, Sydney, had been born in India to British parents in 1870 and married Selina in Calcutta when he was twenty-two. Following a career in the Indian Army, Sydney had worked for many years as an eastern representative for a woollen firm in Calcutta. He'd often travelled to England with his work and still owned a small amount of property there. His firm used the fleeces of mountain goats, raised in the colder regions of India, from which they spun wool. This wool was then used to make carpets, rugs, shawls and blankets, which Sydney organised to be shipped, primarily to England.

Selina had given Sydney five children, all of whom had been baptised at St John's Church in Calcutta. When her children had been young, it had been Selina who had spent most of this time with them. Sydney worked hard all day, and when he arrived home at night, all he wanted to do was eat then go to bed. He became stuck in a cycle of long working hours and frequent drinking sessions, which he claimed helped him to relax, resulting in him having less and less contact with his family. On occasion, his temper would flair and he would lash out at Selina and their children. It was during these times that Frank had been summoned. Sydney had a great deal of respect for Frank, and thankfully for Selina her husband would usually listen to Frank's advice.

Frank had been introduced to the family some years ago, and they had all got to know him well. He had grown up in England with his family, who had always lived in the London area, but he had moved to India around 1911 and found a job in customs at the port of Fort William, where he also joined the Calcutta Volunteer Battery. He and Sydney had met through their work. Sydney used the port of Calcutta regularly for transporting his company's produce and Frank was a preventive officer in the Calcutta customs, so their paths had crossed regularly, and over the years they had become firm friends.

Frank's relationship with the family was unusual. He had no family of his own in India and mostly kept himself to himself, but Sydney's family appeared to like his company, especially Selina, who freely opened her home up to him. This was most likely because over the years, Sydney had not treated her as well as he might have done and Frank had often stepped in to nudge his friend and remind and encourage him to treat his wife with respect.

After having three sons, Selina had quickly fallen pregnant again. This time she had given birth to a daughter, much to Sydney's delight. Ellen had always been Sydney's favourite child. He had formed an instant bond with their daughter, far more easily than Selina ever had. She had put this down to her always feeling exhausted because of her growing family's demands, but if the truth be known, Selina preferred her sons. Ellen was the only girl, so it stood to reason that her father would be more protective over her and want to keep her close. As she had grown older, the pair were almost inseparable.

At times, Selina had felt rather envious of the relationship her husband had with their daughter. He would never hear anything bad said about the girl. Ellen could do no wrong; Sydney would always blame Selina if anything went wrong. So over the years, Selina and her daughter had grown further and further apart.

While Selina had thrown herself into her work as a nurse, Ellen had taken over much of her mother's role within the family home. She would often cook for the family, carry out most of the household chores and was the person her father and brothers would seek out to spend time with, as Selina was always too busy somewhere else.

Six years after having a daughter, and quite by mistake, Selina had a fourth son. She and Sydney had no time for this child. Fred was an inconvenience to them both. Selina believed her husband saw Fred as an intruder. He hadn't ever asked her as much, but she suspected that he thought the boy might not be his. Fred appeared to irritate Sydney, who felt he often got in the way of him being able to spend time with his only daughter.

With their elder sons working all day, their daughter being the apple of her father's eye and Selina rarely at home, Sydney often took out his frustrations on Fred. Fred spent most of his childhood in constant fear of his father, as he could be an unpredictable bully. He learnt from an early age to conceal his feelings, refusing to let anyone in. Selina seemed unaware this had left her youngest son feeling isolated and had undoubtedly affected his self-esteem. Selina was well aware her son would often take himself off somewhere to be alone, creeping back into the house late at night. No one seemed to care enough about where he'd been or what he'd been up to. His mother had no time for his antics.

Selina knew Frank had tried his best with her youngest son. He had noticed Fred becoming more and more withdrawn, so he had attempted to include him in things whenever he was visiting the house. But the boy was having none of it. On one occasion, Frank had found a young dog wandering the streets on his way over to Selina's house, so he'd picked it up and taken it with him, thinking that Fred might want to look after the creature. When Frank arrived at the house, he'd called Fred in from the back garden and presented the boy with his gift. Fred accepted the pup and promptly took the animal outside. Frank and Selina thought he had gone off to play with it, but Selina was later to discover that Fred had forgotten about the dog and it had drowned in the fast-flowing stream which ran along the bottom of their property.

Frank had also helped Fred to evade getting into trouble with the police on a number of occasions during his schooldays. Frank never informed Sydney about these incidents, as he knew his friend would beat the child. He had also managed to conceal many of these events from Selina after the first couple of times when she had thrashed Fred for stealing a teacher's purse and again for stealing food from a local shop. Following these occasions, Frank had insisted the police notify him first. That way if Fred did anything again, which he did, Frank could deal with him in a more appropriate way. Frank had tried to reason with the boy on numerous occasions, but struggled to get through to Fred.

Selina knew there had been one occasion when Frank had come very close to hitting Fred himself, when her son had been caught with his hands around another child's throat. He had pinned a young boy to the floor of the classroom, and all because he had playfully hidden his pencil. The teacher, and undoubtedly the young boy, had been pretty shaken up by Fred's behaviour that day and Frank had been forced to threaten Fred with his belt. Fortunately, he had not had to follow through with his threat, and for a time Fred's behaviour had improved. There had been other occasions when she had questioned Fred's behaviour, but he always had a reasonable and believable explanation for his mother.

***

Selina's first three sons had all left for England as soon as they were old enough, urged to do so by their father. This was something he encouraged all of his children to do. He felt it was important for their futures to experience what life was like in England. Her husband had always told them how very different it was in England and often shared his own experiences with them, amplifying their curiosity enough for them to want to witness the country for themselves.

Alex, Ralf and Joseph had all left India, one year after the other, having already established themselves as clerks, but it was Alex who was the first to join the British Army in London in 1912. Ralf followed at the outbreak of the war in 1914, and Joseph as soon as he was old enough in 1916. Calcutta, West Bengal, had been their home for the first eighteen years of their lives, and one by one, encouraged by their father, they had left their parents to travel overseas.

Although Selina's three sons wrote to her as regularly as they could, she missed them all terribly. It physically hurt her to think about her boys and what horrors they would witness during the war, but her main concern lay with Joseph. He had always been a sensitive child, and she worried he would not cope well being away from home.

As a child, Joseph had been forced to show great courage when his father had launched into one of his rants. Over the years, Selina had witnessed a deterioration in Joseph's spirit and realised Sydney's behaviour had greatly affected him. Sydney could be a bully where his sons were concerned, but she believed he only wanted the best for them and it was his way of pushing them to achieve. However, Joseph was a gentle child and often found his father's character overbearing. Alex and Ralf were far better equipped to handle their father's moods, often giving back as good as they got.

Her daughter, Ellen, loved her elder brothers a great deal. They had always been there for her and watched over her, protecting her when she was little. But, like her mother, it had been Joseph with whom she was closest, and she had missed him terribly when he had left. They wrote regularly, and Joseph had promised that as soon as the war was over he would return to India and escort her to England to show her

5

the sights. They had made many plans in their letters to one another, which went back and forth regularly.

The war had not started long when Selina received news from her eldest son, Alex, who had been injured and forced to leave the army prematurely. Her relief was minimal, as her two other sons continued with their journeys. As the war persisted, Selina had her two younger children to occupy her time when she was at home, and this went some way to taking her mind off her elder sons.

However, the situation at home for Selina only worsened. Still relatively young, Ellen and Fred both clung to their mother, while the uncertainty caused by the war continued year after year. Selina detested this weakness in her children. In an attempt to toughen them up, she withdrew almost all of her limited love for them. Fred turned to Ellen for support, but she too appeared to reject him in favour of her father's attentions. This made Fred withdraw even further, but Selina was too busy to notice.

Much to Selina's horror, Frank too had enlisted and joined the war, leaving Calcutta in July 1915. He did not return until September 1917, after being badly injured. Selina was delighted to have him back in Calcutta. She vowed to nurse him back to full health after his traumatic ordeal, at further cost to her children. Selina and Frank had known one another for a number of years, and Selina had always enjoyed his company. Gossip was rife at this time around Frank, Sydney and Selina's relationship. Selina had been embarrassed by the local gossip. Rumours quickly spread that perhaps Frank and Selina were more than just friends, but people had little evidence upon which to base these assumptions.

Ellen and Fred had never known any other life than the one in India, so when letters arrived from their brothers on leave in England, they sparked a desire to learn more about this country their parents had often called home. Ellen had never understood why they called it that, for as far as she was aware, both her parents had been born in India and never lived in England.

"Why do you call it home, Father, if you have never lived there?" Selina could recall her daughter asking one day.

"Oh, I don't know," replied Sydney. "I suppose it's because England is where my family were from. Both your mother and I have always thought of England as our homeland."

"Do you think you will ever go there again, Father?" Ellen dared to enquire further.

"I might, if this war ever ends," he'd replied.

When news of her eldest son's marriage reached the family in 1917, Selina found it difficult to feel any emotion. She felt little connection with England any longer, and certainly no desire to visit it. She felt almost estranged from her sons. The war had been going on for too long. The only son she worried about still was Joseph. It frightened her how much she missed him.

Joseph had joined the 13th Battalion Rifle Brigade, serving most of the war in France. He had come home on leave during Christmas 1917 and spent two weeks at home before returning to duty. He had been injured a couple of times before this, having to spend time in a military hospital, and then in the March had written to say he was again in hospital, this time with influenza. His health at this time had worried Selina terribly.

As news of the end of the war reached Selina, so too did a letter from Joseph. His correspondence was difficult for her to read. He told of how he had been shot at and still had some gun shrapnel lodged in a wound on his right hand. He expressed a wish to his mother that she should not worry and that he was quite all right and would write again soon. He asked that she let Ellen know he was quite well and not to worry her with his news, but to tell her he would be home soon in order for them to travel back to England together.

Ralf too had been injured and had suffered, but had also shown great bravery in France as the war was nearing its conclusion and was to be honoured for his actions. Both Selina and Sydney were very proud of their sons' achievements before and during the war, but neither were able to share their feelings emotionally with their children.

***

When the war was finally over, there was some joy in Selina's home as the family adjusted to the news. However, this was short-lived. Waiting for news of Ralf and Joseph's return from war was troubling Selina. She did not know why, but she suddenly felt a great despondency. No matter how many times she told herself it was all in her mind and her boys had made it through and it was all over now, it was no use. Her feelings of hopelessness would not go away.

Then it arrived. The telegram. At first only some of the words jumped out at her: 'deeply regret to inform you', 'Joseph' and 'died of wounds'. She fell to the ground. She made a noise an animal might make as it knows it's going to die. Her beautiful son! Joseph was dead.

This devastating news hit the whole family hard. Ellen was as distraught as her mother. Sydney did his best, but he felt as though the wind had been knocked out of him. Fred and Ellen had no idea how to make things better. Things would never be the same again for Selina, and this was when Frank had once more stepped in and held the family together.

It was March 1919 before Ralf left the army and returned to London. He had written to his mother, explaining that his brother Alex had told him about Joseph. He was deeply saddened by the news. His family in India were relieved to discover that Ralf was well, but Selina showed little emotion over his correspondence.

In the autumn of this year, Selina was obligated to write to her sons to inform them that their father was seriously ill. Sydney's health had deteriorated recently, and Selina had thought her husband's demise was due to them having lost Joseph, but the doctors diagnosed him with tuberculous enteritis.

Frank was there again to support Selina as she attempted to seek medical help for Sydney. The doctors said Sydney had probably ingested bacteria through some contaminated food some years earlier. There was little they could do for him. He was going to die, but they weren't sure when.

As her father's illness worsened, Ellen spent more and more time with him in his room, often refusing to come out, even for meals. Her father was unable to eat much, and that made *her* not want to eat. It seemed only Fred was able to get through to his sister during this time, encouraging her to walk with him to the market for supplies then insisting she eat something to keep up her strength before she returned to their father. She would not listen to her mother.

Selina was forced to observe her forty-nine-year-old husband become thinner and weaker. He was in a great deal of pain, and there seemed to be little she could do to ease it. He had been forced to give up his work, and Selina too had reduced her hours, as she was now needed at home to nurse her husband. The situation at home, with the reduction of their two incomes, also added to Selina's pressures.

"Before Sydney loses control of all of his faculties, it is important I speak with him," Frank told Selina one day. The two men had been talking for quite some hours before Frank finally left Sydney's room in search of Selina. When he reappeared, Frank looked as though he'd had a weight lifted from him.

"Is everything all right?" enquired Selina.

"I hope so," replied Frank.

"What's that supposed to mean? What have you two been plotting?"

"Sit down, Selina. I need to talk to you."

Selina quickly sat, as she saw the urgency in Frank's eyes. "Is he dead?" she asked, terrified of the answer.

"No. He's not dead."

"I just wish he would hurry up and die," she sobbed. "For all our sake."

"I completely agree, Selina. No man should have to go through what he is. It's such a terrible illness. It takes away a man's dignity," observed Frank.

A moment of silence sat heavily between them, then Frank continued. "I've just had a long talk with Sydney. And he's in agreement."

"About what?" interrupted Selina.

"He has agreed I can marry you. If you want me to, that is," he added quickly.

"Marry me? But, how can you? I'm already married."

"We can arrange a special licence which will name you as a presumptive widow."

Selina needed a moment to gather her thoughts. "Sydney has agreed to this?" she asked.

"Yes. You can ask him if you don't believe me."

"I do believe you; but how long have you two been plotting this?"

"It's not like that, Selina. Come on. You know me better than that. I see someone I care very much about slipping further away from his family on a daily basis and his wife in turmoil about how she will pay for his funeral, never mind how she will manage after he has gone. It seems the most practical thing to do, and Sydney agrees."

"Practical?"

"Yes, realistic."

"I know what practical means, thank you, Frank."

"Sorry," he sighed. "I only want to be able to help."

Eventually, Selina broke the silence which had filled the room again. "No. I'm sorry. You're right. I should be thanking you, not criticizing you. If Sydney is in agreement, then so am I."

She had never seen Frank look so happy.

"I will make all the necessary arrangements," Frank insisted. "You and Sydney can count on it. Don't worry about a thing."

"Thank you, Frank. Thank you."

***

Selina and Frank married on 10 December 1919. There were just two of them at the registry office. Ellen was at home and Fred at school. In fact, they would not learn of their mother's marriage until after their father's death. Selina and Frank had thought it better that way. Frank moved into the house on Park Lane, Calcutta, watching on as his friend gradually deteriorated over the coming months; all the time his feelings for Selina growing in strength.

As her husband reached his final weeks, Selina stopped her children from seeing him. He had lost control of all his bodily functions, and she believed it would have been too much for them to bear. Sydney had lost so much weight, that it was difficult to still see the man she had first fallen in love with. She did not want her children to witness or remember their father in this way.

Ellen accepted her mother's wish, although it pained her terribly not to see her father. Fred, on the other, hand sneaked into his father's room on many occasions during his final weeks. His curiosity had got the better of him. It seemed he wanted to see his father in this weakened state in order he be able to tell him about all the things he wanted to do with his life. But his father had no idea Fred was even there, and this frustrated and disturbed Fred further.

Sydney hung on for as long as he could, taking his last breath in June 1920. Selina and Frank had him buried the very next day in Calcutta's cemetery. On this occasion Ellen and Fred were allowed to attend, and this was also when their mother told them she and Frank were now married. Ellen had felt numb as her mother shared this news with her and Fred. She'd had no time in which to grieve for her father, yet she was now expected to accept a new one. Fred showed no emotion over the death of his father or to his mother's news.

Within the house, Selina and Frank experienced very mixed feelings, but most of these were of relief, for Sydney was no longer suffering. But Sydney had died without knowing what had happened to his son Joseph, and this greatly bothered Selina. It would be another year before she would receive all the information regarding her son's death, and only then would she realise Sydney had been better off not knowing.

Selina's life had dramatically changed, and she knew it would only be a matter of time before her daughter would be the next to leave India for England. Two of her sons already lived there, and Ellen had expressed that wish too. She knew her husband's death had only caused to bring this event further forward in Ellen's mind. Selina had known that Joseph and Ellen had often talked about travelling to England together, and now, as that was no longer possible, she assumed Ellen would wish to fulfil their travel plans in his memory. In reality Ellen couldn't stand to be around her mother another minute longer.

Selina knew Alex and Ralf would look after their sister if she chose to stay in England, but she hoped her daughter would one day return to her and Frank in India. If she chose not to return, Selina suspected Fred would soon try to follow in his sister's footsteps. That would leave her and Frank alone together in India. Would Frank wish to return to the country of his birth one day? She wasn't sure. All she was sure of was that *she* had no such desire.

Mary

———◁◦▷———

The SS *Orsova* was one of a quintet of 12,000 GRT liners which all began with the letter 'O' and were owned by the Orient Steam Navigation Company Ltd. She had been built in Clydebank, Scotland, in 1909, and since then had endured a colourful history. Originally built to carry passengers between Australia and London and to do trade with the commonwealth, she was requisitioned during the First World War and turned into a troop ship. In March 1917 she was torpedoed by a German submarine in the English Channel. The torpedo penetrated the port side of the engine room and caused considerable loss of life. She was towed back to Plymouth Harbour, where she was eventually repaired, resuming her service with the Orient Line in November 1919. During her lifetime, she would be described as a floating palace, making seventy journeys back and forth from London to Australia and carrying more than 70,000 passengers.

The *Orsova* had started this particular journey, in early February 1927, from Sydney, Australia. She had hugged the Australian coast, stopping at Melbourne, Adelaide and Freemantle, picking up passengers, cargo and mail. Next she crossed the Indian Ocean to Sri Lanka, stopping at Colombo, and that had been where Mary had seen the man embark. For the remainder of her journey, via the Suez Canal, the *Orsova* would also stop at Port Said, Naples, Gibraltar, Plymouth and, finally, Tilbury, London.

Her master for this journey was Evan Cameron, an experienced seaman. He had registered as an apprentice in 1895, aged fifteen years, and signed an indenture bounding him for four years to Thomas Shute and Company of Liverpool. During this time, he had mastered his trade, then working his way through the ranks of lieutenant, commander and, eventually, captain. He now had full responsibility for the *Orsova*.

The *Orsova*'s eight-cylinder quad expansion steam engine could reach a speed of eighteen knots, taking just over six weeks to reach her destination on this occasion, and passengers on board could enjoy her splendid facilities and well-organised activities. The *Orsova* had a substantial number of crew on this trip but was carrying a fraction of her 1,100-passenger capacity, so there was plenty of space for everyone on board. Once out at sea, passengers were able to take part in a number of activities, from wheelbarrow and three-legged races along the promenades to fancy-dress events. They could watch humorous sketches and enjoy whist-drive tournaments, dances and piano solos inside the ship's lounges. Adults and children alike were kept well entertained throughout the journey.

She had five decks, A to E. Each deck offered something a little different, depending upon whether you were travelling first, second or third class.

A Deck was known as the games deck. The wireless operators worked from this deck, and it was also where the officers' quarters could be found. Normally only first-class passengers were allowed on this deck. It was also where the twenty lifeboats were stored.

B Deck accommodated a number of cabins for first-class passengers, along with ladies' and gents' lavatories, complete with baths. The larger cabins, which had their own washing facilities, were known as state rooms. The Veranda Café, a smoking room, shop, barber's shop, drawing room and lounge could also be found on this level. These rooms were lavishly decorated and well equipped with complete relaxation and comfort in mind for the traveller. If one desired to walk around its promenade deck seven and a half times, this would be ample exercise; it being equal to one mile.

Decks C, D and E were used mainly for third-class passengers and decorated in a more modest way, using everyday furniture. However, there were also a number of larger, special state rooms on C Deck. Accommodation across these three decks included a smoking room and bar, two lounges, two dining rooms, a doctor's room, a nurse's room, two purser's rooms, many smaller cabins, ladies' and gents' bathroom facilities and smaller promenade decks. Each deck gave stair and lift access to the other decks.

Mary had boarded the ship in Australia with her mother. They were travelling third class to England. Whenever the ship stopped at a new port, Mary demanded that her mother take her out onto the deck, so that she could watch the new passengers as they climbed the boarding ladders. As Mary hung over the edge of the deck rail, safely supported by her mother, she was on the lookout for new friends with whom she could play for the duration of the trip.

Mary was friendly, kind and appreciative of others. She was extremely confident and outgoing for someone so young, and people took an immediate liking to her because she was always so happy. She made friends easily. She was six years old, and although there were plenty of other children on board, only a small number of these were girls, and even fewer were around the same age as her.

"There, Mother. Look!" Mary exclaimed. "She looks nice." She had spotted a young girl of similar age, wearing smart clothes, boarding in Colombo with her parents.

"Yes, darling, she does. But I suspect she is a first-class passenger. I don't think we will see much of her." Mary sighed. She couldn't understand why people travelling together on the same ship never mixed or spoke to one another. It was all rather silly and confusing for her. Then she spotted someone else, shrieked and pointed. "Look, Mother, there's another girl!"

"Darling, can you please stop wriggling so much. I'm going to drop you if you keep getting this excited every time you see another child."

"She looks nice, don't you think?"

"Yes, Mary. She looks nice."

This child was also travelling with her mother and two elder sisters. "Do you think she'll be in a cabin near ours?"

"She might be, darling. We shall just have to wait and see."

Mary waved frantically at her possible new friend, but the other six-year-old was unaware she was even there. However, there was a man a number of passengers behind this family who had spotted Mary waving, and he began to wave back. He stopped waving but continued to look up at her intermittently and smile as he made his way along the boarding ladder. Mary smiled back but soon lost interest in the man, as he was not a potential playmate.

The man boarded the ship at Colombo. He was twenty-two years of age; a British citizen born in India. He had left behind his mother, but was travelling to England to visit his sister and brothers whom he had not seen for a number of years. He had been planning his trip for some time.

The man was smartly dressed, and although he was travelling third class, could easily have been mistaken for a first-class passenger. He wore a narrow-cut suit with a tie. A watch chain could be seen as his jacket flapped open in the breeze, and his dark hair was cut short, parted at the side, smoothed down with oil and swept back over the top of his head. His well-trimmed moustache looked flawless, a cigarette protruded from his mouth and one could be forgiven for ever-so-briefly being distracted by his considerably large nose. He carried a Homburg hat in his right hand, along with a large suitcase with the initials 'FA'. He used his left hand to intermittently remove his cigarette from his mouth, but quickly replaced it to continue to use this hand to hold onto the ladder rail. His shoes were black lace-ups and polished to perfection. He walked with an air of authority, and anyone who did not know him could not have been blamed for thinking he was someone important.

The man's business was in insurance, which he neither liked nor disliked. It was a job and paid enough money until a time when he could do better for himself. He knew he was meant for bigger and better things and that these would come to him in time.

The insurance man was allocated a cabin on D Deck, towards the stern. He quickly made his way there and unpacked his few belongings. Once settled into his cabin, he went for a walk around the ship to familiarise himself with its accommodation. He used the stairs just outside his cabin, near to the dining saloon, and climbed to C Deck. Passing a number of larger cabins than his, he arrived at a set of doors which took him out onto the promenade deck. He walked towards the bow of the ship, past the doctor's cabin and dispensary, peered in through the lounge windows then continued towards the smoking room and bar. It was here he stayed for a good many hours until the ship was well out to sea. He enjoyed a game of cards with a number of other gentlemen on board then left for the dining saloon in search of a meal.

***

Mary was delighted to discover that the child she had spotted coming aboard was indeed staying not far from her and her mother's cabin on D Deck, near the bow. She asked her mother if she could speak to the other child. They quickly introduced themselves, becoming good friends, and their mothers did the same. Both mothers were travelling without their husbands and with their children, so they too were glad of one another's company. Over the coming days, the two families became well acquainted. They would soon discover that they would enjoy one another's company a great deal throughout the trip.

The girls spent much of the time in each other's cabins. Margaret's cabin was close to the small promenade deck, and Mary was allowed to leave her cabin, walk along the corridor beside the lavatories, through some double doors and along another corridor to Margaret's cabin. Their mothers had told them they should always stay together and never wander around the ship by themselves.

Margaret's two elder sisters, who were fifteen and twelve, were on occasion asked to look after the two younger girls in order that their mothers might be able to enjoy some of the ship's entertainment. While on board, the two women experienced a piano solo, an evening of song and a night of comedy sketches.

The two families' mealtimes were mostly spent together in the dining saloons on D Deck. The party of six, two adults and four children, would share a table each day, and the staff allocated to their table always found them gregarious and easy to please. Never did they complain about anything and they always showed their appreciation to the staff.

Mary was a ray of sunshine on board the ship. Her laughter and mischief were contagious among the other passengers. There was an elderly gentleman who had taken a liking to Mary and her friend Margaret. He introduced himself to the girls' mothers and commented on how well behaved they were. Both women noticed and commented upon the nasty cough the gentleman had and suggested he seek some assistance from the ship's doctor. He thanked them and they only saw him once more in the dining saloon after that.

There was another gentleman the families took a liking to. He sat near them on a number of occasions at dinner and performed some magic tricks for the girls, which they thought were marvellous. He told them he worked for a theatre company in London and had recently been to Australia for a well-deserved holiday. However, he had missed his trade and enjoyed using this opportunity to be able to entertain his fellow passengers.

Mary's mother was beginning to find the attention her daughter was attracting quite embarrassing. So many of the passengers had commented on her. It seemed these comments were almost continuous: "Isn't she a delight" or "You must be very proud" or "Such a kind and happy little girl".

Mary and her new friend, Margaret, had attracted even more attention when they had taken part in some organised games on C Deck during their second week on board. The pair had worked so well as a team that they had won the wheelbarrow and three-legged races. During the tug-of-war contest, a growing crowd had gathered to watch, and many people were cheering for their team. Mary and Margaret had given it everything they'd got, and just as they had won the struggle, they both tripped over each other's feet, sending the whole of their team collapsing into a heap on the deck, and the crowd let out a roar of laughter.

As Mary lifted herself up and brushed herself down, she noticed the man she had seen embarking the week before. He was staring straight at her and smiling. His demeanour stopped her in her tracks, and in that split second, he waved at her again. She smiled and briefly waved back, before turning away to help Margaret get up. When she looked back afterwards, he had gone.

The following day, while in the dining saloon, Mary noticed the same man again. He was walking towards their table. She watched him as he seated himself just across from them into the only empty chair around that table. He quickly said hello to everyone seated beside him and then Mary caught his eye. She flashed him a smile.

"Hello, young lady. Are you enjoying your meal?"

"Yes, thank you," Mary beamed.

"What are you having to eat this dinner time?" he enquired further. By now both mothers were intrigued as to how Mary knew the young man. Margaret's mother whispered into her daughter's ear, "Do you know who the man is?" Margaret shook her head.

"We're having roast turkey and stuffing today," replied Mary.

"And would you recommend it?"

"Oh yes. It's very delicious."

The man noticed the look of interest upon the two women's faces and apologised.

"I'm sorry if I have interrupted your meal."

"That's quite all right," reassured Mary's mother. "How do you know my daughter?" she enquired.

"Well, I don't really. We waved to each other over a week ago now, when I was climbing aboard, and then I was watching the tug-of-war the other day. Your daughter's team caused quite a commotion. But I haven't been formally introduced to her."

Mary held out her hand and politely announced, "I'm Mary. Pleased to meet you." Her mother had stopped being surprised by Mary's self-confidence and directness a long time ago. She envied her daughter's relaxed attitude to life.

"Very good to meet you at last, Mary." The man took her hand and shook it gently. "And this is your mother?" he asked her. Mary nodded. The man got up out of his chair and, leaning over Mary, he offered his hand to her mother. "How do you do, madam?"

"Very well, thank you," she replied, taking hold of his hand to shake it.

"Well, I don't wish to disturb you any further, so I shall let you get on with your meal." And with that, the man returned to his chair and began a conversation with a waiter.

Mary grinned at her mother and continued with her meal.

It wasn't until later in the comfort of her own cabin, just before she fell asleep, did Mary's mother realise the young man had not told them his name.

***

Some days later Mary asked her mother if she could go and call on Margaret. "Of course, dear, but make sure you go straight there."

"I will," she called back as she disappeared through the cabin door.

Mary walked along the corridor and through the double doors into the next corridor, but this time, instead of going directly to her friend's cabin, she decided she would like to go out onto the promenade deck. The sun was bright, and she could see it shining through the glass panels in the door to the outside. As she walked through these doors, she looked up and the sun blinded her. It was warm on the deck, even though there was a slight breeze. Some passengers were enjoying the fresh air and warming sunshine as they sat in a number of deckchairs which had been placed upon the deck earlier that day.

In the far-right-hand corner Mary spotted the man again. He was sitting in a deckchair, smoking a cigarette. She caught his eye and he waved and stood up. She felt compelled to go over to him to say hello. As she approached him, he asked her, "Where are you off to, Mary, on this glorious sunny day?"

"I'm going to my friend's cabin," she answered.

"Oh yes? And where is that?"

Pointing, she replied, "Back through the doors over there, but first I wanted to see if it was warm outside."

"Well, it is, isn't it? It's a beautiful day. And just look at that view. You can see for miles. Here, let me lift you up and you'll be able to see a little better." And with that, the man took his cigarette out of his mouth and threw it out to sea. The breeze immediately caught it and disposed of it with great speed. With ease, he lifted Mary into the air, gently placing her feet upon the metal railing, which was high enough up to enable her to hold the wooden handrail and look out to sea. The man stood behind her to support her.

"There you go. Now what can you see?" he asked softly into her right ear, leaning over her from behind.

"Lots of water," Mary answered, and this made the man laugh.

"You are funny," he said. "Can you see anything else?"

"I think I can see something over there, but I'm not sure what it is."

"That's another ship," said the man.

"It's not as big as our ship, is it?"

"It could be bigger. It just looks small because it's so far away," he attempted to explain.

"Where are we?" asked the inquisitive Mary.

"We are travelling on the Red Sea at the moment, but soon we'll be in the Mediterranean."

"But it's not red," argued Mary.

"No, it's not," laughed the man again. "Anyway, what are you going to do when you get to England?" he asked, trying to change the subject.

"My mummy and I are going to visit my aunt in Southampton. Where are you going?"

"I'm off to Wales to visit my sister."

"Is that far from Southampton?"

"Quite far."

"We might see each other."

As the man and child continued their conversation, neither noticed the time slipping by. Mary's friend Margaret had become bored inside her cabin and asked her mother if she could go and call on her friend. Minutes later, when she arrived at Mary's cabin, Mary's mother was a little surprised when she opened her cabin door to find Margaret standing there.

"Is everything all right?" she asked.

"Yes, thank you," replied Margaret. "Can I come in and play with Mary?"

"But I thought she was with you?"

"No."

"But ... have you seen her today?"

"No."

And with that, Mary's mother took Margaret's hand and they quickly made their way back to Margaret's cabin.

Mary reached Margaret's cabin door at the exact same moment her mother did with Margaret. She had suddenly realised her friend would be waiting for her and she had better go. She thanked the man politely for talking with her, asked him to help her down, said goodbye and rushed off.

"Where on earth have you been?" demanded her mother. "I've been so worried since Margaret turned up without you."

At that moment Margaret's mother opened the door. "Hello," she said. "Is everything all right?"

"Where have you been?" demanded Mary's mother again, ignoring her friend. Margaret slipped under her mother's arm and gave her a hug. Her mother hugged her back, realising what must have happened. "Come inside and we can talk about it," Margaret's mother suggested to her friend.

That was what they did, and Mary was relieved that Margaret's mother was able to calm the situation down quickly and that she didn't get into too much trouble.

"There's no harm done now, is there? Mary is safely returned." But Mary's mother insisted she went in search of the young man to give him a piece of her mind. She searched the deck, and when she couldn't find him, she went to the deck above and to the smoking room on C Deck, all without any success.

"When we see him next in the dining saloon, I shall give him a piece of my mind," she told Margaret's mother when she returned. Mary was confused by her mother's behaviour and didn't understand why she should be so upset. Her mother made Mary promise never to speak to the man again, unless she was with her, and never to go wandering around the ship by herself.

Mary, Margaret and their families were able to enjoy the rest of the journey. The two women kept their daughters very close after that and made sure there was always one of them, or one of Margaret's elder sisters, with them at all times.

The day before they were due to arrive in Plymouth, Mary's mother was trying to restore some order to her cabin, when there was a knock at the door. It was Margaret's mother. She was all in a fluster, with her three daughters in tow.

"Have you heard?" she asked.

"Heard what?" replied Mary's mother.

"A child has gone missing. They are asking for as many people as possible to help search the ship. Apparently, she is the same age as our Margaret and Mary."

Mary's mother was quite taken aback and unsure as what to think or say.

"Are you feeling all right?" asked Margaret's mother, noticing her friend's colour suddenly fade.

"Yes, I think so. Would you stay with the children while I go and help with the search?"

"Of course."

So that was what Mary's mother did for the next couple of hours. The crew were very good, well organised and reassuring. 'She can't be far' and 'I'm sure she'll turn up soon' were two of the most common phrases they were heard saying during this time. They searched everywhere: all the dining areas, smoking rooms and lavatories; all the decks, stairs and lifts; any cupboards; and even inside the lifeboats, the engine room and the officers' quarters. There were a great many people who had volunteered to search, and she had been surprised at how many of these were first-class passengers. Then Mary's mother realised, after spotting the distraught parents, that the child who was missing was the first-class passenger her daughter had first spotted coming aboard. She felt physically sick and quickly went to find a seat upon which to compose herself and gather her thoughts. Those thoughts were interrupted by a familiar voice.

"Hello. Are you feeling unwell?"

Looking up, Mary's mother was surprised to see the young man she had taken a dislike to. "No, I'm quite all right," she answered.

"Have you been helping to look for the missing child?" the man enquired.

"Yes. Have you?" Her tone was rather accusatory.

"Yes. Isn't it terrible? I've been helping for over an hour now. We can't find her anywhere. There's talk that perhaps she's gone overboard. Is Mary all right? I haven't seen her for a while."

A little troubled by his directness and then his enquiry after Mary, she replied, "Yes, she's quite safe. I think I should get back to her now."

"I don't know," he continued. "First there's a death on board, and now this."

"A death?" Mary's mother was shocked.

"Yes, some elderly chap who had a cough. Bad case of bronchitis, so they say. He died a couple of nights ago."

Mary's mother had thought she was beginning to feel better, but now she felt even more unwell. "I must get back to my daughter."

"Yes, and I must get back to helping with the search. I'm sure they'll find the child soon."

"We're starting to search the cabins," announced a helpful crew member passing by. "You'll need to go back to your cabin now please, sir, madam."

Mary's mother had no idea how she made it back to her cabin, but thankfully she did. Her mind was in turmoil over the young man. She really didn't like him, but couldn't quite put her finger on why that was, concluding that he probably wasn't as bad as she imagined, as he too was helping to look for the missing child.

Two hours after leaving her cabin, Mary's mother returned. Margaret's mother was pleased to see her friend and eagerly wanted to know if the child had been found. Mary's mother quickly updated her and quietly informed her about the old man's death, as she didn't wish to upset their daughters. Margaret's mother said she would return to her cabin so that it could be searched, and promptly left with her three daughters. Half an hour later she returned with good news.

"She was found on C Deck, locked inside one of the cubicles of the gents' lavatory."

"But I'm sure I was told that was one of the first places that were checked," announced Mary's mother.

"Yes. Someone else said that. I suppose they must have just missed that one."

"Who found her?"

"A member of the crew, by all accounts. They heard her sobbing. Apparently, when she was asked how she got there, she said she couldn't remember. It's all a bit of a mystery. I'm just pleased she has been returned safely to her parents."

"So am I," agreed Mary's mother. "So am I."

The following day the ship docked at Plymouth and a number of passengers disembarked. Thankfully, for the remainder of their journey there was little for Margaret and Mary's mothers to worry about.

Ellen

———◦———

In 1927 Ellen lived with her Welsh husband in a bungalow in Flint Mountain, North Wales. It was a charming property, exhibiting two large chimneys and a shady veranda with an overhanging roof which ran across the front of the property, giving excellent views of the surrounding countryside. The word 'bungalow' evolves from *'bangla'*, meaning anything from Bengal, and this design of house had been commonly used in India to house British officers and their families. Ellen had been born in India, and when she had moved into this property with her husband, it could not have felt more perfect. Characteristic of the many dwellings found in India, Ellen's home sat on a brick base, two or three feet off the ground, was one storey high and exhibited a large living room at its centre, with smaller rooms in each corner for sleeping. Of course, Ellen had only views of the Welsh countryside from her current home. She and Gwilym had quickly begun to fill their home with children.

In 1927 they had a son of four years and a one-year-old daughter. Ellen carried her daughter on her hip as she walked towards the front door. Her son was following closely behind.

"You know I wrote to my mother, sharing our news with her?" Ellen called out to her husband from the hallway. She picked up a letter from the front door mat, instantly recognising the handwriting and the Calcutta postmark. Ellen remained rooted to the spot as she attempted to tear it open with the help of her daughter. She briefly scanned its contents.

"Yes, dear. Has she replied to you?" enquired Gwilym from their central sitting room. They had been married now for four years, and Ellen had recently discovered she was to have another child. Both she and Gwilym's family were very excited. "No, but my brother's coming to visit us in March."

Gwilym appeared in the hallway, complete with overcoat and briefcase. He reached behind Ellen for his hat from the hatstand, and placing it on his head, said, "We can discuss it later in more detail, as I have to get to work, but that is good news, isn't it?"

"Yes. I think I'm excited. Yes, I'm sure it will be good to see him."

"We'll talk about it later, darling. I'll see you this evening."

"Have a good day, dear," replied Ellen, her eyes remaining fixed upon her brother's letter as her husband kissed her and his daughter gently on their cheeks.

"I will. And you be good for Mummy," Gwilym told his son. He gave him a cuddle then left.

Gwilym worked for an established and well-regarded firm of solicitors in North Wales. He had been born in Flintshire; his parents having moved to Wales from Liverpool before he was born. While growing up, his father had established a number of pawnbroker businesses in Bangor, Holyhead and Colwyn Bay. Aged fifteen, Gwilym had been sent to Anfield to live with his aunt and uncle while he was educated at the Liverpool Institute High School for Boys. With its rather long title, the school was often referred to by its pupils as the 'Inny'—this being the name he would use in his letters home. While there, he had studied law, which would lead him into his chosen career of solicitor.

Both he and his father had joined the army together in 1914, and both had been wounded. His father received a serious wound to his lower back, losing his life later at home in Wales, in September 1917. Gwilym was wounded in October 1918 while in France. He had recovered from his wounds after spending time at a hospital in Rouen.

It had been during the war, that Gwilym had met Ellen's brothers, and afterwards, through their continued friendship, was introduced to Ellen in 1921. She had grown up in India along with her four brothers. Their childhood had been a fairly happy one. Their father having a good job meant the family could live comfortably. They had attended church regularly, and Ellen enjoyed school. Her mother was a nurse, but Ellen had spent little time in her mother's company as a child and had grown much closer to her father.

When her three elder brothers had joined the British Army in 1914,

Ellen had been sixteen and her brother Fred ten. The war significantly depleted Ellen's family, and the house in India had suddenly felt empty. At this time, she and her father had grown close, Ellen having always been his favourite.

As the end of the war was announced and England and the British Empire attempted to recover from the devastation, it was Ellen's mother who felt the greatest loss when one of Ellen's brothers was killed in action. As Ellen attempted to support her mother through one of the worst times in her life and worried about her father's health, she was rejected by her mother and prevented from seeing her father.

Her two surviving brothers had decided they wanted to remain in England. With their father owning property in Kentish Town, London, this was where her brothers had decided to begin their married lives. Ellen had wished she too could have left her home in India at this time.

The war was over, and everything that Ellen had once been familiar with appeared to have changed overnight. Her mother was distraught at losing a favoured son, giving little thought as to how Ellen might have felt. Her surviving brothers had decided not to return to the family home and then her father had become terminally ill, leaving Ellen feeling very alone. Every doctor her father had seen said there was nothing that could be done for him. Ellen felt as though her life had been turned upside down.

Just as Ellen thought her life could not get any worse, her mother announced that her father's closest friend, Frank, was to move into the family home. Ellen wasted no time in writing to her brothers, begging them to return and talk some sense into their mother. But it was to no avail. Both refused to return home once Ellen had explained to them the unusual situation.

Ellen did not realise at first that it had been her father who had been instrumental in this arrangement and had given his blessing. This was before he had become too ill to know his own mind and no longer recognise Ellen or her mother. She was forced to go along with this sad state of affairs for the sake of her father. His illness and rapid demise had put an end to their close relationship much sooner than Ellen had anticipated, and she suddenly found herself feeling isolated.

As the months passed and Ellen waited for her father to die, she had plenty of time to formulate her escape plan. She decided that after her father's death, she too would be heading for England. When her father finally succumbed in June 1920 and her mother announced that she and Frank had already married, Ellen left for England as quickly as she could.

Ellen headed for London and stayed with her brothers. She had spent a couple of months with Alex, her eldest brother, but because he was so busy with his work in the rubber industry, they hardly got to see one another. When she then went to stay with Ralf, although a company director of a ladies' coat manufacturers, he was able to give his sister more attention. Ralf had not been married long, and Ellen got along with Ralf's wife very well. The two women ganged up against him most evenings, but the house was always full of laughter when the three of them were together.

Ellen and Gwilym were introduced by Ralf, who was in no doubt they would get along like a house on fire. They did, and among the many things they had in common was the strong bond they had shared with their fathers and the loss they had felt when bereaved too early. Ellen and Gwilym married in London, in December 1922, and her brother Alex gave her away, while Ralf was their witness.

Now, left with thoughts of Fred's imminent arrival while her husband was at work all day, Ellen found herself wondering how her mother would be taking the news of Fred's visit. She believed her mother would not have wanted Fred to leave India. He would be the last to do so, and although Ellen knew it would affect her mother greatly, she also knew her mother's pride would not stand in his way. In his letter, Fred had not made it clear how long he would be staying, or indeed if he had plans to return to India. Ellen was concerned about what her mother's reaction would be if Fred decided to stay in England. She knew her mother would blame her for encouraging Fred to stay. She was used to being blamed for most things which did not go her mother's way.

Fred arrived in March at the bungalow, and Ellen and her family gave him a very warm welcome. Ellen had not seen him for more than five years and hardly recognised her twenty-two-year-old brother. It was clearly evident that he had undergone the transformation from boy to man. His features had changed, his nose was larger and he had grown a moustache.

Fred approached his sister, embracing her carefully, for he could see instantly her condition.

"You look great, Ellen," he laughed. "All this mountain air must agree with you."

"We just love it here, don't we, Gwilym?"

"Don't really know much else," Gwilym replied. It was his way of explaining he had never seen the likes of an exotic country such as India.

"Your house is beautiful. It reminds me of the houses back home," continued Fred.

"It did me the first time I saw it," agreed Ellen.

"And who's this?" asked Fred, stroking his niece's face.

"This is Betty. Say hello to Uncle Fred, Betty." Of course, she couldn't, as she was too young, but she managed a smile.

"And this is Ralf," Gwilym introduced his son. Fred bent down to shake the boy's tiny hand. "Very nice to meet you, Ralf. I'm your Uncle Fred."

Fred was welcomed inside and shown to a bedroom which was to be his for as long as he needed it. Ellen had thought of everything, and Fred knew he would be well looked after during his stay. She was overjoyed to be spending time with her brother again. She hadn't realised just how much she had missed him. Ellen and Fred quickly managed to rebuild some bridges, enabling them both to feel more relaxed in each other's company.

Fred was soon introduced to the members of Gwilym's family, who all lived locally. He was offered a job by Gwilym's brother-in-law who owned a local garage and ironmonger's shop on Holywell Road. Evan's had run their business from here for many years and were well regarded in the town. Fred settled quickly and appeared to enjoy his new motor sales job, and the other Evan's employees all appeared to get along with him.

Gwilym, on the other hand, did not warm so easily to Fred. Although he did his utmost to keep his feelings from Ellen, she was aware her husband was experiencing some difficult moments during her brother's stay. Gwilym tried so hard to get along with Fred, for Ellen's sake, but there was just something about him which made Gwilym feel uncomfortable. Fred was never unpleasant to him—in fact, he was the perfect gentleman—but something prevented Gwilym from feeling as enthusiastic about Fred as his wife did. At one point, Gwilym had thought it might be he who had the problem. Was he jealous of Fred? But that thought quickly passed, as he had never been the resentful, possessive type.

Ellen witnessed some awkward conversations between her husband and her brother. She had realised very early on that they were both very different men. Gwilym was content with his existence, that of husband and well-established solicitor, whereas Fred was still seeking a life which would suffice him further. Gwilym expected nothing from anyone and accepted people for who they were. Fred, on the other hand, expected everyone should be more like him: extrovert, discontent with the simple life and always pursuing advancement.

Fred remained in Wales until the end of the summer. He had found work locally, with the help of Gwilym, but it was not what he wanted to do, and he had recently started to complain to Ellen about this. Fred felt his opportunities were restricted in Wales and believed he could do better for himself elsewhere. After only a few months spent with Ellen and Gwilym, he wrote to his brother Alex. He was sure London could offer him greater prospects.

***

Ellen's third child arrived at the end of July and was baptised at St Thomas's. Ellen decided to name him Fred, after her brother. Everyone was overcome with joy at the child's arrival. Baby Fred could not have wished for more doting parents and grandparents. As Gwilym and Ellen relished their role as parents, wholeheartedly devoting all their love and time to their children, Ellen's brother quickly began to feel neglected. To him it seemed that everything now revolved around the new baby and no one had time for him any longer. Fred would quickly lose patience whenever the child became upset, and one morning in August he had a go at Ellen for seemingly being unable to soothe her baby during the night.

"What was the matter with him last night?" demanded Fred. "Couldn't you have fed the little sod to shut him up?"

Ellen clutched the baby close, tears beginning to fill her eyes. "He has six feeds a day, Fred. That's more than enough. Anyway, it wasn't because he was hungry."

"Why was he crying so much then?"

"He must have had a belly ache. He was constipated, because as soon as he'd filled his nappy, he quietened down again."

"Well, perhaps you are feeding him too much then," suggested Fred.

Ellen turned and left the room before she said something to her brother she might regret.

Seconds later she heard him exit the front door.

When Gwilym found her crying in the kitchen, still clutching the baby, he asked her what was the matter.

"The baby disturbed Fred last night and he's pretty grumpy about it this morning."

"What did he say?"

"He suggested I was doing it all wrong. I can only do what I think is best," Ellen continued.

"Of course you can. You are an excellent mother, and don't let anyone tell you otherwise," assured Gwilym. "Now give me the baby and go and wash your face. I'll see to this little mite, won't I?" Gwilym smiled down at his youngest son as he took him out of Ellen's arms. As Ellen left for the bathroom, she heard her husband say, "Mummy shouldn't listen to silly Uncle Fred now, should she?"

"Silly Uncle Fred," repeated their son Ralf.

Ellen considered her husband's comment and concluded that perhaps Gwilym was right. Fred had been quite cruel to her that morning.

On his way to work, Gwilym took a detour via Evan's Garage. He got on very well with his brother-in-law's family and guessed his sister would most likely be there as well. She spent quite a lot of time at the garage, as she often helped her husband out with the paperwork. Gwilym was correct and asked his sister, Merthyr, if it would be all right for him to have a private word with Fred.

"Is everything all right, Gwilym?" Merthyr enquired.

"It will be," he answered. Merthyr went to fetch Fred. Eventually, she returned, with Fred following closely behind her.

"You can go in there if you wish," Merthyr said to her brother, pointing to a small, partly glass-partitioned office which happened to be empty. Piles of papers sat neatly stacked upon a single desk. Gwilym held the door open for Fred and he walked inside. Gwilym closed the door behind him.

"Is everything all right, Gwilym?" enquired Fred. "It's not the baby, is it?"

"Now look here, Fred. You quite upset your sister this morning. Was that really necessary?"

"That baby of yours kept me up half the night," Fred retaliated.

"What do you expect? It's a baby. They do that every so often."

"I can't function properly at work if I'm tired."

"I manage all right, and I suspect my job is a little more demanding than yours," replied Gwilym. His comment triggered a reaction in Fred that neither of them had expected.

"Well, I shan't be here for much longer," announced Fred.

"No? Why not? Where are you planning on going?"

"I'm off to see my brother in London."

"I see. And what will you do for work there?" enquired Gwilym.

"My brother Alex will be able to fix me up with something. It won't be difficult to find work in London."

"Were you going to mention this to your sister?"

"I was, when I'm ready."

"Let me suggest you do it sooner rather than later, because if we ever have a repeat of what happened this morning, it will be me who throws you out, not you who chooses to leave. Do you understand what I'm saying, Fred?"

Fred nodded, unable to think of a flippant answer quick enough. He was sufficiently embarrassed by his brother-in-law's attitude and behaviour towards him and this made him angry. The conversation over, Gwilym left the office, closely followed by an angry Fred. When Merthyr returned later, she discovered that the pile of papers which had been stacked neatly on the desk had been scattered chaotically all over the floor.

Less than a month later Fred was on his way to London. Gwilym was greatly relieved to have his home back to normal and not to have to worry about his house guest any longer. Ellen was less pleased to see her brother leave, but thankful she would no longer have to pacify her brother's often unreasonable behaviour. She wrote to her mother informing her of Fred's departure and letting her know that he was heading to London to visit Alex, believing that Fred would not have written to her himself. Ellen and Gwilym could finally feel more relaxed about life and relished in the comfort of how much calmer things would be without Fred around.

***

Some months later, within the space of less than a week of one another, Ellen received letters from both her brother Alex and her mother in India. She was not surprised by the letter she received from Alex because he had very little that was positive to say about their younger brother. Alex explained that he had been able to find Fred work at the Continental Tyre and Rubber Company, where he was a salesman. Alex's job took him travelling abroad quite regularly, so it had mostly fallen on his wife, Helena, to look after Fred during this time. He went on to explain that Fred's job was that of office clerk, but no sooner had Fred started with the tyre company, it was clear he was not going to fit in easily. Fred had struggled to get along with the other male clerks, expressing to them that he was more qualified than they and bragging about how he would soon be travelling abroad like his brother. There had also been a number of complaints by women who worked in the same office as Fred regarding his inappropriate behaviour towards them.

Alex explained how he had become quite irritated by Fred, as he constantly pestered him about travelling abroad, and in no uncertain terms had been forced to inform his brother that he could not have him along for any of the trips. Upon his most recent return from Canada, Alex had discovered that Fred had made advances towards his wife, Helena, in his absence, and this had been the final straw. He also explained how he had given Fred one week to find somewhere else to live and how he now felt uncomfortable about leaving his wife at home with Fred. He went on to explain how Fred had then left without warning, walking away from his job and causing Alex much embarrassment within his company.

Ellen was extremely disappointed in Fred and could not understand why he should behave in such a way. But it appeared Fred was the least of her problems. The letter Ellen received from her mother later that same week was a further shock. The first time she'd read it through, she couldn't quite believe what she was reading. The second time she'd picked it up, it had made her weep, and that had been when Gwilym had arrived home.

"Whatever has happened?" he asked, genuinely concerned for his wife. "Is little Freddie all right?"

"Yes, he's fine. Listen to this." Ellen began to read the letter a third time—his time out loud to her husband—and this time it made her feel angry. "Dear Ellen, I am dismayed you should treat your younger brother so cruelly when all he has ever done to you is treat you kindly. In his last letter to me, Fred was quite beside himself with concern for you and the baby, and upon giving you advice, feels he was very poorly treated by that husband of yours. I told you no good would come from marrying a Welshman. I am appalled to hear that you and your husband have forced Fred to leave, and in doing so lost him what sounded like a perfectly good job—"

"Stop!" Gwilym shouted, clearly very irritated by his mother-in-law's letter. "Please do not read out any more to me."

"Oh, but there is plenty more. She goes on to accuse me of poisoning Alex against Fred, saying that I have made things difficult for him there as well." Ellen then went on to remind her husband about the letter she had received from Alex earlier that week.

"I have never written to Alex and told him what Fred was like while he was here, so my mother can only have heard that from Fred," she began to sob.

"Give me the letter!" demanded Gwilym, and he snatched it out of Ellen's hand. He proceeded to vigorously rip up the three sheets of writing paper. He threw the pieces into the waste-paper bin.

"There. We'll hear no more about it. I'm sorry, Ellen, but I want nothing more to do with your mother, or Fred for that matter, and I shall be writing to Alex to inform him of this."

Ellen was shocked by her husband's unusual and forceful reaction. He was normally such a placid, patient man, but seeing Ellen so hurt had wounded him too.

"You do not deserve to be treated in such a way, especially not by your own flesh and blood. I think it best if we cut all ties with them both."

"I don't think I can do that," sobbed Ellen.

Gwilym took her in his arms and held her as she let out all the hurt she was feeling. "No. I don't expect you can. You are far too sweet a person to bear a grudge. What I should have said was 'Let's not react to this letter. Hopefully, it will all blow over and we can forget about everything that has been said'."

"I'll do my best," replied Ellen.

But Gwilym did write to his old army pal and brother-in-law to inform him of how upsetting Fred's visit had been for them too.

Alex

————◄○►————

Alex had been born in Calcutta, West Bengal, and encouraged by
his father, he had travelled to England as a teenager and worked
as a correspondent and salesman. He joined the British Army, enlisting
into the Herefordshire Yeomanry, and became a trooper in November
1912, aged nineteen. His medical in London found him physically fit
for duty. The following year, in May, he received two weeks training.

After being posted to Putney in London, he transferred into the
London Yeomanry, who were commonly known as the 'Rough Riders.'
This had been intended as a home defence force, but with the outbreak
of war, many had volunteered for overseas service, so the unit was
split into first line for overseas service and second line for service at
home.

Alex had completed almost two years with the army before he was
called for active service in August 1914. He passed a further medical in
September and joined the second-line regiment.

At the end of December he was given the task of drilling, when he
rather clumsily tripped over a bench, twisting his right leg. He was
sent home to recuperate. The doctor said there was some enlargement
to the internal condyle of his right femur. This derangement to his right
knee joint made it impossible for him to stand for any length of time, or
ride, resulting in him becoming unfit for service. He was eventually
discharged as unfit for military service at the end of January 1915.

Because Alex was the eldest of his siblings, he had always felt a
responsibility to lead the way and hoped his brothers would follow by
his example. They did; firstly by joining him in London, then joining
the army in quick succession. But what kind of example had he set
them after his accident? Alex had been exceptionally unlucky in the
army. He had always regretted not being able to do very much during
the First World War. He felt humiliated that he had been discharged

without accomplishing anything for his country. He had felt the need to prove himself, so that his father would not be disappointed.

During the war, Alex was living on Bartholomew Road in South Kentish Town, London, in a large property his father owned. He found work as a salesman in the rubber industry, and it was during this time, he met his future wife. Helena worked as a shop assistant at a draper's shop on Oxford Road, Marylebone. She had fallen for his deep, dark brown eyes and auburn head of hair the moment he had limped into her shop, but both she and Alex were too anxious to do anything about their feelings at first. Alex would often find an excuse to visit the shop and soon started walking out with Helena's fellow assistant, Joan, much to Helena's surprise. When Alex eventually asked Helena to accompany him to the theatre one evening, he confessed to her that he had been too nervous to ask her and had asked her friend instead.

Helena thought the whole episode amusing, confessing how she too had felt the same as Alex. They wondered if they had just wasted the previous six months, but then decided it had given them a chance to get to know each other well, as they had often gone out in a foursome: Alex taking along his colleague Will, and Helena accompanying Joan. In fact, they had recently discovered that Joan and Will had been seeing each other, so it appeared everyone was happy.

In October 1917 Alex and Helena married at St Peter's Church, Belsize Park, in Hampstead. They moved into a house on Belsize Lane, and at this time Alex had started working in South Kensington for the Continental Tyre and Rubber Company. The firm was a German company and in the past had made the rubber fabric for airship balloons, footwear, balls and toys, waterproof fabrics, cart and bicycle tyres. Then they had begun the production of pneumatic tyres. It was in Germany that the company first presented their treaded car tyres in 1904, and in 1908 surprised their competitors with the removable wheel rim. The company's achievements in Germany allowed them to open a branch in London in 1909, as well as others across the world, and it was at this time, they began to focus on exports. Their tyres were used on cars with great success in the French Grand Prix in 1914, but production was held back with the onset of the war. After the war Alex received a promotion within the company and was considered a rubber-tyre expert. He became increasingly involved in exports and would often travel abroad on business.

***

In 1927 Alex and Helena lived twenty miles south of London, in Orpington, Kent, where they'd bought a semi-detached property on a delightful street. At this time, Alex's job was taking him abroad regularly. They'd never had any children and they were comfortably well off. On occasion, Helena would accompany her husband on his trips abroad, which she might not have been able to do if they'd had children.

On his most recent trip, Helena had chosen not to go with Alex. She had recently begun to think about starting her own business with her sister Gladys. The sisters had always enjoyed needlework and working with wool and decided to turn their enjoyable pastime into a business. With financial help from her husband, Helena intended to purchase a small shop from where the two sisters could sell their fancy goods; something else she may not have been able to do if they'd had children.

That year, Alex's younger brother Fred had written a couple of times asking Alex if he could come and stay and enquiring if Alex knew of any work available within the offices of the rubber company. Alex and Helena welcomed Fred's visit, and Alex was able to find his brother some work.

Fred had previously visited their sister in Wales and arrived in London in mid-September, shortly before Alex was due to leave the country again. Alex was able to settle his brother into his home and introduce him to his fellow workers before he had to leave. However, it soon became clear that Fred was going to be more difficult to live with than Alex and Helena had first anticipated.

From the moment he arrived, Fred caused upheaval within their typically peaceful household with his confrontational behaviour. He was always disagreeing with and challenging their housekeeper, and was even rude to Helena on a couple of occasions. Alex was somewhat reluctant to leave his wife in the company of his younger brother.

"I shall be quite all right, darling," reassured Helena. "Yes, your brother is a little challenging, with his old-fashioned attitudes and immature behaviour, but he's harmless. I've always got my needlework to keep me occupied; and Gladys, who is used to listening to my complaining."

"Are you absolutely sure, darling? I can always see if I can rearrange the trip."

"Stop worrying, Alex. I'll be just fine, but hurry back to us when you have completed what you need to do."

"I will, my darling. I promise."

The next few weeks felt incredibly long for Helena, and time passed very slowly. She couldn't wait for her husband to return. Alex was due to arrive home at the end of October 1927, having spent time in Canada. Helena had missed him greatly during his absence, mostly because of how difficult she had found it to keep her brother-in-law happy.

Before his departure Alex had been able to find Fred a job working as a clerk at the Continental Tyre and Rubber Company. While he had been away, it had fallen on Helena to keep him entertained and assist her brother-in-law in keeping hold of that job. From the start, it had been clear to her that this was going to be difficult because he was so frequently objectionable.

It would be true to say that Fred did not fit in easily. He struggled to get on with people, often believing he was more qualified than his fellow clerks, bragging about how he would soon be travelling abroad like his brother and refusing to take on work he felt was beneath him.

After Alex had left for Canada, there had been a number of complaints by women who worked in the same office as Fred regarding his inappropriate behaviour towards them. Helena had attempted to advise Fred on this matter, but instead of taking heed, he had attempted to turn his unwanted attentions onto her. She made it quite clear to him from the start that if he persisted in this manner, he would be asked to leave, and thankfully he had stopped.

When Alex returned home from abroad and discovered what Fred had been up to at work, he was both embarrassed and appalled by his brother's behaviour. It had been the final straw when Helena had informed him that Fred had also made advances towards her in his absence.

Alex wasted no time in talking to Fred and gave him a week to find somewhere else to live. Fred hardly reacted at all to his brother's ultimatum.

"Fine. If that's how you want to play it," was all he had said before storming out of the room.

Alex wrote to his sister in Wales, informing her of their brother's objectionable behaviour. He explained in his letter to Ellen how he had given Fred one week to find somewhere else to live and how he no longer felt comfortable leaving his wife at home with him. He went on to explain how Fred had then scurried off without as much as a word of thanks to him or Helena, walking away from a perfectly good job and home and causing Alex much embarrassment at work.

"What the hell is the matter with him?" Alex asked Helena after completing his letter to his sister. "What makes him think he can treat people in this way?"

"I'm sure I don't know, Alex."

"I wouldn't be surprised if it's all Mother's fault. She and Frank both spoilt the boy too much when he was younger. Now he's a man, he thinks he doesn't have to conform and can behave exactly as he pleases. He's no brother of mine. He won't get anything more out of us. I want nothing more to do with him."

When Alex received a letter by return post from his brother-in-law Gwilym, he was shocked to hear how Fred had also behaved when he had stayed with them. Mention of the contents of a nasty letter from his mother, which had upset Ellen, had also shocked him.

"You see, Helena. Is it any wonder Fred is the way he is? Mother and Frank have given him excuse after excuse for his bad behaviour. The things Ellen has told me about what Fred got up to in India. I tell you, it's no wonder my father would get so angry with him. If I'd been around, I would have given him a sound thrashing as well."

"Oh, Alex. Was he really that bad as a child?"

"I only have Ellen's word, of course, as I had already left home, but my mother would never have a bad word said against Fred. Now, after seeing the aggravation he can cause with my own eyes, I have no reason to doubt my sister."

"You could have a point, darling. Let's not think about Fred any more. What would you like to do this weekend?" asked Helena in an attempt to change the subject.

It wasn't long before Alex received another letter. This time it was from his brother Ralf, informing him that Fred had turned up on his doorstep a little worse for wear, but how he had managed to talk some sense into him and get him to turn himself around. According to Ralf, Fred now had a job, which he seemed to be enjoying, working as an insurance agent.

"Just listen to this, Helena." Alex read out loud part of the letter Ralf had written to him. "I don't understand, dear brother, why you should treat poor Fred in such a ghastly way."

"Poor Fred?" questioned Helena.

"I dread to think what story he's told Ralf," worried Alex.

"And fancy Ralf believing him," said Helena.

"I suppose he has no reason to doubt him. But he will soon realise what he's like."

"Perhaps he will put it all behind him now and settle down under Ralf's supervision," suggested Helena.

"Perhaps," replied Alex sceptically, but hoping his wife was correct.

Alex wondered if he should write to his brother to explain what had really happened between him and Fred and about how Fred had behaved when he had stayed with Gwilym and Ellen. But his brother Ralf could be headstrong and most likely would give Fred the benefit of the doubt. Alex thought better of it. Ralf would just have to discover the truth for himself. Alex knew Fred could be a pain in the neck, but what he hadn't considered was the potential danger he might be putting Ralf's wife in.

***

Shortly before Christmas Alex arrived home from London to discover his house had been broken into. Helena had finished her chores and left the house that afternoon after locking and bolting the doors and windows, as was her way. She had not been home at the time of the break-in, as she had been visiting her father, a furniture manufacturer and importer who lived in Essex.

Alex reached his home at around five o'clock that evening to find all the rooms in his house in a state of utter turmoil. At that point he could not tell what, if anything, was missing because everywhere was in such chaos. However, he made no hesitation in contacting the police.

The following day, when Helena had arrived home and Alex had got her to calm down, they worked out between them what was missing and made a list of those items together. Among them were many items of jewellery, including a brooch and a tiepin, as well as money, including a number of Dutch guilders Alex had kept since his last trip to the Netherlands. The strangest item to have gone missing, though, was a torch which Alex usually kept in the pantry in case of an emergency.

Alex and Helena estimated that the items that were missing came to the value of £75. Within days the police had returned to Alex's home to ask him if he could identify any of the items they had so far seized. He could, and arrests were made.

Alex was informed by police that two local men named Armstrong and Johnson had been arrested and charged with breaking and entering his house. They were held on remand for one week at the local police court, and a week later committed for trial at West Kent Assizes. It transpired that these two men were well known to police in the area. They both lived about a mile and a half away from Alex's home. Only the month before, the pair had been in trouble with police after an incident in a public house. An argument had ensued between them at the bar and witnesses said they kept referring to a 'stuck-up fella' and that Johnson accused Armstrong of 'giving too much away to that stuck-up fella'.

The police returned to Alex's home to discuss the matter further. "It appears they were disagreeing about whether they could trust him or not," mentioned the police constable to Alex. "Can you think of anyone to whom the description might represent, sir?"

"No, constable. It could be anyone," replied Alex.

The police constable described how Johnson had taken hold of a glass, smashed it with his fist and then shoved it into Armstrong's face. He said that when he was later asked by the magistrate why he had done it, Johnson said it was because Armstrong had opened his mouth too wide.

The constable then concluded, "Johnson eventually pleaded guilty and was fined and ordered to pay damages for the glass to the landlord of the pub. It was when we went round to search Armstrong's and Johnson's properties, that we discovered a number of items there which had been listed by you and your good lady wife."

These items were later taken to Alex's home and he was asked if he could identify them. He told the police that they did indeed belong to him. Alex then attended the court during Armstrong and Johnson's trial. He was asked to give evidence. The judge asked Alex, "Sir, can you identify the pin?"

"Yes, your honour."

"But you have no means of saying that that particular pin is yours?"

"I am certain it is my tiepin, your honour. I have had it for ten years. It was a gift from my wife," Alex replied. He was almost made to feel like a criminal himself.

Both the accused men argued in court that they had not committed the burglary, but admitted they had received the stolen items from a third party. They claimed they did not know the name of the man in question, but they referred to him as a 'stuck-up fella with a big nose'. They went on to further describe the man, and it appeared to Alex that the description was very similar to that of his brother Fred. Alex's blood suddenly ran cold. Was he imagining this? Could this seriously be something his brother would be capable of? He was, after all, very angry when he had left Alex's home. Alex put all of these thoughts quickly out of his head when the police and the court did not believe the two men and they alone were found guilty of the crime.

Having their home broken into, followed by the court case, had taken its toll on Alex and Helena, and they soon decided to put their house up for sale. They no longer felt happy or safe in their home, knowing that a thief had gained access to it and rummaged through their personal belongings. Both were having trouble sleeping at night, so they decided that moving house would be the preferred option.

Helena's sister Gladys had proved a great support to Helena during this time. She knew what the two of them had gone through with Fred, and then after the break-in she had a surprise for them both. Gladys had news of a potential property purchase. She had found the perfect shop premises, which were vacant, but they would have to move fast. The only problem she could foresee was that it was almost ten miles away, in Sevenoaks.

"A change of area is just what we need," suggested Alex. "I think it's an excellent idea."

"What do you think, Helena?" asked Gladys.

"I agree completely. In fact, I feel rather excited at the prospect of these new horizons."

Alex wasted no time in supporting his wife's dream and purchased the shop on High Street, Sevenoaks, which Gladys had found, along with Cedar Lodge—a property for them all to live in—one mile away, on Kippington Road.

Helena and Gladys were kept busy producing many new goods to sell, and their shop was soon a great success. Helena had not felt this happy and content before. It bothered her less now when her husband had to travel abroad, which was lucky, for over the coming years he would travel to Singapore, Japan and Hong Kong regularly. On some occasions, when Alex had to be away for over a year, Helena would accompany him, leaving her sister in charge of their fancy-goods shop, but mostly she was content to stay at home. Finally, Alex and his wife were able to put their upsetting experience with Fred behind them.

Ralf

—◄◊►—

Following a childhood in India, Ralf followed in his brothers' footsteps and headed for England, where he found work as a clerk before joining the 3rd Battalion of the Norfolk Infantry shortly before his twentieth birthday. Ralf had deep brown eyes like his brother Alex, but his hair was much darker, almost black, giving his appearance a sallow complexion. Ralf was the tallest of his brothers.

Once in London, he too had headed for one of his father's properties in Kentish Town and was there at the time his brother Alex had injured his knee and was forced to leave the army. Ralf had offered Alex encouragement to be more positive during this time. After Ralf had joined the army, he attempted to continue to reassure Alex by letter. At this stage Ralf had not yet been posted abroad. He was undergoing training, but had only been able to visit Alex the once before he'd left for France in May 1915.

Ralf's war was very different from that of his brother. He saw a great deal of action. He was involved in many battles in France. He worked his way up through the ranks, being promoted from lance corporal to corporal, and then to sergeant by March 1916. While attending trench mortar training at a camp set up in France behind the front line, he learnt how to use various weapons.

In 1917 Ralf had been wounded. However, he made a speedy recovery and five days later rejoined his regiment. Shortly after this Ralf was mentioned in the *London Gazette* for his courage during another battle. He was discharged from the army in March 1919, returning to London.

Ralf was awarded the Star, the British War Medal and the Victory Medal, which were affectionately known as 'Pip, Squeak and Wilfred'. He had been deserving of a special mention in despatches by Sir Douglas Haig and also received the Distinguished Conduct Medal.

This was awarded to him for his gallantry in the field in the face of the enemy.

In September 1918 Ralf had been south-west of Cambrai, France. During operations, when the enemy had made a counter attack, Ralf had collected a few men and re-established a stop in a communication trench that the enemy was bombing down. In spite of heavy bombing and machine gunfire, he maintained his post against all attacks for a considerable time until the enemy withdrew. He showed the utmost gallantry and coolness to his party before their counter-attack. For these actions, Ralf received the Level 3 Gallantry Medal, awarded to soldiers for acts of gallantry and devotion to duty under fire or for individual acts of bravery. He shared some of these experiences with his brother Alex, but played down his part in the war, as he did not wish to upset Alex by appearing to boast about his achievements.

When he returned to London, Ralf lived close to Alex, in Kentish Town. One year later he had married. His wife, Florence, had grown up in the London area, where her father was regularly employed as a dairy farmer. During the war, she had worked for a funeral director who lived on Lower Mall, overlooking the Thames. She and Ralf had become better acquainted as they spent many hours walking alongside the Thames.

By 1924 Ralf and Florence had moved to Guildersfield Road, Streatham, where they would remain for the next ten years. Ralf was now working for a company which made ladies' coats. He was well respected within his workplace and would soon be promoted to company director, but unlike his elder brother, Ralf would have two children.

Ralf kept in contact with Alex and they saw each other as often as they could, but with Alex travelling abroad as much as he did, those times were not as often as Ralf would have liked. With a busy working and married life, the two brothers did not correspond as often either. However, in November 1927, when his younger brother Fred had knocked on his door, intoxicated and upset with Alex for treating him so appallingly, Ralf had taken pity on Fred and invited him to stay. He had promptly written to Alex to express his disappointment in the way Alex had apparently treated their brother Fred.

Once Fred had sobered up and was making sense, Ralf had been able to establish that there had been a misunderstanding at the tyre company where Alex had found Fred a job. Alex had got the wrong end of the stick and reacted too hastily, explained Fred. The brothers discussed calmly what Fred would prefer to do for work, and Ralf was able to secure Fred a job, working for a well-established insurance company in the city.

Ralf explained in his letter to Alex how Fred had taken to it like a duck to water and was now quite settled. He had written, 'Perhaps, dear brother, you were too eager for Fred to fit into your place of work rather than find him something he enjoys'. He had gone on to say that he didn't understand why Alex had treated Fred so poorly and hoped his brother would take his words in the way they were intended. The last thing he wanted to do was upset Alex.

Ralf had found it fairly easy to satisfy his younger brother. Once he had calmed Fred down and they had been able to discuss rationally that drink was not the answer to a problem, he had felt assured he would be able to help Fred. Together they had found Fred a job which he seemed to have settled into well, and everyone was happy.

Ralf could recall from letters sent from his mother during the war that she had found some of Fred's behaviour challenging while he was growing up. He hoped this was now an end to his brother's unconstructive behaviour, but couldn't help recalling some of the things his mother had mentioned to him in her correspondence. He shared his concerns with his wife.

"Mother had written to me during the war, concerned about Fred's schooling. I must admit I had quite enjoyed reading her letters, as they had taken my mind off the losses we had suffered earlier that day."

"Do you still have your mother's letters?" asked Florence.

"Not all of them. I'm not sure where I was when I lost them. You know how it is."

"Can you recall many of their contents?"

"Oh yes. Quite clearly. Fred had always been a bit of a loner, you see. Never seemed to have many friends at school. He was a high achiever, mind, unlike Ralf and myself; we just did what we had to, whereas Fred didn't seem to try and always came out with high scores in most subjects. Mother and Father were very proud of his academic achievements at school."

"Do you think it was the war that changed things then?"

"Who knows? It was around that time, after the three of us left for England and joined up. Around the time when my father had started to become unwell. Something changed. I can recall my mother writing to tell me about him getting into fights at school, mixing with some unsavoury Indian boys and I think he was on occasion cruel to animals. I recall my mother mentioning that she saw him batter a snake to death in the back garden with a stick. It wasn't a venomous snake and had been quite harmless. You see, we boys had learnt from an early age which snakes to avoid."

"Perhaps he just made a mistake," suggested Florence innocently.

"That's not what my mother thought. She also made mention that he had let a puppy drown in the stream which ran along the bottom of the garden."

"Oh, that's terrible, Ralf."

"But she was never really sure. Anyway, there was other stuff as well. He started breaking into property and stealing. When Mother found out, she saw to it that Frank was there to bail him out and eventually he just stopped."

"Well, let's hope that is what has happened now. He seems quite happy in his new job, doesn't he?" asked Florence.

"Yes, I think so. I'm not sure what went on at Alex's house, but I suspect it was something and nothing. Nothing for us to worry about anyway."

***

A month later, with Christmas fast approaching, Ralf was busier than ever at work. Fred was now part of the family, and on the evenings when Ralf made it home in time for dinner and the children were in bed, the three of them would enjoy Florence's fine food and ample conversation.

During Christmas 1927, Ralf had the feeling that something was bothering his brother. Fred had started drinking again; not excessively, but enough for Ralf and Florence to have noticed. Some evenings he would not arrive home for his evening meal and some nights he would not return to the house until after dark, after they had retired to bed.

One evening, the two brothers found themselves in each other's company for the first time in quite a while. Ralf seized this rare opportunity and enquired after his brother's drinking habits. Fred attempted to reassure Ralf, saying that he could control his drinking, explaining that it was just his way of letting off steam after a busy day at work. Sufficiently convinced, Ralf continued his conversation by asking respectfully, "And how are you finding the insurance business, Fred? Is it keeping you busy?"

"Yes. It keeps me extremely occupied most days."

"Good," nodded Ralf, waiting in the hope that Fred would offer some more information, but he did not. A couple of days later when Fred returned home drunk again, Ralf pressed his brother further.

"If you must know, dear brother, that job you found me has become a bit of a noose around my neck."

"What on earth are you talking about, Fred?" Ralf enquired.

"I'm sick to death of being treated like the new boy who knows nothing. I have a shadow who assists me all the time, whether I need it or not. He thinks he knows everything, and he's a real pain in the arse."

"Who are you talking about?" asked Ralf.

"He's called Wilfred. According to him, he's taken me under his wing and has been showing me the ropes."

"That's very obliging of him."

"The job's not that different from what I was doing in India really, so he's not teaching me much I don't already know. I guess it makes him feel valued. He likes to think he knows everything about everything."

"Perhaps, but he doesn't have to do it, I suspect," reasoned Ralf.

Fred chose to ignore this comment and continued. "Bit of a lonely chap by all accounts. No wife; no family. He lives alone, not far from here, I think. He insists I accompany him on his rounds until I find my feet. I reckon I could do it with my eyes closed now, but I don't want to upset the old fella."

"Best not, Fred. If you can put up with him just for a short while longer, I'm sure he'll eventually leave you to it."

"He's a couple of sandwiches short of a picnic if you ask me."

"Best not to upset him though, Fred. Just go along with it. Perhaps you could try and stay off the drink. It's not helping the situation, is it?"

"I suppose I don't have a choice," replied Fred, irritated by his brother's insistent manner.

What Fred didn't know was that it had been his brother who had set him up with this gentleman in the first place. Fred also didn't realise at this time that the man in question only lived a short walk away from Ralf's house.

When Ralf had first made enquiries into the company on Fred's behalf, he had been introduced to the gentleman, and they had discovered they lived a road apart from one another. He had promised Ralf that if Fred managed to secure a job at the firm, he would gladly supervise him and take him under his wing until the time when Fred felt confident enough to go it alone. Ralf had called round to the gentleman's house shortly after Fred had started work with the company to see if his brother had settled in all right. The elderly gentleman had reported that both he and the company were pleased with Fred's early progress.

For the next couple of years everything in Ralf's life appeared to be perfect. His job was challenging and he worked long hours, but he did enjoy it. His wife was happy to stay at home and tend to everything there, or so he thought. They enjoyed holidays with their children at least once a year, and even Fred appeared to be very settled with them, coming and going as he pleased. It appeared Fred also enjoyed his work in insurance and was making good money from it.

In November 1929 Florence asked Ralf if they might employ some help for her around their home. She explained to her husband that Christmas was fast approaching and if he was to entertain his work colleagues at their home, as he had last year, she was going to need someone to help her. She had found the whole experience rather overwhelming the previous year and was not prepared to endure the sleepless nights which would inevitably happen, especially now, as they were suffering with what everyone was calling 'The Depression'. Ralf agreed without question, as they were fortunate and could afford it. Florence soon began the difficult task of interviewing potential candidates.

It wasn't too long before she found a suitable candidate, named Edie Smith, to help her prepare food, clean and tidy the house, make up the fires, repair and wash the clothes and, of course, help with her sons. The twenty year old was a godsend from the moment she entered their premises. Although young, she and Florence got along well. 'Young Edie', as Ralf had named the girl, was a hard-worker, but also a pleasure to be around. She was great with the children. She sang beautifully to herself as she went about her chores, bringing with her a ray of warm sunshine and brightening up the whole house.

December was indeed a busy month for the household. Florence and Edie were kept extremely busy in preparation for a number of dinner parties which Ralf had arranged to hold for his fellow directors. Ralf was rushed off his feet, arriving home late most nights; even on one of the nights he had planned a dinner, and poor Florence had been required to entertain their guests as best she could until he had arrived home. When their guests had departed, full of good cheer and excellent food, Ralf had congratulated his wife on providing a successful occasion for them all and the following day presented her with a top-of-the-range fur coat from his workplace, along with a diamond brooch to display upon it.

**

During most of December Fred managed to make himself scarce. He had agreed willingly to this when asked by his brother. Ralf believed Fred when he said he disliked these types of occasions. However, when Ralf and Florence weren't entertaining, Fred often wasn't around either. They suspected he may have started drinking again, and Florence wondered if the time of year had anything to do with this habit.

"I suspect it is just a coincidence, my dear. Nothing more. All the same, I think we should keep an eye on him," suggested Ralf.

"I think that is a good idea. I shall ask Edie if she can as well. After all, she goes to bed after we do and is more likely to hear him come in than we are."

Fred had indeed begun to drink again and was frequenting several public houses in the London area, some of which were well known for attracting unsavoury characters. It had been Edie who had informed Florence of this fact. Fred had arrived home one evening after Ralf and Florence had retired upstairs. Edie was still up, banking up the fire with slack in the living room fireplace before she too was planning on going up to bed. She hadn't heard Fred come in and he had startled her. She turned to see him swaying in the doorway, watching her. "Oh, sir, I didn't see you there. Is everything all right? Can I get you a hot drink to take up to bed?"

"I don't want a hot drink," he replied rather grumpily, falling into the armchair beside the door.

"Well, I'll be off to bed then. Goodnight, sir."

But as Edie attempted to walk past him, he grabbed her arm. "Stay and talk for a while, would you?" he begged, looking deep into her eyes.

"Of course, sir," she replied politely. "What would you like to talk about?"

"I don't know," he replied abruptly, slurring his words.

"Why don't you tell me where you've been tonight or how your work is going?" suggested Edie helpfully.

And Fred began to rant. At times it was difficult for Edie to understand some of what he was telling her, but she managed to grasp the gist of it. He told her he had been asked by a colleague at work to cover his workload for him, as he was feeling a little under the weather. Fred was moaning because he had agreed to it and was now regretting the amount of time it was taking him to get round all of the other man's customers as well as his own. To make this tiresome chore more appealing, he told Edie, he had called into a couple of public houses after completing his collections. When he told her where he had been that night, she was a little shocked, as she knew the places had terrible reputations and that her employer would not approve.

Edie then suggested to Fred that perhaps he should not drink in such places.

He reacted aggressively to this suggestion and told her she should mind her own business. "And don't go saying anything to my brother either," he added. "My brother is also too fond of interfering. He apparently knows the old chap I'm covering for. Asked him to keep an eye on me, he did. The cheek of it. As though I can't be trusted." And Fred went on and on and on.

When the moment felt right, Edie managed to slip away upstairs to bed, leaving Fred prattling on to himself. He eventually fell asleep in the living room armchair, and that was where Edie found him the following morning. She tapped him lightly on the shoulder to wake him up and told him his brother would be down soon. Fred quickly composed himself, and she didn't see him again until the following day.

Edie informed Florence of the conversation she'd had with Fred, and having done so, felt the matter over with. It was up to her employers how they chose to handle the situation. But it soon became apparent they had chosen to do nothing.

Ralf and Florence turned the matter over and over, and in the end they decided they should just keep a closer eye on Fred. How they intended to do this would soon prove challenging, as Fred continued to stay away from the house for long hours at a time. They often suspected his bed hadn't been slept in at all on some occasions. As Christmas came and went, Ralf and Florence would wonder about Fred's strange behaviour. However, before they could discover the truth, he would horrify Florence by putting her through a terrible ordeal.

***

One evening in late January, Fred arrived home worse for the drink again. There were only Florence, the children and Edie at home. Ralf was working late. Florence was upstairs seeing to her boys and had not heard Fred arrive home. When she heard raised voices coming from the kitchen and the smashing of what sounded like a ceramic plate, she assumed it was her husband arguing with Edie but could not understand why, as this was very out of character for him. She raced down the stairs, and upon entering the kitchen discovered Edie pinned up against the kitchen cupboards and Fred attempting to do unspeakable things to the girl.

"Get away from her right now!" she demanded. Florence had no idea where the voice she had just used had come from. She had never been forced to use it before and was unaware it even existed within her. What she did recognise, though, was the immense anger she was feeling.

Fred spun around and faced her. She hardly recognised him. His eyes were dark, almost black. "Why? Do you want some?" he boomed.

Florence held her ground. "Get out of my house!"

At this point, Edie had composed herself enough to slip past Fred, and quickly moved to stand beside her employer, brushing down her skirt, which Fred had just had his hands up. The two women stood in unison, ready for whatever might happen next, knowing they had one another for support.

Fred fumbled with the fly of his trousers as he realised the two women were too much of a challenge for him. "I'll collect my things then, and I'll be out of your hair," he snorted, heading towards the door. As he left the kitchen, Florence thought she heard him mutter 'bitches' under his breath, but she couldn't be sure.

The two women fell into each other's arms and Edie began to quietly sob. Florence sat her down on a kitchen chair, reached inside one of the kitchen cupboards and poured a small amount of her husband's best brandy into two glasses.

"Drink it," she insisted. Edie did as she was instructed and abruptly shivered as she swallowed the liquid. "Now just sit there for a moment." Florence swallowed her drink in one go then got up and made her way to the door.

"Don't leave me," cried Edie.

"I'm not going anywhere," replied Florence. She watched and waited for Fred to return from upstairs.

After a few moments, he appeared on the stairs carrying the suitcase he had arrived with three years earlier. As he passed the kitchen door, he spotted Florence and said, "Good luck explaining this to Ralf. He's not going to believe a word you tell him." Then he laughed unreservedly and opened the front door, slamming it hard behind him.

Wilfred

Wilfred was an insurance salesman and collections agent in London. With the help of his father, he had obtained this position some years previously, and by 1930 he was a well-regarded employee. As an insurance salesman and collections agent, it was Wilfred's job to travel around the London area, making hundreds of collections each week. He had got to know the city well and was used to travelling by foot or using the train and tram systems.

Wilfred was respectable and trustworthy, and this had also won him the admiration of his fellow agents. Owing to his decent character, he would tirelessly offer his support and encouragement to the younger, timider or more insecure newcomers to this role, taking them under his wing until they no longer needed his assistance. Fred had been his most recent triumph, and Wilfred had been shocked to discover how seriously mistaken he had been about this young man.

Wilfred had never married. He lived alone in a reasonably large house on Pennistone Road, Streatham, left to him by his father, who had bought the house from new. It was an attractive house, with mock-Tudor architecture, and the two men had lived there together until his father's death in 1925. Since then Wilfred had tended to let the house go a little. He mostly lived within just two rooms of the property. The front bedroom was where he slept. It had wooden beams across the ceiling, an oak perimeter shelf and an attractive, dark, oak-panelled fireplace. Wilfred felt comfortable, secure and able to relax in this room. But it was the kitchen where he spent most of his time. This housed a table at its centre, with a number of non-matching chairs: a comfortable cane, a leather armchair, a dining-type chair and a couple of less comfortable wooden kitchen chairs. In the centre of its main wall was the chimney breast, which housed a large, black, lead, range fireplace, complete with firebox, ash pit and oven. This was usually lit daily, as it heated the room, dried Wilfred's clothes, heated the water to allow him to wash and was also where he did all of his cooking.

Since the death of his father, Wilfred had done little with the property. He rarely cleaned it, nor could he afford a cleaner. As he lived mostly out of his kitchen, this was where he kept most of his paperwork, so the room appeared busy and full. He had two large bookcases either side of the chimney breast, but although these were kept exceedingly tidy and ordered, they gave the appearance of being cluttered. However, he did have a great deal of this paperwork, and finding space for it all was becoming more and more of a challenge.

His kitchen was lit by a single gaslight which protruded from the ceiling, casting a meagre light directly over the kitchen table. Above the fireplace stood an antique clock which had once belonged to his grandfather and still kept good time. Apart from an old kitchen cupboard, the odd vase and a couple of inexpensive pictures on the wall, the only other significant item in his kitchen was a birdcage.

Wilfred had purchased two green budgerigars a few years after his father's death, and they had proved great company for him. He adored the birds and would sit in his kitchen for hours watching their antics. When he cleaned out their cage, they would fly around his kitchen, enjoying their moment of freedom, but they always came back to their cage and their master when he eventually called them. The two birds brought Wilfred great pleasure.

Wilfred had no family. His mother had died a number of years before his father, and as he had never married, he had no children. He had never met the right woman. Or rather, he had never met an obtainable woman. The women he came into contact with were usually married to his clients and were, therefore, unavailable to him.

Wilfred rarely mixed with anyone outside of his work. The only other activity besides his insurance work which brought him close to any other kind of human contact was the chess club he attended most Wednesday evenings. There, it was usually men only. On the odd occasion when a woman had been in the vicinity of the building during a chess night, it had been clear to Wilfred that she was not a woman with whom he would wish to acquaint himself.

Wilfred was a man of high standards, and he had high expectations of other people as well, especially the ones he chose to mix with in his personal life. Over the last couple of years, Wilfred had got to know Fred well. It had been Fred's brother with whom Wilfred had first become acquainted, when he had visited the office in search of work for Fred. During their conversation, the two men had realised they lived in close proximity to one another, and Wilfred had agreed to oversee and guide Fred if his interview was successful.

Wilfred had believed from day one that Fred was someone who had great potential for insurance work. Although he was young, and at times could appear troubled, Fred was very polite and could soon have most potential customers eating out of his hand. He especially had a way with the ladies, which Wilfred had never been able to achieve. Although Fred had shadowed Wilfred on his rounds to begin with, he had quickly taken to the job and managed to establish a good client list for himself.

Once Fred had established himself, Wilfred only really saw him if they were both at the office at the same time. This happened in November 1929, and on this occasion Wilfred invited Fred to join him at his chess club the following Wednesday evening. He wasn't sure why he had done this. Perhaps he felt he had seen little of his young friend recently.

Wilfred thought Fred found him a little odd, but Fred was pleasant enough to Wilfred, so it obviously didn't bother him too much. He had, after all, been the only one to make Fred feel welcome when he had started working for the insurance company. Wilfred wondered if Fred thought he owed him for this kindness, and that by accompanying him to his chess club, he was repaying the favour he had done for Ralf. He felt the need to explain himself.

"I really didn't mind helping your brother out, Fred. It was a pleasure to assist you when you first began with the company."

"How do you mean, 'help my brother out'?" Fred enquired.

"He asked me if I would show you the ropes and keep my eye on you. You didn't know?"

"No. He kept that quiet."

"I do hope I haven't spoken out of turn," worried Wilfred.

"Don't be silly. I wouldn't have had it any other way," smiled Fred.

When he had returned home from his club that Wednesday, Wilfred reflected upon his evening with Fred, believing they'd both enjoyed each other's company equally. Theirs was an unlikely friendship, but at this time it appeared to work for them both.

***

By the end of this year, Wilfred's health had started to deteriorate. He had often suffered with his health, and his trouble would usually flair up during the winter months, so he'd been expecting it. In December Wilfred was feeling less and less able to visit his customers and asked Fred if he might fill in for him; to go house to house to collect money from his regulars. Fred agreed, and Wilfred believed he was glad to help.

After Fred had performed this task on Wilfred's behalf, and this happened a number of times alongside having to collect from his own clients, Fred would call in at Wilfred's house with the takings from his rounds and the pair would enjoy a cup of tea together and a brief chat about their day.

Fred appeared to enjoy their chats, but he had not taken a liking to Wilfred's budgerigars. Wilfred had asked Fred on more than one occasion not to rattle the cage or poke things through the bars at them, as this would frighten his pets, but Fred appeared to enjoy upsetting his birds. On this particular day, though, Fred was more interested in watching Wilfred as he checked and double-checked the takings Fred had collected on his behalf.

"There appears to be a number of pounds short from your collections this week," commented Wilfred.

"Oh yes. I can explain those," replied Fred, very matter-of-factly.

Fred explained to Wilfred how a number of Wilfred's regular customers had not been able to make the full payment this week, giving their names and reasons why.

Once satisfied that his own and Fred's totals tallied, Wilfred got up from the table, unlocked the kitchen cupboard, reached inside and pulled out a tin. This was where he kept his collected insurance money. He added the money Fred had collected on his behalf to the tin, then replaced it inside the cupboard, locking it afterwards and replacing the key inside his trouser pocket. Wilfred noticed Fred observing him and said, "You can't be too careful these days."

"Absolutely," replied Fred.

During another visit to Wilfred's home with the insurance money he'd collected, which again was short, Fred disclosed that he had recently treated himself to a number of expensive new suits and shoes for work. At first Wilfred had thought how practical and sensible it was of Fred to purchase these items. But after Fred had left his home, Wilfred pondered over the cost of these extravagant items and speculated how Fred could possibly have afforded them.

Wilfred knew he would have to investigate further and it wasn't long before he discovered that Fred had been 'dipping his fingers into the till'. Fred had been accumulating this money for quite some time, most likely right from the start of working alongside Wilfred. Wilfred was horrified by his findings and promptly informed his superiors about Fred stealing from the company. A separate investigation by the company was launched in the new year, and within a week Fred had been dismissed from the firm. Wilfred had felt very disappointed and betrayed by Fred.

***

Christmas came and went, and it was now mid-January. Fred's dismissal had happened on the quiet, as the company could not risk the story reaching the newspapers. It undoubtedly would have done them much harm. Wilfred never saw Fred again. He felt terrible about the whole thing. How could he have been so wrong about Fred?

The worry of bumping into Fred, or him finding out that it had been Wilfred who had informed the company about him stealing, was constantly on Wilfred's mind. As his health deteriorated further, he was unable to find anyone else to cover his rounds for him. As the days passed, Wilfred became further and further behind with his collections, to the point that a number of his regular clients with whom he had been doing business with for many years had complained and had been allocated a new agent.

It was no use. Wilfred had to pull himself together and get back out there or he stood to lose his job. Mustering all his strength, Wilfred started back to work during early February. He travelled across London, going house to house, collecting from his remaining customers. By the Wednesday of that week, he felt exhausted, yet forced himself to attend his chess club, which he had not done now for quite some weeks. He walked the mile to the White Lion, situated on Streatham High Street, where his fellow players were delighted to have him return. As he began a new game, the landlord approached him, handing him a message which had been received by telephone about twenty-five minutes before Wilfred had arrived. The message requested that Wilfred call at 54 Corunna Street, Crestwell, at seven-thirty the following evening to discuss insurance with a man who had given his name as Edward Benton.

The following evening, Wilfred set out. He had never heard of Corunna Street and had never received a call like this at his chess club before. He was tired and had endured another busy day, but he decided to keep the appointment, as his customers had been significantly reduced recently and he hoped there might be some valuable commission in it for him.

He caught the train to Clapham Junction, then jumped on a tram for another two miles along Wandsworth Road. Unsure where to get off the tram, he asked both the conductor and the ticket inspector, explaining that he did not know the area well. At this stage Wilfred was becoming increasingly agitated, as it was almost seven-thirty, and he realised he was not going to make his appointment on time. Both men told him they had never heard of such a street but gave him directions as to where they thought it might be. He got off the tram when instructed and walked for a quarter of a mile further before coming upon Corunna Terrace.

Wilfred knew immediately this was the wrong street, as there were only a small number of houses on it. There was definitely no number fifty-four.

He decided to call in at the public house on the corner of this street and ask. The landlord told him, "The next road along is Corunna Place, but that has even less houses on it. After that there is only Corunna

Road. I suspect that is where you're after. There is no Corunna Street. Not around here." Wilfred thanked the landlord and continued with his search.

Before crossing over to Corunna Road, Wilfred thought he should quickly investigate Corunna Place to make sure the landlord was correct about the number of houses there, and he was. There were even fewer houses on this street. Both of these smaller roads backed onto the railway line. This was a noisy, dirty and unpleasant area of Crestwell. Crossing the road, he was now pinning all his hopes upon Corunna Road, and he quickly made his way to number fifty-four, as by now it was seven forty-five. Corunna Road crossed Patmore Street, then he eventually arrived at number fifty-four. He knocked on the door. A woman answered.

"Good evening, madam. I have an appointment with a Mr Edward Benton. Is the gentleman at home?" asked Wilfred.

"Sorry, love. What name did you say?"

"Benton? Edward Benton?"

"There's no one here who goes by that name," replied the woman.

"This is number fifty-four?"

"Says it on the door, don't it?"

"Yes," agreed Wilfred reluctantly. "You see, I've been asked to meet an Edward Benton at 54 Corunna Street."

"This is Corunna Road."

"Yes, thank you, madam. I am aware of that. It appears there is no Corunna Street, so I thought they must have meant road."

"There's no one here who goes by the name of Benton. There's me and the husband and our two lads, surname of James, and our lodgers are Mr and Mrs Hadley. If you ask me, someone's playing a nasty trick on you, love." And with that, she closed her front door.

At the end of this road there was another pub. Wilfred thought he would check with the landlord there, just in case. Once again, he was told there was no such place.

Wilfred spent two hours looking for Corunna Street, including taking the train and tram journeys, only to discover that while there was a Corunna Terrace, a Corunna Place and a Corunna Road, there was no Corunna Street. He made enquiries in public houses, spoke to a policeman on his beat and asked several other passers-by in the neighbourhood for directions, but nobody was able to help him in his search for the mysterious address. He was lost in London on a cold night, trying to find an address that seemed not to exist. Wilfred eventually gave up and decided to return home.

Whoever had made the call to his chess club appeared to be pulling Wilfred's leg, sending him on a pointless journey to a fictitious address. On his way home Wilfred wondered if this appointment was merely a joke or something more sinister.

When he arrived home, he realised there had been more to it. He quickly observed that his house had been broken into. Wilfred never used his front door, but always entered through the back, where he found the door hanging off its hinges. As he entered his kitchen, he noticed his insurance collection box was on the kitchen table, open and empty, and to his horror he saw that his two precious budgerigars had been killed in their cage. Wilfred didn't care about the money, but he was utterly devastated about his birds.

When he was able to gather his thoughts, Wilfred checked the rest of his house. Nothing else appeared to have been touched. Only the kitchen had been ransacked, and nothing else had been taken. Wilfred informed the police, and they sent a constable round to his house within the hour. Around midnight, he was taken to the police station to make a formal statement.

Wilfred told the police about the phone call to his club and explained that he'd left his house on Pennistone Road at around six forty-five and caught the train from Streatham Common to Clapham Junction at seven o'clock. From there he'd caught a tram along Lavender Hill and Wandsworth Road until he'd got to Stewarts Road, where he'd walked to where he thought he'd needed to be.

At first the police thought the call made to his chess club was an attempt to lure Wilfred away from his house, in order to steal his insurance money when no one would be at home. They believed, like Wilfred, that he had been tricked into leaving his house by a man asking to meet him to discuss insurance. There had been a number of burglaries in the local area in the previous months, so they could not rule out the usual suspects at first.

During the interview, Wilfred was asked if he could think of anyone who could have broken into his home and stolen the money. "I suspect one man only," said Wilfred, and he went on to explain his association with Fred.

"It was when Fred was collecting money on my insurance round that I first noticed money was missing from the ledger. I thought Fred had been dipping into the takings and confronted him, but he convinced me there were legitimate reasons for the reduction and that it was down to my customers. This happened on more than one occasion," explained Wilfred.

"There was just something about the man, but I couldn't put my finger on it. I believed he was continuously short of money, but I can't prove that. I now believe Fred decided to rob me because he must have found out that it was me who reported him for fiddling the insurance books and lost him his job. It must have been Fred who sent me on that wild goose chase around Crestwell on a cold winter's night as revenge for getting him the sack. Fred also knew my home well; he had visited it on many occasions. And he was also aware that I kept large sums of insurance money in a tin in my kitchen cupboard. Oh, and he also disliked my unfortunate birds." Wilfred was keen to offer as much information to the police as he could.

The police investigated Wilfred's claims, but they were unable to trace Fred, although they did get to speak to his brother with whom he had been staying. His brother had no forwarding address for Fred, explaining that they had fallen out and lost contact. Their enquiries met a dead end.

The tram conductor recounted to the police how Wilfred had pestered him and his ticket inspector to notify him where to get off and that he'd seemed strangely agitated as he rode on their tram. He added that when he had eventually pointed out to Wilfred the correct stop, Wilfred had seemed particularly keen that he should know he was a complete stranger to the area.

It occurred to the police that the caller to the chess club appeared to know Wilfred would be there that night, but in fact, this would have been impossible to know, as he had not been to the club for a number of weeks before. When the police discovered the location of the phone box from where the call had been made, they began to change their minds, choosing to believe that it was Wilfred himself who had made the call. They believed he'd had the opportunity to place the call himself, as the phone box in question was the one outside the public house where his chess club met each week.

The police now thought Wilfred had staged the whole elaborate evening in order to keep the takings he had collected that week for himself. They had noted the way he was living and that he must have been struggling to make ends meet. Perhaps he had murdered his birds, as he was no longer able to afford to look after them. The police also noted the number of people Wilfred had spoken to that evening—asking for directions—all of whom added to their suspicions, making them conclude that Wilfred was attempting to create a watertight alibi.

As the police could find no concrete evidence that Wilfred had taken any money, he was eventually only charged with wasting police time. But by then Wilfred was a man worn down by poor health and disappointment. He returned to his job in insurance after this incident, but he was never the same again. His illness returned and he was forced to give up work altogether, living out his days alone and penniless.

Anthony

———◄◦►———

"The last thing I expected to 'ave when I entered through the gates of Brixton Prison was a fan club. There's this one bloke 'oo just won't leave me alone," Anthony moaned to a fellow inmate. "I've told 'im what 'appened about four or five times, but 'e keeps coming to find me and ask me all these questions."

"Do you think he knew the bitch?" asked his cellmate.

"I 'adn't thought of that. Maybe."

"Who is he anyway?"

"Don't know 'is name. I'll point 'im out to you next time I see 'im. You'll not be able to miss 'im. 'E's got an enormous 'ooter."

Brixton Prison was London's oldest prison. Built in 1820, when Brixton was a small village, it had originally held 175 inmates. In 1932 it could hold up to 800 prisoners. At one time it had housed a treadmill, where prisoners would pace its revolving steps for up to ten hours a day, powering the prison flour mill from where their daily bread was made. *Thank Christ, they got rid of it thirty years ago,* thought Anthony each time he passed the footings which remained in the yard outside.

The prison at this time held a mix of offenders on remand: thieves, armed robbers, rapists and murderers. All were male, as female prisoners had not been seen at Brixton Prison since the 1880s. The assortment of society within the walls of Brixton Prison were not the types of people anyone of an ordinary character would choose to mix with, and there was never a dull moment inside its walls, as there were always fights, hunger strikes, stabbings or sexual assaults. Anthony had been charged with housebreaking and murder and was now awaiting his trial. His cellmate had been charged with armed robbery and his so-called fan had been charged with larceny and receiving stolen goods.

Since his schooldays, Anthony had been living a life of crime. He frequented the same places other criminals visited, mixing with the undesirables of human society, and gradually, over a period of time, his crimes had become more serious. Although he pretended his new-found fan irritated him, Anthony had actually become rather dependent upon his admiration. He would, when allowed out of his cell, seek out this new-found friend, pretending to come across him by accident.

"How do?" enquired his fan when he next saw Anthony, who just happened to be hanging around waiting for him.

"I suppose. As much as anyone who's waiting to be tried for murder can be," Anthony replied. The two men sat down in unison at a table where a number of other prisoners were reading and playing cards. "I didn't mean to do 'er in, you know. I'm innocent," stated Anthony.

"Really?"

"Yeah. I was just after a bit of, you know," he winked. "'Ow's your father, you know?"

His fan nodded. "I guess she was having none of it then? All the same these women, aren't they?"

"No. It wasn't like that."

"What do you mean then?"

"She was the other way. She wanted to do all manner of sordid things to me. She was disgusting, she was. Never known anything like it."

Anthony could tell his fan was keen to find out more details regarding this woman's promiscuous sexual behaviour, but he was not willing to discuss this subject any further. His fan was forced to alter his approach.

"So, what was her name?" he asked.

"Didn't really ask 'er name. But I think the police said 'er name was Ada."

"And how did you meet her?"

"It must 'ave been about midnight when I saw 'er. Followed 'er, I did. All the way from Piccadilly for about a mile, till we got to Lambeth Bridge. Then I spoke to 'er. I'd watched 'er wiggle in front of me for more than 'alf an hour and couldn't stand it any longer, so I picked 'er up. We walked along the embankment, chatting, ya know, and she asked me back to 'er flat in Brixton. Couldn't say no, could I? Wish I 'ad now though."

"Is that where you killed her?"

"Ya don't mince your words, do ya? Anyone'd think you're the plod."

"Sorry, I just meant—"

"I know what ya meant. You wanna know 'ow I did it. I did it with me bare 'ands. I warned 'er first, like. I told 'er I'd choke 'er. We argued, ya see, about what she wanted to do. So, I 'it her then got 'old of 'er throat, and she struggled for a bit, but then she just went out. I didn't think it was so easy to kill someone."

"What did you feel afterwards?"

"What d'ya reckon I felt? I panicked, didn't I. I never meant to kill 'er. I just wanted to frighten 'er. Get 'er to stop what she wanted to do."

"So, what did you do next?"

"I thought about it for a few seconds, then knocked over a table and made a mess of the room to make it look like a break-in. But she only 'ad a ring worth taking, so I changed me mind and put the furniture back and straightened the bed clothes. Then I thought I'd make it look like she'd done 'erself in, so I got one of 'er silk stockings and tied it round 'er neck to make it look like she'd strangled 'erself."

Anthony's story was interrupted at this point as all prisoners were instructed to return to their cells.

"See ya tomorrow, no doubt," he called after his fan, who waved back at him and smiled. *That should keep 'im going for a while*, thought Anthony.

***

The following day Anthony was outside in the prison yard getting some exercise alongside his fellow cellmate when his fan caught up with him again.

"All right?"

"Yep," replied Anthony.

"All right?" the fan asked Anthony's cellmate.

Realising that this must be the fan Anthony spoke of, because the

SARAH LYSAGHT

chap definitely had a larger nose than most, he nodded to the fan in response then walked off. He had no desire to listen to Anthony's story again. He'd heard it too many times already.

Getting straight to the point, Anthony's fan began to ask more probing questions. "So, how come you got caught then?"

"Bet ya've been thinking about this all night, ain't ya?"

"I'm just the curious type, that's all."

"Well, I made a mistake, ya see. I should 'ave just left and got right away from there. Bet I would 'ave got away with it then if I 'ad. It might 'ave been one of them unsolved crimes you 'ear about in the newspapers. Anyway, I saw an opportunity, with it being the middle of the night an' dark an' all. I put me shoulder to the door of this small shop, broke it open and went in. Trouble was, one of the plods spotted me and chased me. Quick bugger 'e was. Arrested me in no time. I blame it on the drink from the night before. Weren't quite feeling me ol' self, ya see."

"But I still don't understand how you can be arrested for breaking in somewhere but charged with murder."

"Well, if ya just let me finish."

"Sorry. Do go on."

"Listen to you, all la-di-da. Do go on, indeed." Anthony attempted to speak in a posh voice.

His fan's expression changed. He was not impressed with Anthony making fun of him, but Anthony was enjoying the attention, so he quickly reassured his fan and said "I'm only joking, me ol' mate", patting the man on the back to reassure him. "Let me explain. I'm an idiot. I don't mind admitting it. I confessed, ya see. On the way to the police station, I told the constable that I'd just done somebody in. He didn't believe me though. I 'ad to convince him."

"But why did you confess?"

"Guilt, I suppose. Because I never meant to 'urt 'er."

"But you might have got away with it."

"I suppose I thought that when they found the body, they'd think it was me anyways, 'cause I'd been arrested nearby on the same night. I thought that if I confessed and told 'em the truth, they'd believe me."

"They might not have found the body for days, or even weeks, after."

68

"Perhaps, but knowing my luck, they would 'ave found 'er the same night, so I came clean. But I don't really care now anyway. What will be, will be. It's out of me 'ands now, and I'm stuck 'ere."

There was a moment's silence between the two prisoners, then Anthony asked, "So, it's your turn now, mate. What you in 'ere for?"

"Receiving," his fan answered.

"That it? Not very daring, are you?"

Anthony was unimpressed, and noticing this fact, his fan cockily admitted, "I did my brother's place over first. They never caught me for that. And I'd been taking insurance money for months and nobody noticed. That amounted to hundreds of pounds."

"Now you're talking, lad. Pray, do continue," joked Anthony in a false posh voice. "Tell me why ya would rob yer own brother though. Not sure I understand that one."

"I have two elder brothers, you see, and they both think they know better than me, but I showed them."

"Well-off, are they?"

"Yes. The eldest is always travelling abroad, and his wife often goes with him. They have this grand house and never seem to be there. What's the point in that, I ask you?"

"Nice if ya can get it."

"So I decided to help myself when they were out one day. They've got enough stuff not to notice, I thought."

"So, what did ya get?"

"A torch—"

"A torch?" Anthony interrupted, laughing loudly. "Well, ya ain't gonna make yer fortune like that now, are ya? What did ya want with a torch of all things?"

"It was dark outside, and I didn't want to turn on the house lights, so I used the torch and just put it inside my pocket as I left."

Anthony laughed again, unimpressed. He could tell his fan was desperate to impress him and he was loving every moment.

"There were also gold rings, a wristwatch, a gold brooch, a tiepin, some other jewellery and some cash and foreign coins," insisted his fan.

"That's more like it. Now calm down or ya'll 'ave the screws on us. So where did ya get rid of the gear?"

"Well, it was my first job, and I hadn't really thought it through. It wasn't until later that I realised if I got caught with the stuff, I'd be in trouble, so I took it to a pub I know, where I'd previously met some fellas who I knew would buy it off me. I made sure I got a decent sum for it all."

"Glad to hear it. So after ya'd knocked off yer brother's place, ya thought ya'd try something more challenging?"

"You mean the insurance money?"

"That's right."

"That was a pushover, not really a challenge."

Anthony couldn't make out if his fan was lying to him or not. But he was going to have to wait to find out, for just as his fan was about to explain more, all prisoners were told to return to their cells for the day.

***

Anthony couldn't find his fan the next day, or the day after that. He was too proud to make enquiries as to the chap's whereabouts and so was forced to wait patiently for another few days. When his fan finally resurfaced in the dining area one lunchtime, he was looking a little worse for wear.

"What 'appened to you?" Anthony enquired as he sat down next to his fan.

"Some chap didn't take kindly to me asking too many questions, so he thumped me. Next thing I remember was when I came round on the floor and my face hurt like hell."

"That's what it's like in 'ere. Ya meet all kinds of nutters. Ya'll learn. Anyways, tell me all about this insurance money ya got yer hands on before we get shoved back into our cells again."

The pair huddled in close together, so as not to be overheard.

"All right then. I was working with this old boy who thought he knew it all. He thought he was the only one who had ever collected insurance money, so you had to do it his way or he'd get really upset with you."

"Yeah. I've met 'is sort, all right."

"I got really fed up with it. I couldn't seem to get anything right, and he treated me like a child."

"So, what did ya do?" Anthony pressed his fan, realising that his fan was enjoying how the tables had turned now that all the attention was on him.

"The old boy became ill and asked if I would visit his customers and collect their money for him. I agreed, but I soon found I was working later and later because I had so many collections to make, and most were right across the other side of the city."

"So ya started pocketing the old chap's earnings? As payment for your inconvenience?"

Anthony's fan glared resentfully at him for guessing his story before he could tell it.

"You guessed it," replied his fan sarcastically. "I was getting away with it for quite some time as well, until I got hauled in to see the boss. I could afford whatever I wanted one minute, then it was all taken away from me. But I taught the old man a lesson, I did."

"What did ya do, mate? See him off, did ya?"

"I showed him who was really boss. I robbed him; that's what I did. I sent the stupid sod off on a fool's errand then broke into his house and took all his takings from inside the tin he kept hidden in his kitchen. He never even had time to suspect me. Once he'd reported it to the police, he was too busy attempting to convince them he hadn't done it himself. It was the company's money, you see."

"Yeah, I get it. Clever little sod, ain't ya?"

"Well, I got away with it. The last I heard, the police had charged him with wasting their time and all but given up on finding the money."

"So 'ow much do ya reckon ya got away with then?"

"Ah, well that would be telling now, wouldn't it?"

"So why ya in 'ere? What did ya get caught stealing this time?"

"I was in the pub, helping a mate to get rid of some gear. Big job, it was. Involved quite a few of us across London. Just as I was about to leave with my gear, the cops arrived and filled the pub, arresting the lot of us. Someone had tipped them off."

"Got a bit cocky, did ya?"

"You could say that. I put my trust in a couple of idiots who promised everything would go smoothly and I'd make a killing."

"Obviously those two idiots couldn't keep their gobs shut," commented Anthony.

"The police said they'd been heard discussing the robberies and bragging about the pretty sum they were going to make."

"Are those two fellas in 'ere?"

"No. They were sent to Wandsworth. Apparently, they'd committed armed robbery a few months prior and attacked a policeman before getting away. When the police searched their flats, they found items from that burglary, which was how they got them."

"Idiots. Ya can learn from that."

"Oh yes. I have."

"So, 'ave ya any plans for when ya get out?"

"Not really. I'm still trying to work that one out. You?"

"Me? Yep. Got big plans, I 'ave. Met this woman, ya see. Says she'll wait till I get out."

"That's nice," replied his fan, unsure as to whether Anthony was being completely honest with him or just fooling himself.

"Listen, mate. If ever ya need any 'elp once yer out, I can let ya 'ave the names of some reliable chaps I know who'd sort ya out, no questions asked. They'd not let ya down."

"That's very kind of you. Thank you. I'll give it some consideration."

"'Ark at you. Gone all la-di-da on me again, you 'ave."

"Right, gents, back to your cells, please. Quick as you can now!"

And that was the end of their conversation once more.

***

Anthony and his fan would meet a few more times before his fan was released, having served six months in prison. Anthony's sentence was far longer for his more serious crime. He had never stopped to consider the consequences of his crime. It had been his impulsive and irresponsible behaviour which had landed him in prison. The police believed he felt no remorse for what he'd done, and they also did not believe him when he told them it was accidental.

Over the years, as his crimes had worsened, so too had his drink problem. He had lost his job and had nowhere to live. He wandered the streets most nights and had to steal to pay for the alcohol he was now dependent upon. That was how he had come to be where he was today.

Having spent six months in prison with Anthony, his fan was informed on the day before he left prison that although Anthony had been charged with wilful murder and found guilty, a successful appeal had reduced his sentence to manslaughter. Anthony informed his fan that he would only have to spend the next eight years in prison.

The two men never saw one another again. But before they had parted company, Anthony had ensured that his fan had full knowledge of a number of contacts he could make if ever he needed to do so.

Selina

———◇———

In April 1932 Selina and Frank made the decision to move from India to England. They had been married for thirteen years and were now in their fifties. Their relationship after the death of Selina's first husband had rapidly developed, and Selina had grown to love the tattoos which covered Frank's body. At first she had thought them rather vulgar. Now she was able to stroke and admire the stork and snake designs he had across his upper body and arm and believed she loved Frank more than she had ever loved her first husband. It had been Frank who had got her through the most difficult times in her life: the unruly behaviour of Fred during his youth, the suffering and loss of her first husband and when she had discovered what had really happened to her son Joseph.

Frank had been there when she had discovered her son had died from a neck wound two days after the war was declared over. He had supplied the strength she needed when she'd received Joseph's war medals and memorial plaque, issued to commemorate all of the war dead. And a further year later, in January 1922, when Joseph's belongings were finally returned to Selina, Frank had supported her again. As she'd tightly clutched and examined her son's belongings—his watch, his ring, his diary, photographs of the family, his Stylo pen and his purse—it had been Frank who had held her when she had wept for hours.

By 1932 Selina had not seen any of her children for more than five years. Fred had been the last to leave India, in 1927, and although she had corresponded fairly regularly with most of her children since then, often reading things she found hard to accept, she had never visited any of them. Selina missed them but had never once considered moving to be nearer them. It had been Frank who was instrumental in the move to England. He was enthusiastic about moving back to his country of origin.

As they caught the Ellerman City Line passenger steam ship from Calcutta to London, Frank was excited to be returning to England, while Selina endured the long journey as best she could. Upon their arrival they stayed with Alex and Helena in London for a short time before finally settling in a place called Willesden, an area in North West London about five miles from Charing Cross, where Frank had grown up. After the First World War, Willesden had grown rapidly. Many factories had opened, and flats and houses were built to accommodate the workers who flooded into this area. Irish immigrants also moved here, many of whom were in the building trade, and they too needed to find places to live, as well as work. By 1933 there was little green space left for the people here to enjoy, as the council had been so set on rushing through numerous building schemes, they had neglected to leave any space for parks and leisure. Selina and Frank moved into an overcrowded and diverse area. It was all they could afford, but Frank instantly felt as though he had come home.

They rented rooms in a property on Bramston Road, owned by a Mr and Mrs Jenkins. Mr Jenkins was a retired caretaker of a local school and he rented out rooms in his house as a means of extra income. The Jenkins were an amiable couple, and Selina and Frank got on well with them. They took the rooms on the upper floor, while the Jenkins had the ground-floor rooms.

The four adults were around the same age, and both couples had children who were now grown-up and living independently of them. Most evenings, they would eat a meal together and enjoy a game of cards. The women shopped together at weekends and shared the housework, while the men occasionally visited a local pub and enjoyed a beer. Times were hard for Selina and Frank at this stage in their lives; money was scarce and there was also the recession to consider. They would have to be prudent with the little money they had left from Frank's family's estate if it were to see them through to their old age.

Most of the houses along Bramston Road had more than one family living in them at this time. The neighbours either side of the Jenkins' household had families with young children, so it could often be quite noisy, and there were always people coming and going up and down the street. But Selina and Frank settled here and appeared to be happy.

When her son Fred turned up on their doorstep one afternoon in 1933, Selina was overcome with joy to see him. He had discovered where Frank and his mother were living when he had re-established contact with his brother Ralf. While staying with Alex, Selina had sensed they'd had a falling out, and all Alex could tell her was that he'd not seen or heard from Fred in some time. She was now pleased to discover that Fred had at least been in contact with one his brothers.

Fred arrived complete with suitcase, and as the afternoon progressed, Frank established the true reason Fred was there. After a cup of tea and general chit-chat, Fred eventually admitted that he had lost his job and lodgings and had nowhere else to go. He explained that he had asked his brother Alex if he might stay with him, but he had refused and told Fred where their mother and Frank were now living.

"I wondered if I might stay with you and Frank; just until I can get myself organised," enquired Fred.

"I would love you to live here with us—of course I would—but it's not our house, Fred. We will have to see what Mr and Mrs Jenkins have to say."

"Can we ask them now?" demanded Fred.

"They're out," replied Frank abruptly.

Selina shot her husband a glance. "They should be back any time now," she assured. "They're only a few doors away, visiting a neighbour who's just had a baby."

Selina had discovered this fact only the day before when she had bumped into the young couple as they took their baby out for its first push in a pram. She had returned home and immediately informed Mrs Jenkins, who madly finished knitting a pair of booties to go with the lemon cardigan and bonnet she had already completed.

Ten minutes later Mr and Mrs Jenkins arrived home. Selina met them in the hallway as they took off their coats. Frank and Fred remained seated in the upstairs sitting room without speaking to one another. Selina explained the situation, and Mr and Mrs Jenkins were more than happy to accommodate Selina's son. They explained that Fred was welcome to use the smallest room on Selina's floor, which at that time was mainly full of their son's things.

"If Fred is happy to clear the room himself and bring everything downstairs for us to go through, he would be most welcome to the room," said Mrs Jenkins.

"He will only have to pay a nominal amount for the little room," added Mr Jenkins.

"I'm sure that will suit," replied Selina. "You are both very kind. Thank you."

Selina raced to the top of the stairs and called out to Fred. "Fred! Come and meet Mr and Mrs Jenkins."

Fred did as his mother requested.

Shaking hands with Mr Jenkins, he and Fred arranged a payment upfront for the room. Fred politely complimented Mrs Jenkins on her beautiful home, wrapping her around his little finger, the way he did with most women he met. He agreed to every little favour she asked him as he emptied the small room of her son's belongings. Women seemed to just melt into Fred's hands the moment he smiled at them, and Fred had learnt over the years that he was able to manipulate certain situations to his advantage. He did just this with Mrs Jenkins, so that from then on he had her, just like his mother, eating out of his hands.

Fred quickly settled into his new home, and his mother was delighted to have him under her roof once again. The same could not be said of Frank. He'd learned from Alex about all the things Selina's youngest son had been up to since arriving on British soil, and Selina had chosen to sweep all of this under the carpet. It was as though she did not want to believe her son was capable of such things so chose to believe he wasn't.

Fred appeared to cause trouble wherever he went, but for the last two years no one in the family had known his whereabouts. He had turned up on Alex's doorstep, only to be told in no uncertain terms that he was not welcome and then informed, much to his surprise, that his mother had recently moved to the area and might take him in. After learning his mother's new address, he had headed straight there.

Frank had always found that Fred could easily influence Selina and soon realised that while Fred was around, he was no longer as important to her. Having Fred at home with them all day, every day seemed to go on for ever, so each night Frank started to pester Fred, asking if he had found himself a job yet.

***

For the next year, Fred was in and out of work. Not one of the jobs he had been able to find was permanent, and he was restless and bored with life. He just did not know what it was he wanted to do. By 1934 even his mother had started to become concerned about his behaviour, especially when Fred started to refuse to eat his meals with them. He rarely washed or shaved and it seemed he had stopped looking for a job. He appeared to have given up on life and filled most of his day staring out of the window. Whenever Selina and Frank left the house, this was what he was doing, and when they returned, he appeared not to have moved from his seat beside the window.

"Frank and I are popping out to the shops. Would you like to come?" Selina asked her son one Tuesday lunchtime. Fred shook his head from side to side without answering, continuing to stare out of the window at the street below.

"Is there anything you need then while we're out?"

"No, I'm fine," he snapped back at his mother, lighting up another cigarette.

"We'll see you later then," replied Selina, hurt by her son's curt manner.

Selina and Frank left the house. Fred was quite alone, staring vacantly out of the upstairs window. He sat there watching a stray dog walking the length of the street, cocking its leg randomly in gateways. A delivery van passed by, calling at a house further down the street, and then an elderly woman walked past carrying some shopping. The bag she was carrying looked far too heavy for her to manage.

Fred yawned. A young child caught his eye. She had come out of a gate about five doors down and was skipping. Suddenly, she stopped, and Fred thought she was going to be sick. Then she continued on her journey, but at a much slower pace. She was a pretty little thing and reminded him of his sister. Her long dark hair was swept back off her face and tied into plaits with two blue ribbons. She had milky white skin and her eyes were dark. She passed by under his window. Fred leapt to his feet, hurried downstairs and out of the front door as though he had forgotten to do something.

Selina didn't need too many things from the shops. Frank was pleased about that. He was just there for the fresh air and the walk. He hated shopping. Selina usually shopped on High Street, but today she had decided to go to the shops on Harrow Road, as it was a little further to walk. They went to the newsagent's for a paper and at the butcher's bought pork chops for tomorrow's dinner. Next they visited the chemist to pick up some cream for Mrs Jenkins' leg. She had asked Selina if she wouldn't mind doing this for her, as she and Mr Jenkins had a prior engagement and wouldn't be able to get there before closing and she needed it. Selina had willingly agreed.

After the chemist, they entered the greengrocer's. It was very busy in there, and Selina and Frank reluctantly joined a long queue. "Is it normally this busy in here?" he asked his wife.

"I haven't seen it quite so busy as this," she admitted.

Frank soon became fed up and started to annoy Selina by shuffling his feet around on the floor. "Why don't you go and sit on that chair near the door?" she said, thrusting the newspaper from her shopping bag into his hands as the queue slowly moved forward an inch or two. Frank did as his wife suggested. He sat down and began to read the paper. Selina turned occasionally to check up on her husband as she waited patiently in line. Then, as she glanced over her shoulder for a third time to make sure Frank was all right, two figures caught her eye as they passed hurriedly on the pavement outside the shop. At first, she thought it was Fred, but as she couldn't see the man's face clearly, she dismissed this thought. What did strike her, though, was that the child he had with him bore an uncanny resemblance to her daughter, Ellen, when she had been the same age.

Something didn't feel quite right to Selina about the man and this child being together. She sensed even from that distance that the child was unhappy. She pushed all silly thoughts from her head and, turning back to the queue, she supposed he must be her father who was cross with her for some silly reason or other.

Selina was finally able to purchase the fruit and vegetables she needed and left the shop, with Frank following close behind with his newspaper. Outside the shop Frank replaced the newspaper into Selina's shopping bag and offered to carry the heavy purchases she had just made. Selina glanced up and down the street, but there was no sign of the man and his daughter, so she and Frank started to make their way home. They had just reached Wrottesley Road when they were approached by two policemen.

"Excuse me, sir, madam. Have you seen a young female child wandering or looking lost?" asked the taller policeman of the two.

"No," relied Frank.

"How old is the child?" asked Selina.

"She's six years old, madam. She has long black hair, pale complexion and dark brown eyes. Her mother and her school have reported her missing."

There was a short pause while Selina thought. "While I waited in the queue at the greengrocer's, I did see a young child being almost dragged along Harrow Road by a man."

Both policemen and Frank looked at Selina, surprised. "Did you not think to intervene, madam?" the shorter officer asked.

"I almost did," she said, "but then I thought I was being silly and imagining it. And I didn't want to lose my place in the queue."

"Do you think it could be the same missing child?" asked Frank.

"Possibly, sir. Did you see anything while waiting in the queue with your wife?"

"No. I was sitting with my back to the window and door, reading my newspaper while my wife was waiting in the queue."

"Well, it is most likely an unrelated incident, but if you wouldn't mind going to the nearest police station, madam, and giving a short statement, that would be most helpful. We should be on our way now. Have a good afternoon."

"Thank you," replied Selina.

"I hope you find the child," remarked Frank.

The officers nodded and went on their way, and Selina and Frank continued with their journey. When it was clear Selina was heading home and not to the nearest police station, Frank enquired as to why.

"The more I think about it, the more I think I was wrong. The man and child I saw were just going about their own business."

"But if the child was six, shouldn't she have been at school?"

"I suppose so." Selina started doubting herself again. "She could have been with that man for any number of reasons. He could have been her father, and he was taking her to see the dentist and she didn't want to go. Or the doctor. I'd feel silly now if I went to the police station. They would think I was stupid and interfering."

"I'm sure they wouldn't."

"I don't want to waste their time. Besides, I want to get home for Fred."

"All right," conceded Frank. "Let's go home."

When they arrived back at the house, Fred had gone out. It appeared he had gone out in a hurry, as he had left his cigarettes behind on the table in the front room. He did not return home until much later that day, looking clean shaven, but offering no explanation as to where he'd been, and clutching a fresh packet of twenty Player's cigarettes about his person. He went to bed early that evening, saying that he was tired.

***

Two days later Mrs Jenkins shared some news with Selina in her downstairs sitting room over a cup of tea. This news greatly shocked and worried them both. As Mrs Jenkins read aloud from her newspaper, Selina instantly knew that the incident she was reading about was regarding the same child she had spotted while waiting in the greengrocer's queue.

"The child left her mother's house after lunch on Tuesday to return to school. Two friends were waiting for her a couple of hundred yards away, but she never arrived. They then raised the alarm." Mrs Jenkins looked up at Selina. "It's terrible, isn't it?"

"Yes, quite terrible," agreed Selina.

"The police seem to think she may have been spotted with a man walking along Harrow Road."

"Really?" replied Selina. "Does it say how they know that?"

"No. It just says she may have been seen. Oh my goodness me! Oh no! Dear, dear me!"

"Whatever is it, Mrs Jenkins?" enquired Selina reluctantly.

"I have just realised I know this child. It's little Rita from five doors down. You must know her. Long black hair and piercing dark brown eyes. You must have seen her. She's always playing outside on the street and I thought it odd that I'd not seen her these last couple of days. You must know who I mean?"

"I'm sorry. I can't say I do."

"Rita is rather a shy little thing. She wouldn't have just gone off with someone she didn't know."

Selina felt queasy, and as Mrs Jenkins read on, she thought she was going to be sick.

"It says the police are looking for a well-dressed but unshaven and untidy male of slim build, between the age of twenty-five and thirty years, who it is believed tormented her for more than an hour in the cemetery."

As Mrs Jenkins looked at Selina, she realised that all the colour had drained from her friend's face. "Are you feeling all right, dear?" she enquired. "Would you like another cup of tea?"

"No, thank you. I suddenly feel quite unwell. If you don't mind, I'm going to go upstairs for a lie down."

"Of course, dear. Do you need me to help you up the stairs?"

"No, thank you. I can manage."

Selina lay on her bed. Her mind was in turmoil. Surely her son couldn't be responsible for something so terrible? She must be mistaken. How could she even think such a thing? But her thoughts kept taking her back to that moment when she had seen the man on the street outside the greengrocer's and how she had instantly thought him to be her son. There was nothing for it. When Fred arrived home, she would have to confront him.

For the next couple of hours Selina worked out what she was going to say to Fred, so as not to arouse his suspicions in case she was wrong.

When Fred arrived home, he was in a good mood. "I have some news I want to share with you and Frank. Where is he?" he demanded.

"He and Mr Jenkins went out just after lunch. They should be back any time now."

"All right. I'll wait," decided Fred.

Selina took this opportunity to tackle her son before Frank returned.

"Fred? Do you remember on Tuesday when Frank and I went to the shops after lunch?"

"Yes," replied Fred nonchalantly.

"When we arrived home, you had gone out."

"Yes."

"I was wondering where you had got to? You appeared to have left in a hurry, and you returned home quite late."

Fred suddenly looked reticent. "Oh, Mother, I really wish you hadn't asked me that."

Selina's stomach somersaulted and she had that sick feeling again. "Why not? What are you hiding?"

"I had wanted to wait until Frank was here, to tell you both together."

"Tell us what?" Selina questioned hesitantly.

"I might as well tell you then," Fred conceded.

Selina wretched and a teaspoon of bile entered her mouth. She swallowed it back down quickly.

"I've found myself a job," Fred finally admitted.

Selina looked confused.

Fred continued to explain. "That's where I was. I was meeting a gentleman about a job."

Selina was unsure whether to believe her son. "I don't understand," she eventually replied.

"What's not to understand?" Fred was beginning to get irritated by his mother.

"Why did you leave the house in such a hurry?"

"What makes you think I left in a hurry?"

"You left your cigarettes behind."

"Oh yes, I did, didn't I? I suddenly remembered I had an appointment with the gentleman I've just mentioned. I lost track of the time and didn't realise I'd left my cigarettes until I got on the train."

"Train?"

"Yes, Mother. I caught the train to Kingston for a job interview. That's the news I wanted to share with you and Frank."

Just at that moment, they both heard the front door open, and Frank and Mr and Mrs Jenkins' voices filled the hallway downstairs.

"At last! Now can I explain my news to you both together?"

Selina was confused. How could she have got it so wrong? How could she have thought Fred could have done such a terrible thing? Her relief was immense, and when Frank entered the room, she rushed over to him, embracing him with such enthusiasm, that one might have thought she had not seen her husband for more than a year.

"What a wonderful greeting. I should go out more often," he joked.

Animatedly, Selina announced, "Fred has some marvellous news he wishes to share with us both."

Frank turned his attention to Fred, who by now had seated himself over by the window.

"Go on then, Fred. What's your news?"

Fred explained his story again, this time in a little more detail, and both his mother and Frank listened intently.

Eventually, Fred stopped talking and Frank spoke up. "What's the job, Fred? You've said you had an interview and that today you've been offered the job, but you haven't actually told us what the job is."

With this realisation, they all began to laugh. "I'm going to be a hairdresser," Fred announced proudly.

"A hairdresser?" both Selina and Frank declared at the same time.

"Yes. Mr Smithers, the gentleman I mentioned, has his own successful business in Kingston, where he employs other hairdressers, and he is willing to train me."

Selina and Frank remained stunned.

"What's the matter? I thought you'd be pleased for me."

"We are, Fred," insisted Selina. "Aren't we, Frank?"

"Of course. If it's what you want?"

"It is. Most definitely. I haven't enjoyed any of my most recent jobs. I can't wait to start this one."

"Then we are both very happy for you," Selina assured her son. "When do you start?"

"First thing Monday morning. I thought I would leave on Saturday, get settled into my new place, investigate the area on Sunday and be refreshed and ready to start on Monday morning."

"You're leaving?" Selina suddenly realised.

"Of course, Mother. I need to be nearer to my work. I'm not catching the train there and back every day. It takes almost an hour. That's why I was nearly late on Tuesday for my interview."

Selina's cheerful mood quickly deteriorated as the realisation hit her that her son would be leaving her soon. He had been living with them now for over a year, and she had become quite used to having him around.

"I'm going to miss you, Fred."

"I know, Mother. But I won't be far away. And if it's all right with Mr and Mrs Jenkins, I'd like to keep my room here, just in case I need it. And I can visit you then, whenever I want."

This seemed to cheer Selina up.

"I'm sure Mr and Mrs Jenkins will be happy with this arrangement," Fred continued. "I'll go and ask them now." And with that, Fred rushed down the stairs. Selina was left wondering if it would be another five years before she would see her son again.

Rita

Rita had been going to Furness School in Harlesden for just over a year, and she had enjoyed it from the very first day. The school was an imposing building, three storeys high, but this had not put Rita off. She had settled quickly, and all the teachers liked her. She was willing to please, and they knew she would be one of the children they'd be able to shape into a star pupil.

In 1934 Rita was six years old. She was an intelligent child; kind and shy. A sweet little thing with black hair that parted down the middle and curled at the sides. She had big brown eyes and a tiny button nose and a mouth that turned down at the ends, which could make her look sad, although she very rarely was. She was usually just deep in thought.

Before Rita had started at school, she had insisted that her mother allow her to complete the five-minute journey by herself each day. Her mother had willingly agreed, as she also had two younger children to take care of. Rita walked to and from school twice a day because she also went home at lunchtimes to eat with her family.

Rita had no father and lived in a house filled with strangers. Her family shared and slept in one room, but they were allowed to use the kitchen and outside lavatory. She had never known a father. She had never wondered where her mother's other babies had come from. She was too young.

Rita had made many friends since starting school. Most of them lived close by, and two of her friends would always meet her halfway, then they all walked to school together.

Barbara and Elsie lived at the top end of Ancona Road. The sisters were usually waiting outside their house for their friend, but on the odd occasion when they were running late, Rita would have to knock on their door to get them to hurry up.

The three girls often played together after school and got along well. Rita had been invited to Barbara and Elsie's house once for tea, but because her mother had never invited the girls to back—as she was unable to afford to feed them all—Rita had never been invited again.

One Tuesday morning, Rita left for school on time, walking from her home on Bramston Road. After crossing over and turning left into Wrottesley Road, she then crossed over again and turned right into Ancona Road, where she met her friends. From there the three walked the length of Spezia Road to their school. At lunchtime they repeated the same journey but in reverse.

Rita's home was always noisy, and today was no exception. Her younger siblings were both boys. One was three and the other still a baby, but there was always someone shouting or crying. She often wondered how there had never been any complaints about the din they all made. None of the other people in the house seemed to make anywhere near as much noise as her family. They all seemed to keep themselves to themselves.

Rita finished her hot midday meal of rabbit pie, which her mother had made for her, and left home to return to school for afternoon lessons. She didn't want to get into trouble for being late, so with an air of freedom, yet urgency, she started to skip along the road. Her stomach was so full of rabbit pie that the jerking sensation made her feel sick, so she quickly slowed to a walk. Rita didn't notice the man from five doors down staring at her, watching her intently from his window. After passing his house, she didn't notice him come out and start to follow her.

Meanwhile, Barbara and Elsie waited patiently at their front garden gate for Rita to appear. They too did not like to be late. There was one particular teacher who always shouted at her pupils if they did not return from lunch punctually. She had always frightened them. Barbara and Elsie waited and waited, but Rita never arrived. Eventually, they went back inside and told their mother that their friend had not appeared. Then they ran the distance to school without her, as instructed by their mother.

As Rita had reached the end of Bramston Road, she had stopped to cross over. After looking both ways, she stepped out into the road, and at the same time a man appeared at her side. He spoke to her as they crossed.

"Hello," he said in a friendly manner as he smiled down at her.

She looked up at the man and smiled back, politely replying "Hello" because she was sure she had seen the man before and should know him. She knew the man from somewhere, but couldn't quite remember where. As they both reached the other side of the road, the man took hold of Rita's hand. "Would you like to go to the park?" he asked kindly.

"I'm on my way back to school," Rita replied innocently.

"Would it be so terrible to miss school for once and go and have some fun in the park?"

But before she could answer, he was pulling her across the road which she should have turned down and was dragging her up Wrottesley Road.

"I'll get into trouble if I don't go to school," she said, trying to pull away from the man's tight grip.

"No, you won't. I'll not tell anyone."

"My mother will be cross."

"Not if you don't tell her. We'll make sure you're back in plenty of time, so no one will get suspicious."

Rita had no choice but to continue with the man. *Will anyone miss me?* thought Rita. *When I don't turn up, Barbara and Elsie will just go to school without me. They won't mind. Not just this once.* As Rita was deciding that it would most likely be all right to accompany the man, he loosened his grip a little. They continued along Wrottesley Road for about half a mile, crossing a bridge over the railway and heading towards Kensal Green Station. Rita knew this area. She knew it well. They passed shops on either side of the road and were heading towards the tube station. She had been here on a number of occasions with her mother to visit her aunt. She definitely recognised it.

Their journey continued along Harrow Road, where a tall brick wall stretched out far ahead on Rita's right side. They followed the length of this wall. It was a long way and Rita was starting to get tired. Her feet were hurting. Her mother had recently bought her a new pair of shoes and they were starting to pinch her toes. Her mother had saved up for ages to buy them, and Rita had been so pleased with them. Her old pair had worn out to the point that they both had holes in the soles and one of the buckles was missing, but right now she wished she had her old pair back on.

The man did not speak to Rita until she began to cry.

"What's the matter with you?" he asked abruptly.

"My feet hurt. I want to go home."

"Look. We're nearly there," he snapped back at her, pointing out an entrance up ahead. Rita had noticed they had already passed a previous entrance. The man guided Rita through a pillared archway complete with a large pair of imposing iron gates.

"Is this the park?" she asked.

"Yes," the man lied to her. He had noticed the sign as they had gone in, which read 'All Souls Cemetery', but Rita had not.

They followed the path ahead, which led into the cemetery, and then the man turned right at a crossroads to continue further along another path, all the time his grip upon Rita's hand becoming tighter and tighter. Quickening his pace, the man veered off to the left where an abundance of trees and bushes had been planted. This was all that stood between them and the Grand Union Canal. Rita began to feel uneasy. All she could see were hundreds of gravestones, and she quickly realised they were not in a park. She pulled away in an attempt to free her hand, but it was no use; the man was far stronger than her.

There was no one else around. No one to see that Rita was in danger. There was no one to ask for help and no one to hear her cries. How was she to get away? Then the man let go of her hand, but before she could even register this fact, he had come up behind her, put his left hand over her nose and mouth to stop her screaming and dragged her into the bushes.

She was pushed face down into the undergrowth. She had leaves in her hair and creepy crawlies on her face. Her new shoes would be filthy and her mother mad with her. She attempted to wriggle free and scream, but it was no use. She was unable to escape the man's tight grip.

Once satisfied they were hidden, the man turned her towards him, pulled her up into a kneeling position and holding tightly onto her shoulders with both hands spoke quietly, yet angrily, to her.

"You can never tell anyone about this. Do you understand me?" he demanded, shaking her roughly by her shoulders.

Rita nodded her head, now completely terrified by this man.

She felt a trickle of warm liquid run down her leg as she wet herself, but this and her dirty shoes were the least of her problems.

"Sit down," he demanded, pushing her down by her left shoulder as his right hand groped at his trouser fly. He placed himself on the ground up close to her and grabbed her hand, placing it inside his trousers.

"I don't want to," squeaked Rita.

"Be quiet or I will have to hurt you," he quietly growled at her.

The man tugged at her arm, forcing her hand further inside his trousers, and he kept doing this for some time.

Rita made no attempt to stop him. She was paralysed with fear. If she had been able to scream, no one would have heard her and the man might really have hurt her. As she knelt there on the cold, damp ground, she attempted to concentrate on the gentle sounds of the canal water lapping the sides of the barges as they passed intermittently. Then she could hear a train pass along the Great Western Railway, which ran alongside the canal. The only other sound she could hear—apart from the birds, and leaves in the trees gently rustling in the breeze—was the sound the man made as he occasionally groaned.

Suddenly the man's whole body jolted and shuddered and he groaned again, releasing his firm grip upon her hand. As Rita's hand became free, she glanced at it, noticing a thick, sticky liquid upon it which was glinting in the daylight. Repulsed, she wiped it onto her skirt. Rita saw her opportunity and ran faster than she had ever run before, heading in any direction, as long as it was away from the man. He had become distracted, released his grip, and Rita had seized the moment.

Rita ran, not knowing where she was running to, and soon found herself at the mortuary chapel, a grand four-pillared monument. At the same moment, an elderly man wearing a long black dress and a woman, also dressed in black, appeared in its doorway. Rita ran up the steps to them and fell at their feet, sobbing. She made an attempt to explain her predicament and control her sobbing as the woman attempted to comfort her and the man suggested he get help. As she glanced up, she spotted the man who had abducted her nearing the pathway.

"He hurt me!" she screamed, pointing in the direction of the man. "He made me do a horrible thing!"

The priest and his mourner could tell instantly that the child was telling the truth.

"You stay with the girl and get her some help," the priest suggested while he began to move in the direction of the man on the path.

"Hey! You there!" he called after the onlooker. The man turned and ran back the way he had come. The priest attempted to make chase. He followed as the man ran behind the chapel then in and out of the gravestones towards the boundary wall.

"Stop!" puffed the priest.

The man ignored him and ran even faster. It was no good. The priest was in poor shape and had to give up the chase. He was much older and losing ground all the time. The man disappeared into some overgrown foliage. Unseen, he scrambled over a wall, appearing in the backyard of the Masons Arms. There he composed himself before rejoining the pedestrians on Harrow Road as if nothing untoward had ever happened.

On the afternoon of her disappearance, an extensive search for Rita was conducted in the area, by both members of the police force and local volunteers. Her two friends had alerted their mother when Rita had not turned up to meet them. She, in turn, went to see Rita's mother, who was beside herself with worry, and the police were called.

"My Rita's a good girl. She wouldn't just go off like that. Something terrible must have happened. You need to find her! You need to find her!" Rita's mother yelled at the police.

"We're doing everything we can. I promise you," the constable told Rita's mother. "We have a team of officers and members of the general public all out there looking for her. Now, you're not to worry. In my experience they usually turn up in the end. She's probably just lost track of the time after buying sweets or something. I'm sure she'll be home in no time."

"She better had. I'll kill her when she gets home. Putting me through all this worry."

Despite their efforts, the police were unable to find any trace of Rita until she was taken to a police station by the priest and the female mourner. From there she was transported to the hospital, where she was examined.

"She's been lucky," Rita heard a doctor telling a policeman. "Things could have been a lot worse," he added.

She was then interviewed by the police. Although they found a young policewoman to do this, the policeman who had sat next to his colleague throughout the interview had terrified Rita because he looked very similar to the man who had taken her into the cemetery. He had the same dark hair and eyes and a similar big nose.

Rita was too scared and traumatised to help the police with their inquiries. She felt unable to give them a description or communicate any details of what had actually happened in the cemetery. When asked if she knew who the man was, Rita had looked away, feeling unable to answer the question. Later that evening, Rita was able to return home to her mother.

No evidence as to the identity of the man in question was ever discovered. However, during the afternoon that Rita had gone missing, a woman did report an odd story to a bobby on the beat. His police report had read that as the woman in question and her husband walked home from the shops, he'd approached them and asked if they had seen a young child matching Rita's description. The woman reported that while in a shopping queue she had seen a young child being dragged unwillingly along Harrow Road by a man and had almost interfered, but hadn't wanted to lose her place in the queue. The woman had never attended the police station to give a statement as she had been instructed. Despite many police appeals, this woman was never traced, and the policeman in question had been reprimanded for not making a note of the woman's name or address.

At the time, newspapers reported: 'A young girl going from home to school was snatched then dragged into the cemetery, where she was tormented by a man for more than an hour. She had left her mother's house after lunch on Tuesday to return to school. Two friends were waiting for her a couple of hundred yards away, but she never arrived. They managed to raise the alarm. Police thought she had been spotted with a man walking along Harrow Road.'

The newspaper had also described Rita as very shy, and for this reason police believed she probably knew the man. They strongly believed that the individual responsible for the child's abduction was someone the victim had met before and thought she knew.

Rita's attacker was never caught. The child had nightmares for many years after the assault, and her schooling suffered as a direct result of her abduction. Rita struggled for many years to form any kind of relationship with men, as she felt unable to trust them following her ordeal.

Rose

———◇———

A simple trip to the hairdresser's during the summer of 1935 had changed her sister's life forever. This had been at Rose's suggestion, and now she blamed herself for everything. Why had it all gone so wrong? she wondered.

Rose had recognised that since the sudden and unexpected death of their mother, their father had become very reliant upon her youngest sister at home and with his business. She felt sorry for her. Lily always looked so unhappy.

Rose had been fortunate to have escaped her father's clutches some years earlier. She had never been able to do anything right in his eyes and couldn't wait to move out of the family home. She had secretly been saving the money her father paid her for working in his shop, as well as money from another part-time job he had known nothing about, and this had enabled her to fulfil her dream. Rose had always wanted to open a bookshop. She had done just that with her best friend, Sophia, and now they were living the dream.

Next it was Lily's turn to feel trapped. Feeling unable to abandon her father for many reasons, not least because she had promised her mother on her deathbed that she would look after him, Lily remained in a state of limbo. And Rose was witness to her sister's rapid decline.

"Lily looks so tired and forlorn these days," Rose told Sophia. So they concocted a plan. Rose talked Lily into accompanying her and Sophia to a local dance.

"It will do you good," insisted Rose.

"I would rather have an early night," pleaded Lily.

"Nonsense. You'll see. It will give you a new lease of life," persisted Sophia.

"It's just what you need. Trust me," continued Rose.

It was no use. Lily finally gave in and agreed to go.

Preparations for the dance began on Saturday afternoon, when Rose insisted she treat Lily to a new hairdo at the salon which had recently opened in their town.

As soon as they entered the freshly painted salon, they were treated like royalty. Rose's requests for them both to have waves put into their hair, as well as a cut, was handled professionally. They were shown to their seats and each had a gown placed about their shoulders. The salon owner appeared behind Rose and introduced himself, quickly making a start by putting a comb through her hair and confirming with her exactly what it was she required.

Rose glanced over at Lily, noticing that her face was rather flushed and realising that she was embarrassed about the handsome, clean-shaven stranger who was seeing to her hair. It was instantly clear to Rose that her sister was attracted to this well-groomed gentleman. He was about five feet nine inches tall, with shiny, thick, chestnutcoloured hair which detracted from his oversized nose. His dark brown eyes sparkled as he spoke to Lily. Rose thought he was probably older than her sister, but only by a couple of years. As he introduced himself and discussed with her sister her requirements, she witnessed Lily's cheeks flush again.

Lily was very quiet when they left the salon some two hours later. Rose asked her if she liked her hair.

"Are you happy with the result?" she enquired hesitantly.

"Yes, I love it."

"What's wrong then? You're ever so quiet."

"I think I must be tired."

"You can't be tired. We have a dance to go to this evening."

"I'll be fine. I'll be all right once we get there."

"Good. We'll have a great time. You'll see."

Rose was right. Once they had hurried Sophia up, who seemed to take forever deciding what to wear, they settled themselves at a table with some drinks, the band started to play and they all began to enjoy themselves.

They discovered they knew quite a number of other party-goers at the dance that evening, and most of these friends came over to say hello, some staying for a drink and a chat. A couple of their friends complimented Rose and Lily on their new hairstyles.

Halfway through the evening Lily leant over to Rose and whispered, "What's he doing here?" Rose looked up, and the hairdresser who had worked on her sister's hair earlier that day was making his way over to their table.

"Oh no. He's coming over," wittered Lily as Rose dug her in the ribs to shut her up.

The gentleman was polite and charming and introduced himself as Fred. He then spent the rest of the evening at their table, but it was obvious that it was Lily he was interested in. Rose did not have a particular problem with this. She had little interest in men, but couldn't help being a little suspicious of Fred's intentions. However, as the evening progressed, she was pleased to see her sister relaxed and enjoying herself for a change.

Rose and Sophia both discovered that they too enjoyed Fred's company and conversation, and they were soon all getting along as if they had known each other for years. Fred appeared to be extremely easy to get on with and obviously made Lily feel completely at ease, as Rose could see her sister was positively glowing in his presence.

Together the group listened to and enjoyed the band who played tunes to which the foxtrot, waltz and quickstep was danced. Fred and Lily were up on the dance floor often, while Rose and Sophia preferred to look on, amused.

Later it became more obvious to Rose that Fred was a bit of a Casanova. He had them all eating out of his hands before the night was over. He relished being the centre of their attentions, keeping them captivated with his endless stories, and he positively encouraged Lily to flirt with him. By the end of the evening Rose was confused about Fred. There was something about him which made her feel uneasy. She discussed this quietly with Sophia, who told her she was imagining things and in no uncertain terms warned her that she should not say anything to Lily, as it would spoil her evening.

***

As the months passed, Rose realised that Lily had become completely infatuated with Fred. She was surprised to discover that they had seen each other regularly since the day of the dance and that her sister was keeping this fact from their father.

"What am I supposed to do, Rose? I've tried explaining my feelings to Father, but he just won't listen. He's too stubborn and selfish to see that Fred makes me happy."

Again, Rose listened to Sophia and felt it would be wrong to interfere, as she had not seen her sister so elated in such a long time. Together they devised ways to enable Fred and Lily to meet one another in secret, without their father's knowledge, and for a time this worked.

Rose felt she was trying to please everyone—protecting her father and satisfying Lily—and soon strong feelings of guilt overtook her and she needed to speak to Sophia again about her sister's situation.

"Obviously, I want Lily to be happy," Rose insisted.

"That goes without saying. I feel the same," agreed Sophia.

"But at the same time, I know it's wrong to be going behind my father's back."

"I agree with you again. But it seems to me that at the moment you are unable to achieve both of these things at the same time. Shall we have another chat with Lily? She and Fred are coming round for their tea again tonight."

"Again?" Rose asked.

"Well, they haven't got many other places they can go. I'll see if I can get her on her own and mention how we both feel."

"Thank you, Sophia. I hope she'll listen to you." The two women embraced one another for reassurance. "What do you make of Fred? Do you like him?" Rose reluctantly asked Sophia.

"He's pleasant enough. Why? Do you have a problem with him?" asked her friend.

"Not exactly."

"What is it then?"

"I'm not sure really. Just a feeling I have."

"What sort of feeling?"

"Just ignore me. I'm being silly. I just don't want to see Lily get hurt."

"She won't. We'll make sure of that, won't we?" replied Sophia.

Soon after her conversation with Sophia, Rose discovered that Lily had attempted to confront their father again, hoping to explain her feelings for Fred. He had declined to listen to anything she'd attempted to say and refused to allow her to see him again or to discuss the subject further.

This event had clearly upset Lily, as the next time Rose saw her sister, she was extremely despondent. Not wishing to leave her sister in this state for any length of time, Rose wanted to help. But she did not know how to do this. She knew her father wouldn't listen to her either. What was she to do to try and help her sister?

Rose pondered the problem again, then came up with an idea. She would secretly pay Fred's employer a visit. He was the gentleman who had cut her hair all those months ago, and upon entering his shop, she felt a little embarrassed that she had not been back since. But he was very pleasant towards her and able to put her completely at her ease.

Rose was surprised to discover that Fred was not in the salon. Apparently, he had offered to purchase some more stock from the suppliers on his employer's behalf, which thankfully made her difficult task all the more straightforward.

"I'm here because I'm worried about my sister. She has been seeing Fred, you know?"

"Yes. I am aware they are close. What seems to be the problem?"

"My father is being quite unreasonable about the whole thing and refuses to listen to anything my sister or I have to say on the matter."

"Yes. I gather he doesn't approve."

"That's right." Rose looked at him quizzically.

"Fred has mentioned something along those lines," he explained.

"My father has no idea Lily is still seeing Fred and refuses to allow her to explain how she feels. I am wondering if it should be Fred who stands up to my father. Being a man himself, my father might take him more seriously and listen to what he has to say."

"I have been having similar thoughts myself," the hairdresser confessed. "Leave it with me. I'll have a word with Fred, and hopefully all this deceit can stop. It's much better when things are out in the open, don't you think?"

"I hope so," agreed Rose.

"I'm sure everyone will feel much better after it is," suggested the hairdresser.

Rose left the salon with more of a spring in her step, although her feelings of relief would be short-lived, for one day later Lily rushed through the door of her sister's bookshop like a woman possessed.

"Lily, what on earth has happened?" asked Rose.

"I'm furious," she screeched at her sister. "Fred has visited Father's shop, and if I hadn't walked in when I did, who knows what might have happened."

"What did happen?"

"Nothing. Haven't you been listening? I managed to stop him before he could say anything or before Father realised who he was. Fred saw me rooted to the spot, unable to move with the sheer terror that he might say something to Father, and thankfully he quickly left. But I'm furious with him for turning up in the first place. After all the conversations we've had about how he needs to let me tell Father in my own time."

Rose felt very guilty about not admitting it was most likely because of her meddling that Fred had entered their father's shop. She did not want to make matters worse by confessing to Lily what she had done.

"What will you do now?" she asked.

"I have no idea, but at this precise moment in time I don't care if I never see Fred again."

"You don't mean that."

"I do!" Lily began to sob.

"No you don't."

"No, I don't," she admitted, wiping her angry tears. She blew her nose loudly on her lace handkerchief.

"That's pretty," noted Rose, trying to lighten the moment.

"Fred bought it for me. Ohh," she sobbed.

"Perhaps you both need a little time apart," suggested Rose kindly. "So that you can think about what you really want."

Lily clearly thought about this suggestion for a moment, and much to Rose's surprise, agreed with her elder sister.

"I'm going to tell Fred I can't meet him any more; not until I have decided what I want to do."

"I think it's for the best," agreed Rose.

A number of weeks passed before Rose and Sophia were able to devise another plan. During this time, Rose was forced to observe Lily's happiness greatly decline, and her father's mood also blackened. Finally, Rose came up with the suggestion that Lily should write their father a letter.

Lily embraced this idea, as she could not think of any other way to deal with the situation. She spent a great deal of time over her letter and told Rose and Sophia she had left it where her father would undoubtedly find it. Days later, when he had still not reacted to her letter, they could only surmise that he had never read its contents and must have destroyed all evidence of its existence, knowing full well what might be written upon its pages.

This had been the final straw for Lily. She explained to Rose and Sophia that she had tried everything she could think of to get her father to listen, but it was too late. Their relationship would never mend. It had broken down completely and now she only had feelings of contempt for her father.

"There must be something else we can try," suggested Sophia.

"What do you suggest? Haven't we tried everything to get Father to listen?" said Rose.

"He's too stubborn and pig-headed," yelled Lily.

"He's a proud man. Not that that's an excuse. He just thinks you should respect his wishes," continued Sophia.

"His wishes mean I have to stay at home for the rest of my life, look after him and run his shop. What makes him think I'd be happy to do that?"

"He's so terribly old-fashioned, Lily," said Rose. "He can't help it. He's so stuck in his ways and still sees things as they were fifty-or-more years ago."

"Mother would be spinning in her grave if she could hear us now," commented Lily.

"I'm not sure she would have allowed him to get away with this. I'm certain she'd be on your side," commented Rose.

"She would, but then if she were alive, perhaps we wouldn't be having this problem in the first place," replied Lily.

Both Rose and Sophia nodded in agreement with Lily's last comment and soon after parted company, still with no resounding solution to Lily's problem.

More days passed, and then Lily paid Rose an unexpected visit.

"Fred and I have made a decision," she announced.

"Oh yes?" replied Rose intrigued.

"Fred has asked me to marry him." Rose looked stunned. "But I have declined," her sister quickly added.

"All right. But why?" enquired Rose.

"We have decided we are going to move away instead."

"Really? But where will you go?"

"Fred has found work in another salon, in Crestwell."

Rose was shocked. "Crestwell?"

"Yes."

"Does Sophia know?"

"Yes."

"What did she say?"

"She said if it will make me happy, then I must do it. She said you both would deal with Father together once I've left."

"But you *are* going to tell him before you leave?" asked Rose.

"Of course. But not until I'm about to walk out of the door. That way there will be nothing he can do to stop me."

"When will that be?"

"We thought New Year's Eve."

"That soon?"

"Now that we've made the decision, there seems little point in delaying."

"You will write to us to let us know how you are, won't you?"

"Of course I will. I'm really quite excited now that I've made a decision. I can't wait to be with Fred all the time. He makes me so happy."

"I'm really pleased for you, Lily. I hope you'll both be really happy."

"We will. I know we will. Be happy for me, Rose."

"I am, truly."

Rose had tried to sound convincing. She hoped it had worked. But deep down she was apprehensive for her sister. She worried about her.

Lily had so little experience of life compared to her and Sophia, and she just wanted her sister to be happy.

Perhaps Fred was the one who could provide that happiness for Lily, but for some reason, and Rose could not explain why, she felt this would not be the case. Rose thought that Fred and her sister's relationship would quickly break down and he would go off with someone else. Rose had a feeling that Fred was just one of those men who flitted from one female to another as and when it pleased him, leaving a trail of destruction in his wake. Her sister would be powerless to stop him and ultimately get caught in the crossfire. Rose hoped she was wrong. God, how she hoped she was wrong.

Leonard

———◇———

L eonard had completed his apprenticeship and previously enjoyed a hairdressing career in Kingston. There, he had secured full-time employment working for the Smithers family from Thames Ditton. They owned a ladies' and gentlemen's hairdressing salon on the High Street, Kingston, a bustling town set alongside the River Thames.

Leonard had worked there for many years, and the Smithers had overseen his training in the early days. Their supervision was strict, and at first he worked long hours for little wages. Over the years, the Smithers had got to know Leonard well, eventually feeling able to leave their business in his capable hands—its smooth running guaranteed with Leonard at the helm. Leonard was completely trustworthy, and excellent in interviews—always able to spot potential and reliable staff in an instant. They had often asked him to attend interviews when new staff were required.

The family salon was always busy from the moment it opened its doors early in the morning until after closing time. Customers arriving at the salon were never turned away, even when they had not made an appointment. The owners believed this was good for business, and over the years this had proven to be the case, as their client list was far greater than any of the other hairdressers in the town. Their reputation preceded them, and all customers left their premises satisfied. Leonard saw to this. All customers were to leave the salon feeling completely happy about the service they had received or Leonard would want to know why.

Leonard had met many interesting people over the years since working at the salon. Many had a story to tell—some funny, some sad and some even alarming—but Leonard was able to remain professional at all times, dishing out advice, reassurance or assistance where needed. He had never allowed his work to cross over into his personal life. That was, until the day Fred had walked into his salon.

During 1933 Fred had become a regular customer at the hair salon, as he was often in the area with his work. Leonard would cut Fred's hair, shave him and tidy up his moustache. One day, Fred asked for his moustache to be completely removed then confided in Leonard about how unhappy he was. He explained how he no longer enjoyed his work in insurance. He found it tiresome and unchallenging and longed to do something different with his life. After much conversation between the two men, it had been Leonard who had persuaded Fred to change his career path. He offered to train him in the art of hairdressing, and with his employer's approval, employed Fred at the salon's premises in Kingston. With Leonard's help, Fred found rented accommodation nearby and soon settled in.

Fred had to work his way up, starting with sweeping the floor and making drinks for clients, before he was ready to cut the customers' hair. But Fred was a quick learner and great with people. Leonard soon discovered that Fred had a way about him which could put a person completely at ease. Charisma and compassion appeared to come naturally to him. He was admired by all, especially the women, who found him captivating and devoted to their individual needs. He had most customers eating out of his hands. Leonard found him to be a breath of fresh air and was pleased he had taken the risk of employing him. Things had turned out well, and many customers soon requested for Fred to do their hair.

Early in 1934 the Smithers had a business proposition for Leonard. Their business in Kingston had become so successful that they wanted to expand. They informed Leonard that they had found new premises thirty miles away, in Frimsham, and asked him if he would be prepared to move there and run it for them. A new business contract was soon drawn up and signed on the understanding that Fred could relocate along with him. Leonard felt he could not achieve this move alone and knew Fred was the perfect choice. The Smithers agreed, as did Fred, and everyone was happy with the new arrangement.

Fred and Leonard had no dependants to consider, whereas none of the other salon staff had the desire to uproot their families, as they were firmly settled in the Kingston area. As the salon in Kingston was not closing, all existing staff remained, some gaining promotion.

Before his departure, Leonard advised the Smithers about who from the existing staff would make the best manager, and they went with his suggestion. Leonard and Fred spent a couple of weeks supervising their replacements before it was time for them to depart.

Both men were very excited about their new challenge. They boarded temporarily at the Coach and Horses public house while the new premises were given its finishing touches. Soon after, Leonard was able to move into a small property on The Street and Fred had rooms above the new salon. The two men could not have been more content in their work. They adored their jobs and the delightful surroundings in which they found themselves. Their commitment to their new and exciting venture could not be faulted.

The new salon was more modern than the one back in Kingston. The Smithers had ensured they had all the latest up-to-date equipment and décor. There were separate areas for ladies and gentlemen, with modern streamlined display units in both. Everywhere was clean and organised, so as to produce the most efficient outcome. The washable wallpaper and Formica panels ensured the utmost of hygienic surroundings. Frosted-glass partitions gave privacy between cubicles, yet let in plenty of light, and a comfortable sofa and reception area greeted each customer upon entry. Leonard had found the perfect receptionist: an enthusiastic, yet quietly spoken, local woman.

The salon was soon busy with the most inquisitive of the town's residents, who couldn't wait to get a glimpse of the salon's latest gadgets and experience the most fashionable of hairstyles. In no time at all Leonard had established a great number of regular clients, much to his business partner's delight.

Leonard tended to take care of the gentlemen clients in the room towards the back of the building, while Fred saw to the female customers, sweeping them off their feet with his perfected charm. On occasion, when the salon was particularly busy, Leonard would help out Fred in the ladies' side of the salon.

During the spring of 1934, Leonard and Fred welcomed a customer who would eventually have a great impact upon both their lives. She was a local girl—single and slightly younger than Fred—who had entered the shop somewhat reluctantly along with her elder sister. The pair were pleasant enough, but after they had gone, Leonard felt Fred had become a little preoccupied and asked him if everything was all right.

"I must confess that I'm a little taken aback by the feelings I have suddenly experienced for one of our customers," admitted Fred.

"You do surprise me, Fred. I've never seen you so distracted."

"I don't seem to be able to concentrate on anything now."

"Except her, of course," smiled Leonard.

"Yes, except her," agreed Fred.

"Was it the young lady who came in with her sister and wanted her hair styling in the same way?"

"Yes. How did you know?"

"Just a lucky guess. Look, it's gone quiet now. No one is booked in for another half an hour. Let's go and take a break, and we can chat about it."

Fred nodded in agreement.

"Give us a shout if anyone calls in," requested Leonard to the receptionist.

"Yes, sir," the woman replied.

Sat together in the back room, Fred opened up to Leonard as never before. Many suppressed feelings suddenly came rushing to the forefront, and he confided in Leonard as he might a father. Until that moment, Leonard had gained little understanding of his colleague's private life, but past events poured out of Fred as though someone had opened the floodgates.

Leonard learned about Fred's unhappy childhood, the death of his father, his ability to disguise well his lack of confidence, how he had been in and out of work which didn't suit him since moving to England, his feelings of never being able to settle anywhere and, most importantly, how he had never had a serious relationship with a woman. The feelings Fred was experiencing clearly terrified him and excited him at the same time, and Leonard was acutely aware that neither he nor Fred knew what to do about them.

"Well, this is possibly one area where I'm going to find it difficult to advise you, Fred, having not had much experience with women myself."

"What a pair we are," smiled Fred. But it appeared a weight had been lifted from him during his conversation with Leonard.

"I understand there is a dance on this evening at the village hall. I keep seeing the posters for it everywhere."

"Yes, I have too."

"You should go," insisted Leonard. "It will do you the world of good."

"Perhaps," replied Fred a little reluctantly.

"You might see that young lady there. If it's meant to be, it will be," suggested Leonard. He had overheard the sisters discussing their plans for the evening, and they had mentioned the dance.

"I'll see how I'm feeling later," smiled Fred.

At that moment, they heard the sound of the shop's doorbell as someone entered, followed by the receptionist's voice calling them.

"Thanks for the chat though," said Fred. "I feel much better."

"No problem. I'm always here to listen," Leonard reassured.

***

The following week, Leonard discovered that Fred had attended the dance and that he had indeed met the same woman whose hair he had transformed that very day. Fred was now a different person. He told Leonard he had met up with the woman the day following the dance, when they had enjoyed a pleasant stroll around the park together. Apparently, they got along like a house on fire and had plenty of things in common. Fred confided in Leonard, saying that for the first time in a while he felt his future looked more promising.

Leonard was pleased for Fred. He'd passed this particular stage many years ago and was quite content with his present position but could understand that at Fred's age he needed more.

For a number of months Leonard was led to believe things were good between Fred and his young lady friend. He would often take over the final finishing touches of a client's hair, so that Fred could leave on time to meet her. He gained pleasure from seeing his employee so happy.

Leonard was surprised to discover that all was not as it seemed.

According to Fred, his young lady had a father who was far from happy about the situation his daughter had got herself into and had forbidden her from seeing Fred. According to Fred, this was because she was the youngest of his children, and now being a widow he expected his youngest daughter to say at home and look after him and the family business.

In the spring of 1935 Fred admitted to Leonard that he and his young lady, Lily, had continued to see one another behind her father's back, informing Leonard that her father was a well-known figure in the town.

"I do believe I have seen him on a number of occasions, but only to speak to while in his shop. He seems like a decent chap. Why don't you go and introduce yourself to him? I'm sure he'll soon come round to the idea," Leonard had suggested.

Fred was reluctant to do this at first, but the more he thought about it, the more he thought Leonard was right. After many more discussions, Fred told Leonard he'd decided he would pay the man a visit, but Fred neglected to inform Lily of this decision. When Fred recounted the events to Leonard later that day, he was quite upset about the whole episode. He had not considered what degree of anxiety his actions might cause Lily. She'd made him promise never to attempt to speak to her father again unless she asked him to do so, and she'd refused to see Fred for a while.

Towards the end of July Leonard noticed a dramatic change in Fred, and there seemed little he could do to lift his friend's spirits. One moment Fred would be quiet and subdued, disappearing all hours of the day and night, and the next he would be flamboyant and exaggerated in his work. He suspected that Fred's unusual behaviour was due to his turbulent relationship with Lily.

Fred had taken to drinking and was frequently spending time in a number of public houses. Leonard had been able to smell the drink on Fred's breath some mornings and was concerned his clients would be able to do the same. He worried about the company Fred was keeping in these places and realised that he might soon have to have a word with his friend if the situation did not improve.

When a customer who had regularly visited the salon since it had first opened, and whose husband was well known in the town, entered Leonard's salon one morning in August displaying severe bruising to her face, momentarily Leonard forgot about Fred's problems. Leonard saw Fred spot their customer enter the salon and was surprised to see him suddenly disappear, leaving Leonard to deal with her.

"How are you, Mrs Hind?" enquired Leonard, having read in the newspaper the previous week that she had been assaulted.

"I'm getting there, thank you."

"It's good to see you out and about. And I'm pleased you managed to make your regular appointment with us. I was unsure if you would."

"It will take more than a cowardly attack to stop me from getting my hair done," she bravely joked.

Mrs Hind had always been very polite and friendly. She often chatted about her children and the important work her husband did. She had been married for fourteen years and lived close by in Clover Cottages. Today, however, she appeared more interested in the whereabouts of Leonard's employee.

"How is Fred? Is he all right?" she enquired.

"Yes, he's well, thank you," replied Leonard, wondering just where Fred had disappeared to.

"It was very brave of him to do what he did. I haven't had chance to thank him properly yet."

Leonard must have looked confused enough that Mrs Hind felt the need to explain further. "It was Fred who came to my rescue last week."

"It was?" Leonard asked, surprised.

"Yes. Has he not told you?"

"No. He hasn't mentioned a thing."

Leonard knew Mrs Hind had been savagely attacked the week previously on her way home as she was crossing over Bushy Common. He had read all about it in the newspaper, which had informed him her assailant had leapt on her from behind, grabbed her by the shoulders and thrown her to the ground. When having failed in an attempt to gag her with a handkerchief, he had begun punching her in the face, neck and body, inflicting serious bruising. The attack had shocked Leonard and the whole community.

"When I screamed for help, it was Fred who heard my cries and came running to my assistance." Leonard was lost for words. "Then he made an attempt to chase the man across the common, but he got away," continued Mrs Hind.

"I had no idea. Fred never said a word." Leonard said eventually.

"The police believe he must have been hiding in a clump of trees or bushes, waiting for me to pass."

"The whole episode is just too terrible to think about. I am so sorry for your injuries, Mrs Hind."

"I'm all right, but I would like to see Fred to thank him properly."

"Of course. I'll go and find him for you."

Leonard eventually found Fred in his flat upstairs. "Mrs Hind wants to see you, Fred." Fred appeared to stare right through Leonard, as though he had not heard what Leonard had just said. "Why didn't you tell me?" Leonard continued.

"There was nothing to tell," replied Fred.

"That's not what Mrs Hind says. She wants to thank you. You'd better come down and see her."

Reluctantly, Fred went to see their customer and struggled to disguise his shock when he saw she was covered in bruises.

"Hello, Mrs Hind."

"Oh, Fred, I just wanted to thank you for last week. I was too shocked at the time. Today is the first time I've felt strong enough to venture out."

"There's nothing to thank me for. Anyone would have done the same."

"I think we both know that's not true, Fred. You were very brave. I want you to have this." Mrs Hind handed Fred an envelope containing a sum of money. Fred was embarrassed, but took it from her.

Leonard saw Fred's face flush and wondered if he should step in, but Fred seemed to have the situation under control.

"I would appreciate it if we could put this behind us now, Mrs Hind. I'm not one for fuss."

"I understand, Fred. We'll say no more about it then."

"Thank you, Mrs Hind. Now, what can I do for you today? The usual, is it?"

"Yes, please, Fred. That would be wonderful."

Realising Fred's reluctance to have shared his recent experience with him, Leonard wondered if he too should commend Fred for his helpfulness and say thank you to Fred for his kindness towards their customer. He thought long and hard about how he might achieve this. He wanted to lift his employer and friend out of his present state of despondency.

Leonard decided to take it upon himself to attempt to reconcile Fred with Lily. He paid the young woman a visit to see if he could help in any way. Lily was embarrassed at first and then shocked to learn of Fred's bravery. She confided in Leonard that she was to make a further attempt to inform her father of her feelings for Fred by writing him a letter. Leonard assured Lily that he thought this would work and told her she could always turn to him if she needed any further support.

The following week Leonard assumed Lily must have carried out her promise, for soon the couple were seeing one another again: going out for meals, visiting the picture house together and meeting regularly. Leonard was relieved to see Fred happy once more. In actual fact, it soon transpired that Lily had still not found a way to appease her father. By all accounts, the man was being extremely difficult about the whole situation. However, Lily continued to reassure Fred, telling him she would speak to her father soon about their relationship. Fred confessed to Leonard that he was tired of their secret rendezvous and wanted everything out in the open but didn't know how he should go about it.

"Perhaps you should take matters into your own hands, Fred," suggested Leonard.

"What do you suggest? Haven't I tried just about everything? The last time I did that, it upset Lily so much, she didn't want to see me."

"You could try a marriage proposal."

Fred was momentarily stunned into silence. He had not been expecting such a suggestion.

"Marriage?"

"Isn't that normally the case when two people love each other and want to be together?"

"Yes, I suppose so."

"What do you have to lose, Fred?"

Some days later Fred informed Leonard he had taken his advice and asked Lily to marry him.

"You'll never guess what she said," he teased Leonard.

"Yes?" Leonard asked hopefully.

"No. She refused me," Fred announced.

"Oh, Fred, I am sorry." Fred grinned at Leonard. "You don't seem as upset as I would expect," continued Leonard.

"That's because Lily and I have made a decision."

Leonard was intrigued. At their first opportunity the pair sat down together in the back room of the salon to discuss Fred and Lily's decision in more detail. What transpired was difficult for Leonard to swallow, and he couldn't help feeling a little injured by his friend, but he continued to support him because he truly cared about Fred.

Although Lily had declined Fred's offer of marriage, she had agreed to move away with him. Fred was now asking Leonard to help him find new employment away from Frimsham; somewhere around the London area. Leonard couldn't help feeling that his colleague and good friend had suddenly become very single-minded and hadn't even considered his feelings. The only thing Fred seemed concerned about was Lily's wishes.

Leonard understood this must have been a difficult decision for them both to make under the circumstances, and being a kind-hearted man, he promised he would do everything he could to help Fred. Leonard was true to his word, first contacting his business partners to inform them and then a fellow hairdresser whom he'd known well for some years who owned a salon in Crestwell. He was able to secure an interview, and after that it was up to Fred.

Over the last couple of years, while working with and getting to know Fred well, Leonard had believed he'd found the son he'd never had. Fred had often confided in him and come to him for advice, and Leonard had thought that Fred felt the same way about him.

When the pair had made the move to Frimsham, Leonard had

considered that Fred might be the one to take over the business when the time came for him to retire. The strong, almost parental, feelings Leonard had for Fred, he now realised had not been reciprocated.

Things changed quickly for Leonard after this. Once Fred had decided he was leaving Frimsham, Leonard didn't wish to be there either and decided to contact his business partners in order to make the necessary arrangements to dissolve their business partnership. This was to coincide with Fred and Lily's departure in December 1935. Although the two men had promised to remain friends, they never saw one another again and soon lost contact. Leonard never heard from Fred again.

Constance

———◄○►———

It had been Constance's husband who had suggested she try the new hairdresser's which had recently opened in their town in 1935. Her children had been particularly difficult the previous week, and she was quite exhausted by them. Her teenage son and daughter were becoming more challenging by the day, and Constance had complained to her husband most evenings that week about their ungrateful and selfish behaviour.

"All that I do for them and never a word of thanks."

"Constance, you should treat yourself. God knows you deserve it. Why don't you give that new hair salon a try? The one that's just opened in the town?" suggested her husband, Henry.

"I suppose I could. If it was a morning appointment, I could be back in time for the children when they get home from school."

"You should make an afternoon appointment, so that you're *not* here when they get home. That would surprise them. Make them appreciate you more as well."

"Do you know what? I think I will. It's about time they started to learn to fend for themselves."

"You do far too much for them, Constance. They're big enough now not to rely on you so much. It will do them both good to see you have a life too."

So that's what Constance did. She enjoyed her first visit to the salon so much that she became a regular customer there and was soon good friends with Fred, who cut and styled her hair each visit.

Constance had lived in Surrey all her life. She had been born in Aldershot, grown up in Frimsham and now lived with her husband in Clover Cottages, not far from Bushy Common. She had married Henry at St John's in 1920, and although her father had died the year after she had married, Constance's mother was still alive, living close by. Over the years, her mother had been a great support and helped out with the children.

Constance's husband was a dealer of antiques and a pawnbroker. He had made a small fortune over the years, but was extremely frugal with their finances. He saw his family never went without, yet they lived in a small cottage which displayed none of their wealth. As well as this cottage, Henry had purchased another small property near to the coast, where the family spent most of their holidays. The rest of his money he kept in savings, ready for his son, if he should choose to attend Oxford, and for both of his children's futures.

Both parents cared for their children immensely and loved them dearly. They worked hard to give them everything they'd never had, which might explain why their children had become rather self-absorbed over recent years. Constance and Henry would see to it that they put a stop to this behaviour and make their children realise how lucky they actually were.

After her initial visit to the hairdresser's that day, Constance's children had been surprised not to find their mother at home preparing them an evening meal upon their return from school. Constance had spoken to her children that evening about them helping her out more around the cottage and how they could start by cleaning their bedrooms. At first the children had not been impressed with this new regime and rebelled, but when their father had threatened to stop their weekly allowance, they had quickly complied, realising that both their parents were aligned in these new rules. Things began to change for the better.

Constance soon enjoyed regular visits to the hairdresser's. She got along well with the two gentlemen who ran the business, and she looked forward to her visits as much as they looked forward to seeing her. Once a regular customer, Constance felt quite at ease in Fred's company. He made her feel special, treated her with admiration and often complimented her on her looks, making a fuss of her. He indulged her by listening intently and interestedly to everything she had to say. He hardly spoke to her as he performed wonders with her hair. A nod of acknowledgement to what she said was enough to suffice her. Constance would talk for hours about her husband, his job, her children, her mother and her friends. She had become a bit of a village gossip, if the truth be known, and seemed to know everything about everyone in the town. It didn't bother Constance to be called this. She rather liked the attention.

Constance did not think for a moment that Fred and his fellow hairdresser thought of her in this way, or that they might discuss her behind her back. They were always the perfect gentlemen towards her, and she relished having someone special to talk to. Each visit, Fred would toy with her in an attempt to share information regarding the town. More often than not, he failed, as Constance was usually one step ahead of him. Constance was too wrapped up in her own life to notice how much this irritated Fred.

As Constance found she had more time on her hands, now that she needed to do less for her children, she found herself becoming more bored at home. One evening she mentioned this to Henry.

"We can soon sort that," he replied. "I've got so much work on at the moment, I don't know if I'm coming or going. I was thinking about taking on another assistant."

"Really?" answered Constance, surprised. She knew her husband would not have taken this decision lightly, as it would mean another wage going out.

"Would you be interested in helping me out?" he asked.

"What would you want me to do? I'm not sure I could work in the shop all day."

"No. I guessed that much. I could do with someone to take the various items into Aldershot for me to get them valued. We seem to be getting a lot of antique jewellery at the moment. It would usually only be once a week, but it would help me out, as this can take me away from the shop for a few hours. Would you be interested? I can explain it all in more detail if you are."

"Yes. I think I could do that. I could combine it with a trip to the shops each time."

"That will fill your whole day then," laughed Henry. "But don't go too mad, will you?"

"I'll only buy what we need. Don't panic," smiled Constance, knowing her husband well.

In July 1935, during a visit to the hairdresser's, Constance shared with her stylist, Fred, her new role in her husband's business. She discussed the many items of jewellery she now handled and how surprised she was by some of their value. Fred remained quiet throughout, and Constance thought she must be boring him, as he appeared to show little interest in their conversation.

"Are you all right today, Fred? You seem a little preoccupied," she enquired.

Fred appeared startled by her observation. "I'm sorry, Mrs Hind. I just have something on my mind today," he answered.

"Anything I can help with?" Constance enquired.

"I don't think so. It's a young lady I know."

"Oh yes? Tell me more. Perhaps I can help."

"Thank you. But this is something I have to sort out myself. You were going to tell me about those antique rings you had the other week. Were any of them worth anything?"

"Oh, Fred, you wouldn't believe it. Do you remember I told you about the sapphire one?" And Constance began to divulge her story, quite forgetting about her hairdresser's problems.

As Constance left her home some days later, taking the route across the common—the way she always walked when visiting Aldershot—she carried inside her handbag eight rings, two brooches, two pearl necklaces, a watch, a compact, two chains and a pendant. Her journey was around three miles, but she was able to catch a bus for most of it, which was a good job, as her handbag felt extremely heavy.

She had her day planned. She left home once the children had gone to school and after completing a small number of chores. Once she had taken the pieces of jewellery to be valued, she would then need a couple of things for her family's evening meal before she could head home again. She also needed to remember to call in on her mother on her way home. Her mother had been feeling a little under the weather recently, and Constance wanted to make sure she was all right.

It was a relief to rest her handbag on her knee during the bus journey. It was heavier than she'd anticipated. Constance thought that perhaps it wasn't such a good idea to carry around so many valuables in her handbag. Henry would be cross if she were to lose any. The thought that someone might attempt to steal them from her never even crossed her mind.

The valuation had taken longer than expected, but the dealer told Constance that the value of her items exceeded £1,000. This should not have surprised Constance, judging by their weight. Whatever had she been thinking, taking them all at once? Never mind; it couldn't be helped now. They were quite safe in her handbag. No one could tell she had jewels to that value in her bag just by looking at her. She would quickly pick up the few things she needed for home and make her way back to the bus stop.

Constance relaxed again once on board the bus, clutching her handbag and shopping bags close to her chest, so as not to let them out of her sight. No one was the wiser. The other passengers just assumed she was doing this in order to free up the seat next to her. At the next stop an elderly woman climbed onto the bus and sat next to Constance. They chatted briefly about their shopping trip and then moved on to children, grandchildren, knitting and the state of the country. Before Constance knew it, it was time for her to get off the bus.

She had her usual walk back across the common to complete, then a short diversion to her mother's house, where she looked forward to receiving a hot cup of tea and perhaps a piece of her mother's delicious fruit cake. She certainly felt as though she could do with a treat after the day she'd had.

As Constance crossed the common—an open grassy area surrounded by clumps of trees and high bushes—she had no idea about the two men hiding, waiting for her to pass. The larger and rougher looking of the pair squeezed himself out from between the shrubs and leapt on her from behind. His slenderer accomplice remained hidden and observed from a distance.

The well-built man grabbed her by the shoulder and threw her to the ground. She dropped both her handbag and shopping bag, the contents of the latter emptying itself across the grass. The man then attempted to gag her by roughly shoving a handkerchief inside her mouth, and she thought for a split second that she was no longer able to breathe. When she realised she could breathe through her nose, she attempted to get free from her attacker. While wrestling with him, she managed to remove the handkerchief and started to scream for help.

At this point the man realised he needed to shut her up, so he punched Constance in the face, then in her neck and body a number of times, sure that this would do the trick. All the while, Constance continued in her attempt to break free from the man's grasp, screaming as loud as she could. Realising he had taken on more than he could chew and was sure to be caught if he continued, he finally let go of Constance. Moving quickly to where her handbag lay, he grabbed it and ran off.

Constance realised her attacker had left, yet she continued to shout for help. Close to losing consciousness and covered in blood, Constance was surprised to see her hairdresser appear from nowhere and rush to her assistance.

"Are you all right?" he asked, clearly as shaken as she was.

"The brute's taken my handbag, Fred!" And with that, Fred attempted to make chase.

Constance's assailant made off across the common followed by Fred. He'd made too good a start on Fred and was soon lost to view. Her assailant had managed to get away. Fred soon returned to where he'd left Constance. By then a couple walking their dog had come across her after hearing her cries for help.

Constance had managed to pull herself up into a sitting position and was being comforted by the couple when Fred returned. She heard someone come up behind her, panting heavily. She spun around, terrified her attacker had returned.

"Are you all right?" Fred enquired.

"Did you get my handbag?" Constance asked.

"No. I'm sorry. He got away."

"I think we should call the police," suggested the elderly dog-walker.

"Yes, of course," said Fred.

"I just want to go home, Fred. Would you take me?" Constance pleaded.

"Of course," Fred replied.

***

As Constance was helped through her front door by Fred, her children became almost hysterical because of the way their mother looked. Apart from being covered in blood, one of her eyes was badly swollen, she had a fat lip, ripped tights, and cuts and bruises to her legs and arms.

Constance took her son's hand in an attempt to let him know she was all right.

"Telephone your father at work, would you, dear? Tell him I've been attacked and they have the jewels. That should bring him home quick enough."

Fred then helped Constance into an armchair in her front room, while her daughter fussed and panicked over her mother.

"I'm all right, darling. Could you put the kettle on and make some tea? You'll have one won't you, Fred? My husband will be home soon. He'll want to know what happened."

"Of course," Fred replied reluctantly.

Constance guessed he was probably in shock, but he would have to look after himself. She had suddenly come over extremely tired and her face and body hurt like hell.

Constance drifted in and out of consciousness, seemingly unable to stay awake. Fred went out into the hall and she could hear him speaking to her son about when his father would be home.

"He's on his way," was her son's reply.

"Do you know the number for your mother's doctor?" Fred enquired.

"Yes," replied the boy.

"Then I suggest you call and tell him what has happened and ask him to visit as quickly as he can."

Minutes later Henry arrived home, crashing in through the front room door and waking Constance. When he saw the state of his wife, he didn't know what to do. He knelt beside her, held her hand and started to cry.

"You can stop that right now," she said to him. "I'm not dead yet."

"Are you all right? You look terrible."

"Thank you very much. I feel fantastic," Constance remarked sarcastically.

"I'm afraid the man who attacked your wife got away," said Fred.

Until then, Henry hadn't even noticed the slender stranger in his front room. All of his attention had been focused upon his wife. Henry looked confused. "Who are you?"

"This is Fred, from the hairdresser's," Constance explained. "He came to my rescue and chased the man who attacked me."

"Have you sent for the doctor?" Henry asked his wife.

"Your son has," replied Fred. And at that moment there was a knock at the door.

The doctor was shown into the front room by Constance's son.

"Well, well, well. What have we here? You've gone and got yourself into a bit of bother by the looks of you. Anything broken?" he asked.

"I don't think so, Doctor."

"Can you manage to get yourself upstairs if Henry and I help you, Constance?" the doctor asked kindly.

"I think so."

"I think that would be the best place for you right now, don't you?"

Constance was not about to argue.

"Thank you, Fred, for all your help," Henry said on his way out of the room with Constance and the doctor.

"Oh, I did very little."

"No, son. You may just have saved my wife's life, and for that we are both very grateful." Fred looked embarrassed. "Once I have my wife settled, I shall be speaking to the police, so expect a visit, won't you?"

"If it's all the same to you, sir, I will go directly there now and make a statement."

"Good man. Thank you, Fred. I'm sure you'll see my wife up and about again in no time."

It took Constance a number of days to recover from her injuries and the shock of exactly what had happened to her. But she was a strong woman, and it would take more than that to keep her bedbound or housebound. She was enduring nightmares almost nightly about the attack. She saw things in her dreams: things that she was unable to distinguish were fact or fiction, a real memory or made up. She needed to believe they were not memories but dreams, as during most of them, she had seen Fred crawling out from behind some bushes as he feigned coming to her assistance. Deep down she knew this not to be the true course of events that day and chose to erase these dreams each morning from her memory.

She'd had plenty of time while recuperating to consider how to repay Fred for his bravery. She and her husband had discussed it many times, and they had reached the decision that they should like to give him a sum of money for his kindness.

When she felt up to it, Constance went to visit her favourite salon. As she entered the premises that morning, she immediately spotted the elder hairdresser, not noticing Fred disappear into the back room.

"How are you, Mrs Hind?" enquired the elder man she knew as Leonard. He had obviously read about the attack in the local newspaper the week before, as had the rest of the town. For once, it was *she* who was the topic of everyone's conversation, and she was rather enjoying it.

"I'm getting there, thank you."

"It's good to see you out and about. And I'm pleased you managed to make your regular appointment with us. I was unsure if you would."

"It will take more than that to stop me getting my hair done," she bravely joked. "How is Fred?" she enquired. "Is he alright?"

"Yes he's well, thank you," replied Leonard, looking around for his colleague.

"It was very brave of him to do what he did. I haven't had chance to thank him properly yet."

Leonard looked confused. Constance was surprised that Fred obviously had not told him what had happened. She explained, "It was Fred who came to my rescue last week."

"It was?" Leonard was surprised.

"Yes. Has he not told you?"

"No. He hasn't mentioned a thing."

"When I screamed for help, it was Fred who heard my cries and came running to my assistance." Leonard looked lost for words. "Then he made an attempt to chase the man across the common, but he got away."

"I had no idea. Fred never said a word."

Constance asked if she could speak with Fred, and Leonard went to find him. Fred appeared reluctant to approach her. He was clearly shocked by the way she looked. It shocked her every morning when she looked in the mirror, but she knew the bruises would go eventually.

Constance thanked Fred again for coming to her rescue. Fred was clearly embarrassed, and when she handed him an envelope filled with money, he blushed and quickly disposed of it into his trouser pocket. They agreed that no more would be said about the attack, and Constance left the salon feeling on top of the world. Fred had worked his magic once more, and she would never forget what he had done for her on that terrible day.

Lily

———◁◦▷———

L ily had been born in 1906; the youngest of eight children. She had grown up in Frimsham, where her father ran a successful business. As his family had grown, they had all been expected to assist with his retail establishment and serve his customers. Lily was no exception, and she had been happy to spend time with her father in his shop as a teenager. She was a quiet, yet content, girl who allowed nothing to get her down. She always made the best of life and never complained about anything.

Over the years, she had watched on as her elder siblings developed into adults and became more independent. Some found love and left the family home to set up their own, while others found exciting work opportunities which allowed them to move away from the area. Her sister Rose had been the last to leave. They had always been close, and Rose had been there for Lily when their mother had suddenly become ill and died in January 1933. Most of the family had been at their mother's bedside as she had passed away, but instead of the family then pulling together, the opposite occurred.

After her mother's death, everything appeared to change for Lily. Although Rose was just along the street, running her own business, she was often too busy to make time for Lily. Her father had also dramatically changed since the death of her mother and tended to cut himself off from everyone and everything, except for his shop and its customers. As his working day came to a close, all he wanted to do was be alone, which meant Lily was also alone.

She soon began to feel isolated, miserable and despondent. She started to loathe her life and crave new horizons, but at the same time experienced massive feelings of guilt towards her father for feeling this way. She was in turmoil. She had a responsibility to her father, especially as he no longer had her mother for company. Being the youngest child and the last to remain at the family home, she saw no way of ever being able to live her own life. Then she met Fred.

Fred had an instant affect upon Lily. He swept her off her feet. He stirred feelings and desires inside her she never knew she had. Her stomach would do somersaults whenever she saw him, and she knew they were meant to be together. She was unable to get him out of her head. But her father stood in the way of her happiness and forbade her from seeing him, so in the end she believed she had no other option. Lily moved away from Frimsham in December 1935—from the only life she had ever known—leaving her father, to start a new life in Crestwell with Fred.

The basement flat into which Lily and Fred moved stood opposite a large public park. The park accommodated a bandstand, a drinking fountain, subtropical and rosary gardens, a boating lake and ponds. They enjoyed many walks around its grounds together throughout the year and in all weathers. On their very first visit to the park, Fred had insisted Lily join him in a boat, and after some encouragement, as she was unable to swim, she had allowed him to row her out onto the lake. It had been cold, but excitingly romantic.

As Fred established his trade as a hairdresser, Lily found work as a waitress. Fred teased her over her uniform and expressed concern over the other male customers she came into contact with. Lily enjoyed his over-protectiveness at first. Both of them worked long hours. They needed to in order to pay for their flat and other necessities. But Fred soon hinted that he would rather have Lily at home all day. Hadn't she just escaped that life in Frimsham? Why would she want to go back to it?

When news of the King's death reached Lily in 1936, the event made her think about her father and what she had left behind. Her father had always been a strong advocate of the royal family, and she knew he would be mourning the loss of the King. She wondered if he was giving her as much thought as she was him. Lily attempted to push thoughts of her father from her mind, as they only upset her, and instead tried to concentrate on her new life with Fred.

By March Lily had a more pressing dilemma to deal with. She had discovered she was going to have a baby and was unsure as to how

Fred would take this news. Pessimistic thoughts of Fred rejecting her and of having to return to her father full of remorse filled her head with horror. When Lily eventually told Fred about the baby, she had been surprised at how well he had taken her news. He had been reassuring and positive and somewhat thrilled by her news. She would soon discover she had played straight into his hands. He had always wanted her to remain at home. Now she had little choice.

Fred had done the respectable thing, and they had got married. Lily's wedding day was one of mixed emotions as she shared it with the man she loved and her best friend from work, but no one from her family. Fred was the same. He had insisted it be a small affair at the registry office, with just two witnesses. No one from his family attended either. *What a pair we are*, she thought.

Soon Lily was forced to leave her work because of her condition. Once at home alone all day, with only her own thoughts for company, her life promptly started to unravel. When the baby had been born, the situation went from bad to worse.

***

Lily suffered terribly from guilt about the way she had left things with her father. She had deceived him for so long, seeing Fred behind his back and all the time knowing he didn't approve of him. How could she have left her father at a time in his life when he was getting no younger and would soon need all the help he could get? She had encouraged her sister to conspire along with her for her own selfish reasons, so that she could be with the man she thought she loved. Some days the guilt she felt was almost unbearable, and the desire that she might be free of it, even more overwhelming. These feelings were never more pronounced than after the birth of her son in late September 1936.

Lily would wake up feeling low, and the day would gradually get worse. When Fred's mother had paid them a brief visit, Lily had found it extremely difficult. His mother had made it quite clear that she didn't think Lily was coping very well. There often appeared nothing in particular which triggered these feelings, but it was something that

Lily had to deal with on a day-to-day basis. Some mornings she could wake and feel positive about her life, but then if she thought about her father again, or if her son was not well, she might quickly find herself feeling hopeless and despondent. She could not control these feelings, and Fred did not seem to understand her.

Lily mentioned to Fred that she thought his smoking around the baby was making their son's illness worse. Fred laughed this off, telling Lily she was being ridiculous. Not having her husband's support made her feel worse, and she often felt she wanted to escape from the life she had chosen. Lily would take herself off for long walks, leaving her baby with a neighbour for hours at a time as she tried to work out what was wrong with her.

Lily quickly began to lose interest in her new life with Fred and the baby. She neglected her flat. It had been her pride and joy when she had first moved in. Now it was untidy, with dirty cups and plates in need of washing and clothes and baby equipment strewn across the furniture. Lily was not sleeping properly and felt consistently tired. She had lost her appetite and rarely had a meal ready for Fred when he arrived home after a long day at work.

Fred eventually became fed up with the situation at home. At first it seemed he had tried to help Lily, but there was only so much he could do when he was out at work all day. She knew he had asked various people for advice, and most had said it was most likely something Lily would get over in time. When he had told Lily this, she had been unconvinced.

When Fred suggested she take their son to a hospital because she was concerned for his health, she had listened. She took the baby to two separate hospitals during October and November, and both times her son was discharged with a clean bill of health. But Lily still worried about the child. Fred even suggested that Lily see a doctor herself, but she refused, claiming she was just tired and would be well again soon. She thought she could manage things without anyone's help.

By the end of November it was clear Fred was at the end of his tether with her. He started to blame Lily for everything that went wrong. He told her it was her fault their son was always crying and that she was a bad mother. He said it was down to her that there was no food in the house, down to her that his shirts weren't washed and ironed on time and it was her responsibility to get the flat tidy.

As Lily's self-confidence diminished, her self-loathing increased. She told herself she wasn't good enough at anything. She was a terrible daughter, who had let down her father at the worst time in his life. He had depended greatly upon her. He had provided for her all her life and she had deceived and plotted against him. She was failing as a wife, unable to care for her husband who worked hard all day to provide for her and their son. He loved her, and in return she resented him for having brought her to this place and got her pregnant. She had also failed as a mother. She had no idea how to bring up a child, never mind how to keep it healthy and happy. Her son would often refuse to take his bottle from her, and on the occasions when he did, he would usually bring it all straight back up again. What was the point?

Lily started to leave the baby more regularly with her neighbour, in order to have a break and visit friends. That in itself was a joke, for she had only made one friend—apart from her neighbour—since moving to Crestwell. She had met Ruth while waitressing, and they had become good friends. Ruth had been her witness at the registry office on the day she had married Fred and visited her in hospital after she'd had the baby. She was a true friend; someone she could trust. Ruth had visited her at the flat on a number of occasions since she had left her job to have her son.

She knew Ruth had never warmed to Fred, although she was unsure why, but she was relieved that this had never altered their friendship.

In early December Fred had unexpectedly contacted Ruth when he had been concerned about Lily's emotional state. According to Ruth, Fred had telephoned her because Lily had accused him of having an affair. Lily had come across a note in his trouser pocket before washing them. It had been from a girl at work, confirming that she would be able to meet up with him after work. According to Fred, it had been completely innocent, as he had needed to speak to her about staffing issues within the salon, but at first Lily had not believed him.

Ruth had gone round to the flat and spent time with Lily that day. They had chatted about Fred and the note. They had played with the baby and reminisced about work. Ruth had tidied the flat while Lily got some rest. She had been a tonic to Lily that day.

Only days later, Lily's mood had depleted once more after listening to the King's abdication speech on the radio. Fred didn't understand why his wife had suddenly become so glum again. He didn't know that the King's actions would be having a grave effect on her father and how she again felt guilty about not being with him at this time.

Over the following weeks, her husband's fuse grew much shorter and his patience with her moods wore thin. He became irritable about everything and critical and sarcastic over anything Lily said or did, resulting in him spending less and less time at home.

On the morning Lily received a letter from Ruth inviting her to meet in The Piccadilly, she felt as though a weight had been lifted, and she was floating on air. She was looking forward to spending time with her friend again. They were to meet after Ruth's shift at work, and Ruth had asked her to bring along the baby. However, by early afternoon Lily was having second thoughts about meeting her friend.

She didn't understand why she had suddenly started to feel this way. When she'd received her friend's letter, she had felt excited and was looking forward to it. Now she felt pessimistic and miserable. She didn't want to let her friend down. She wanted to see Ruth. She missed her friend. Perhaps she would go by herself and leave the baby with her neighbour. Yes, that was what she would do.

Thinking she might enjoy a coffee and uninterrupted conversation more if her son did not accompany her, Lily left him with a neighbour she had got to know well. Ruth was surprised at first not to see Lily with the baby, but she understood and they sat down to enjoy a chat. Lily felt uncomfortable from the start, but did her best to hide her negative feelings from her friend, as she herself did not understand why she was feeling that way. She talked to Ruth about her son and how worried she was. Lily explained that she felt unable to look after him properly, and they discussed her concerns about her husband working all hours to make ends meet.

"I worry about everything, Ruth, and I don't know why."

"I'm sure it will pass in time, Lily. It's most likely how every new mother feels. You'll feel better soon. Try not to worry."

As they parted company, Ruth mentioned, "I finish early on New Year's Eve. I'll pop over if that's all right?"

"Thank you, Ruth. I'd like that. I think I'm going to find it difficult that day, as it's a year since I left my father."

"I understand, Lily. It will get easier in time. You'll see."

Lily hugged her friend then turned away quickly to leave before Ruth could see she was crying.

Lily should have been looking forward to Christmas, but it was a difficult time for her. She hated every second of it. The only two positive things about it were that she had Fred to herself for a couple of days and the baby's cold seemed to have improved. Fred tried to lighten the mood by suggesting they have a game of cards, go for a walk or visit their local pub, and for a time these suggestions had worked. Lily had been able to temporarily forget her troubles and enjoy their time together. But the second she let her guard down, those feelings of anxiety, guilt and distress came flooding back and she plummeted back down into a pit of despair once again.

All the while Fred was at home, Lily seemed able to cope, but when he had to return to work on the Monday morning, her mood quickly deteriorated. Fred worked late into the evenings, as party-goers wanted to look their best. Meanwhile, Lily tried to figure out a way through her impossible situation. She couldn't go on like this any longer. She was at her wits' end.

When Fred was ready to leave for work on New Year's Eve, Lily begged him to stay at home. "I'd love to, but it's going to be really busy at work today. We have many more clients than usual, with it being New Year tomorrow."

"Please, Fred," she begged him again.

"Don't you have Ruth calling in today? She'll keep you company until I get home."

With Fred at work and the baby having a sleep, Lily was left with her thoughts. She began to feel overwhelmingly suffocated inside her little flat. She needed to escape. Popping out to see her neighbour, she asked if she could look after the baby again. She told her neighbour she wanted to visit some friends, but in reality she just needed to get out of the flat and away from everything.

Before she left, she wrote a quick note to herself: a reminder to get some more cough syrup for the baby, as his cough seemed to have returned. She placed the note inside her handbag. Then she wrote another note to Fred, telling him where she was leaving the baby, and left that note on the table where he would see it. It read, 'Fred, I need to get away. I have left the baby with our neighbour on Howard Road. I cannot go on like this. You have not helped. I am finding it all too difficult. Lily.'

Lily gathered her son's things together and put him in his pram. She wrapped him in plenty of blankets and grabbed her coat and gloves. Her mind was elsewhere as she left the flat, and she had completely forgotten that her friend Ruth was supposed to be calling round.

Lily pushed the pram past the Royal Oak, along Parkgate Road, left the baby with her neighbour in Howard Road and then headed into London across Crestwell Bridge. As she reached the middle of the bridge, she stopped. She turned and looked down into the water. It was a long way down and the water looked freezing. She stayed there momentarily, staring into the depths below, then she continued on to Chelsea, then Kensington. After that, it all became a bit of a blur.

Lily had no idea where she was going. The further she walked, the more despondent she became. Feelings of utter inadequacy washed over her. She was no good to anyone. She couldn't do anything right. They would all be better off without her.

Lily walked for hours around London, not noticing the evening drawing in and the streets becoming dark. She hadn't noticed the street lights coming on or the temperature dropping. In fact, she no longer felt very much at all. She was in a world of her own, alone and isolated.

She gave little thought to Fred, wondering only once if he were home from work and if he'd been round to Mrs Wesley on Howard Road to collect their son. Had he read her note yet? If he had, he would most likely be angry with her again. She could never get it right. She didn't think he would go out looking for her, after all he'd have the baby to look after. He wouldn't leave the poor little mite alone, would he?

Lily felt worse about letting down her friend Ruth. She had promised to call round today. What had she thought when she had discovered Lily was not there? Lily hoped her friend would understand and not feel too cross with her.

Lily arrived back on Osborne Road just as her friend Ruth was leaving the flat and walking off in the opposite direction. They did not see one another. Fred had followed Ruth out and was standing in the doorway of the flat, smoking a cigarette. She did not notice him either, but Fred had spotted Lily.

Lily was in a trance, looking as though she knew where she was going, but really there was little going on inside her head that made any kind of sense to her. She had realised she was in the vicinity of her flat, but made no attempt to head in that direction or even glance over. She knew she didn't want to return home just yet.

As Lily reached the gate of Crestwell Park, she discovered they had been locked for the night. She continued to walk on a little further to where she knew there was a gap in the wooden fencing and squeezed through. Once inside the park grounds, she went in search of a park bench and sat down. She was exhausted. She must have been walking for hours.

The moonlight shone brightly overhead, but she did not notice its beauty or the detail of its craters and seas, clearly visible in the star-speckled sky. There was nothing but silence all around her. There was no one else in the park, or so she thought. She sat still among the tranquillity of her surroundings, dwelling and worrying, wondering how it had come to this?

Suddenly, the sky was flooded with a rainbow of colours as fireworks went off in all directions, and she was briefly distracted by the shouts and cheers of party-goers as they welcomed in the new year. She tilted her head backwards to look up, but she was unmoved by the shimmering colours that lit up the night sky. Lily could bear it no longer. She knew she couldn't face another second in this world, never mind a whole year. Her mind was made up.

As the fireworks fizzled out, Lily stood up and walked towards the boating lake that lay only yards in front of her. She stepped over the low picket fence, nearing the water's edge, and stared down deep into the dark pond water. She briefly turned, thinking she had heard something in the bushes behind her, but there was nothing there. She bent down, gently placing her handbag on the ground. Then Lily removed her gloves and coat, dropping them to the ground in a heap. Slowly, she moved forward into the pond. She felt nothing as she entered the water. She thought nothing as she disappeared beneath its surface. Soon she would be at peace.

Ruth

———◁◦▷———

Ruth had first met Lily in early 1936. They were both working as waitresses at The Piccadilly Hotel. They had been moved to work together in one of the massive restaurants the building housed, where they served afternoon teas promptly and efficiently to guests. With most of their shifts coinciding, they had quickly got to know each other well. They formed an instant friendship, enjoying one another's company while sharing their breaks together. On occasion, they went together for something to eat after work or met up for coffee before their shift was due to start.

Ruth was slightly younger than Lily, but most people would have assumed they were the same age. Both women were petite and attractive. Whenever they were together, they roused the attention of gentlemen. But neither were interested in this response. Lily lived with Fred, albeit a secret from her other work colleagues, and Ruth had recently divorced after a short, abusive marriage; information she too had chosen not to disclose to her employer.

The two women had become close extremely quickly and entrusted their secrets to one another. Ruth told Lily all about her malicious, violent husband's behaviour towards her and Lily disclosed how her father had treated her and why she had been forced to run away with Fred.

One day, Lily had turned up for work looking quite dreadful, and later that morning Ruth had discovered her in the toilets being sick.

"What's the matter with you?" Ruth asked.

"I think it must have been something I ate," replied Lily.

"As long as it's not catching. Do you think you should go home?"

"No, I'll be fine. I think it's passed now."

"Best clean yourself up then. We're back on in five minutes."

"I'll be right with you," Lily called after her friend.

When Ruth had walked into the toilets a few days later and found her friend suffering with the same symptoms, she asked, "Do you think you could be pregnant?"

"No. I don't think so."

"When was your last bleed?"

"A couple of months ago, but I've never been terribly regular with them."

"Perhaps you should get checked by a doctor."

"Do you really think so?"

"I think it would be best."

Ruth knew her friend must have been frightened by the prospect. She was living with a man who people thought was her husband, but the hotel management believed she was single and, more importantly, living alone. And now she might be pregnant? Ruth felt for her friend.

A few days later Ruth enquired as to whether Lily had seen a doctor yet.

"I feel much better now, thanks. I don't think it was what you thought. I'll be fine."

"If you're sure."

"I'm sure. Thanks, Ruth."

On some days, Ruth thought Lily looked pale again, then on others she was lively and cheerful. When Lily disclosed some weeks later that she and her fella Fred were to be married and that they were also having a baby, Ruth was shocked.

"I'd like you to be a witness. Say you will, please, Ruth."

"Of course, I will," replied her stunned friend, with tears in her eyes. "How long have you known?"

"Not long. I was afraid to have it confirmed at first, and then I needed to pluck up enough courage to talk to Fred."

"How did he take the news?" Ruth asked sensitively.

"It was his idea to get married."

"Rightly so."

"We're going to need all the money we can get now, so I'm going to have to hide my situation from everyone here for as long as I can. You won't mention anything, will you?"

"Lily, it upsets me that you have to ask me that."

"Sorry, Ruth. I'm just all over the place at the minute."

"I understand. You can rely on me."

"Thanks, Ruth. You're a true friend."

Lily introduced Ruth to Fred for the first time in the April. She invited Ruth round to their flat and cooked one of her favourite meals for her friend. Ruth and Fred got along well, and the evening had been a success until Lily realised she had run out of milk for the coffee.

"I just need to pop out for some milk. I shan't be long."

"I can go for it," Fred suggested.

"No, no. You entertain Ruth. I'll only be five minutes." And she had gone.

Fred and Ruth were discussing some of the customers who frequently visited The Piccadilly. They sat beside one another on the settee.

"Do any of them harass the women there?" asked Fred.

"You don't need to worry about Lily. She knows how to look after herself," Ruth assured him.

"But would she know what to do if one of them touched her?" he asked, placing his hand upon Ruth's knee. Ruth froze, completely stunned by Fred's brazen move. His dark eyes locked with hers and she felt unable to move. He puffed on his cigarette, his other hand still resting on her knee. He said nothing, just grinned. It was as though he was speaking to her through his eyes. He frightened her. He was intimidating. His eyes were warning her off, telling her not to get too close to his wife. As he moved his hand further up her leg, she wriggled free from her temporary paralysis and jumped up from the settee.

"What do you think you're doing?" Ruth demanded.

"Just seeing how you might respond," Fred replied calmly.

The front door to the flat opened and Lily walked in. "I'm back," she announced as she entered.

"I'm really sorry, Lily. I won't be able to stay for coffee. I completely forgot I was supposed to call in on my mother today. She hasn't been well and I promised. I'm sorry to have to rush off like this."

"What a shame. Just as we were getting to know each other," smiled Fred.

"Never mind, Ruth. I understand. You'll have to come over another time. You and Fred seem to have hit it off."

"You've found a good friend there, Lily," mocked Fred.

Lily retrieved Ruth's coat and hugged her friend goodbye at the door. "I'm so pleased you and Fred get along. He's great, isn't he?"

"You're very lucky, Lily. I'll see you on Monday."

"Bye, Ruth. Thanks for coming," Lily shouted after her friend as Ruth quickly disappeared down the street.

You're very lucky? Why had she said that? What she had wanted to say was run for the hills and never look back! She hadn't taken to Fred. There was clearly something not quite right about his behaviour. But how on earth could she say that to her friend. After some hours of further consideration, Ruth wondered if perhaps she had totally misread the situation and over-reacted. She was prepared to give Fred another chance for the sake of her friend.

Over the coming months, Ruth listened to Lily's plans for the wedding with enthusiasm, but inwardly dreading each time her friend would invite her round to her flat. She needn't have worried though, as both times Fred had not been there because he'd been working late to earn extra to pay for the wedding and the baby.

Ruth knew her friend was short of money and kindly offered to loan Lily a plain silk gown and veil from her sister's recent wedding the previous November. Lily was relieved. "I had no idea how I was going to be able to afford one. You do think it will fit me? I've got a bit of a tummy now."

"It will be perfect. Trust me."

***

When it had started to rain on the June morning of her friend's wedding, Ruth had wondered if it was an omen. She hoped her friend was doing the right thing. She certainly seemed happy enough, and on the two recent occasions when she had come into contact with Fred again, he had been the perfect gentleman. But there was just something about him which made her distrust him and his motive. And she was unable to explain this feeling.

Lily's dress fitted perfectly and her small bouquet did an excellent job of hiding her little bump. The ceremony inside Crestwell Registry Office was brief. After the short service, Ruth signed the register along with the bride and groom and second witness. Fred's witness was Will, who apparently worked with Fred and came across as a much more genuine person than his colleague. Fred seemed to have a hold over this man. Will jumped to it whenever Fred asked him to do something. He seemed a little afraid of Fred, not wishing to upset him and fussing over him all the time. Will appeared to take his best-man role extremely seriously.

As the four of them left the registry office, Ruth handed Will a fistful of rice and together they showered the newlyweds with rice and laughter. She was determined to remain cheerful for her friend on her special day, even though there was a storm brewing. The sky lit up before the distant rumble of thunder reached their ears, and it was difficult for Ruth not to feel a sense of impending doom about her friend's marriage. As long as she didn't show these negative feelings, Ruth knew she would get through the day.

The small wedding party made their way to Fred and Lily's local, the Royal Oak on Osborne Road, where they all enjoyed some food together. Lily and Ruth joked about the landlady, who had met their every request with speed and efficiency, saying that she would be an asset to the hotel where they worked. The wedding party were jovial and animated throughout the afternoon and into the early evening.

By eight o'clock Ruth could see her friend was in need of her bed and decided to call the proceedings to a conclusion, as it appeared Fred could have gone on for many more hours.

"Would you like me to walk you home, Lily?" asked Ruth.

"No, I'll do it," interrupted Fred.

"Why don't we all walk you home," suggested Will.

"No, I'll do it. You walk Ruth to the bus stop," insisted Fred.

"All right, mate. No worries," replied Will.

There were some awkward moments as they all said their goodbyes outside the pub, and then Will walked Ruth to the bus stop while Fred and Lily disappeared in the opposite direction.

"Is Fred often like that?" Ruth asked Will.

"Can be, sometimes. Just likes to do things his way, that's all. He's a good guy really."

"Umm." Ruth was not convinced.

***

Lily returned to work after her marriage, but it wasn't for long. Ruth could tell her friend was always exhausted after her shift and was relieved when in July Lily decided to hand in her notice. Ruth felt that if she had left it much longer, her employers would definitely have realised her friend was expecting a baby. Ruth missed her friend terribly after she left.

She managed to work her shifts to allow her to visit Lily on a number of occasions before the baby was born, but shortly after this, they had changed her shift times once more and visiting Lily had become more difficult.

Ruth managed to visit Lily in hospital a couple of days after her son had been born in October, when she found her friend very tearful. She put this down to her friend having the baby blues. After that, she had only managed to get over to the flat twice. During those times, the friends had discussed Lily's difficult birth and cooed a great deal over the baby. Her friend seemed perfectly happy on both of these occasions, except for some money concerns, and Ruth had no reason to be concerned about Lily or the baby. But this had obviously been before the baby had become ill. Ruth didn't see her friend then until early December. She had no idea her friend had become so low with it all.

When Ruth received a telephone call from Fred, explaining his concerns for Lily's health, she was immediately suspicious. *Things must be bad if he's calling me,* she thought.

Ruth managed to arrange her visit to Lily's flat when she knew Fred would be at work. When she arrived, she was surprised to find her friend and the flat in such disarray. Lily appeared exhausted, and Ruth suggested that she slept whenever the baby slept.

"But I might not hear him crying and sleep right through it. And what about all this ironing?"

"Look, Lily, I'm no expert, as you know, but I'm sure you are only experiencing what every other new mother goes through. The trick is not to let it bother you. Who cares if the flat is a little untidy? Who cares if Fred's dinner is not ready when he gets home? He'd understand, wouldn't he?"

"Yes, of course. I suppose you're right."

"Go and get your head down while I look after the baby. He'll be fine. I'll make him up some more bottles and finish your ironing."

"You shouldn't have to do that."

"I want to. Now off to bed you go."

Too exhausted to argue with Ruth, Lily gave her a cuddle and disappeared into the bedroom. When she reappeared a couple of hours later, the flat was tidy, the ironing complete, dinner had been started and the baby was fast asleep after having his bottle.

"You're a miracle worker," said Lily when she saw what her friend had achieved.

"Not really. I'm just pleased I could help."

"Can I ask you something?" enquired Lily.

"Of course. What is it?"

"I know Fred cares about me because he called you to see if you could cheer me up, but I think he might be having an affair."

Ruth was shocked by what her friend said. "What makes you think that?" she asked.

"I found a note in his trouser pocket from a young girl he works with. It said she could meet him after work."

"Have you asked him about it?"

"Yes. He says it's completely innocent and that he just needed to speak to her after work about some staffing issues."

"Umm, could be completely innocent."

"Apparently she's the owner's daughter."

"I suppose that might make more sense then, so that they could speak in private without the rest of the staff overhearing."

"Do you think I'm worrying over nothing?"

"Yes, most likely. You need to concentrate more on yourself and the baby. Forget Fred. He's a big boy and can look after himself."

Lily managed a smile for her friend.

When Fred telephoned Ruth again the following week, asking once more for her help and to visit again, she informed him in no uncertain terms that it should be *he* who should offer more support to Lily, by getting home from work a little earlier in order to help with the baby. "I will visit and help when I can, Fred, but you need to do your share."

Fred did not take this advice well. While Ruth knew she had offended Fred, she also felt she had little to lose, so asked, "Are you seeing another woman, Fred?"

"Don't be so ridiculous. Whatever gave you that idea?"

"Well, I'm very pleased to hear it. Lily deserves better than that. Go home and take better care of her. Goodbye, Fred." And with that, she hung up the phone.

Ruth wished she could have seen Fred's face. She knew he would have been fuming with her telling him what to do. This had been her revenge for the time he had run his hand along her leg. As she replayed their conversation over again in her head, she hoped he had not returned to the flat and taken out his temper on poor Lily.

Ruth found it difficult to visit Lily much during December, due to the extra shifts she had been allocated at work. She wrote to Lily, inviting her to The Piccadilly, so that they could meet for a coffee after she had finished work. When Lily had turned up without the baby, she was pleased to see her friend but surprised she did not have him with her. Lily was chatty enough, but she was different. She appeared anxious and a little jumpy. She spoke negatively about her ability to care for her son and talked about never having enough money for even the basic things. She had become emotional every time Fred's name was mentioned. Ruth had tried her best to make her friend feel reassured during their short meeting, but as they parted company, agreeing to meet again on New Year's Eve, she was sure Lily had been in floods of tears. That meeting would turn out to be the last time Ruth ever saw Lily. How she wished she could turn back the clock and keep her friend with her, safe.

Ruth eventually made it round to her friend's flat on New Year's Eve at about nine o'clock. Work had been extremely busy, and she had been forced to work later than anticipated. When Ruth arrived at the flat, there had been no one in. She'd knocked for some time, thinking

Lily might have been asleep with the baby, but still no one answered. As Ruth stepped back out onto the dark street, contemplating her return trip by bus, she hadn't noticed Fred approach. He had thought she was Lily and had been rude and abrupt with her.

Reluctantly, Ruth followed Fred into the flat. As she lifted the baby from his pram, Fred thrust a piece of paper in front of her face. Most of the evening after that was a blur. All she knew was that her best friend was missing and her friend's jittery husband feared his wife might do something terrible.

***

The inquest into the circumstances of her friend's death in January 1937 left Ruth frozen to the core. She struggled to comprehend how it had come to this. Her constant feelings of mistrust towards Fred unnerved her. She didn't know what to do.

Fred appeared very calm during the first part of Lily's inquest, glancing around the room and nodding at the spectators he recognised. It had started promptly at ten that morning, and Ruth had been glad she'd allowed enough time to get a seat, as the room had quickly filled. The clerk told everyone to stand, the coroner took his seat at the bench and then he opened the inquest.

Fred was first to give his evidence. He spoke of how Lily's health had been good until after the birth of their son. He explained how she had experienced some problems during the birth and named the doctor who had been present. At this point the inquest came to an abrupt halt when a note was handed to the coroner explaining how the doctor in question was ill and would not be able to attend for some time. If they wanted the doctor as a witness, there would need to be an adjournment. The court agreed, and the inquest was adjourned for a couple of weeks.

Ruth left her seat and waited outside for Fred to exit. When he appeared, he had a young woman with him. Ruth stepped forward.

"Could I have a quick word, Fred?"

The woman smiled and stepped away, giving them some privacy. Fred lunged forward and embraced Ruth, which took her by surprise.

"I have managed to get this morning off work, Fred, but I have to work tomorrow, so I won't be able to make Lily's funeral."

"I understand, Ruth."

"Truth is, Fred, I don't think I would cope terribly well tomorrow."

"No."

"I'm sorry, Fred. I feel I should have done more to help."

"I won't have you blaming yourself. There was nothing any of us could have done. We tried, didn't we?"

I did, thought Ruth. *Did you? Really? And who was that woman on your arm?*

"Goodbye then," said Fred, moving in for another embrace.

"Stay in touch, Fred. And give the baby a kiss from me," said Ruth, breaking away from his grasp.

"I'll do that," Fred shouted as Ruth rushed off down the street, tears streaming from her eyes. Why on earth had she said 'stay in touch' to Fred? She didn't wish him or the baby any harm, but at the same time she had no reason to stay in touch with him. She hoped her comment hadn't given him the wrong impression and suspected he had already moved on anyway.

Ruth never went to the second part of Lily's inquest. She was too distraught to attend. She had lost a very special friend and partly blamed herself for not doing more to support Lily. When she later read the details of Lily's inquest in the local paper, she was shocked to discover Lily's baby son had died, and she now saw things very differently. Seeing it all written down on paper made it somewhat clearer to her. Once again, she had a bad feeling about Fred. She was convinced he had more to do with Lily's death than it appeared, except there was no proof and it seemed no one else suspected him. She doubted his actions and attitudes towards her friend. It seemed she was the only one who suspected he might have assisted in Lily's death.

The newspapers reported all manner of things, some of which added up and others that did not. Ruth had not realised how sick the baby had been. Each time she had seen him, he had seemed fine, but then, what did she know about babies?

Statements quoted directly from the inquest suggested to Ruth that Fred was making out that Lily was much sicker than she was. Ruth had found her friend bogged down with the responsibilities of being a new parent: nothing more. Lily had definitely not been in 'poor health,' as stated by Fred, and she did worry about money, but according to Fred, she had 'no money troubles'.

Fred had described his wife as 'a little strange' after the birth of their child, saying that other people had told him she would be all right in time. *I would have told him to take her to the doctor if I'd have thought for one minute she was acting strange*, thought Ruth. Lily was described in the newspapers by one of her neighbours as 'always singing' and 'always cheerful'. Another had said she was 'devoted to her son and husband'. That was the Lily Ruth had known. Something was definitely amiss.

Yes, her friend had allowed things to get on top of her and allowed the flat to become untidy, but she was worried about her ability to look after her son and the family's lack of money. Instead of supporting his wife, Ruth wondered if Fred had more to do with her friend's decline. Had he accused Lily of being inadequate? Had he convinced her she was a terrible mother who could not keep her child healthy and didn't know how to look after him properly? Could it have been Fred who had pushed Lily into taking her own life? Had he also got rid of his own son? Or was her imagination running away with itself?

Ruth read every single newspaper report about her friend, and by the end of it all she was completely confused. She was distraught that it had come to this. There were two things which had been reported that she didn't understand. They just didn't seem to add up. The first was the note, supposedly left by Lily. Part of the note had read, 'Please forgive me for doing this. You have been wonderful all through. No blame attached to you.' Ruth thought she had known her friend quite well and believed the words used in the note didn't ring true to how Lily might have spoken. It sounded to Ruth as if someone else had written it and was trying to remove any blame from Fred.

The second piece of information was regarding Lily's clothes left beside the pond. According to reports, these were a coat, which had been neatly folded, with a pair of gloves placed on top. With Lily's mind being in the turmoil it so obviously was, and her flat in such a jumble, then why would she bother to fold her coat neatly? Surely, she would have just dropped it in a heap on the floor when she'd taken it off. And there was no mention of her handbag. Clearly, she would have had that with her.

Nothing made any sense. All the thoughts she had going round and round in her head about her friend Lily were starting to make Ruth ill. She had reached the point where she knew that if she didn't do something quickly about the way she was feeling, it might be too late. Ruth visited her doctor, but when he offered her shock therapy for what he called 'her depression', it was enough to shock her into taking matters into her own hands.

Ruth decided to move far away from London, leaving her memories of Lily behind her and starting afresh in a new town. She found a new home and a new job. In time Ruth managed to turn her life around. She thought of her friend intermittently. She never forgot Lily, but never lingered too long in the past, for the past had gone and no one could ever change what had happened.

Frank

———◇———

Frank's family had lived in Crestwell for many years. He had been born there in 1882 and had grown up north-west of the city. He had gone to school at Sleaford Street when he was five, then Saunders Road at eleven. His father had been a waterman, transporting people across the Thames, and when Frank had left school, he too had worked on the Thames as a labourer.

By 1911 Frank had joined the army and was living in India, while his family remained in London. Once in Calcutta, Frank found himself a job with the British government, working as a preventive officer for the Calcutta customs, where he was responsible for managing the import and export of goods. He was expected to search vessels for illicit goods on a regular basis and needed to be able to detect and prevent any attempts made to smuggle goods in or out of the port.

While working for customs, he met and became good friends with Sydney. Sydney worked in the woollen industry and used the port weekly, sometimes more. They had quickly developed a firm friendship, and Sydney welcomed Frank into his home as if he were a member of his own family. Sydney had five children, who over the years Frank got to know well. He also had a soft spot for Sydney's wife, Selina. In time Frank would become Selina's closest confidant; someone with whom she would share her most intimate thoughts and feelings.

Frank became part of the Calcutta Port Defence Volunteers and in July 1915, aged thirty-three, he enlisted as a gunner into the Calcutta Volunteer Battery, which was formed from volunteer regiments based in Calcutta. He enlisted for two years; firstly, travelling to Bombay en route to British East Africa. In Burma, during December, he was hospitalised for a month with dysentery. He would suffer with this more than once during his military service, and also from malaria.

From Bombay he went to Dara-Salaam, and by April 1917 he had travelled along the Suez and was in Cairo, Egypt. There had been plenty of hard marching during this time. It was estimated that he and his fellow soldiers had trekked for over a thousand miles, often having to cut their way through dense jungle. They had come across many animals during this time, such as deer, zebra, gnu, rhino and lions. On one occasion they had discovered two ostrich nests, one of which contained fifty-five eggs. They had all enjoyed a supper of scrambled eggs that evening, forced to admit that their strong flavour had taken a little getting used to.

Along with many other men in the army, Frank had a number of tattoos etched upon his body. A stork strutted across his chest, while a snake slithered along his left arm. He had many other smaller images about his person. They all reminded him of his experiences during this time, and he was very proud of these tattoos.

By July 1917 Frank was heading back to India, where he was finally discharged from duty at Fort Wilfred on 11 September 1917. While away he had been badly injured, and his friend's wife, Selina, assisted with his recuperation. He then continued to work for the British customs in Calcutta.

Selina and Sydney were both delighted to see him return, but Selina had changed greatly. Three of her sons had also gone off to war at the same time as Frank and she had not handled their absence well. Although she'd had her daughter and youngest son at home to keep her busy, she had worried greatly about her other three sons.

Frank had become very fond of all of Sydney and Selina's children over the years. He had missed them all while he'd been away. When Frank returned to the town, he noticed a change in the family. Sydney was always working long hours. He was also drinking too much, which often resulted in Selina requiring Frank's assistance with her husband's undesirable behaviour. On one occasion, Sydney had become violent and Frank had been summoned and forced to warn his friend that his behaviour was not acceptable. Thankfully, Sydney had taken heed.

Frank believed Sydney behaved in this way because he hardly ever heard from his sons and missed them all. When news reached the family that one of Sydney's sons had died, the household seemed to fall apart. Frank believed this was the trigger which then quickly changed everything for the family.

By the autumn of the following year, Sydney had become ill, and the doctors had been able to do very little for him. Selina was beside herself with worry. Their daughter Ellen was spending every possible waking hour in her father's company, as she did not know how long she had left with him, and their son Fred began to misbehave.

Fred had never truly been accepted by his parents. Frank believed this was possibly because his arrival into the world had not been planned. He realised that both Sydney and Selina found their youngest son a challenge.

Frank had always tried his best with the child. It had been he who had noticed Fred becoming more and more withdrawn after his father's illness was diagnosed, so he would always try to include him in whatever he was doing. He had once found Fred a sweet little puppy to care for, but within hours of presenting him with it, the poor creature was dead, and Frank never did discover whether it had been an accident or not.

Once Sydney was unable to discipline Fred, it was left for Frank to see to it that he did as he was told. On the occasions when Fred did misbehave, Frank rarely informed Sydney, as he did not wish to make his friend's suffering any worse. While still at school, Fred had been in trouble with the police a number of times, and Frank had often helped him to evade punishment for his petty crimes. It had proved useful to have the right contacts and know who to speak to, but Frank wondered if perhaps this had given Fred the wrong message.

Selina, on the other hand, had thrashed her son on more than one occasion. When she had discovered he had been stealing from his teacher, she had left Fred in a bad way. Frank felt it more productive to reason with Fred, and slowly he gained some trust from the boy. Fred would, on occasion, seek out Frank if he thought he was going to get into trouble for something. However, there had been one time when Frank himself had come close to giving Fred a taste of his belt after he had been caught with his hands around a girl's throat at school. Instead, Frank had given Fred a strong talking to, which seemed to have done the job, and Fred's behaviour appeared to have improved for a time.

Frank saw Fred as a troubled teenager who was unaware of where he fitted in. He realised Fred found it difficult to make friends. He recognised Fred was usually up to no good if he was absent from home, which was most of the time. The only person Fred seemed to have any time for was his sister, but even she had neglected his affections since their father had fallen ill.

Frank's marriage to Selina had occurred with mixed emotions. They both knew they were doing it for the right reasons—these being financial, for Selina and her children's security, but also because it had been Sydney's dying wish. However, they had done it in secret without informing Ellen and Fred until after the death of their father, and this news had not been welcomed by either child.

The day his best friend had died had been one of mixed blessings. Frank had been devastated to lose Sydney, but finally he could feel at peace in the knowledge that his friend would no longer suffer and be in pain. It had been near impossible to hold the family together during this time, but somehow they had made it through.

***

When Ellen announced she was to travel to England, in 1921, to visit her brothers, both Frank and Selina had known that Fred would soon follow. Six years later, the same age as when his sister had left, Fred also left for England. Both Frank and Selina had been surprised that Ellen had not returned home to India but married one year after arriving in London and then moved to live with her new husband and his family in Wales. Selina decided she did not wish to make the long journey to England for her daughter's wedding, or when her grandchildren had been born. When Fred had left for England, Frank began to discuss with Selina the possibility of them also making the trip to England one day. Frank secretly longed to return to the country of his birth.

It took a great deal of Frank's patience, but eventually Selina came around to the idea of moving away from India. On 5 April 1932 Frank and Selina travelled on board the *City of York* to England. Until they were able to find somewhere more permanent to settle, they went to stay with Selina's eldest son, Alex, in Sevenoaks. While Selina settled into England for the first time, Frank felt as though he had come home. He wanted to live in the same area as he had grown up in, and he quickly found a house in Willesden, where he and Selina were able to rent out a number of rooms. The area had changed greatly from when he had lived there previously, some thirty years earlier, but in other ways it was just the same, and he instantly felt at home there.

Frank had managed to find them accommodation with another couple of a similar age who were agreeable and friendly. They owned the property and rented out their upstairs rooms as a way to achieve an income. The four adults enjoyed each other's company, sharing their mealtimes and socialising together over a friendly game of cards. Frank didn't mind when the women began to spend more time in each other's company, as this meant he and his landlord could take regular trips to the local pub.

Frank and Selina had been at this property less than a year when Fred turned up out of the blue wanting to move in. Frank was not impressed. He thought the lad had some cheek, but Selina welcomed her son with open arms, fussing over him as if he were still a child. She hadn't seen him in more than five years and had obviously forgotten how difficult he had been. Her two other sons had lost touch with Fred, and they didn't know where he had gone. It had seemed that he had vanished off the face of the earth, so Selina had been completely overjoyed to see him when he had turned up, and she wanted him to stay.

Frank had previously been made aware of a disagreement between Fred and his sister when Fred had first reached England and visited Wales. Selina had received a letter from Fred explaining how unfairly his sister and her husband had treated him. At the time, Frank had found it difficult to believe Fred's version of events and sided with Ellen, but Selina would hear nothing bad said about Fred. He had been unaware that Selina had responded to this incident by saying a number of nasty things in a return letter to Ellen. Selina and Ellen had corresponded little since then, and Selina had never visited Ellen or her grandchildren in Wales.

Frank was now sceptical about Fred's version of events during this visit to them. While staying in Sevenoaks, Alex had confided in Frank about the things his brother had got up to, so Frank knew to take Fred's stories with a pinch of salt. Frank questioned everything Fred told him, much to Selina's dislike. Fred told Frank that he had lost his job and lodgings and had nowhere else to go. He told Frank that he had paid a visit to Alex who had passed on their mother's new address in Willesden. But even though his story seemed believable, Fred appeared a little uneasy when telling it. Frank suspected there was more to his stepson's story than Fred was willing to share.

Fred was offered the small spare room in the property his parents rented and quickly made himself comfortable. Frank didn't like the way Fred immediately took advantage of his mother or the way he managed to sweet-talk his way round her and their landlady. Both women were like putty in Fred's hands. He had definitely honed his skills when dealing with women and seemed able to manipulate them into doing just about whatever he wished. But Frank was not falling for Fred's charms. He wouldn't be able to pull the wool over his eyes.

Frank took an instant dislike to Fred. His lackadaisical behaviour could no longer be excused as Frank had done when Fred had been younger. Frank tried talking to Selina about his concerns and shared the information Alex had told him about Fred, but Selina would have nothing bad said against her son. She refused to believe that Fred was capable of any wrongdoing. Frank knew this was because her son had returned to her and she didn't wish to lose him again.

With Frank now retired from his work with the British government, he spent most days at home. Fred always seemed to be there as well, with his laid-back attitude to finding a job, and this annoyed Frank immensely. Frank felt Selina was spoiling her son, allowing him to feel too comfortable in her care, as if he had no need to seek paid work. Each day, Frank pestered Fred, enquiring if he had found employment yet. His plan was to enrage Fred enough that he would want to leave.

Frank's plan worked, and Fred soon became irritated by his stepfather's interference. He eventually found himself a job. Annoyingly, he was unable to keep this job for long. His explanation as to why this was, was rather vague. A long succession of other jobs followed quickly, but all seemed to last no longer than a matter of weeks.

Frank was deeply concerned about Fred. He appeared to be unable to stick at anything for very long, seeming restless and bored with his life. Frank spoke to Selina again about his concerns, but she disagreed with him, saying that Fred was just a little down on his luck at the moment and she believed things would pick up for him soon.

Not until Fred refused to eat or spend time with his mother did Selina start to become concerned about his behaviour and attempt to do something about it, although she had little success. Selina then went to Frank to express her concerns, saying that all her son did all day was stare out of the window. "He shows little interest in anyone or anything," she told Frank. Rather than say to his wife that he had told her so, Frank agreed to talk to Fred. Frank soon realised that he too was unable to reach Fred.

Some weeks later Frank and Selina had left the house to do their weekly shopping. They invited Fred to join them, but he refused, so they reluctantly left him behind. When they were on their return journey, they were stopped by two policemen and asked if they had seen a young child who had gone missing. Selina had enquired as to the age of the child, and once confirmed, explained how she had thought she'd seen a child matching the description being unwillingly dragged along the street by a man. Frank had been surprised because Selina had not mentioned this to him while they'd been out.

After being asked by one of the policemen to attend their nearest police station to give a statement, Selina had convinced herself and Frank that she had been mistaken and refused to go. When they had arrived home and Fred was nowhere to be found, Frank could tell his wife was again troubled by these events. He suspected that Selina thought Fred had something to do with the child's disappearance. Frank too had later become suspicious of Fred's movements that day, after he had returned home late with no explanation and looking bedraggled.

A few days later, when Frank returned to the house, he'd gone upstairs to find Selina and Fred locked deep in conversation. Selina rushed over to him and hugged him as though she had not seen him in weeks. She was strangely animated as she announced that Fred had something to tell them. Fred had at last found himself a new job, and his mother's relief was immense, but Frank sensed, not for the first time, that there was probably more to Fred's story than he was letting on.

Frank found it difficult to stifle his laughter when Fred announced he was to become a hairdresser. He sensed Selina was also bemused. Fred had never shown any interest in this line of work before. Frank successfully suppressed his amusement and congratulated Fred on finding work. When Fred followed this by announcing he was moving out, Selina's mood deflated rapidly and Frank was left to pick up the pieces.

Frank's mood improved at the thought of his stepson's departure, while Selina's deteriorated further. She had got used to having Fred around all the time, but now it was clear that he no longer needed her and Frank. She told Frank that she felt he was casting them aside like an old coat, with little thanks or appreciation for what they had done for him.

***

Frank and Selina would hear little from Fred over the next few years; that was until he reappeared one day with a pregnant woman in tow and introduced her as his future wife. Frank had liked Lily from the moment he'd met her. She was clearly besotted with Fred, and he with Lily. Even though Selina appeared happy for her son, Frank could tell his wife was less than impressed.

It seemed that Fred had at last found happiness. Selina no longer needed to feel as much concern about her son as she had in the past. She eventually accepted that he had a new life as a hairdresser and that he was to marry Lily. She seemed thrilled when Fred told her that he and Lily were expecting a child, due in the October of 1936.

Soon after the baby was born, Selina paid Fred a visit, but she had returned home to Frank feeling rather subdued. When he'd asked what the matter was, she explained how she had felt surplus to requirements. Selina said Lily had made her feel welcome but would not let her help with her baby son, and she had only held the child for a few moments before its mother had whisked him away again. Selina said she had not been allowed to feed the child or change him and Lily had appeared rather anxious.

"Fred is understandably cheerful and delighted at the fact he is now a father. They've called the child after him, and he looks just like his father did at that age."

"You can remember that long ago, can you?" enquired Frank cheekily. "I have trouble remembering what we did yesterday," he laughed.

"I knew you wouldn't understand," complained Selina.

"I'm pleased for them. Of course I am. I hope it will be the making of him. God knows, you could do with a time when you are not worrying about him. I'm very happy for them both. Truly I am, Selina."

"I'm not worried about Fred anymore. It's the baby that concerns me."

"Why? What's wrong with the baby?" Frank asked, believing his wife always needed something to worry about.

"I can't quite put my finger on it. I suppose I didn't get to spend long enough with him. It's just a feeling I have. Nothing more."

"You and your feelings."

Only, months later Fred had lost both his wife and child and Frank recalled what Selina had told him. She had been right about her feelings. The news of Lily's suicide and then their grandchild's death had hit them both hard. As Selina attempted to support her son during this time, he rejected her help, and this upset Selina even more. Frank could not stand to see Selina so distressed. The whole episode had made Frank begin to feel unwell. Fred was still nothing but trouble. He would never change. Frank suggested that he and Selina move away from Willesden and away from Fred and go and live near the coast.

They moved to Bournemouth in 1937. No sooner had they moved there, then Frank started to feel unwell. He was now in his mid fifties and Selina in her sixties. All those years of gallivanting across the world during the war had obviously caught up with him.

Frank no longer worked, and they had used most of their savings to finance their move to the coast. They lived in rented accommodation on Buchannan Ave, Boscombe, with an elderly widow named Alice who also took in a number of Christian missionaries. Although they both felt it was the right move to make at the time, they quickly realised that Frank's health was becoming more of a problem.

By December 1938 Frank and Selina had been forced to come to terms with the fact they may not have as much time left together as they had planned. Time was now extremely precious, and Selina had finally begun to put Frank first. This was confirmed to him when she next received news of Fred.

"Thank God he's only writing to you," Frank grumbled. "I'm not sure either of us could deal with a visit from him at the moment, or have to listen to his problems."

"There's no need for that, Frank," Selina scolded.

"So, what does he say? Don't keep me in suspense."

"He says he's getting married again."

"Well he doesn't let the grass grow, does he?"

Selina gave Frank one of those looks which said 'don't start'. "It sounds like they work together at the salon. She's called Betty, and she's the owner's daughter."

"Fallen on his feet then?"

"Why can't you just be happy for him, Frank?"

"Sorry. It's just that there's usually a hidden agenda where Fred is concerned."

"What on earth do you mean by that?"

"Oh, nothing. Just ignore me."

"No. Tell me. What do you mean?"

Frank managed to deflect his wife's questioning with one of his own. "Will you be going?" he asked.

"To the wedding? I shouldn't think so. Fred says it's not far off. He also mentions it will be a small affair." Selina looked back at Frank and smiled. "You are my priority at the moment. I wouldn't dream of leaving poor old Alice with such a responsibility."

"Don't leave me alone with those do-gooders either," Frank quipped.

"I wouldn't dream of it. You could turn a saint, you could, Frank." They both laughed.

Selina was true to her word and did not leave her husband's side to attend her son's wedding. When he was admitted into the Royal Victoria Hospital the following year, she walked the mile from their home to sit with him every day until he was eventually allowed home. However, Frank's recuperation was short-lived. His complaint made a rapid return the following year, when he finally succumbed and Selina was made a widow once more.

Betty

By 1940 it was difficult to imagine that when Betty had first met Fred she had no specific feelings for him. He was someone her father employed to oversee the running of his salon—a member of staff she had very little to do with. She had kept herself to herself over in the beauty therapy side of the salon, where her father allowed her to run things the way she saw fit. She had been doing this successfully for a year before Fred had arrived.

Betty's father had owned a salon in Brixton for many years. She had often visited it while growing up. After leaving school her parents supported her when she chose to begin a course in beauty therapy, and afterwards her father adapted his salon in order to accommodate her new skills. The rapid success of the beauty side of his business had been overwhelming for her father, and he soon advertised for a salon manager to oversee the day-to-day running of the hairdressing side of his salon. Fred had come highly recommended, enabling Betty's father to concentrate more on the accounting for his business.

Aged nineteen, running a beauty business took all of Betty's energy and time. Her days were so hectic that she did not get to socialise with her colleagues much and learnt little about the salon staff's personal lives.

On New Year's Eve 1936, that all changed when Fred hammered on her family's front door in Kenton Street, Brixton. His frantic knocking had shaken the whole house. The family had not yet gone to bed, as they had wanted to see in the new year together. Greatly alarmed, he told them his wife had gone missing. Betty's younger sister, Marie, had been swiftly directed up to her bedroom by their mother, and Betty had been charged with making a cup of tea for Fred; "With plenty of sugar," her mother had instructed. Meanwhile, her parents, Vincent and Eliza, listened to Fred's tale and attempted to comfort him.

Until then Betty had given Fred's private life little thought, never considering he might have a wife and family. Betty could hear the panic and desperation displayed in her colleague's voice as he frantically tried to explain to her father the circumstances of his wife's disappearance.

Fred only stayed long enough to gulp down the hot, sweet tea Betty had made for him and to explain his troubles, leaving her family in dismay. It appeared his wife had vanished, and after looking everywhere, he had been unable to find her. This incident would prove to set Betty off along a path where she would learn much more about Fred's life but ultimately end up with little influence or control over her own.

Fred's visit had ruined her family's enjoyment of New Year's Eve. Betty's father was beside himself with worry for an employee he'd known for less than a year, and Betty did not know what to do to help. Her father suggested that he might go out into the night to help Fred look for his wife.

"Do you know what this woman looks like?" Betty's mother asked realistically, and her father was forced to admit that he did not. In fact, Betty nor her father knew anything about Fred's private life. "Then there is little you can do to help," her mother replied.

The salon remained closed over the new year and was not due to re-open until 4 January. Betty and her father heard nothing further from Fred during this time, and both expected him to turn up for work as usual on the Monday morning, with the concern for his wife a distant memory. Upon their arrival at the salon that morning, they were shocked to discover that Fred's wife had been found dead.

Betty's father was quite beside himself and openly admitted to his daughter how guilty he felt for not helping Fred more on the night he'd called at their house. Betty attempted to comfort her father and organised to send a small bouquet of flowers to Fred's home address from all the staff at the salon. "It's a small gesture, but it will hopefully allow him to realise we are all thinking of him during this difficult time. I will make sure the card says that he should take as long as he needs."

"Thank you, Betty. You are very thoughtful," said her father.

The following day Betty's father allowed her to take some time off from their salon to attend the inquest into the death of Fred's wife in an attempt to support their employee.

The harrowing account of the drowning of Fred's wife was outlined, then postponed until 19 January in order to gain a medical report from her doctor and for her funeral to take place the following day.

Betty approached Fred afterwards. "How are you, Fred?" she asked without thought. Fred did not reply. Instead, he forced a smile and asked, "Can I return to work after I have buried my wife?"

"Of course," agreed Betty. "You are welcome to return to the salon whenever you feel ready to do so."

Fred returned to work on 11 January, having left his young son in the care of local midwives, and disclosed to Betty that he hoped his work would take his mind off things. She kept a watchful eye on Fred, leaving him to his hairdressing, yet stepping in when she noticed him struggling. Betty did her utmost to be understanding and supportive. She undoubtedly achieved this, as Fred invited her to his flat the following weekend to meet his baby son. Betty felt compelled to accept his invitation. She was surprised to discover that she enjoyed the visit. Fred was more relaxed in his own home; a different person from the one she had recently experienced at work. His young son was a delight, even though he was constantly struggling with a chesty cough and runny nose.

Fred was back at work again on the Monday morning and asked Vincent if he minded if Betty accompany him to the court again the following day. Betty's father agreed, as it was clear to both Betty and Vincent that Fred needed their support. Moments later a telephone call came into the salon for Fred. Betty stood beside him as he was informed by a local midwife, caring for his son, that the child had taken a turn for the worse. Fred rushed from the salon. "Telephone me later, Fred, and let me know how he's doing, won't you?" Betty called after him.

It was around six that evening, just as Betty was locking up, that Fred startled her as he noisily entered the salon.

"Fred! You gave me such a fright. How's the baby?"

Fred broke down.

"Sit down, Fred. Sit down here." Fred slumped onto the salon sofa and Betty sat next to him. She cradled him in her arms as he told her how his son had died earlier that day from bronchitis. He was extremely despondent. Betty and Fred remained in the salon until late that evening as Betty attempted to comfort and reassure Fred. "You must somehow find enough strength to carry on, Fred. I will be by your side tomorrow. You can get through this, Fred," she encouraged.

The following day Betty attended the inquest. As more evidence was provided by a number of new witnesses, Betty gained a great deal of intimate knowledge about Fred's personal life, which under normal circumstances she most likely would never have known.

It was established that Fred's wife had drowned herself due to depression after having their baby boy and him being in ill health soon after his birth. The whole situation was very upsetting, and at one point Betty found herself wishing her father had been sitting next to her. As she listened to the details of the poor woman's demise, it was difficult to hold back her tears.

Betty glanced intermittently over at Fred, careful not to stare at him for any length of time. It was plain to see that he was under a great deal of stress and deeply overwhelmed with sorrow. When he was forced to explain to the court that the previous day his young son had succumbed to his illness and died, Betty had wanted to get up and leave. Her heart ached for Fred, a man she hardly knew, and the need she had inside her to comfort him was overwhelming.

Something powerful inside Betty stirred and was roused that day. She experienced feelings she never knew were possible and didn't quite know what to do about them. At first Betty tried to ignore them, but at work and at home all everyone wanted to talk about was Fred. While she continued to support and motivate Fred at work, she also encouraged him to continue with his life and made him realise there was more to be had from it. Betty was unsure if it had been she who had put the thought into his head, but Fred decided that a change of career might help him heal more quickly. He made the decision to leave the salon and found work as an insurance clerk in an office. By then her feelings for Fred had increased. This move appeared to have the result Fred desired, although it had left Betty's father with staffing issues, which took some time to resolve, and Betty with a dilemma.

With Fred's different job and fresh confidence and positivity, Betty's concerns for Fred rapidly changed from those of sympathy to feelings of desire. Each day, she found herself completely unable to get thoughts of Fred out of her head. A change had taken place in Fred as well. He suddenly wanted to spend more and more time with Betty. He'd changed almost overnight. Something between them had ignited. Unexpectedly, Fred energetically swept her off her feet, romancing and seducing her with his faultless, charming personality, of which she had seen little of before. Betty found him irresistible.

Before Fred had entered her life, Betty's closest male friend had been Alan, a boy with whom she had grown up and shared much of her life. Betty had been out with Alan to the cinema on many occasions, and her family had thought the two would eventually marry. But suddenly all this had changed. Betty began cancelling planned dates with Alan in preference of seeing Fred. Fred would take her out for romantic meals and walks and kiss her passionately, unlike anything she had ever experienced with Alan. Betty quickly succumbed to Fred's charms. In no time at all, she had been trapped like a beautiful butterfly paralysed inside a spider's web.

***

It had been both a difficult and exciting couple of years for Betty, culminating, in December 1938, with her marriage. She and Fred had been planning it for some time, but at first Betty's parents were not happy that she had begun a relationship with Fred. Fred's life appeared very complicated to them, and they believed their daughter was too young to deal with his problems. Betty realised that the thirteen-year age gap between her and Fred also concerned them. She too had fears, but Fred had a way of making her feel as though she was worrying about nothing. Betty's parents asked her time and time again to reconsider her plans, and now in hindsight she had started to wish she had listened to them.

When Betty and Fred had originally announced their plans to marry in a registry office, Betty's parents had become rather upset at this prospect, explaining they had always thought their daughter would want to get married at the family's local church—the same church in which they had married.

Betty did not wish to upset or disappoint her parents. It had taken some doing, but after discussing her dilemma with her good friend, Alan, together they had managed to change Fred's mind about where they should marry. And it was also decided that Alan would be perfect as Fred's best man. Fred appeared reluctant about both decisions at first, but Betty soon won him round.

In the run up to their wedding day, Betty and Fred worked as hard as they could, saving up enough money to afford to rent their own home. Betty's father was to pay for the wedding, so they did not have this expense. They never seemed to have much time for socialising, so Betty never really got to meet any of Fred's friends. Shortly before their wedding, Fred explained that no one from his family would be able to attend. His sister lived in Wales, and it was too far for her to travel; his two brothers were unable to get the time off work; and according to Fred, his mother didn't like occasions such as weddings, so there had been no point in inviting her. Fred also told Betty that he had invited a couple of colleagues from his insurance work, so at least she would get to meet them.

Alan had been there to support Fred on their big day, which had been filled with laughter and joy. Betty's extended family, including many aunts, uncles and cousins, had spaced themselves out in the church, making it less obvious how little representation Fred had from his family. Her younger sister had been by her side, fussing over her all day, and her parents had shown great pride in their two daughters. Betty could not have wished for a happier occasion as she embarked on her new life married to Fred.

Married life at first was all but perfect. Betty knew she was fortunate. When she moved into her first home on Leigham Avenue, Streatham, it seemed that Fred had put all his sadness behind him and life was now being good to them. His relationship with her parents also appeared to improve at this time, or so Betty had thought. In reality, Eliza and Vincent found it difficult to accept Fred into their family and only tolerated him because they did not want to upset their daughter. Betty knew that now. He had brought turmoil and chaos to Vincent's home and business, leaving him short-staffed after he'd decided to walk away from the salon, and Vincent found it difficult to trust him after this.

Betty was aware that Fred had upset her father shortly before their wedding day, when he had announced he no longer wanted to work at the salon and had found himself a job in insurance—he could earn more money through his insurance work—but she was unaware he had boasted to her father about how he was more than capable of providing for himself and her, refusing any financial assistance from Vincent. This had offended her father greatly.

Although Betty remained at the salon full time, Fred had insisted they move further away from her family's home, and her work, to live in Streatham. It wasn't an ideal situation, as there were many others also sharing this property and Betty had further to travel to work, but Fred had explained that it was all they could afford at the time and it was important they were able to stand on their own two feet, without help from her father. Betty had agreed.

It wasn't long before Fred convinced Betty that she should also give up her work at the salon. In fact, he insisted upon it. He said it wouldn't be long before they would have a baby and he wanted her to get used to staying at home and looking after him before one arrived. He was able to convince her that this was a very practical solution. He reassured her that he was earning enough to pay for everything and this would give them time to get used to having just the one salary coming in.

Everything changed when in 1939 war was declared. Fred was laid off and forced to seek work elsewhere. Thankfully, he found another job quite quickly. Betty had been adamant she had not wanted him to join the army. However, Fred's new job did not cut it for him and he soon became despondent. Betty began to dread the mood her husband would be in each night when he arrived home. He seemed to have nothing good to say about his office job and would continually moan on about it to her. This would happen most nights, and one Friday evening he was late home. When he finally fell through the front door shouting and swearing, it was clear to Betty that he had been drinking.

Betty was twenty-two at this time, and feeling frightened by her husband's drunken behaviour, she quickly left their home, walking the mile and a half up Streatham Hill and Brixton Hill to her parents' home. Fred made no attempt to follow her or find her that night.

Once in the safety of her childhood home, her mother comforted Betty. "He most likely needs time to sleep it off, dear, so you can stay here with us tonight."

Betty attempted to justify her husband's behaviour. "I'm sure it's because he feels worthless at work. I know he hates his job at the moment. He often says he's really bored with it and how it doesn't challenge him."

"Then perhaps he should join up and help his country get the bloody Germans out of Poland," suggested her father.

"Oh no. I don't want him to join the army," Betty replied rather horrified.

"It might make him appreciate you more," continued Vincent.

"Vincent, you're not helping," said Eliza, noticing the panic in her daughter's eyes.

Betty's emotions were all over the place, and her panic was due to the fact that she had recently discovered she was pregnant. However, she chose not to disclose this fact to her parents that evening. She wished to inform Fred first.

***

In the early days Betty had been naïve about sexual intercourse. She had heard her girlfriends discuss some aspects of it, but she could only go off her own experiences of intimacy with Fred. He had stipulated early on that there was no way he was ever going to use a sheath. His primary method of birth control was to withdraw, and it should be her responsibility not to get pregnant until the time was right.

At first she had wondered if Fred wanted any children with her. He would often avoid intimate contact with her during certain times of the month but want to be with her more when she was most likely not to conceive. Fred seemed to know when Betty's period had ended, and a couple of days later would entice her into the bedroom for sex. But this time Betty had been caught out, and she didn't know how Fred would react to her news.

The following day, when Betty returned home, the flat was spotless, the washing had all been ironed and put away and Fred was attempting to make a meal for them both. Betty approached him tentatively, but Fred was the perfect gentleman. He was acquiescent about his bad behaviour the previous day and promised it would never happen again. They enjoyed a meal together, and after the meal Betty shared her news with Fred. He appeared to be delighted, but Betty could tell he was apprehensive after having lost a previous child. She attempted to reassure him. They talked for most of the evening, and Fred decided he would start to look for another job. He kept insisting this would be a fresh chapter for them.

Hitler had other ideas. He put a stop to Fred finding another job when, in the autumn of 1940, the Germans systematically bombed London night after night for weeks and weeks. Many were killed and injured and much of London was destroyed. Raids upon the city continued throughout the war, with hundreds of bombers pounding the area, causing widespread destruction.

One September evening Crestwell was hit badly, and the following day Winston Churchill arrived to inspect the damage. "Good old Churchie," Fred commented to Betty when he read this information in his newspaper. "Keeping up our spirits; that's what he's doing. Just let me get my hands on that Adolf Hitler chap. I'd show him a thing or two."

"Don't talk like that, Fred."

"Well, it's about time we put a stop to all this."

Betty was terrified, not only of the bombs but of losing Fred. Every few days he would threaten her, saying that he was going to join the army; and each time he did this, she battled to talk him out of it. It was almost as if he enjoyed these conversations. She prayed the war would be over soon so that Fred would no longer be tempted to leave her. What was she thinking, bringing a baby into the world at such a horrendous time?

With no job to keep him occupied during the day, Fred's mood rapidly deteriorated. His temper flared further when he discovered that Betty had been to see her father about money for their rent.

"What did you do that for?" he demanded.

"It's only temporary, until you find some work. Then we can pay it back. I'm struggling with what little we have at the moment," she reasoned.

"We wouldn't have to pay it back if you hadn't borrowed it in the first place. It's *my* job to provide for you, not your father's." Fred was clearly angry about her going to her father for help.

"He was glad to help. Honestly."

"I bet he was. Gloating, was he?"

"No, Fred. Father's not like that."

"Of course he isn't. I'm off to the pub. If you don't need my money, then I might as well spend it on myself." Slamming the door as hard as he could, Fred left and didn't return until after Betty had gone to bed.

That night was a blur. Fred woke her up when he arrived home. He stank of alcohol. After she had refused his amorous attempts to get her to have sex with him, he had forced himself upon her. The following morning she started to have unbearable pains in her stomach.

Fred left the house early, seemingly unaware of his actions the night before. Betty used the outside toilet in the hope she would not be disturbed. Inside the house, there was never long enough to use the bathroom before someone else wanted to get in there, so she opted for the one outside. She sat, rocking to and fro, clutching her stomach as it contracted every few seconds. Then, unwillingly, she gently expelled her twelve-week-old foetus. Silent tears streamed down her face as the foetal sac plopped into the bowl of water below her.

Fred returned later that day apologetic about his behaviour from the night before, assuring her it would never happen again and repeatedly asking her if she was all right. Betty attempted to reassure him that she was, trying to remain positive and hoping that when the time came, Fred would cope with the news she needed to share with him. She had decided she would leave it a couple of days before she told him about losing their baby.

Alan

———◄○►———

A lan had grown up in the same street as Betty. He was the same age as Betty and had always had a soft spot for her. They had gone to the same school and he had followed her everywhere, attaching himself to her side each playtime and in the classroom. They had quickly become good friends.

Alan was a gentle, kind person who was always willing to help others. He was never demanding in any way, but he was painfully shy, especially in his teenage years, and most girls found him rather tiresome. Betty had always treated Alan differently. She was sympathetic to him, patient and understanding, which may have been why he became so infatuated with her.

In 1936, when his father had died suddenly, it had been Betty who had visited regularly, helping his mother with the household chores and cheering Alan up. She convinced Alan that he would do well in his life, encouraged him to follow his dream and persuaded him to fulfil his desire to become a scientist.

Alan had always been interested in chemistry, and often discussed this topic with Betty. Occasionally, she would be attentive to the information he had to share, especially when it was related to her work in the beauty industry. Often he would go out of his way to discover something new to tell her, just so he could have her full attention and spend time with her.

Alan enjoyed Betty's company immensely, and when both were in their early twenties, he finally plucked up enough courage to ask Betty out on a date. After that they often went to see films at the pictures, where Betty would allow Alan to hold her hand in the dark, but he was too shy to take this relationship any further and was content just to be with her.

Alan could remember taking Betty to see *The Lady Vanishes* in 1938, starring Margaret Lockwood. The evening had been wonderful, just the two of them, but this had been one of the last evenings they had spent together before everything had changed forever.

Betty had started spending more time with an older man named Fred. She let Alan down on a number of occasions, saying that she needed to spend time with her father's employee because he was suffering after the loss of his wife and child. At first Alan had admired Betty for her thoughtfulness and compassion, but soon it appeared to Alan that Betty was spending more time in this other man's company than she was in his.

Alan had arranged, in August 1938, to take Betty to see the American comedy *Bringing up Baby*. Betty had let him down at the very last minute, saying that she was going to meet Fred that night, and Alan had ended up taking Betty's sister Marie instead. Although he and Marie had enjoyed the evening, it was not Marie that Alan was interested in.

As time went on, Alan realised Betty was falling head over heels in love with Fred. He was unable to tell her how he felt about her because he could see she was happy with this other man and he didn't want to spoil that. It upset him greatly that her relationship with this other man appeared to make her much happier than when she was with him.

Betty had always shared personal issues with Alan, so it followed that he should be the first person she turned to when she had a problem. Betty told Alan how she and Fred wanted to marry but her parents were being difficult about the relationship. Her father wanted them to marry in church, but Fred didn't want to, and she didn't know what to do. Alan agreed to help and managed to convince Fred that he and Betty should marry in church, much to Betty's relief. Betty then suggested to Fred that Alan be his best man, explaining quietly to Alan that Fred had no one else who could to do this for him. Alan believed that everyone was happy with these arrangements and was pleased to go along with it.

He was willing to forgo his own happiness, as he could clearly see that Betty was content to be with Fred. On the day of her wedding, as Betty and her sister walked up the aisle together, Alan wished it were he she was marrying. He tried so hard to make Betty's day perfect for her, but every time he attempted to communicate with the groom, he was rejected, mocked or made to feel humiliated by Fred. It quickly became apparent to him that theirs was a friendship that would never blossom.

***

Alan did not see Betty for some time after she was married. War broke out and everything changed and many people lost touch with one another. Alan heard things through the grapevine and on one occasion bumped into Marie on the Underground and asked after Betty. Marie told him very little about her sister's life, but he sensed all was not as it should be. Then a week or two later, in the autumn of 1940, and quite by chance, he met Betty as she was walking home one lunchtime. He had been on his way to visit a colleague, which he quickly postponed.

Alan and Betty decided to enter a tea room whose windows had been boarded up after a recent explosion had caused them to shatter. They sipped tea together and enjoyed egg sandwiches. They talked all afternoon about nothing and everything, and up until then Alan hadn't realised just how much he had missed Betty. They were meant to be together. Why had he not seen this? Why could she not see it?

"It's my twenty-fifth birthday the month after next," Alan announced as they were gathering their coats and about to part company.

"Let's do something to celebrate," said Betty. "I'll have a think. In the meantime, why don't you call round to the house? You have my address now. When is your next day off?"

"Thursday fortnight."

"I'll make sure I'm at home then. Take care, Alan. I'll see you again in a couple of weeks." Betty gave him a peck on his cheek as she left.

True to his word, Alan called at Betty's house on Leigham Avenue in November. He knocked loudly and with confidence on her front door, excited to be seeing Betty again. The door opened ever so slowly and slightly. Betty's face appeared around the doorway, looking very serious.

"I'm very sorry, Alan. I can't let you in. You see, Fred has told me I'm not to see you any more."

Alan was shocked, but he should not have been surprised. "What do you mean? We're not doing any harm, are we?"

"He's told me in no uncertain terms, Alan. He's my husband. I must do as he asks."

Betty seemed petrified.

Alan was concerned. "Has he hurt you?"

"No, Alan. It's nothing like that. Fred can be a little difficult at times, that's all."

"So he hasn't hurt you?"

"Not at all. It's just easier to do as he asks. Now please go."

Alan could see that Betty was clearly becoming more distressed the longer he lingered on her doorstep. She kept looking beyond him, as if to check if anyone was watching them.

"So, you would like me to leave?" he asked, already knowing the answer.

"I'm sorry, Alan. I don't think we should see each other any more. I'm married now. It wouldn't be right. Please understand."

"If that's what you want?"

"Yes. I'm sorry, Alan."

Alan didn't want to leave Betty in this state, but agreed to do so because he was concerned for her. "Are you sure you're going to be all right?" he enquired before he turned and left.

"I'll be fine, thanks, Alan. I'm really sorry."

Alan felt that Fred's demands were unreasonable. He had only agreed to leave because he was concerned for his friend and wanted Betty to be happy. Now, he had no idea if he would ever see her again.

Alan had a miserable birthday, and Christmas was just as bad without the knowledge of how his friend was. Fortunately, he was able to throw himself into his work at the hospital during this time and spent many extra hours there, working long into the night; more than he would have done if there hadn't have been a war on.

***

Alan was used to travelling by bus to his place of work, which was in the chemistry block of St Bartholomew's Hospital. By now he was also used to having to dash to find shelter as the night-time bombs dropped. On more occasions than he cared to remember, he had been forced to spend the night in the Underground tunnels with many other innocent civilians caught up in the war. At the start of the war the government had locked these stations, but when the Germans had begun dropping bombs on London relentlessly for weeks on end, they had been opened up and used as shelters ever since.

Each day after work Alan walked from St Bartholomew's back to the bus stop, but on that Saturday, in January 1941, having worked late again, he headed to the Underground station at St Pauls and took the Central Line on an errand for his mother. He was drawing close to a result after a long and difficult investigation into a substance whose compounds had been complex and which had proved difficult to work with. He had been arriving home exhausted each day and had been promising his mother all week that he would collect the item she needed.

Due to the war, the Underground stations were usually crowded, and this evening was no exception. He travelled the two stops, got off, collected the item from a shop in Old Broad Street and headed back to the Underground at Liverpool Street. He was completely unaware that there had been a man following him since he'd left the hospital. Alan boarded the train along with a number of other passengers. The train was heading for Bank Station, so called because directly above it stood the Bank of England. On this very same evening, German bombers were heading straight for the bank, as this was their chosen target.

Alan was fortunate to find a seat in a carriage that wasn't very full. The man following him climbed into the same carriage, seating himself some distance away at the opposite end, so that Alan did not notice him. The train pulled out of Liverpool Street and headed the short distance to its next stop. The time was just before eight o'clock.

As the train slowed on its approach into Bank Station, the Germans struck above ground. Alan and his fellow passengers had no idea what was unfolding above them. The German bomb just missed its target and exploded outside the Bank of England, where the road collapsed. A huge crater appeared, with rubble disappearing into the subway and station below.

SARAH LYSAGHT

In the tunnel, Alan's train came to an abrupt halt. The lights in both stations and on the train went out. Bank Station's booking hall had received a direct hit. It had been full of people at the time. A muffled boom could be heard below ground, which was followed by a rush of air and a dust cloud that raced through the tunnels. The blast travelled down the escalator shafts, instantly killing everyone sheltering there, then it continued directly on to the two station platforms, causing devastation among the passengers.

Seconds passed then the emergency lights came on, but what illumination they gave was useless. The air was thick with dust and all that could be heard was the screaming and shouting of the injured and scared.

Alan did not make a sound. As passengers began to move inside other carriages, he and his fellow commuters did not. He was drifting in and out of consciousness. When his eyes finally opened, no one around him was moving. They all looked as though they are sleeping, but in that split second he could tell they were all dead. His eyes shut again.

At Liverpool Street Station a voice could be heard over the loudspeaker system asking for men to volunteer to walk through the tunnel in the direction of Bank Station, as an accident had occurred and their urgent assistance was required. Some time later the sound of voices could be heard travelling slowly along the dark tunnel towards Alan's train. Then flickers of torchlight in the distance could be spotted slowly approaching.

The next time Alan opened his eyes, they were quickly covered by a gloved hand. At first he assumed this was someone coming to his aid, but then he realised something was also now covering his mouth and nose. He couldn't breathe. Alan attempted to free himself. He struggled for a number of seconds, but he just didn't have the strength.

When Alan opened his eyes for the last time, the man quickly placed his gloved hand back over them, so that he could not be seen. Then he firmly held his scarf over Alan's mouth to prevent him from breathing. The man did not have to apply much pressure, for in a matter of seconds, after a brief struggle, Alan was dead.

The man had made a hasty decision and acted upon it when the opportunity had presented itself. Now he needed to get back to his seat and sit down as though nothing had happened before the rescue team, who were making their way along the tunnel to the train, arrived.

Once the main power to the rails had been disconnected, the volunteers could safely begin to walk the half mile through the dark tunnel down the line to the next station. They finally reached the back end of the train. These men entered the train, walking carefully through the carriages and checking each passenger for signs of life as they came upon them. Almost all were dead. As one volunteer entered the carriage in which Alan sat, one of the passenger's eyes opened. He was quickly dealt with and assisted off the train.

As these brave rescuers reached the front section of the train, they could see it had been lifted and thrown onto the platform. Complete devastation and confusion met their eyes. They had volunteered, but they had received no training for this type of event. However, they helped as best they could in an impossible situation.

By now medical people were gradually arriving on the scene. The volunteers helped to comfort the wounded, most of whom had been hit by falling debris. Others assisted stretcher-bearers with the more severely injured, getting them up to the surface and off to hospital. The main casualties were those who had been at the bottom of the escalator. A number had also died on the platform, and it was these two groups who had received the worst of the injuries. The few dead bodies which had been carried from the train showed no physical signs of damage and looked as though they had just quietly fallen asleep.

At first the estimated number of deaths had been around thirty-five. That soon rose to fifty-six. More bodies were discovered later, having been buried under debris. Forty people were taken to hospital and another sixty had been slightly injured. The final death toll came to 111, but it should have been 110. Alan should have survived.

When the man from the train was escorted to the street above, he turned to his rescuer, brushed himself down and explained, "I will be fine now. I can make it home from here. Thank you for all your help."

The man felt no remorse. If anything he felt relief. While he made his way across the city, returning safely to his home and wife, Alan's body was collected and brought to the surface along with ten others from the train. Alan was buried on 18 January, after a short service at his family's church. His mother saw to it that he received a fitting obituary in the local newspaper. She would never recover from the loss of her talented son.

Betty

When Fred read out loud from his newspaper, informing Betty of the death of her dear friend Alan, she'd burst into tears.

"Pull yourself together, Betty," Fred demanded unkindly. "I would never have read it to you if I'd known you were going to react in this way."

"I'm sorry, Fred. It's just such a shock. Poor Alan."

"A case of being in the wrong place at the wrong time, that's all. These things happen in wartime. It says here that they had estimated the number of deaths to have been around thirty-five to begin with but that had quickly risen to fifty-six, due to more bodies being discovered buried under debris—"

"Oh, Fred, stop it. I don't want to hear any more."

"The final death toll came to 111," he continued.

"He was such a lovely person. And had so much more to give. He was very clever, you know. It's such a terrible waste. I hate this war!"

"Pull yourself together. There's nothing you can do about it," Fred insisted.

"I must go and see his mother. She must be devastated."

"I'd rather you didn't go round there, Betty."

"Why not? It's not as though Alan will be there now, is it?" she shouted back at Fred.

He looked angrily at her. "I'd just rather you didn't open old wounds."

"I won't be opening anything. I'll be visiting a grieving mother who will be missing her beloved son. Wouldn't I do the same for you if it were your mother?"

Fred tutted loudly, threw down the newspaper and stormed out of the room. Betty was later shocked to discover that he had gone directly to the army headquarters in London and joined up. He had then returned home without her knowledge, packed a bag and left her a note. She was devastated when she realised what he had done.

Although Betty knew her husband was training somewhere in the country, he never informed her where and he only wrote one brief letter to her shortly after he had left. She lived one day at a time, never knowing if she would see him again.

Betty worried for her parents and sister during the relentless air raids upon London. After giving up her work, she spent more and more time at her family's home. Her parents would never let her walk home after dark in case there was an air raid. Instead, they would all huddle together inside the partially submerged bomb shelter her father had helped to install in the back garden. Most nights the church bells would ring out their warning of a raid, that was until the bells were needed for the war effort.

The German targets were supposed to have been the industrial works and places like the docks, but night after night Betty's family would emerge from their shelter to discover the next street had been hit, the local picture house flattened or a row of shops was now a pile of smouldering bricks.

Rationing was bad enough, as they struggled to get hold of enough butter, sugar and ham, but soon the government announced that they were to ration meat as well. The country was in a mess. Innocent people were being killed or severely maimed most nights. Fires were out of control across the city. Betty and her family felt as though they were living through a terrible, relentless nightmare.

Things became too much for Betty's parents. Her mother was a nervous wreck with the constant air raids and her father was trying to sell his business, as it had never been the same for him since Betty had left. Her parents made the decision to move away from London to the country, taking Betty's younger sister with them. Her father left the sale of his business in the capable hands of his solicitor and they temporarily moved into rooms on Buckthorne Road. Eventually, her father's business sold and Betty's family moved away to safety, with little intention of returning to London until after the war was over.

Betty suddenly found she was alone. She had been completely reliant upon Fred. He had always had the strongest influence over her. That was, until he had joined up. Did he really expect her to sit at home doing nothing, dodging the bombs and waiting for his return? It was he who had insisted she not find work but remain at home all day, where he said she would be safe. When she had showed an interest in joining the WVS (Women's Voluntary Service), Fred had convinced her otherwise, saying that there was no point if they were to try again for a child. She could recall having been surprised by this comment. She had never pressed him on this issue. With Fred having lost his first son under such harrowing circumstances, and when she'd miscarried their first child, Betty had decided she would let nature take its course. But once Fred had made up his mind about something, there was no stopping him.

***

When Fred returned home on leave during the summer of 1940, his appetite for sex was insatiable. At first Betty enjoyed her husband's compulsive attention. She missed her parents and sister terribly and had been lonely since Fred had joined the army. The consideration her husband now seemed to be giving her made up for all of that. He made her feel special again, taking her out and treating her. He was the perfect gentleman for a time, but sadly this behaviour did not last long.

Fred informed Betty that he had been posted into the Anti-Aircraft Division and was now located in Clapham; not far from their home. He was to be working one of the many searchlights which were dotted across London and used in the detection of enemy aircraft. The problem was that this meant Fred just wouldn't leave her alone. He turned up at all hours of the day and night wanting her to have sex with him, often remarking in his superficial way, "We need to do our bit for the country. I'm more than happy to supply England with a future. Aren't you?" He enjoyed turning it into a game.

When Fred wanted to experiment sexually, Betty didn't like it. It was clear he was after more excitement from their love-making than she was willing to give. Some of the things he wanted to do to her really troubled Betty, and she often refused him. On more than one occasion he forced himself upon her. Because she feared he might hurt her again, she consented most times without a struggle.

One day Fred requested they make love outside among the bushes and shrubs of a local park. Betty was having none of it, but he kept bringing up the subject for some weeks later and this really upset her. When he again mentioned this desire, and Betty again refused, he pushed her up against the bedroom door and put his hands around her throat. At the point when she thought she was about to pass out, he released his grip and forced her again to have sex with him. When she later plucked up the courage to confront him about his behaviour, he denied having done it at all.

It was soon after this event that Betty discovered she was pregnant again. She reluctantly shared news of her condition with Fred, and he replied flippantly, "At last! I wondered how long it was going to take you." Betty was quite taken aback by his comment, but Fred continued regardless. "Does that mean we'll get the milk for free now? That's something the government offer pregnant women, isn't it?"

Annoyed, but attempting to keep the moment cheerful, Betty replied, "Yes, and orange juice, cod liver oil and vitamin tablets." Fred made no further sexual demands upon Betty for a time.

Although the bombing around London had eased, the area remained a key target for the Germans and no one felt safe. Once again Betty wondered what on earth she was thinking, bringing a child into the world at such a terrible time. So many parents had sent their children away to live in safety with other families in the country, or even sent them abroad. How on earth was she to keep her baby safe?

Fred obviously had a plan in mind when he moved them into the same rooms her parents had rented in Buckthorne Road. Betty had realised he was trying to save them money, but hadn't realised to what lengths Fred was prepared to go to in order to do this. Their landlady, Dorothy, was pleasant enough. She and Fred appeared to get on very well. At times they were as thick as thieves, and Betty suspected she might be selling things on the black market. She just hoped Fred was not getting involved in anything illegal.

Betty knew Fred was despondent over the lack of action London had seen recently, realising that this was because he wanted to do his bit and feel valued. She hoped his boredom would not encourage him to get mixed up in whatever it was that Dorothy was up to.

When Fred joined the Indian Army the following year, completing his training in Aldershot, she was relieved to have him away from Dorothy and the house on Buckthorne Road. It wouldn't be long before Betty would be making plans of her own to leave the house.

Over the next few months, Betty became more and more concerned about her baby's imminent arrival. Her doctor advised that when her time came, she would need to have her baby in a hospital. He had discovered that Betty's heart was making an unusual sound and suggested he keep a close eye on her. There had been a recent trend towards hospital births, and her doctor and midwife had assured Betty that it would be far safer to have her baby at hospital, especially due to her complicated circumstances.

Betty had been devastated when Fred had joined the army. She had been shocked by his sudden decision and the way in which he had gone about it, but ever since she had discovered she was pregnant, she felt as though Fred had become even more detached from her. He obviously felt he needed to get away, and the war was able to give him that valid excuse when he joined the Indian Army. She worried about how she would cope when the baby arrived and hated to admit that perhaps it was for the best that Fred was not around.

Betty was accommodated at a maternity hospital in Woking to have her baby. The government requisitioned many nursing homes and large houses during the war, so that expectant mothers could be evacuated away from the cities to have their babies in safety and extra beds in the larger hospitals could be freed up for emergencies.

By then Fred had almost completed his army training and managed to get some leave to visit her and the baby for a couple of hours. However, she could tell he would much rather have been back at barracks. He paid little attention to his new daughter and fidgeted uncomfortably for most of his visit. When the bell was rung to signify the end of visiting, Fred couldn't get out of the ward fast enough.

Betty named her daughter Juliet. A week after her birth, she and the baby were allowed home. She hated being on her own at Buckthorne Road, even though Dorothy, her landlady, was very good to her. When Marie announced she was moving back to the area that summer, it made perfect sense that she should move in with Betty. The two women continuously fussed over Juliet, as any new mother and aunt would, but Dorothy started to interfere more than they both would have liked, and soon they were looking for somewhere else to live.

Fred had received an emergency commission into the Indian Army in May. Betty eventually received word from him in the August, informing her that after completing his officer cadet training, he had ascended to the rank of second lieutenant. He was obviously very proud of his achievement and would retain this rank until the end of the war. Betty knew very little else about what Fred got up to during the war. She barely had any other communication from him during this time; a handful of letters and one difficult visit home was all she got. If she ever enquired after his experiences, Fred always refused to discuss his role in the war.

During his only visit home, Fred turned up at the house on Buckthorne Road unannounced, only to discover someone else was living there and that Betty and Juliet had moved out. He was not pleased. Having little or no communication from her husband during this time, Betty had made the decision with her sister to rent rooms in a different house. She had left a forwarding address with Dorothy, their old landlady.

Fred turned up at her new home on Athlone Road, only to discover they had gone out with Juliet. The landlady there welcomed him in, explaining that she was an usherette and had to go to work but that he could wait in Betty's room for her if he wished. When Betty and Marie returned, they were both shocked to discover they had a visitor. Fred quickly became objectionable, sarcastic and critical of the way the sisters were living. This upset Betty. She didn't realise that this was because Fred could see they were coping perfectly all right without him.

As the conversation became more heated, Marie made the excuse that there was some washing up to be done in the kitchen and left them to it. Once Fred had Betty to himself, his behaviour changed again. He began to take an interest in Juliet, who was toddling around the room, clutching a soft toy. Then he complimented Betty on her looks, and Betty knew instantly where this was leading. His sudden charm was superficial and she predicted he was attempting to manipulate her into sleeping with him. Betty was not prepared to do this with her daughter in the same room, so Fred insisted she ask Marie to take the child into another part of the house for an hour. Fortunately, Fred's love-making did not last very long and afterwards he fell into a deep sleep.

"Are you all right?" asked Marie with concern when Betty knocked on her bedroom door later that evening.

"I'm fine. Honestly. He's too tired to cause any more trouble," smiled Betty. "Can Juliet stay with you tonight, just in case he wakes up?"

"Of course."

"I've brought her some things," Betty said, handing a pile of clothes to her sister.

"She's already fallen asleep on my bed. Do you want to come in?" Marie offered, beginning to open the door wider.

"No. I don't want to disturb her," she whispered. "I'll see you both in the morning." And with that, she leant forward and kissed her sister on the cheek. The following morning Fred left early, and Betty did not see him again until 1946.

***

During the war, Betty and her sister moved together into a slightly larger property in Athlone Road, near Brixton Park. With Juliet now aged three, they were glad of the extra space, and as it was positioned close to the park, it was ideal for trips out with Juliet. For one year everything was perfect. Both women joined the WVS and found part-time jobs. Betty was able to split the care of Juliet with her sister. She found temporary work as an air-raid warden, while Marie worked driving an ambulance. Both women were happy with this arrangement.

Betty had been made to feel obliged by Fred to inform the army of any change of address, she being his next of kin. He had insisted upon this after turning up the last time and discovering she had moved without informing him. When he eventually arrived home in June 1946, Fred had known where to find Betty and Juliet.

It appeared that Fred had been in no particular hurry to return home to Betty. He had visited his sister in Eastbourne first. She had recently remarried after the death of her first husband and was now living near the coast. Fred explained to Betty how he had enjoyed being beside the sea. He said long walks along that part of the British coastline had helped him to regain some strength and perspective after the war. It had crossed Betty's mind that Fred had been a POW, and this had been his reason for staying away so long, but she felt unable to ask him about this.

According to Fred, he had also chosen to visit his mother after the war, then helped her with a move to live with his sister in Eastbourne. He had then remained in Eastbourne in order to attend his sister's wedding in the April. Fred insisted that they had made him feel very welcome. He disclosed this information to Betty in a way which was clearly intent on hurting her feelings. She knew Fred was letting her know he had been in no hurry to return to her side. His words were designed to make Betty feel worthless and unimportant.

***

Fred had not been home long when it became obviously apparent that he was unhappy about leaving the army. "Released to unemployment, they call it," he kept telling Betty, often threatening to opt for a short service commission whenever he felt she was becoming difficult to handle.

Betty was sure that, as with many men after the war, Fred found it hard to make the transition back into civilian life and to find a permanent job. He was in and out of work almost on a weekly basis. He felt unappreciated and often took out his frustrations on Betty and Marie when he got home. He lost his temper on many occasions, ranting and raving for no particular reason. Four-year-old Juliet was quite disturbed by the aggressive stranger who had entered her world. She started to wet the bed and suffer with nightmares, and this upset Betty more than anything. When Fred put his fist through the living room door after he had lost yet another job opportunity, it was the final straw for their next-door neighbours. The couple made a complaint to Betty's landlord about the noise coming from their house, and to Betty's embarrassment, they were asked to vacate the property.

Marie felt she had no other option than to move back into rented accommodation on Buckthorne Road, and Fred moved Betty and Juliet into a rented house around the corner in Leander Road. Although this house was larger than their last, there were many more people living in it. Fred and Betty were given two of the second-floor rooms. Another room on this floor was rented out to a young woman called Isabella, who was a shorthand typist. A couple with two children were in the ground-floor rooms. There was one man in the attic room and another gentleman in the basement room. It was often a very noisy house. Betty found it difficult to get Juliet to settle at first, but Fred seemed to like it there, so things became a little easier.

Fred was finally able to find permanent employment in nearby Clapham. Isabella explained to Betty how she worked at The Cooperative, and the company was about to advertise for a clerk to work in the insurance department. Betty informed Fred, and after a brief interview he was taken on.

The year 1947 was a better one for the family. Fred appeared to be enjoying his work. He was putting in long hours, so was able to bring home enough money for the family to consider moving somewhere with a little more space. This was fortunate, for by the end of the year, Betty had discovered she was pregnant again.

The family moved into New Park Parade, a busy shopping street with an array of shops. The new flat was spacious, with three bedrooms, and situated above a grocer's shop. It was only a mile away from her sister, so Betty was still able to see Marie on a regular basis. This would prove critical, as a few months later, Fred had begun to behave oddly again.

Betty chose not to share her pregnancy with Fred at this time, mostly because of his strange behaviour but also because she needed time to adjust to the idea herself first. She chose to confide in her sister. Betty was worried. The last time she had been pregnant, the doctors had discovered she had an unusual heartbeat. This time, as soon as her condition was confirmed, they started talking about all manner of things that could go wrong.

One doctor advised her against having any more children because of the strain she would be putting on her heart. Another doctor was more sympathetic.

"You should try to avoid any unnecessary stress or emotional upset," he advised. "Any kind of stress or trauma could cause you serious problems." Betty must have suddenly looked deeply concerned, because the doctor added, "I'm not having you worry about all of this unnecessarily. This is what we shall do. I'm going to monitor your blood pressure and heart rhythm regularly, if for no other reason than to put your mind at ease," he reassured her. "Go and see my receptionist and she will book you an appointment each week for the foreseeable future or until we feel you no longer need it."

"Thank you, Doctor. I'm really grateful to you."

"Nonsense. I'm just doing my job. Now promise me you won't worry?"

"I'll do my best."

"Good girl. I'll see you next week."

***

Marie was a huge support for Betty at this time. She went along with her to most of her appointments, and on the days she couldn't, she went straight round to the flat afterwards to see what the doctor had said and to make sure her sister was all right. Betty didn't know what she would have done without Marie during this time. She was the only person Betty was able to confide in. Together they agreed not to mention anything to their parents, who at this time remained settled in the country. The last thing Betty needed was her mother fussing around her or getting upset about things.

One afternoon in late March, when Marie had been unable to attend a doctor's appointment with Betty, she raced round to the flat to see how her sister was doing. Once reassured everything was all right, the two of them sat down with a cup of tea while five-year-old Juliet played in the corner of the room with her dolls.

"I don't wish to cause you any distress, Betty, but you are going to have to tell Fred about the B-A-B-Y." She spelt out the word in a whisper, in case Juliet was listening. "If you don't, you run the risk of him working it out for himself."

"I know. You're right, Marie. I will soon. I promise."

"It's my birthday soon, Aunty Marie. I'm going to be five," piped up Juliet from the other side of the room.

"No, darling. You're going to be six," corrected Betty.

"Six I mean," continued Juliet.

"That's such a big girl. How did you get to be so big?" asked Marie.

"I don't know. I just grew."

Heading over to where Juliet was sitting, Marie asked, "Now what do big six-year-old girls like for their birthdays, I wonder?"

"I'd like a pram for my dolls," smiled Juliet.

That sounds like a very practical idea, doesn't it, Mummy," hinted Marie, looking back at Betty.

"It certainly does. We will have to pay a visit to the pram shop."

"Don't you mean the toy shop, Mummy?"

"Of course. Silly me." Marie and Betty both sniggered.

Marie remained at the flat until just before Fred was due to arrive home. She always tried to avoid him as much as possible. As she left, she reminded her sister, "Remember what you need to do."

"I'm not about to forget now, am I?"

"Good luck."

"Thanks."

"Goodbye, Juliet. Be good for Mummy now."

"I will."

When Betty told Fred about her pregnancy, she was surprised by his reaction. "That's wonderful news. Are you happy?" he asked.

"Of course."

"Come over here, Juliet, and sit on Daddy's lap. I've got something to tell you," said Fred.

"Have you got me some more sweets?" Juliet enquired. Betty noticed her daughter glance across at her and appear a little tense.

"Have you been buying her more sweets that I don't know about?" enquired Betty.

"Betty, don't fuss so." Fred dismissed his wife's concerns. He lifted Juliet up onto his lap and she wriggled to get comfortable. "Are you listening?" he asked his daughter in a quiet, almost whispering, voice.

"Yes," Juliet replied apprehensively.

"How would you like to have a new baby sister?"

Juliet looked stunned.

"Or a baby brother?" added her mother.

"Yes, or a brother?" Fred agreed.

"I'd like a brother best. Can I have a brother, please?" Juliet asked, looking towards her mother.

"I'll see what I can do," replied Betty. "I can't promise it will be a boy though."

"I don't want a sister," declared Juliet. "She'll want to play with my dolls, and I'll have to share them." Juliet wriggled down off her father's lap and the conversation came to an end.

It had surprised Betty that it had been her daughter who had reacted more negatively to her news, but she was relieved that Fred had seemed pleased at the prospect of another child.

Within the space of a fortnight, Fred's behaviour had changed again. Betty recognised this shift in her husband's mood. She had seen it before. He'd become very cold towards her and Juliet. He would arrive home late from work most evenings long after Juliet had gone to bed. At weekends he would often go for walks alone, returning as and when he felt like it or when the pub landlord had ushered him off his premises. On these occasions he would fall asleep in a chair; he said so as not to disturb Betty, although she often heard him come in.

One afternoon, Juliet asked her father if he would take her to the park and he refused, saying that he had to go out to meet someone.

"Who are you meeting, Fred?" asked Betty.

"Nobody you know. Just someone from work," had been his dismissive reply, and then he had left.

"Can you take me, Mummy?"

"I'm sorry, darling, I can't. Mummy wouldn't be able to lift you onto anything at the moment." Juliet looked dejected. "Aunty Marie should be calling round later. We could ask her," suggested Betty. Juliet nodded enthusiastically.

***

It appeared that Fred's behaviour changed whenever Betty became pregnant. She discussed this with her sister, and together they concluded that they should give Fred the space he obviously needed during this time in the hope he would revert to the more charming, caring Fred once the baby arrived.

When Betty's baby was born, it was a boy, much to the delight of her daughter. Betty and Fred named their son Rupert. He was born in August 1948, at a time when the Olympic Games were taking place in London. Late July and early August had been abnormally hot, so Betty was glad when there was a change in the weather a few days before Rupert had been born. Thankfully, her son's birth had been straightforward and no complications had arisen from her irregular heartbeat. A week later, she brought her baby home from the hospital, pleased that the huge crowds which had descended upon London for The Games had all dispersed after the closing ceremony the Saturday before.

Fred remained unpredictable in the weeks that followed his son's birth. Betty wasn't sure if she was coming or going. One day Fred appeared happy and enthusiastic with life, the next he seemed rather depressed and distant. It was difficult for Betty to remain positive about life under these circumstances, and after another discussion with Marie, they decided to confront Fred about this disruptive behaviour.

Marie insisted that she be there when her sister spoke to Fred. She did not want Betty getting unnecessarily upset, nor did she want Fred doing anything stupid. If it looked as though things between them were going well, then she would take the children out for a walk and leave them to it. What ensued resembled a disorganised bombardment on Fred, which he immediately took offence to.

"Will you talk to us, Fred? Help us to understand what's going on?" asked Betty.

"We just want to help, Fred," assured Marie, clutching at Juliet for comfort.

They were getting nowhere. Fred had completely shut down his thoughts and feelings.

"Think of the children, Fred. All this falling out and bad feeling must be having an effect on them. Can we please try to work it out for their sake?"

Mention of the children jolted Fred into reacting. "When I found out I'd be home early today, my first thought was of the children. I was going to take Juliet to the park and leave you with some time alone with Rupert, but you've kept me here listening to this rubbish."

Juliet jumped down from Marie's knee and ran over to her mother. "Please can I go to the park with Daddy? Please?" she begged her mother, tugging at her skirt.

Betty looked at her watch. "It's too late now, sweetheart. It's almost time for your supper and Rupert's milk."

Juliet looked so disappointed.

"Now who's upsetting the children?" Fred hurled back at Betty.

Betty and Marie stared at one another, neither of them knowing what to do or say next. Before they could think of anything, Fred stood up and grabbed his coat and hat from the arm of the chair, where he had placed it upon his arrival home.

"I'm going out for a walk," he announced.

"Please don't go, Fred." Betty knew he would most likely end up in a pub all night.

"Can I come for a walk, Daddy?"

Fred bent down and kissed his daughter's soft cheek. "Mummy won't let you, darling." And with that, he slammed the door to the flat behind him.

Marie managed to console her niece while Betty sorted them all out with something to eat. Marie stayed with her sister long after the children's bedtime, leaving only after Betty had insisted that she would be all right and wanted to go to bed herself.

Fred chose to sleep in the armchair that evening. The following morning he washed and changed his clothes before kissing his wife and two children and leaving for work.

Jean

———◄◦►———

Jean and Pamela had known each other for almost two years. The girls were exactly the same age and had just completed their second year at school together. They had become friends on their first day at school and were delighted to discover they lived just a few doors away, their houses almost backing onto one another in Ferndale.

During the summer of 1948, when school was closed, they'd promised each other they would spend as much of the holidays together as they were allowed. Because they were only young and had to do as their parents instructed them, they often found life restricting, but they were determined to enjoy their new-found freedom, playing out together near to their homes when permitted to do so.

Jean had lost count of how many times since school had finished that she'd asked her mother if she could go to the park. Her mother was always too busy to take her, and if it hadn't been for her friend Pamela, she didn't know what she would have done with herself.

Jean lived with her mum, Eileen. Her father had walked out on the family around the same time she had started at school. She couldn't remember him much. Her brother Brian, who was an eleven-year-old pain in the neck, was their mother's favourite. Then there was nine-year-old Virginia and two-year-old Davy.

Her mother had been forced to take in lodgers after her father had left, so now they also lived with a Mrs Wood and a Mrs Shaddick. Mrs Wood kept herself to herself, but Ethel Shaddick was very friendly and had insisted that the children all call her Aunty Ethel.

On this particular Thursday evening in August, the family were all at home in their compact terrace, eating supper together.

"Why are we 'avin' supper so early?" complained Virginia. "It's before six."

"'Cause Brian and I are gonna see a film at the cinema," Eileen replied.

"That's not fair. 'E always gets to go. I never get to see a film. You like 'im more than me," protested Virginia.

"What you gonna see?" asked Jean.

"What's it called, Bri?" asked Eileen.

"I told you, Mum. It's called *My Brother's Keeper*, and it stars Jack Warner and George Cole. I've been wanting to see it since it came out ten days ago."

"What's it about?" asked Virginia.

"Why? D'you wanna come too, Sis?"

"I might if you tell me what it's about."

"It's about two criminals who are being transported to prison, when they escape."

"Sounds pretty dull if you ask me."

"We didn't," replied Brian.

"I'll give it a miss then, if it's all the same to you."

"No skin off my nose," retaliated Brian.

"That's enough, you two. 'Elp me clear the table and wash up, Bri, or we'll be late."

"I suppose I 'ave to look after Davy again," moaned Virginia.

"No, I'm leaving Davy with Aunty Ethel."

"Can I go round to Susan's 'ouse then?"

"Yes, but make sure you're 'ome by eight-thirty"

When Jean could get a word in edgeways, she asked her mother, "Please can I call for Pamela?"

"Yes, but don't wander too far. Stay on the block."

"I will," shouted Jean as she disappeared through the front door.

"And be 'ome by eight," she heard her mother shout.

Jean skipped off down the street to call on her friend.

Pamela's house was around the next corner, and the front door to this property was on the side of the house. Jean climbed the two red, highly polished steps, reached up to the knocker and bashed it loudly. After a couple of seconds Pamela opened the door.

"Hello, Pamela. Can you come out to play?"

"I'm just helping me mum with the washing up."

"Who is it, Pammy?" shouted her father.

"It's Jean. She wants to know if I can go out."

There was a pause, followed by, "All right, off you go. I'll finish helping your mother."

"Thanks, Dad," Pamela shouted back.

The two girls skipped off together hand in hand, chatting as they left. Both were dressed in similar cotton frocks which their mothers had made for them. Pamela's was knee length and blue with short sleeves, a full skirt, lace trim and collar. Jean's dress held more features, as her mother was a more accomplished seamstress. It was pale yellow with a white collar, some detail down the front and a layered skirt. Both girls pranced along the street, almost as if they were modelling their summer dresses for an audience.

By the time they reached the turning into The Grove, they had slowed to a walk, giggling loudly at something funny Pamela had just said but still holding hands. They rounded the corner then stopped for a while, letting go of each other's hands. Leaning against a neighbour's garden wall, they continued to chatter, deep in conversation about school and their teachers, their other friends, the boys in their class and what the next school year might hold for them.

After a few minutes a woman from the house knocked loudly on the window at them.

"Get off my wall," she shouted at them through the window.

"Misery guts," replied Jean. Pamela giggled and they both continued on their way.

The girls knew they were always to remain close to their homes and not wander too far. But in their excitement at seeing each other and because they were so deeply locked in conversation, they soon found themselves nearing the end of the road. They were not allowed close to the main road, called Acre Lane, without their parents, and Pamela came to a sudden stop.

Jean continued walking on.

"I'm not allowed to go any further," Pamela shouted after her friend.

"Don't be silly," replied Jean.

"I'm not. My dad will kill me if he catches me."

Jean spun around. Walking backwards towards the end of the street, she shouted back to her friend, "Come on, just to the end and then we'll turn back. 'E won't catch us."

Jean spun back around then continued walking ahead, expecting her friend to join her. Pamela hesitated, and in doing so allowed the distance between them to increase even further.

Pamela decided she would rejoin her friend at the very moment Jean had reached the end of the road. She could only look on as a man approached Jean from the right. He spoke to her friend, who nodded at the man, and then he took Jean's hand and together they crossed over the top of the road and disappeared up Acre Lane. Jean had not even bothered to wave goodbye to her. She had just left with a stranger. Pamela knew something was wrong. She ran home as fast as her feet would carry her.

Pamela hammered on her front door as hard as she could. Her father opened the door for her. "Calm down," he said as Pamela rushed past him. "Where's the fire?"

It took him and Pamela's mother a few minutes to calm their child down and for her to make any kind of sense. Eventually, Pamela was able to explain. "Jean's gone off with a man. A stranger. I don't think she knows him. He just took her hand and they disappeared around the corner. Will she be all right?"

When it dawned on Pamela's parents what had happened, the police were called and a frantic search ensued. Pamela could only watch from the window. She had been told not to go outside. Her father went with the police to search for her friend. Pamela had never seen so many police down her street. She could hear the call of their whistles coming from all directions. Jean's mother was eventually contacted by the police at the cinema, and upon hearing of her daughter's disappearance, she collapsed. The next couple of hours were seemingly unbearable for her.

***

The man who had approached Jean had asked her if she would like to go for a walk with him. "We could go to the park and you could have a go on the swings," he promised.

Jean was not about to turn down the man's offer. She had been asking her mother to take her there for weeks, but she was always too busy. Together, the plausible-looking pair continued along Acre Lane, passing the shops then crossing over and turning right. At the end was Brixton Road, where the noisy trams ran past at speed. Jean became frightened when the man's grip tightened and she had to run across this road in front of an oncoming tram. She thought she was going to fall under the tram, but the man somehow managed to scoop her up and run with her. Once safely on the other side, he put her down and loosened his grip. She managed to wriggle her hand free. "Not far now," the man said reassuringly, reaching for Jean's hand once more.

Jean smiled up at the man. He seemed quite friendly. She knew her mum would be cross with her if she were to find out, but the attraction of the park swings was far greater, and she knew her mother would never be able to find the time to take her herself. She would be home again before her mother missed her.

They eventually left this main road, turning left then crossing another busy road where more trams regularly passed. Here, The Brockwell Pub loomed large on the corner. Jean briefly wondered if this was where her father used to drink and then wondered if this man drank in here too. She couldn't remember what her father looked like now, and in her young head, she began to pretend she was walking to the park with her father.

As they continued, the man spoke to Jean again. "What's your name?"

"Jean," she answered.

"That's a nice name. We're almost there, Jean."

"Can I go on the swings?" Jean asked nervously.

"Of course. That's why we've come, isn't it?"

It had taken them more than half an hour to get to Brixton Park, and they had walked for more than a mile. Jean felt tired but also excited as they entered the park through iron gates flanked by large, white painted houses on both sides. Upon passing through the gates, the man released Jean's hand. She started to run along the path in front of him, the man following quickly behind her.

The narrow pathway soon opened out into the park, splitting in two directions. As Jean reached this point, she turned and asked the man which way she should go to the swings. She had only been to the park once before, and it had been so long ago, she had quite forgotten. He pointed her in the correct direction, and soon the swings were in sight. In no time at all she had scrambled up into a swing and the man began to push her higher and higher. She felt elated as the breeze blew wildly through her hair. The skirt of her dress lifted at the front as the swing flew forward, and she experienced a cool breeze rush up her dress and tickle her stomach. A feeling of exhilaration took over her whole body. She loved the swings. She squealed with delight each time the man pushed her. Higher and higher she went. He smiled whenever she squealed and appeared to be getting as much pleasure from the experience as she was.

The park was quiet, but not empty. Most people were at home having their supper at this time, but there was the odd dog-walker or person crossing the park on their way home from work. Jean was still enjoying her ride on the swing some minutes later when the man suggested they walk over to look at the ponds and the lake.

"I don't want to. I want to stay on the swings," she shouted back from up high.

"No," the man replied firmly. Grabbing Jean's swing, he brought it to an abrupt halt. Looking directly into her eyes, he spoke quietly, yet forcefully, "I want to go over by the water. I've pushed you on the swings long enough. Now you have to do something I want to do. That's fair, isn't it?"

Jean nodded, and the man lifted her off the swing, brushing down the back of her dress for her as he did so.

The man took a firm hold of her hand again, and they walked away from the swings, towards the water. They made their way over to the larger lake first, following its path all the way around its edge. A number of ducks splashed into the water as they passed, and Jean smiled at their antics.

Suddenly, the man pulled Jean off into the direction of the smaller ponds. He said very little to her at this point, but she was conscious of him glancing down at her regularly. As they arrived at the point between the two smaller ponds, the man stopped. He turned around and, holding tight onto Jean's hand, turned to retrace his steps back to a point where the path had forked. He chose the path along which they had not yet walked, checking behind him and looking around him, as if searching for someone or something.

Jean began to feel uneasy. Her mother might be wondering where she was. She had no idea what the time was and didn't know how long she had been gone.

"Can we go 'ome now?" Jean asked nervously.

The man looked at her, his eyes dark and menacing, piercing her very soul. "You have to do something for me first," he grinned.

The man led Jean away from the path and into the dense bushes among the trees, where no one would spot them. He made Jean kneel down, and he kneeled in front of her. Then he made her do something to him she didn't like. All the while he was forcing her to do this terrible thing, he had one hand up her skirt and inside her knickers. Sometimes what he did hurt her.

He had a firm hold of her head with his other hand, pressing it down, his fingers tightly clutching at her hair. She couldn't get away. She could hardly breathe. She had to try and breathe through her nose because it was impossible to do so through her mouth. She thought she was going to be sick. She gagged many times.

When her ordeal was finally over, the man told Jean firmly that if she ever told anyone about what they had done today, she would get herself into the most terrible trouble and he would come back to where she lived and hurt both her and her mother. The child was terrified. Her blue eyes began to fill with tears. The man then told her that if she didn't cry, he would walk her safely back to her home.

"Do you understand, Jean?"

Jean nodded.

The man grabbed her hand and began to lead her away from the park. The solitary man they passed walking his dog never realised the distress Jean was experiencing. She was doing her best not to give anything away, to ensure she was returned to her home safely.

The man held tightly onto Jean's hand as they turned right sharply, then she suddenly felt unwell. There was a nasty taste in her mouth and she was tired. Every part of her body ached and she felt bruised and sore inside. All she wanted to do was to have a drink of water and go to bed.

After waiting for a tram to pass, the man crossed them safely to the other side of the road. Jean recognised this road. They were near to the prison. She had passed it many times before on a tram with her mother. The man crossed them over this road before turning left and walking past the post sorting office. Then they joined a long, straight road which seemed to go on forever, and Jean thought she would never get home. It was at this point she felt she could go no further and kept tripping over her own feet.

"What the hell is the matter with you? Pick your feet up, girl," the man demanded. He became cross with her for being so slow and he kept tugging at her arm to make her keep up with him.

Jean was unsure as to where she was half the time, as most of the roads they had walked along she had never been down before. Finally, she recognised Acre Lane. The man crossed her over this busy thoroughfare and then just left her standing there alone. He turned without saying anything and walked away in the opposite direction. Jean realised she was finally free of this man and continued on by herself as quickly as she could in the direction she believed her home to be.

Three hours after she had disappeared, Jean was spotted by a neighbour, Marjorie Parker. The woman had a reputation for being nosey and had been given the nickname locally of 'Nosey Parker'. She had heard the child had gone missing, and it was around nine o'clock when she noticed her wandering along the road and looking upset. When the woman spoke to her, Jean burst into tears. Mrs Parker returned the child immediately to her mother, who also broke down. The relief of seeing her daughter home safely proved too much to bear for Eileen.

A policewoman was at her home, and Jean was asked to give details of the man who had abducted her. She reluctantly told the policewoman that the man had taken her to Brixton Park for rides on the swings. He had brought her back to Acre Lane and left her there to find her own way home. She revealed nothing about what the man had done to her in the bushes.

It was later reported in a local newspaper that Jean was unable to give any more details to the CID officer and uniformed policewoman, but according to her friend Pamela, the man who had taken her friend away wore a dark suit and had a big nose. Jean never disclosed to anyone what really happened that day in the park and the terrible thing the man had made her do.

Betty

When Betty's husband had left the army, he had struggled to find regular employment. During this time, their relationship had been strained. Fred eventually found a job in insurance and they moved to New Park Parade in Brixton, but Betty observed her husband's demeanour change as his attitude and actions rapidly became more challenging.

After their son had been born, things appeared to improve and they had seemed happy for a time. Rupert had been born in August 1948, but before their son had reached his first birthday, Fred had become restless and unfulfilled and decided to return to the army.

"The army have given me a short service commission. We're moving again," Fred announced one evening, completely out of the blue.

"What are you talking about?" Betty asked nervously.

"I've been thinking about it for some time now. You must have realised I was fed up with the insurance work."

"How could I? You never speak to me about your work."

"What am I doing right now then?" Fred was becoming annoyed. "Do you want to know or are you going to continue to interrupt me?"

"Sorry, Fred."

"I've joined the Pay Corps and have to complete some short but intensive training first, in Devizes, and then if all goes well, I've been promised a job as paymaster at the Kingston Pay Office."

"Where is Devizes?" Betty enquired tentatively.

"Wiltshire."

"But that's miles away. It will be a terrible upheaval for the children, Fred. What about Juliet's schooling?"

"The army will sort out all that, but you and the children can stay here until I move to Kingston, then you can join me."

Plenty of uncertainty followed Fred's decision, and Betty often found herself feeling downhearted. Her sister Marie once again came to her rescue, reassuring her and enabling her to stay positive. "Kingston's not too far from here. I can catch a train or bus to see you. I don't intend to abandon you, Betty," reassured Marie.

"I know. I'm just being silly. Just ignore me."

"I could never do that," smiled Marie.

"Marie, what would I do without you?" Betty gave her sister a squeeze.

By the October, Fred had moved his family to Kingston. Betty and the children now lived at the barracks in married quarters with Fred. The barracks were off Kings Road, where an arched gatehouse, known locally as 'The Keep', showed off the barracks' grandeur and status in the town.

The army had indeed kept its promise and looked after Juliet's education, but Betty really disliked this way of life, for herself and her children. Fred spent all day in the pay office and most nights in the bar, leaving her and the children feeling rather isolated.

Fred had made an effort at first and tried hard to make everyone happy. He would on occasion come home with flowers for Betty and sweets for Juliet. However, whenever Marie paid them a visit, he would always revert back to his objectionable self. This made it difficult for Betty to look forward to her sister's visits, and she felt guilty about feeling that way. Her father had visited once, but Fred had not been happy to see him either, so Vincent hadn't stayed long.

The family had not been at the barracks long when Betty discovered she was pregnant. All the concerns about her health came flooding back, and once more she found that she could only disclose her fears to her sister.

Fred arrived home one evening carrying a number of army briefing booklets in his hand, entitled *Guide for Families Proceeding to the BAOR* (British Army of the Rhine). He casually stated to Betty that as soon as the army could organise their travel, they would all be leaving for Germany. "It's an accompanied posting to Germany. That means you and the children can join me," proclaimed Fred excitedly. Her husband's announcement sent Betty into a blind panic.

"We can't, Fred. I'm going to have another baby," she blurted out.

"And how long have you known about this?" he demanded.

"I've just found out," she lied.

"Well, it's not going to happen overnight. It will take some time for the army to organise this trip. But I reckon we should be there for Christmas. That should give you plenty of time to sort everything out."

Betty was beside herself with worry. She really did not want to move to Germany. It was bad enough being ten miles away from her sister, never mind in another country. The thought of not knowing when she might see Marie again, or indeed if she ever would, distressed Betty greatly. Marie also worried for her sister during this time, and together they managed to convince Fred to go to Germany ahead of Betty, promising that she and the children would follow him in the new year, once Betty's pregnancy was further established.

Betty was reluctant to have her baby in Germany because of the possible complications with her heart. The doctors in England knew her situation, and she felt comfortable that they could care for her appropriately. She had no idea if the army doctors in Germany had even heard of her condition, never mind know how to deal with it.

The new year came and went, and Betty managed to keep putting off her departure for Germany. Both the army and Fred had become a little irritated with her changing her mind all the time. By March Betty could sense her husband's anger growing with every letter he wrote and the strained telephone calls he made to her. There was nothing for it. She would have to inform her husband of her heart condition and hope he understood.

At first Fred had been angry that she had never disclosed her problem to him before now. He slammed the phone down on her. During subsequent conversations, he insisted she join him immediately in Germany, reassuring her that the army doctors were all well equipped for her type of problem and that the hospital staff in Germany were excellent.

"I want you here so I can look after you properly," he said. She believed he was sincere.

Betty felt she had little choice and left England to join her husband. She and the children arrived in Rinteln, Germany, tired and hungry, in the spring of 1950. The journey had been long, with both children irritable during most of it. Juliet had asked her mother on more than one occasion why they had to go there, and Betty found herself struggling to explain a good enough reason for their upheaval.

The married quarters were basic but comfortable, and arrangements had been made for Juliet to start at the garrison children's school the following week. Fred was there to meet them and was allowed to show Betty where he worked, which was referred to as 'the cash office' and situated in a small building with the number 112 above the door.

It was clear to Betty that her husband had settled quickly into this new role and at last had found a job he enjoyed. Working for the RAPC (Royal Army Pay Corps) and running the cash office, it was up to Fred to pay the soldiers' wages during pay parades, issue cash to authorised officers and convert all currency into German marks. The cash office would also receive money from the Army Post Office and the NAAFI (Navy, Army and Air Force Institutes) canteen and officers' shop.

It appeared that Fred took his job extremely seriously, as with it came great responsibility and trust. He told Betty how at last he felt important enough that people were taking notice of him. He said everyone in his division wanted to be his friend, as it was he who dished out their wages. Fred relished this new-found popularity.

Having Betty and the children arrive gave Fred the opportunity to show off to his fellow comrades. He wasted no time in introducing her to as many of his pals as he could, and the following week he organised for her to visit a specialist army doctor based at the military hospital.

In July 1950 Betty's third child was born. She named this daughter Anne. The birth had gone smoothly, and afterwards Betty had wondered why she had worried so much. It had been the easiest of all of her children's births so far, and Fred had been waiting outside the room, rushing in when he had been given the nod by the staff nurse on duty. Later that afternoon he had brought Juliet and Rupert to meet the latest addition to their family and sneaked both excited children onto the ward. As the pair bickered with one another and Rupert attempted to climb onto the hospital bed to hold his tiny new sister, a nurse entering the ward put a stop to their disruptive behaviour. She fetched

Juliet and Rupert a chair, insisting that they sit quietly or leave the ward. Betty wrote to her sister with news of Anne's birth, clearly relieved that everything had gone so well. Her sister's prompt reply mirrored Betty's feelings.

In October Betty wrote to her sister after discovering she was pregnant again. She was beside herself with worry. She was convinced she must have conceived the night Fred had insisted she join him on a night out with other army officers and their wives. The evening had been enjoyable until Fred had become aggressive towards another officer when he thought the man was giving Betty too much attention. He had completely misread the situation, as Betty had also been talking to the man's wife, who it turned out, could recall her family's salon in London.

When Betty had finally managed to get her husband home, Fred had insisted they made love, even though Betty hadn't wanted to. He had been rough and inconsiderate, all the while accusing her of flirting with his pals. If she tried to deny it, he became loud and aggressive. Not wishing to wake the children, she kept quiet and went along with it until her ordeal was over. Now that Betty found herself pregnant again, she would have to endure another nine months of worry about her health and about how to manage Fred's difficult character.

Betty knew she gave her husband too many excuses for his disgraceful behaviour and his treatment of her, but what could she do? She refused to see that her need to remain with him was a weakness. She thought it had more to do with protecting her children, and so she chose to forgive him each time he behaved badly towards her. She believed her children needed their father, and for all his faults, they loved him very much. She did too.

Betty would continue to make excuses for Fred. She reasoned that his drinking, although a problem, was only to be expected from a man who had seen and experienced so much sadness in his life. She believed he had never accepted the loss of his first son and wife, or the baby Betty had lost. She accepted it when he refused to discuss what he had experienced during the war. Betty firmly believed that deep down her husband was a decent man who simply struggled to come to terms with his feelings. She knew that each of her pregnancies brought all of

Fred's raw emotions to the surface again. She truly believed that once they had finished having children, Fred would become more relaxed in his role of husband and father and that together they would grow old, content in each other's company. How could she have been so wrong?

***

Betty was about seven months pregnant when Fred decided he'd had enough in Germany and requested a posting back to England. He gave no consideration to Betty's condition and expected her to follow him wherever he went. Betty had reached the end of her tether. She had no intention of going anywhere at that time; not until after the birth of her fourth baby. She let the army know this in no uncertain terms, and her doctor agreed this was for the best. Fred's transfer was put on hold until after the birth of his child.

It angered Fred that Betty was now the one in control. Instead of him being supportive, he was never around to help with the children. He was usually out drinking until late, and when he was at home, all he seemed to do was upset everyone. Betty and the children suffered a roller-coaster of emotions during this time, never knowing what mood Fred would be in when he did eventually come home and constantly living in a nervous state of anticipation that he might.

By the time her baby was due to be born, Betty felt completely exhausted with the situation at home and had no idea how she had managed to maintain her composure for so long. Telling herself that they were all soon to return to England, and knowing she would see her family again, was the only thing which kept her spirits up.

Betty gave birth to a son in June 1951. Fred insisted his son be named after him and it was on the tip of Betty's tongue to ask why this was so important, especially as he would not allow her to have their children baptised. She knew he wasn't a religious man—he had made that quite clear right from the start—but she and her family were religious, and it had always felt terribly wrong to Betty not to have her children baptised. However, Fred was having none of it and she no longer had the strength to argue with him. She would need the last of her strength for the return journey to England in two months' time.

The family arrived back in England during the autumn of 1951. They moved into a shared property named White Gates—on account of its white, gated entrance—situated in a small village called Brambleton, some thirty miles from the Aldershot barracks where Fred was now stationed. The family shared their home with an army accountant, his wife Peggy and their two children and his sister-in-law Barbara and her two children. It was a busy household and thankfully a large property.

Betty made friends quickly in the village, becoming close to a couple called Richard and Molly, who had two delightful children. For the first time in a very long time, Betty found herself more able to relax and enjoy her life. The children were certainly more settled, especially with having other children of similar ages for company in such close proximity. Betty wrote to her sister, informing her of where she was now living. Marie promptly replied with some alarming news.

According to her sister, their parents had decided they no longer wanted to live together. Marie assured Betty that their parents were not getting a divorce, informing her that their mother now lived with her in rented rooms on Buckthorne Road. Their father was living in rented rooms one and a half miles away, on Norfolk House Road. Marie wrote:

It has been an amicable decision, agreed by them both, and there appears to be no animosity between them. I have no indication as to what has triggered their decision and do not feel brave enough to ask. All I will say to you though, dear sister, is that I have not seen either of them as happy in a very long time as they are now. Who knows? Perhaps they will come back together at some later stage and we will wonder what this has all been about. I will keep you well informed of any future developments. Much love to you and the children. Mother and I hope to visit soon.

***

A couple of months later Fred was sent temporarily to the Command Pay Office in York. It seemed to Betty that the whole house appeared to breathe a sigh of relief after his departure. She could tell that her fellow housemates struggled to take to Fred and his opinionated ways. Betty had been made to feel instantly welcome by Peggy and Barbara, and she quickly discovered she had two new companions and supporters. Fred, on the other hand, had taken an instant dislike to these two women and their strong views. His behaviour at times towards them had been rude and unnecessary, which Betty found embarrassing.

Unfortunately, the position offered to Fred in York was only for the short term, and he quickly returned to the army base at Aldershot, re-establishing himself at their new home in White Gates. He quickly became objectionable again towards his fellow housemates, and tensions began to rise. When Barbara remembered that she recognised Fred from when she had lived in Crestwell, it seemed to put him back in his place for a while. He proceeded to avoid any further intimate situations where he might be called upon to explain himself and spent more and more time down at the village pub.

However, it appeared that this incident had set Fred off on a new path of destruction, and he began to drink more heavily than ever before. Just as Betty thought she and her children may have found somewhere they could be happy, Fred wreaked devastation upon his family like never before. The humiliation, shame, pain and suffering he brought to them all, her wider family and their friends was just too much for Betty to withstand.

If it had not been for her friends and her family, she knew she would never have got through it. They all kept her sane, while her children gave her the strength she needed to continue with her life. Surely, under these current circumstances, her life could only get better?

Juliet

———◇———

Juliet couldn't remember that as a young child she and her mother had moved house many times. As she grew older, she had a sense she did not belong anywhere in particular. When she was young, it was quite normal for Juliet to sleep wrapped in a blanket, huddled between her mother and aunt for warmth, inside a dark, damp air-raid shelter. She usually slept through an entire bombing raid without a care. Some nights she spent in the cellar of a neighbour's house or an Anderson shelter in her neighbour's back garden. Other nights she could be sheltering in one of the many tunnels of the London Underground or a purpose-built street shelter made with a concrete roof. But no matter where she was, she always felt safe, as long as she was with her mother and aunt.

Juliet had experienced some very happy times during the war. Through her naïve and innocent eyes, Juliet's few memories of this time were happy, filled with laughter and song. Then, unexpectedly, everything had changed. The war ended and everyone was suddenly celebrating, and she hadn't realised they had all been pretending to be happy. She didn't understand what had changed, as she didn't understand about the war. Both her mother and aunt had tried to explain to her how the German soldiers wanted to hurt the English soldiers, so they could capture Britain, keep it for themselves and make slaves of the people. But a three-year-old child can have little insight into this sort of situation, and Juliet thought it was a silly story which her mother and aunt had made up.

Juliet's world was turned upside down the day her father returned home from the war. She had been just four at the time, and suddenly there was a stranger in her home who her mother said she was to call 'Daddy'. He appeared to be making all the decisions that her mother and aunt had previously made together. All of a sudden she was no longer her mother's main priority.

Juliet could remember feeling frightened at first by the strange man who had entered her life and the assertive influence and power he had over her mother. Her mother would remind Juliet constantly, "We need to ask Daddy first." Her mother always needed to check to see if it was all right with her daddy before they could go anywhere or do anything.

This man, a complete stranger, now lived at her house, and both he and her mother had instantly expected her to accept this change. She couldn't. She didn't know this man. She didn't like him. He could be loud and bossy. He frightened her and he smelt funny. His eyes burnt right through her if she didn't do as he asked, and her mother was like putty in his hands. He could often be aggressive towards her mother, and this soon resulted in Juliet suffering with nightmares and wetting the bed. This, in turn, made life more difficult for her mother, and it seemed to Juliet that no one was enjoying having this man around.

One of her earliest memories of her father was of him lying in her mother's bed, a thing she was no longer allowed to do, even though she had done it regularly during the war. When they had not been forced to spend the night in a shelter or in the Underground, Juliet would usually fall asleep in her mother's arms, in her mother's bed, listening to bombs dropping in the distance. It had been the one place where they had both felt completely safe from everything. Both of their lives had changed dramatically the day her father had returned.

Juliet and her mother were soon forced to move into another property with this loud, scary man. Juliet wasn't sure why, but she thought it had something to do with her father making a lot of noise and the neighbours complaining about it. When Juliet's aunt had announced she would not be moving with them, Juliet had wanted to go with her instead. She was too young to recognise or express these feelings, and obviously this did not happen. From then on, Juliet felt isolated and lonely. She no longer had the same regular contact with the aunt she adored, nor the same relationship with her mother. It appeared to Juliet that her mother had chosen her father over her for companionship and he had driven away her aunt.

Juliet hated the new house. There were too many people living in it. There was never any peace. Another family with children lived on the ground floor, and they were always shouting and making a racket. Juliet found it difficult to sleep at night and continued to wet the bed. Her mother often seemed very distant towards her, and Juliet remained hesitant around her father, as she could never tell from one day to the next what sort of mood he would be in.

Things slowly started to improve for Juliet. Life at home became more relaxed. It seemed her father's mood had changed when he found a new job, which also meant the family had less money worries. Her mother and father both seemed happier for most of the time. When Juliet's father was not at work, he started to pay her more attention, and on occasion would even take her out for walks. Sometimes her mother would join them and other times she would stay at home and get a meal ready for when they returned. Juliet began to enjoy the new attention she received from her father. She enjoyed their walks and visits to the local park, where her father pushed her on the swings for ages and they fed the ducks.

Juliet was almost six years old when her father decided they were to move again. This time it was into a flat above a row of shops. Juliet preferred it here. Although they were above a row of busy shops, it was much quieter within the flat. From the window, she liked to watch the tiny people down below in the street, bobbing in and out of the shops, pausing to chat to one another. Inside the flat she enjoyed playing picnics with her dolls and having a bedroom to herself. She loved her new school, where she made lots of friends. But most of all, she looked forward to visits from her aunt. As her father worked long days, he was usually out when her aunt called round, but that didn't matter to Juliet. She realised it suited everyone that way.

One afternoon her aunt called into the flat to visit her and her mother. Her aunt and mother were chatting over a cup of tea as Juliet played with her dolls. They started talking in whispers, and Juliet could tell they were keeping something from her. Her birthday was coming up and she suspected they might be talking about that, so in a loud voice, to interrupt their conversation, she informed her aunt that it was soon going to be her birthday. Juliet's exclamation had the desired effect, and her aunt came over to sit with her. They talked for some time about her dolls and what she would like for her birthday.

The birthday present she received jointly that year from her parents and aunt was a brand-new pram for her dolls. She loved it, wheeling it around with her everywhere she went. She would have taken it to school if she had been allowed. It was the best present ever.

No sooner had her life improved, then everything changed again. Her father called Juliet to come and sit on his knee, as he had something he wanted to tell her. She often sat on her father's knee. These times usually happened when her mother had to pop out to the shop or go on an errand. Sometimes he would read her a book while her mother was gone and sometimes they would just talk about school, but always he would tell her to make herself comfortable, sliding his hand beneath her bottom as she did so. His hand would constantly fidget underneath her, his fingers moving slowly, gradually working their way inside her knickers. Afterwards he would reward her with sweets, for sitting so still on his lap, and tell her he loved her very much. She was his special girl and he insisted this was their secret. She mustn't tell anyone because no one would understand the way they felt about each other and she might be taken away from Mummy and Daddy if anyone ever found out.

That day was unusual though. When her father had asked her to sit on his lap this time, her mother had also been in the room. As Juliet climbed up onto her father's lap, she enquired as to whether he had more sweets for her, to which her mother reacted crossly towards her father. Instead of telling her to make herself comfortable, her father quietly asked her if she would like a new baby brother or sister. Juliet thought about her answer. She much preferred the idea of a brother, knowing she wouldn't have to share her dolls with a boy. Juliet was adamant about that, and when she got down from her father's lap, she was a little surprised she received no sweets.

Although her mother and father had seemed happy on the day they had announced to Juliet that she was to have a new baby brother or sister, this happiness did not last long. Soon her father became rather distant towards Juliet and her mother. He seemed to be working all the time, coming home late and never wanting to take her out anywhere.

Juliet thought she must have done something very wrong for her father to be treating her like this. Even his visits to her bedroom in the middle of the night had lessened recently.

Juliet never knew when her father would pay her one of his visits. She would wake in the middle of the night to find him lying on the bed next to her. Sometimes he would just fall asleep beside her and be gone by the morning. Other times he would wriggle about, making strange animal-like grunting noises which she had grown used to. On most occasions his hands would be rooting under the blankets, his face close to hers. His breath usually smelt funny, and the smell made her feel sick. He had never hurt her during these times. He was gentle and clearly found being with Juliet comforting.

Juliet only wanted to please her father. She had learnt that it was better to lie still and just let her father do the things he liked to do with her. Sporadically, he might whisper things to her and kiss her on her cheek, telling her she was his best girl. But she was very aware that this was their secret and that she must never tell anyone because other people wouldn't understand the love the two of them felt for each other.

Her father's mood swings confused Juliet. When her mother came home from hospital with her baby brother, Juliet was instantly besotted with him. So was her aunt. But her father remained very quiet and subdued for most of the time he was in the house. Then for no apparent reason he would raise his voice at her mother and storm out of the house, slamming the door, and not return until long after Juliet had gone to bed. If he had not visited her in her room that night, the following morning she was unable to determine his temperament, so she started to avoid him whenever these situations occurred.

One morning, before he left for work and while Juliet's mother was busy in the kitchen, her father went up to her and bent down, laying his hands lightly upon her shoulders.

"I'll take you to the park later if you like," he whispered. "I'll be home early today."

Juliet nodded enthusiastically and her father then left for work. It was the school holidays and no one had taken her to the park recently, not since before her brother had been born, so Juliet was very excited about her father's promise.

Juliet's aunt called round that afternoon and they all enjoyed fussing over her little brother. That was, until her father arrived home early as he'd promised. Instantly, Juliet could sense an atmosphere within the flat. She knew her father and her aunt didn't get along too well. When her mother and aunt both started firing questions at her father, he quickly became overwhelmed and angry. Juliet thought how sad he looked. She didn't understand why her mother and aunt were being so cruel to her father.

Her aunt reached out for Juliet and pulled her onto her knee, as if to protect her from the raised voices, as she and Juliet's mother continued to question Juliet's father. When her father mentioned that he had promised to take Juliet to the park that afternoon, her mother announced that it was too late. Juliet was furious with her mother. Getting down from her aunt's knee, she pleaded with her mother, but it was no use. Her father stood up and proclaimed he was leaving. As he grabbed his coat and hat. Juliet asked him if she could go with him. He bent down, kissed her cheek and said, "Mummy won't let you, darling." And with that, he left.

Juliet was furious with both her mother and her aunt and went and hid in her bedroom until her aunt managed to coax her out for her tea. She cried herself to sleep that night, not really understanding the different emotions she felt inside. Juliet began to dislike her mother more and more after this. She also found her aunt's visits less enjoyable from then on. The only person with whom she had complete trust in now was her father. Things had changed greatly from the time of her first contact with him.

***

Over the coming years, Juliet's father would force his family to move house five times before Juliet reached her tenth birthday. This would include a move abroad, which she had disliked the most. Juliet thought her new school in Germany was horrible. The other children were all right but the teachers were very strict, and the children were made to learn the German language, which Juliet found extremely difficult to understand.

She detested the fact that there were soldiers everywhere. They frightened her. And she hated it when her father brought any of them to the house. One of the men had sat her on his knee and her father hadn't liked it and become very angry with Juliet, but she hadn't understood why.

Juliet could tell her mother disliked living in Germany. She wasn't sure whether it was because she didn't have any friends there, because she was always pregnant, or because her mother was unable to see Juliet's aunt. Juliet could remember her mother frequently writing to her aunt while they were abroad. Often she would get Juliet to draw her aunt a picture and they would include it inside the envelope. She could tell her mother missed her aunt terribly, as she would always be looking out for one of her aunt's return letters, but none ever seemed to arrive.

Her father's moods while in Germany were very up and down. He had become a little distant towards Juliet during this time. Juliet put this down to him having to spend so much time working for the army.

Juliet was nine when her father moved the family back to England in 1951. By then she had another sister and brother. Her mother now had four children to care for and Juliet tried to help as much as she could. Her father blamed the move on the army, telling Juliet that they were posting him back to do a very important job for them. "Your mother is happy about it. She'll be able to see her family again and you won't have to learn any more German," her father had declared.

When Juliet was growing up, her father had never allowed the family to stay in one place long enough to feel secure. Juliet always found making friends and trusting adults difficult, and now she was going to have to start all over again. However, where the family ended up next would be different.

Juliet's family moved into a large house with three other adults and four other children. Juliet instantly felt more assured. The adults, especially the women, were very friendly and kind to her. It was clear that they and her mother got along very well, and the house always seemed a happy place. There was plenty of laughter and shouting, but good-humoured shouting, not angry shouting. Her mother and father still fell out, but they did so more subtly, to ensure the other adults in the house were unaware. There was only one other man in the house, who worked for the army like Juliet's father, and although he was pleasant, he tended to keep himself to himself unless her father was also around.

The other children in the house were mostly younger than Juliet, but there was an older girl named Jennifer, with whom she shared a bedroom along with a four-year-old called Janet. Fourteen-year-old Jennifer was kind and often allowed Juliet to join in with whatever she was doing, realising that it was better if they could all get along.

Juliet's new school was small and was situated in the village of Brambleton close by. It was completely different from any of her other schools. There were only a couple of teachers and the classes were of mixed ages because only children from the village attended. Lessons were usually interesting. Juliet even enjoyed mathematics, but she preferred the skipping and team games at break times.

Juliet loved the freedom she now had, being able to explore the countryside. She and Jennifer were allowed to go out for walks across the fields and along the footpaths, as long as they stayed together. Often they would take a picnic and be gone for hours during warmer, drier days. This suited Juliet, as she found being around her mother all the time tedious. Life in Brambleton was very different from anywhere Juliet had ever experienced before, and she was determined to enjoy it.

***

Juliet still adored her father, sometimes more than she loved her mother. From a very young age, she had known her relationship with her father was different. That was because of the way he had made her feel. She was special. He had always treated her differently from her brothers and sister, and she knew she was his favourite.

Juliet had a secret that only she and her father knew about. She had kept this secret from her mother, and this had made her feel superior. When her mother and father argued, Juliet knew it would be her he visited later that night for comfort. She accepted this outcome, believing he favoured her over her mother.

In April 1952 Juliet was ten. Her mother organised a surprise birthday party for her and invited all of her friends from school. Juliet was not told until the morning of the party. She was so excited. While the whole house buzzed with the preparations, Juliet helped her mother prepare some party food in the kitchen. Her father walked in to see where everyone had got to, and before she knew it he was threatening to leave and go to the pub. Juliet begged her father to stay, explaining that she needed his help with some of the games they had prepared. She was relieved when he agreed to stay.

Juliet had fun at her birthday party. All her guests had thoroughly enjoyed themselves, her father included, but after it was all over and the clearing away had begun, he had quickly disappeared off to the pub.

Juliet and Jennifer were asked to tidy their bedroom, which had been well used during the celebrations by many of the other children. Reluctantly, they agreed and disappeared upstairs. As they tackled the mammoth task, Juliet's mind wandered. It concerned her that she had only met Jennifer's father once and that he rarely visited the house. Juliet's father had just managed to make her special day perfect and she wondered why Jennifer's father never seemed to spend time with her or Jennifer's mother.

"Does your daddy not love you?" Juliet asked Jennifer.

"Of course he does," Jennifer replied.

"Then why is he never here?"

"Because he has a very important job which means he's away from home a lot. But it doesn't mean he doesn't love us," Jennifer reaffirmed.

"My daddy says I'm his special girl."

"That's nice," replied Jennifer, a little unsure how to respond to that comment.

"It is sometimes ... but other times I don't want to be his special girl. When your daddy comes home, will he come into our room at night to see you?"

"Probably. Now we'd better sort out this room before our mothers discover it's still untidy."

214

Juliet's father didn't visit her room that night, or the next, but he did on the Monday evening, when he tried to be especially quiet, so as not to wake up Jennifer or Juliet. That evening he was not as gentle with his daughter as he had been previously and he hurt her. She struggled under his weight, moaning and sobbing, hoping he would soon stop. She tried to keep her objections quiet, so as not to wake up the others, but her father was hurting her. Why did he not stop?

When he finally moaned and moved away from her, Juliet suddenly felt revulsion for her father, not love. She started sobbing, but he did not console her. He just left the room.

Jennifer got up out of bed and walked over to Juliet, thinking she'd had a nightmare. She asked her if she was all right.

"My daddy hurt me. I don't want to be his special girl anymore."

"You'll be all right," reassured Jennifer. "Go back to sleep now." And she sat with Juliet until she fell back to sleep.

A few days later Juliet's mother took her into her bedroom and spoke to her. "Now Juliet, I want you to know you are not in any trouble. I just need to ask you some questions. Whatever you tell me will remain between you and me, but you do need to tell me the truth. Do you understand?" Juliet nodded. "And remember, you have done nothing wrong."

Her mother asked her some strange questions about her father and whether he did things to her in her bed at night. Juliet was confused at first, wondering how her mother had found out. She thought that perhaps her father had told her mother because he felt bad about hurting her, so she told her mother the truth. Her mother did not interrupt. In fact, she never said a word. Every now and again she just nodded. Later that day her mother and father had a terrible argument. Her father stormed out and never returned that evening. He did not come back the following day either.

A day or so later her mother took Juliet to the local police station, where she was interviewed by a sympathetic policewoman. Her mother was allowed to stay with her, but she wasn't allowed to speak. Juliet had to do all the talking while her mother constantly blew her nose. Afterwards Juliet thought her mother would be really cross with her, but she wasn't. She just kept hugging her and asking her if she was all right.

The other women in the house began talking in whispers and would go quiet whenever Juliet entered a room. She knew they were talking about her and was upset that her mother had told them and the police when she had promised she wouldn't tell anyone. Now all her mother seemed to do was cry all the time. Juliet knew it was her fault but was unsure as to exactly what it was she had done wrong. She thought her mother hated her because her father had left them. She didn't know how she could make everything better again.

When Juliet found her mother sobbing, sat alone in the kitchen, clutching a cup of tea that had gone cold, she asked her what was wrong.

"I'm so sorry, darling. I let you down."

"Did you send Daddy away?" Juliet asked.

"No, darling. Your father left because he is ashamed of what he has done. He should never have done those things to you. It was his choice to leave because he couldn't face up to things. Daddies who truly love their daughters do not do things like that to them."

Juliet was still unsure whether to believe her mother. She did not want to believe that her father no longer loved her.

Barbara

———◦▸———

$\mathbf{B}$ arbara's sister Peggy and husband Dereck had moved into White Gates in Brambleton in 1949. They had met through the army. He had been working as a treasury accountant when they married in Aldershot in 1947. Their second child had been born at White Gates, but their time there was to be brief, as they would only remain at this property for three years. Barbara would be here for longer. Both women knew that when you had a husband attached to the army, you soon got used to travelling and were rarely able to stay in one place for very long.

It had been the army who had helped Dereck and Peggy find the house. It was extremely spacious, having five bedrooms to fill, so Dereck arranged for another army officer and his family to join them at the house in 1952. The officer worked in the Pay Corps and had recently returned from Germany with his wife and four children.

Barbara had also joined her sister's household in 1952. Her sister had married Arthur in India in 1935, and they had two children. Arthur was a medical man, and Barbara had met him while completing physiotherapy training before the war. He was a qualified surgeon and a colonel in the British Army. He often travelled and was abroad in 1952, so Barbara had taken this opportunity to spend some time with her sister. White Gates at this time housed five adults and eight children. At times it could feel very hectic.

To begin with the three families got along tremendously. While the men were at work, Peggy, Barbara and Betty spent most of the day together. Barbara's two children and Betty's eldest daughter attended the village school, while the younger children enjoyed daily trips into the village with their mothers and had a spacious garden in which to play. At weekends the men would occasionally visit the Vine Inn, while the women made the lunch together. The men would then spend

217

most of the afternoon sleeping off their lunch, while the women took the children out for a walk. Both Barbara and Peggy had noticed that Betty's two eldest children could become spiteful with each other when in close proximity for any great length of time, so regular fresh air and plenty of space between them always seemed to do the trick.

Peggy and Dereck occasionally entertained other house guests. Their good friends and neighbours, Richard and Molly, more often than not would pay them a visit. They lived up at the big house on the hill and Molly and Peggy's husbands also knew one another through the army. Richard and Molly had two children. Richard had left the army after the war, moving his career into the textile industry, and by all accounts was achieving great success. The four couples got along well; the men all having their army experiences in common and the women their children.

***

After a number of weeks of sharing a house together, Barbara, who had always been a straight and direct woman, openly admitted to her sister that she felt unable to warm to Fred, although she explained how she liked Betty. Peggy had to admit to her sister that she felt the same. Barbara explained, "I feel completely at ease in Betty's company and feel like I could talk to her about almost anything. Just in the same way as I can to you, Peg. But Fred makes me feel rather uncomfortable."

"He appears to be trying too hard to be friendly, which makes him seem insincere," Peggy explained. Both sisters thought Fred had another agenda, and they especially didn't like the flippant remarks he often made to his wife. Even though these remarks appeared to wash over Betty, most likely because she was used to them, Barbara and Peggy felt they were unnecessary and portrayed Fred as being from a lower class than they.

Shortly after Barbara had moved into the house, Peggy told her sister that she had noticed a change in Fred's behaviour. One afternoon Barbara, Peggy and Dereck, along with Fred, Betty and their youngest children, were all sat in the living room at the front of the house enjoying a cup of afternoon tea. The rest of the children were playing together in a back room, where most of the toys and games were kept. Barbara and Peggy had been talking about the time when fourteen years ago Barbara had given birth to her first child in Crestwell, where she had lived with Arthur above a car garage, and how she had hated that particular time in her life.

Barbara looked directly at Fred and suddenly announced, "I know where I've seen you before. I never forget a face. You used to live on Osborne Road. I used to see you. Regular as clockwork, you were. The same time each evening. Walking home from work, I presume. I never forget a face," she exclaimed.

"Is my sister correct, Fred? Did you and Betty used to live in Crestwell?" asked Peggy.

All at once the colour drained from Fred's face. Betty picked up her youngest child, saying, "I think you could do with a change of nappy, young man," before asking for Fred's help, and together they left the room.

Until then, the relaxed party of five adults had been enjoying the general chit-chat, most of which was made by the women and listened to intermittently by the men. Occasionally, they had all participated, but suddenly the conversation had been cut dead. Fred looked ashen and quickly made his excuses, claiming that Betty needed some assistance with their youngest child. Leaving their other child behind, he had quickly left with his wife.

"Was it something I said?" enquired Barbara.

"I shouldn't think so," replied Dereck. "Fred can be a bit funny at times, but he doesn't mean anything by it."

"His reaction was a bit strange though, Dereck. Don't you think?" asked Peggy.

"Not really. Perhaps he didn't enjoy his time in Crestwell either," remarked Dereck.

The subject was quickly left behind. Betty soon rejoined them in the living room with the baby, but according to her, Fred had taken himself off for a walk to clear his head.

"I hope I didn't say anything to upset him, Betty. But I was right, wasn't I? You did live in Crestwell?" insisted Barbara.

"I didn't but Fred did, with his first wife."

"Oh. I'm ever so sorry. I didn't mean to pry."

"That's all right. It was a long time ago, and it was a difficult time for Fred."

"And I've just opened old wounds. I *am* sorry, dear."

"It's not your fault. I am amazed you can remember him from all that time ago."

"To be honest my memory can drive me a little crazy at times, especially when I recognise someone like Fred but can't for the life of me remember where I know them from." Thankfully, they all felt able to laugh about Barbara putting her foot in it and the conversation soon moved on again. Fred, on the other hand, appeared to struggle to put this incident behind him.

Fred's behaviour after that day rapidly declined, and Barbara noticed he'd started drinking heavily. It had obviously bothered him that she had a connection to his past, during a time he would rather not remember. From then on, whenever Fred was at home it felt as though the whole house was walking on eggshells around him, conscious not to upset him, or worse, make him angry.

On a number of occasions, Barbara and Peggy were witness to Fred raising his voice at his wife, and neither of them had liked it or wished him to do it to them or their children. The sisters had asked Dereck to speak to Fred about this, and since then, Fred had spent as little time as possible in their company.

***

Barbara and Peggy seemed unable to work Fred out and found him rather peculiar. They realised he must have many demons which he had most likely never faced up to, but was that really an excuse to treat his family the way he did? Barbara saw Fred making his family feel guilty, as though his behaviour was somehow their fault and it was they who were preventing him from doing what he wanted to do. Barbara noticed he was no support to Betty, especially where the children were concerned, leaving her to do everything and to make all the decisions.

It appeared that all Fred wanted to do in his spare time was drink heavily at the Vine, in an attempt to obliterate whatever it was that was bothering him. More often than not, he would arrive home in the early hours very drunk. Crashing into everything on his way up to his bed, he often woke the whole house. In the morning he would act as though nothing had happened and everything was all right. Barbara and Peggy discussed this unsatisfactory situation regularly and did not understand why Betty continued to put up with it.

With the three families living together as closely as they did, it was difficult not to notice what was happening between them. There were few secrets. However, in April 1952 Betty asked Barbara and Peggy if they would help her prepare a surprise birthday party for Juliet. She was to be ten years old in a couple of days' time. Betty's daughter had asked for a party the year before, but Betty had felt too unwell to arrange it in Germany, when she had been heavily pregnant with Freddie. She had promised Juliet she would give her a party the following year when she reached double figures. Betty explained to Barbara and Peggy that Juliet had forgotten all about her promise, so she wanted to surprise her daughter.

It would have been little use to ask Fred for any help with the planning, so she went to Barbara and Peggy with some ideas. They were more than willing to lend a hand, and so the preparations quickly received all their attention. Juliet's spring birthday was to fall on a Saturday this year, so that made things a little easier.

Invitations to the party were written and given to the parents of a number of girls from Juliet's school, along with instructions to keep it secret from their daughters until the day. Party games were organised, presents were wrapped and hidden until the big day and any party food that could be prepared ahead of time was kept well out of sight.

On the morning of Juliet's birthday, the house came alive with excitement, but no one was more excited than ten-year-old Juliet. The younger children helped Dereck blow up some balloons, while the three women were helped in the kitchen by Jennifer and Juliet to prepare an array of sandwiches and scones.

"There's enough food here to feed a small army," commented Fred upon entering the kitchen to see where everyone had got to. "It's not all for the children, is it?" he asked Betty.

"Of course not. There will be enough for everyone."

"Because I'm quite happy to get something to eat down at the Vine," was his reply. *Impossible man*, thought Barbara.

"Don't do that, Fred. Juliet will be upset if you don't stay for her party," said Betty. Juliet overheard their conversation. "Please stay for the party, Daddy. I need you to be in charge of pin the tail on the donkey and the egg-and-spoon race and the wheelbarrow race."

"Sounds like I'm going to be too busy to go to the pub then," conceded Fred, winking at his daughter.

"Thank you, Daddy," said Juliet, and she hugged her father.

"Just until the games have finished," he quickly added.

Fred knows just how to manipulate his wife and daughter, thought Barbara.

When Juliet's friends from school started to arrive, there was not a moment's peace for the adults until they were picked up again some three hours later. Juliet had thoroughly enjoyed her tenth birthday party. They played many party games and wore party hats while they ate too much food and drank lemonade. Barbara thought Betty had excelled herself with the birthday cake, which was smothered in thick, pink icing and covered with sweets, and everyone had received a piece of the cake and a balloon to take home afterwards.

When the last child had finally left, the adults began the mammoth task of clearing up before they would all collapse with exhaustion. It was at this point Fred disappeared. When Barbara enquired as to his whereabouts, Betty whispered, "I think he's gone to the pub." Barbara was not impressed. Dereck had not left for the pub. He was helping to tidy up, and that was what Barbara felt Fred should have been doing.

***

When Barbara had moved into White Gates with her two children, the existing children had been forced to share rooms in order to free up a room for her. Jennifer, Juliet and Janet now all shared one bedroom. The situation was not ideal, but the girls seemed to be coping well with this arrangement. When Juliet's friends had left after the party, the girls had been asked to tidy their room.

"It looks as though a bomb has hit it," said Barbara. "Be a good girl, Jennifer, and help Juliet and Janet to tidy up, will you?"

Ten minutes later Peggy went upstairs to return some of her daughter's belongings, when she overheard a conversation between Juliet and her niece, Jennifer. She remained just outside the bedroom door, so the girls had no idea she was there.

"Does your daddy not love you?" Juliet asked Jennifer.

"Of course he does," Jennifer replied.

"Then why is he never here?"

"Because he has a very important job which means he's away from home a lot, but it doesn't mean he doesn't love us," Jennifer reaffirmed.

"My daddy says I'm his special girl."

"That's nice," replied Jennifer.

"It is sometimes … but other times I don't want to be his special girl. When your daddy comes home, will he come into our room at night to see you?"

"Probably. Now we'd better sort out this room before our mothers discover it's still untidy."

Outside the bedroom door Peggy was rooted to the spot, wondering if what she had just heard, and the huge leap she had just made in her conclusion to it, could possibly be the correct judgement. Had she completely got hold of the wrong end of the stick?

She attempted to put these thoughts out of her head and was successful in this until a few days later when her sister came to her in a terrible state.

"Peggy, I need to speak to you urgently," demanded Barbara.

"All right, dear. Whatever is the matter?"

"It's Jennifer. Let's go out into the garden so no one can overhear us."

"Has something happened?"

"Yes. No. Oh, I don't know," she spluttered as they moved outdoors. "It's probably just me misconstruing things. But I can't help feeling there's something wrong."

Once safely in the garden and unable to be overheard, Peggy suggested, "Start at the beginning, dear."

"I will. Yes. I'll tell you what Jennifer told me and you can form your own opinion."

"I shall do my best. Now, what is it?"

"Last night, in the middle of the night, Jennifer was woken by a strange noise. She said she could only describe it as a grunting noise. She said she was pretty scared to begin with because she realised someone else was in the bedroom with them. She was about to sit up and ask who it was, thinking it must be Betty, when the person got up off Juliet's bed and walked out of the room. She says that at that point she realised it was Juliet's father. As he closed the door behind him, she heard Juliet begin to sob, so she got up out of bed, thinking the child had had a nightmare, and asked her if she was all right. Juliet told her that her father had hurt her and she didn't want to be his special girl any more." Barbara noticed her sister's face change but continued. "I thanked Jennifer for telling me and asked her not to mention it to anyone else. I explained that I would make sure Juliet was all right. Jennifer was most concerned for the child. She kept saying that she felt as though something was not right about Juliet's father being there. What do you think, Peg? Am I worrying about nothing?"

The conversation Peggy had overheard a few days earlier sprang forward in her mind and she shared those feelings she had experienced at the time with her sister.

"We are going to have to talk to Betty," Barbara concluded.

"Oh, dear Lord," replied Peggy.

***

Betty was surprisingly calm when Barbara broached the difficult subject. She explained to Betty about the two incidents, relaying the conversations as accurately as she could remember them. Betty said very little in reply, but it was obvious from her pained expression that she too was having the same appalling thoughts as Barbara and Peggy. She quickly excused herself in order to find and speak to her daughter.

Nothing appeared to happen for the next couple of days. In fact, the house and everyone in it appeared incredibly tranquil, as though waiting for the inevitable nightmare to begin. And it did. Betty spoke to her daughter, and Juliet confirmed her worst nightmare. Then she confronted Fred, but he denied everything, walking out on her and never returning home that evening.

The following morning, when Fred had still not returned to White Gates, Betty spoke with Barbara and Peggy and together they concluded that the police would need to be informed. Betty left her children in the care of her friends while she went to the local police station. Upon her return she was clearly distressed, and she explained to Barbara and Peggy how she had been asked if she realised how serious her accusation was.

"How stupid," declared Barbara.

"I told the officer that I hadn't made the decision to go there lightly. Then he took my statement and told me he would need to speak to both of you and Juliet. I asked if it was really necessary to speak to my daughter, and the officer said it was. 'This is a very serious crime,' he said, 'and we cannot afford to make mistakes.' Then he said he could ask for the interview to be done by a woman police officer if I preferred. But they don't have any at Brambleton Police Station, so he's going to request one from elsewhere."

"Will you be able to stay with Juliet during the interview?" asked Barbara.

"As long as I don't interrupt the proceedings," replied Betty.

"This whole thing is terrible. That poor child," sighed Peggy.

Betty burst into tears. She had held them back for as long as she could.

"You're not helping, Peg. I'll go and make a pot of tea," suggested Barbara.

When Barbara left the room, Peggy put her arms around Betty in an attempt to console her, while their youngest children continued to play happily around their feet with a selection of toys that had been placed upon a rug.

A month later Barbara saw Betty attempting to come to terms with life without Fred. He had vanished that day, and none of them had heard a thing from him since. Betty and her children had begun to attend the local church each Sunday, a thing she had not done for many years. She explained to Barbara and Peggy how one of the last times she had attended church was when she had taken Juliet to be baptised during the war. Fred had been away in the army at this time and for reasons best known to himself had never allowed her to have their other three children baptised. "He never saw the point," Betty informed them both.

"Perhaps you could do it for the children now, without him," suggested Peggy.

"Perhaps," considered Betty.

White Gates had become a sombre place but a sanctuary for Betty and her children: somewhere Fred no longer lived. However, this didn't stop Betty from worrying about him and wondering where he was and what he was doing. Then one day in July he turned up at the house unannounced. Betty later told Barbara that she suspected he had been watching the place, as he hadn't knocked until just after Barbara and Peggy had left, taking all the children with them into the village for some fresh air and supplies. Betty had agreed she would stay behind to prepare the day's meal.

Betty told Barbara that Fred had looked dreadful. "His hair couldn't have seen a comb for weeks. He was unshaven and his clothes dishevelled." Betty explained how she felt she had no choice but to invite him in. He had told her that he was to appear in court on 31 July, charged with incest. She already knew this, as she too had received a letter and was expected to attend. "He begged and pleaded with me to take him back, still denying that any assault upon Juliet had ever taken place. He said he loved his children and would never do anything to hurt them. He told me he loved and missed me and begged me to reconsider the possibility of him moving back in so things could go back to the way they used to be."

Barbara was horrified by Fred's nonchalance. "Please tell me you sent him away with a flea in his ear," she demanded.

"It made me feel positively terrible, but yes, I did."

***

When Fred appeared in court, Betty was also there, having to rely again upon her friends for support in caring for her children. Barbara was always willing to help, but Fred's behaviour was difficult to stomach, and knowing that he had been in their house among her and her sister's children repulsed her.

Barbara knew Fred had been charged with committing a serious offence against his ten-year-old daughter and was to appear in court in Hampshire. She was disgusted that he'd pleaded not guilty. He reserved his defence and was allowed bail. She was also appalled to discover that upon exiting the court he had immediately approached Betty, asking to speak with her. Their neighbour Richard, who had accompanied Betty to the court, had stepped away to give them some privacy. Once again Fred implored Betty to take him back, and Betty said she would think about it.

"You said what?" was Barbara's reaction when Betty told her what she had said to Fred.

"Barbara, we mustn't interfere. This has to be Betty's decision," Peggy told her sister. But the more Barbara entertained the idea of Fred's return, the more she felt repulsed at the prospect.

In an attempt some days later to cheer everyone up and create some sort of normality at home, Betty made her first important decision without Fred's influence. She made a booking with the vicar of St Mary's for her three youngest children to be baptised in August. Dereck, Peggy, Barbara and their children were all to join in with the celebrations, along with Betty's mother and sister and their neighbours, Richard and Molly. By then Betty had been forced to find a new home in the village, as the army had said she could not remain at White Gates if Fred was no longer with her.

It was obvious to Barbara that Betty clearly wanted her children's baptism day to be special for them and for it to signify a new start for them all. Barbara and Peggy did everything they could to help make this possible, but it was a difficult task, especially when the day before the baptism Betty received a letter from Fred which greatly upset her.

In his letter he once again begged Betty to take him back, explaining how he had not touched a drop of drink since the day at court and that he was undergoing some treatment for his behaviour which he was sure would cure him. Betty shared his letter with her friends.

"That's the first time he's admitted his guilt," spotted Barbara.

"Yes," agreed Betty. "It feels wrong to be pleased about that."

"Does he really think you would have him back?" asked Peggy.

"Of course he does," Barbara answered crossly.

"He goes on to say that he plans to plead guilty at the trial in November."

"Good. I should think so," maintained Barbara.

"Will you take him back?" enquired Peggy.

"I don't know what I'll do yet. I can't think about him just now. I just want to concentrate on tomorrow and the children," Betty insisted, and her eyes began to fill with tears.

"It's going to be a wonderful day," reassured Peggy.

"With the promise of sunshine all day," affirmed Barbara.

It was indeed the perfect day. A day they all enjoyed, hardly giving a thought to Fred at all.

It was a wrench to Barbara when Peggy, Dereck and the children all moved out. Dereck had been posted to another county and his family were to follow. Life at White Gates was to change again dramatically. Both sisters were fondly attached and would miss the other immensely. After Peggy's departure the house was strangely quiet. Barbara spent her time helping prepare Betty for Fred's next court appearance in November. She was sorry her sister would not be around to help.

Shortly before his court appearance Barbara discovered that Fred had been relinquished from duty. The army stated this to be on account of his disability, but it was a kind way of saying that Fred was no longer able to complete his job and the army wanted no further association with him.

Fred eventually pleaded guilty, but only after his and Betty's solicitors had agreed the charge be reduced to indecent assault. The court heard how Fred was receiving some medical treatment at Knowle Hospital, where he had access to a library and occupational therapy and he had completed work in the laundry and the greenhouses.

"It sounds more like a holiday camp," commented Barbara sarcastically to Betty when she had shared the day's events.

"His trial was postponed until December in order for the judge to acquire a medical report from his doctor. Apparently, he has been undergoing another course of treatment. I confess I had no desire to see or speak to Fred after the hearing," said Betty.

"I don't blame you. I wouldn't either."

"I was concerned he would ask me to take him back again, so I escaped via a back door from the court, so as not to be seen."

"Very wise, dear."

Betty made a decision later that day, urged on by Barbara. She decided she wanted a divorce from Fred. Barbara encouraged this and did everything she could to assist Betty. By the end of the year, Betty's mother had moved into the village and was now living with her and the children. When the court reconvened in December, Betty instructed her solicitor to drop all charges against her husband and start divorce proceedings instead. In 1953 Betty was finally free of Fred after receiving her decree absolute.

Vincent

———◇———

Before Vincent had met and married Eliza, he had been a chiropodist. He had worked for the Neville family, who at one time had owned around nine Turkish baths across the London area. Some were built for ladies; some for gentlemen. Vincent found himself working inside one of the smaller women's baths, as this was where the chiropodist salon was located. The men's baths tended to house smoking rooms, bars and hairdressing salons.

Vincent had received training, learning massage techniques, and owned his own portable set of tools containing tweezers, nail nippers and an operating knife for work on corns, calluses, bunions and ingrown toenails. Vincent saw his regular customers every two weeks, when he would firstly soak their feet, then provide a foot massage and trim their nails. He was able to advise his clients on the very best way to look after their feet. He had met Eliza when she had come into the baths with a friend and he had worked on her feet.

Vincent married Eliza in 1914 and promptly went off to war. Upon his return, he was able to save enough money, which enabled him to open his own hairdressing salon in Brixton. There he offered his chiropodist services. Their daughter Betty was born in 1917, and six years later they had another daughter, Marie. Vincent's two daughters, although six years apart, had always been devoted to one another. Their mother adored them both equally, but Betty had always been Vincent's favourite. They often seemed to know what the other was thinking and they had similar interests.

From an early age Betty had shown great interest in Vincent's salon and enjoyed accompanying him to work. It was no great surprise to Vincent and Eliza that when Betty finished school, she asked if she could train as a beauty therapist. In 1934 Betty started to offer this service through her father's salon. Vincent was thrilled to be working with his daughter but he had not anticipated the beauty therapy's rapid success and growth. He soon put an end to the chiropody side of his business, as this was no longer viable.

At this time Vincent's business in Herne Hill was prospering. When he found he needed someone competent to take over the running of the hair salon, he had met and employed Fred. This allowed him more time for his bookkeeping.

Fred had come highly recommended by a fellow hairdresser and good friend, whom Vincent had first met during a business conference. They had sat next to one another and conversed about staff and hairdressing matters. They had met a couple of times since and had become firm friends. The timing could not have been better for Vincent when he had heard from his good friend, enquiring about opportunities for a trained member of staff.

However, Vincent now regretted the day he had taken Fred on. Fred had destroyed his family and their reputation. He could never forgive him for the shame and anguish he had caused them all. He thanked God that his friend Leonard no longer walked the earth and was not here to see the devastation his trainee had caused for so many. It undoubtedly would have killed the old man if he had still been alive today.

At first Fred had been enthusiastic and efficient, getting along with everyone. Vincent had felt relieved he had been able to find someone so quickly—and someone who had come so highly recommended. But what Vincent could never have realised was just how much danger he was placing his daughter in.

Vincent's little family had always been solid. They looked after one another. He had protected his girls and was very proud of both of them. They were strong, independent women, like their mother, and he could not have wished for two more adoring daughters.

After letting Fred into their lives it appeared that family life would never be the same again. Once Fred had established influence and power over Betty, she began to drift away from her father and her family. Vincent's colourful sailing boat was swept away by a spiteful gust of wind and eventually freed, but only after her mainsail was shredded, her tiller worn and her hull leaking.

***

Vincent's family had given Fred a great deal of support following the death of his wife and baby son. Vincent had encouraged Betty to attend the inquest into the death of Fred's wife, and Betty had been there to pick up the pieces when Fred's son had died two weeks later. Vincent had felt proud of Betty's maturity in handling the situation, but he was soon to realise that his daughter had become infatuated with Fred. Most evenings, Betty was missing from the family dining table, choosing to spend this time with Fred rather than with her family.

Vincent and Eliza thought Betty had allowed herself to become too involved with Fred and his problems and that Fred was far too old for her. But Betty would hear nothing bad said about Fred. She had already been seduced by this older, charismatic man. Vincent and Eliza discussed what they might do to change the situation. But before they could reach a decision, Betty announced that she and Fred were going to marry.

There were many reasons for Vincent's dislike of Fred as an appropriate suitor for his daughter. Fred was thirteen years older than Betty, and in Vincent's opinion, Betty was still too young to be thinking about marriage. She had only recently had her twentieth birthday. She was just beginning to put her beauty therapy qualification to good use and establish her business. She had such a bright future ahead of her and it seemed she was willing to give this all up for Fred.

Vincent was old-fashioned in some respects. It offended him that Fred had not asked his permission first for his daughter's hand in marriage. It appeared that Fred needed no one's permission to do anything. He pleased himself, without a thought for anyone else. He hadn't even accompanied Betty to their home to make the announcement. He had left Betty to do that alone.

"Fred wants us to marry at the registry office," declared Betty. Vincent's face reddened. "He's not very religious, you see." Betty desperately tried to justify this reason.

"Not acceptable," boomed Vincent from across the room. Vincent had certain expectations which needed to be met. "If you do not marry at the church this family has attended every week since we have lived here, the church in which your mother and I were married and the church in which you and your sister were both baptised, then you will never be welcome in our home again!"

Betty and Eliza were genuinely taken aback by Vincent's sudden declaration, looking to one another for support. Marie started to cry. She had never seen her father so angry. The room fell silent, aside from the quiet sobs Marie was emitting. Eliza attempted to comfort her youngest daughter. Eventually, Betty spoke calmly and quietly.

"I'll speak to Fred again, Father. We'll sort this out. I promise."

"Good girl. I know you will do what's right."

Although Vincent eventually went along with Betty's wedding in church, he had felt sure that his daughter was making a terrible mistake. But Vincent had to admit that his daughter's wedding day in December 1938 had been just perfect. Betty had looked radiant. So had Marie and Eliza for that matter. It had stirred up so many happy memories of his own wedding day which had taken place more years earlier than he cared to remember.

Vincent had paid for everything and, therefore, he and Eliza had been able to do things properly and see their daughter married in the way they believed was right. Betty had worn a V-neck, full-length, satin wedding dress which tapered in at the waist, accentuating her beautiful figure. The dress had long sleeves finished with a wrist point, drawing attention to her hands and bringing focus to her wedding ring—the only thing Fred had paid for. Vincent had also bought her some white gloves to wear in case it had been cold, but Fred would only allow her to wear them from the church back to her father's house, as he had wanted her to show off his lavish purchase. On her head she wore a hip-length veil, and she carried a bouquet of expensive arum lilies, which again her father had paid for.

Betty's only bridesmaid had been her sister, who wore a violet velvet dress with a matching muff and a headdress with a ribbon. Fred's best man was the family's close friend and neighbour, Alan, because it appeared that Fred had no friends or family who could fulfil this role. Vincent had often wondered if it would be Alan to whom his daughter would marry.

On the day, Vincent had teased Alan incessantly about how well he

233

scrubbed up, until Betty had stepped in and told her father off. Alan had blushed with embarrassment when Betty had intervened and again when they had toasted him and bridesmaid Marie after the speeches. Vincent couldn't help feeling that Alan would have made a more appropriate suitor for his daughter that day. And why had he never noticed before how obviously smitten Alan seemed to be with Betty?

After the ceremony family and friends were invited back to Vincent and Eliza's home for cooked ham with salads followed by cake and trifle. Vincent watched uneasily as Fred captivated his guests with his stimulating conversation and magnetic personality.

"Just listen to him," spat Vincent. "He could charm the birds out of the trees," he muttered to Eliza, who was also smitten with Fred, like everyone else. Later that evening Fred, Betty, Marie, Alan and some of their younger guests disappeared to the local pub for a few drinks and a sing-song by the piano. It had been a long day and Vincent and Eliza chose to stay home. Vincent had stomached all that he could of Fred for one day.

***

At the beginning of the war Vincent's wife suffered terribly. As more and more bombs dropped relentlessly every night across London, he noticed Eliza's health deteriorate. She would jump at any slight noise, panic if she hadn't heard from either daughter for more than a few hours and eventually refuse to leave the house at all.

By this time Fred had managed to convince Betty to stop working at Vincent's salon and brazenly informed him and Eliza that they should expect to see some grandchildren soon. Vincent, Eliza and Betty had all been shocked and embarrassed by his rather impertinent announcement.

Within a year of his daughter's marriage to Fred, Vincent was no longer able to recognise Betty as the same independent woman she had once been. She was now allowing Fred to make all the decisions for her. Although Vincent disliked the way Fred appeared to be controlling his daughter, there was nothing he could do about it. Fred was very clever. He was able to make Betty believe she was happy.

Because his daughter no longer worked with him, and because Eliza's nerves were bad, Vincent decided to sell his business and home and temporarily move his family into rented accommodation before eventually leaving London for the country. He felt a strong need to protect them and keep them safe from the bombing. They had all been terribly reluctant to leave Betty behind in London, but she had insisted that she and Fred had made a life for themselves there and wanted to stay. Betty promised her parents she would visit them often, but Fred saw to it that this never happened.

Vincent and Eliza remained far away from London until some years after the war had ended. Their daughter Marie returned as soon as she had turned eighteen, against her parents' wishes, but they were relieved she had gone to live with Betty. This had been when Betty's first child had been born. Vincent had regretted not visiting Betty at this time, but his priority had been his wife. Eliza was still suffering with her nerves and the doctor had been worried about her weak heart. Complete rest and as little excitement as possible had been his recommendation, and Vincent had stuck rigidly to his suggestion, thinking this was the best thing he could do for his wife. In reality Vincent made all the decisions and Eliza had begun to resent him for it. She had been a strong woman up until then. Now she no longer even had a say in what she had for lunch. She knew she was missing out on her children and grandchildren's lives, but at the time she did not have the strength to do battle with her husband or fight her illness.

When Vincent and Eliza finally decided to move back to London in 1949, Eliza told her husband that she no longer wanted to live with him. He was shocked.

"I will never divorce you," he threatened.

"I don't want a divorce, Vincent. I just don't want to live with you any longer."

Vincent did not understand what he had done wrong. While they had lived by themselves, his wife had felt stifled and controlled by Vincent, who had been completely unaware of how she had felt. Now that Eliza felt stronger, she was determined not to allow Vincent to dictate to her any longer. Eliza made the decision to live with her daughter Marie in rented accommodation in Brixton They were not far from Betty, and Vincent was forced to find alternative accommodation at a lodging house in Streatham.

Once back in London, Vincent was able to visit Betty and his grandchildren for the first time in almost ten years, but he received a cold reception. It was obvious that Betty believed her parents' split was down to him, and Fred had been there spouting his own opinions on the matter. Vincent was only able to spend a couple of hours with his two grandchildren, Juliet and Rupert, before he could no longer stand to be in the same room as Fred. His son-in-law was utterly disagreeable. He didn't know what his daughter saw in Fred and couldn't believe he'd actually liked the man when he'd first employed him. First it was Vincent's relationship with Eliza, and now his and Betty's relationship had also broken down. What was he to do?

Vincent soon learned that Fred had organised for Betty and the children to move abroad. It had been Marie who had informed her father that Fred was moving them all to Germany. Marie had also hinted to her father at this time that all was not well with her sister's marriage. But what was Vincent to do? He didn't wish to antagonise Fred or upset Betty any more than he already had.

With his wife now living with Marie and Betty moving away, Vincent made the decision that he must try to get on with his own life. He had always had a head for business and over the war years had become involved with a number of successful companies in which he had invested money from the sale of his salon. Soon after moving back to London, Vincent became a company director, throwing himself enthusiastically into this role.

Over the next couple of years, while his daughter Betty was out of the country, Vincent embarked on a new relationship. He was forced to keep this relationship secret from the rest of his family, as the woman in question was exactly the same age as Betty. Vincent had begun to have feelings for Eileen who lived at the same boarding house as him. Coincidentally, she was also a hairdresser, and this had been what had initially ignited their interest in one another. However, their relationship was inconsistent, as Eileen kept changing her mind about whether she wanted to be with Vincent. Eileen's main problem was that Vincent was still married, so she saw no future for them unless he was to divorce. Vincent had always been honest with Eileen, explaining that this could never happen, which was why their relationship continued to blow hot and cold.

When Vincent was informed by Eliza and Marie that Betty's marriage was in crisis, in 1952, he joined forces with his estranged wife and daughters in an attempt to support them as best he could. It had been a difficult ordeal; one filled with raw emotions which he found impossible to deal with at times. He tried to remain strong for his family, but often felt very alone, angry and frustrated. He had no idea he could feel so much hatred for one person. If he could have got his hands on Fred at this time, he was sure he would have killed him. He detested the man, mostly for what he had put Betty and the children through, but also for what he was putting Marie and Eliza through.

Vincent's family had never been involved in a scandal such as this and he felt ashamed. He suffered terribly with feelings of guilt. He wished he had never let Betty marry Fred. He had not felt right about it at the time. Why had he not acted upon these feelings? Everything would be very different if he had. Instead, his family was in pieces and he was hopelessly trying to fix them all back together again. Vincent knew Betty had always been strong. It was a good job. That monster had put her and her children through hell. As her father, he knew she could get through this. She had to, for her children's sake.

***

The last time Vincent saw Betty, in late 1953, he thought she looked very thin. The court case and her divorce had taken its toll, but she remained positive about her future. She was making plans, and he was pleased she had shared some of these plans with him.

She had her mother living with her for extra support, but Eliza's health also concerned Vincent.

"Have you told the girls about your heart, Eliza?" Vincent asked her quietly during a brief moment when they had found themselves alone.

"Well?" insisted Vincent.

"No, and I have no intention of telling them," Eliza spat back at Vincent.

"I think they should know. All of this must be putting you under a lot of strain," he persisted.

"Betty has enough to worry about without me making it worse. Just leave it, Vincent."

Vincent knew when he was beat, and where Betty got her strength from. It was clear Eliza did not want to trouble their children with her ailments. They all had enough to contend with, and Vincent was forced to respect her wishes.

Vincent was pleased he also got to see Marie during this time. She was visiting her mother and sister, and it was satisfying for them all to have been under the same roof for a few hours, even though the circumstances for them being there were difficult to deal with. They managed to briefly set aside their problems and enjoy each other's company.

Marie lightened the mood by disclosing that she had met someone special. She had been reluctant to share too many details with her family at this time, as she recognised her sister was still in distress about her own relationship, but it had been a relief for those few moments for them all to feel more positive about the future.

Later Vincent was able to reflect upon how important his family still were to him. He believed life had a way of passing you by if you let it. Life would happen all around you, often excluding you, if allowed to do so. Each day could seem filled with important things, and those days quickly turned into weeks, then years. Before you knew it, you realised you'd missed so much. He had rarely taken the time to think about what was important, where he could have made a difference or what truly made him happy.

From that day forward Vincent made a promise to himself. He would always put his family first and nothing would stop him from achieving this. They were the most important thing to him again. He just wished he had realised this years ago. He would endeavour to protect them once more.

Frances

———◇———

At sixty-four, Frances should have been thinking about retiring from nursing. She was originally from the USA, but having lived for almost thirty years in England, little remained of her American roots. After training to be a nurse at Hartford Hospital in Connecticut, she caught a ship to England in 1932 and settled for a time in Lincolnshire. Frances travelled back to New York on a couple of occasions to visit family, but for the last twenty years she had remained in Maidstone, Kent. Alongside her nursing career, Frances also ran a lodging house on Potley Hill Road.

Having never married, Frances was used to being able to turn her hand to most things in order to make ends meet and survive. For a time, she had turned her back on nursing, choosing to part own a tea room on Gabriel's Hill, which had turned out to be one of her better ideas. However, with the start of the Second World War everything had changed and she had reverted to nursing once more.

Frances had been a nurse at Oakwood Hospital for a number of years now. The hospital catered mostly for patients with mental problems and was able to provide a variety of treatments. It was situated two miles away from her home, in an area known as Barming Heath. Frances had become good friends with Mary, one of the live-in assistant matrons. Mary was aware that Frances rented out rooms in her home, and it had been she who had introduced Frances to Fred. Fred had arrived on her doorstep during the autumn of 1954, looking dishevelled, in poor health and in need of a place to stay. She had given him a tour of her home, shown him the room she had available for rent and informed him of some house rules.

"He's had his problems. I'll be the first to admit that," confessed Mary. "But I really believe he has turned a corner. He shouldn't give you any trouble," she reassured her friend.

Mary had not known Fred very long, but she had always found him pleasant—once they had got him off the drink, that was. The two were similar in age, but apart from that they had nothing else in common. Although suffering with depression when he had first arrived at the hospital, Mary had found Fred charming and polite—most unlike many of her other patients. But she knew little of Fred's situation. She was only privy to what the doctors decided to share with her, and of course she shared this with her friend Frances.

Mary knew Fred had received treatment once before and that it was not at Oakwood. She could only assume that this previous treatment had not been successful. She was also aware that Fred had struggled to stay off the drink since his last lot of treatment and that he had recently gone through a divorce. Under these difficult circumstances, Fred had appeared to respond positively to his treatment, and she informed Frances of this fact.

Within the grounds of the hospital, Fred had taken part in various therapeutic workshops and worked on the 300-acre farm site. As his treatment was nearing its conclusion, he had secured himself a temporary, part-time job in the hospital bakery.

Mary had promised to help find him some accommodation upon his discharge. He had confided in her about his brothers' reluctance to take him in and the circumstances of his divorce, although Mary was sure there was more to his story. Fred had shown Mary sincere gratitude when she had informed him that she'd found him a room to rent and introduced him to Frances. That had been back in November 1954, and since then Fred had become a bit of a pest.

***

For the last four months, Mary had confided in Frances about her concerns over Fred. At first he had casually bumped into her in the grounds of the hospital, explaining how he'd just finished work at the bakery. They briefly exchanged pleasantries, and Mary asked after his health and enquired into his accommodation on Potley Hill Road. Fred had appeared more settled, and at first these encounters had not concerned her.

Then, one day it appeared he had made an extra effort to visit the hospital, informing Mary that he now had a new job at a local confectionary factory. "That is good news, Fred. I'm very pleased for you," Mary answered cheerfully.

"It's the factory on the riverbank in the town centre, called Kreemy Works. Do you know it?" enquired Fred.

"Oh yes, Fred. I know where you mean," replied Mary. "Sharps, isn't it? That's great news. Congratulations."

"There is talk of some night shifts soon. Rumour has it they are going to introduce twenty-four-hour production to keep up with the rise in sales. I hope to be able to increase my hours soon."

"Good for you, Fred. I'm sorry. I have dash or you'll have me late for my ward rounds. Take care now. Bye, Fred."

"Bye, Mary. See you soon."

After that they seemed to bump into each other even more frequently. One evening, as Mary was working late, she happened to glance out of the ward window and spot Fred loitering in the hospital grounds. He was stood staring straight at her through the glass windows and it unsettled her. It was at this point she confided in Frances.

Frances warned Fred off, telling him in no uncertain terms that if he did not leave Mary alone, he would lose his room at her house. She was not one to mince her words. But neither of the women had realised at this time just how obsessed with Mary Fred had become. Nor had they realised he had started to drink again.

It appeared that Fred was under the illusion that Mary was interested in him, and by March 1955 he had become completely infatuated with her. He would often hand notes over to other nurses, asking them to pass these on to Mary. In his notes he announced his feelings for her, and on one occasion he asked another nurse to leave a tin of toffees he had purchased on Mary's desk. Mary knew it had to stop but didn't know what to do about it. She didn't want to get Fred into trouble, and she knew that if she said anything to her friend, it was likely that Fred would lose his room in Frances's house.

On a wet Tuesday evening in March, as Mary was approaching the nurses' home across from the hospital, Fred appeared out of nowhere, causing her to jump back with fright.

"Fred! You frightened the life out of me! What are you doing here?"

"I wondered if you would like to come out with me this evening to see a film."

It was very obvious to Mary that Fred had been drinking. "I'm very tired, Fred. It's been a long day, and I've not had anything to eat since lunchtime." She attempted to pass him to get to the entrance of her accommodation block, but Fred put out his arms to stop her, placing his hands upon her shoulders.

"How about we meet later then, at the Fountain Inn?" he suggested.

"You know you shouldn't be drinking, Fred."

"I've only had a couple," he claimed as he gently swayed back and forth.

"Can you let me pass, please, Fred?" Mary attempted to ask calmly, removing his hands from her shoulders.

"Will you agree to meet me later?" insisted Fred.

In order to get rid of him, Mary knew she would have to agree to something. "Fred, if you promise me you will go straight home, I will come to Potley Hill Road later to see you after I have had something to eat."

"Do you promise?" he asked. He looked surprised.

"I promise," assured Mary.

Much to Mary's relief, Fred staggered sideways and let her pass. Once safely inside the nurses' accommodation block, Mary flopped into her armchair, fell into a deep sleep and forgot all about the promise she had made to Fred.

***

Frances believed that Fred had recently been showing signs of depression. He seemed to hate his job at the confectionary factory. He had no friends that she knew of and appeared very lonely, which was most likely why once again he had turned to the drink. Each night after work, on his way back to Potley Hill Road, it appeared that Fred called in at the pub for a drink. Time would often escape him, and it would be late before he arrived home.

The house was situated at the end of a row of terraces. It was compact but looked more like two terraced houses squeezed together. This particular evening, Fred had arrived home before Frances, using his key to enter. He could get into the kitchen but was unable to get into Frances's private rooms, as she kept these locked. He entered the kitchen and was about to help himself to anything he could find in the larder when he heard her put her key in the front door. He was staggering in the hallway as Frances entered through her front door. Half leaning against the wall for support, he demanded, "Where have you been?"

Frances was cross to have been greeted in this way. "Where do you think I've been, Fred? I've been at work. You, on the other hand, look like you've been in the pub all day. Let's get you upstairs."

Frances was a strong woman, which had its uses in her profession. Fred was now of slight build, which made things easier, and in no time at all she had him safely in his room. His hands were freezing and he was making little sense.

"Let me get myself settled, Fred. I'll put the kettle on and bring you up a hot-water bottle. Then I suggest you try to get some sleep." With that, Frances disappeared back downstairs.

Half an hour later, when she returned to his room, Fred was still wearing his overcoat and wandering around. He appeared extremely agitated. He was pacing the room and kept going over to the window and looking out, as though he was expecting someone.

"What is it, Fred? What's the matter?"

"Nothing," was his only reply.

"Right, I've put a hot-water bottle under your covers, so I suggest you climb into bed and get some sleep. I'm sure you'll feel better in the morning."

By this time it was almost eleven o'clock. Frances, like Mary, had endured a busy day and all she wanted was her bed. By eleven-fifteen she was sound asleep. Fred could now put his plan into action. Sitting at the end of his bed, he reached for an envelope which held a letter from the factory regarding him turning up late for work on two separate occasions. The letter warned that if he was unable to turn up for work on time, he would be sacked from his job. This, in fact, was his second written warning. Fred took the envelope, turned it over and on its back he squiggled a note.

***

On Wednesday morning Frances awoke to a strong smell of gas. She instinctively knew what Fred had done. She ran upstairs to his bedroom. She could not look at the body in the bed. She threw up the sash window to let out the choking fumes and contacted the police.

When PC Ballard arrived at her home, Frances showed him upstairs to where Fred's body lay lifeless in the bed. Frances had already turned off the gas and made the house safe. There was nothing else she could do now. PC Ballard confirmed to her that Fred was dead, then he searched the body. Inside Fred's coat pocket he discovered a small book. As he placed it on the bed next to the body, Frances realised it was a diary.

When PC Ballard was content that there was nothing else to find on the body, he covered it completely with the bed covers and left it for the coroner to deal with. He let his eyes scan the room, initially in search of a suicide note. He came across the envelope lying on the floor beside the bed, next to a pair of shoes. He turned it over and read out loud. "It is now eleven-thirty. Where are you, Mary?" PC Ballard looked at Frances. "Do you have any idea who Mary is?" he asked.

Frances was utterly unnerved. "I'm not sure."

It had to be Mary from Oakwood, but she was not about to disclose this to the police. Her friend Mary had nothing to do with this mess, and Frances was not about to drag her into it. This was completely Fred's doing, and no one else was responsible.

"He tended to keep himself very much to himself," Frances offered further.

PC Ballard acknowledged her comment with an expert nod.

After a further brief search the police constable said he would stay with the body until further assistance arrived. He could clearly see that Frances was shaken by the experience.

"If you would prefer to leave the house for a while, I can make sure it is securely locked when we all leave."

"Yes. I think I'll do that. Thank you," replied Frances. She already knew that she must go straight to see Mary. As she turned to leave, the police constable interrupted her thoughts.

"Sorry, madam. I forgot to mention. There will be an inquest into this death and you will most likely be asked to give evidence."

"Will I?" Frances's thoughts were elsewhere. "Yes, I suppose I will," she realised. Stunned for a moment, Frances finally said "Thank you" and left the room, her eyes choosing not to take one final glance at the covered body. Downstairs she grabbed her coat, hat, handbag and keys and left, with her thoughts in disarray.

Frances went immediately to see Mary. Thankfully, she found her friend still in her flat, due to her being on the late shift that day. Understandably, Mary became quite distressed when Frances broke the news of Fred's death to her. Frances herself was still shaken by the event and she suggested she make them both a hot drink.

"The sugar is in the cupboard just above your head," Mary helpfully informed her friend. Frances added a couple of heaped spoons into both cups. "There," she said, holding out a cup and saucer to Mary. "That should help with the shock."

"Thank you," responded Mary rather quietly.

As Frances explained to Mary about the note and diary the constable had discovered, she found herself becoming rather agitated by the cowardly act Fred had just committed. Although she felt him to be spineless and pathetic, she knew it was best not to share these thoughts with Mary. She did not wish to cause her friend any more unnecessary upset.

"I saw him only last night," admitted Mary. "I promised him I would call round to your house and see him later. That must be why he wrote the note. It's all my fault."

"Nonsense. Don't you dare blame yourself. It wasn't you who gassed him."

"Please don't speak like that," begged Mary.

"Well. It wasn't you who made him drink again either now, was it? That was his choice. He could hardly stand up last night when I helped him up to bed."

"He'd been drinking when he was round here earlier."

"There you go. That was his choice. And that was before you had promised to visit him at my house. So you see, it isn't your fault."

"No. I know you're right. It's just that this has really shaken me. I thought he was getting better."

"The police said I would most likely be called to give evidence at the inquest."

"Oh dear," sighed Mary. "Will *I*?" she panicked.

"Not if I have anything to do with it," assured Frances. "I see no reason why anyone else should link the Mary in the note to you." Mary looked relieved. "Do you mind if I stay here until lunchtime? Just to give them all enough time to do what they have to do at my place."

"Of course," agreed Mary. "I'm here until three o'clock anyway."

***

Frances was indeed called to give evidence at the inquest into Fred's death, and much to her and Mary's horror, the inquest was then reported in the *Kent Messenger* the following day. The headline read, 'Where are you Mary? wrote ex-captain found gassed.'

Mary felt unable to visit Frances's home during this time, so two days later they sat together once more in Mary's flat reading what had been printed in the newspaper. 'Former army captain working at a local factory was found dead in bed on Wednesday morning, fully clothed, including an overcoat.' The images of finding Fred flashed back clearly into Frances's mind. The report continued: 'Gas was escaping from a wall bracket and a ten-foot tube was lying on the floor.'

The two women sat closely, sipping from cups of hot, sweet tea which had only limited powers of comfort. "It says here that he served in the last war and held a short-term commission as a captain afterwards. He never told me that," said Mary. "At the inquest did you see his wife?" she asked her friend.

"Yes."

"What was she like?" Mary enquired.

"Attractive, but sad looking," replied Frances. "She told the judge that she had last seen Fred in the autumn of last year, when he'd visited her house in Brambleton."

"Lovely little village, Brambleton," commented Mary.

"I wouldn't know. I've never been there," replied Frances.

"Sorry. Please carry on," insisted Mary.

"His wife said he appeared then to be under the influence of alcohol. He looked poorly and extremely thin. She described him as highly strung and nervous. She also said they had corresponded by letter and she had learned that he had been in and out of work. If I remember correctly, the coroner then asked his wife, Betty I think her name was, if Fred had ever threatened to take his life."

"What did she say?" asked Mary.

"I must admit that I had found her answer a little strange. I felt as though she might have been hiding something. She answered, 'He had often said there was only one way out, but he had never attempted anything.'"

"One way out of what?" asked Mary. "They had already divorced by that time, hadn't they?"

"Yes, I think so."

"Look. There's the bit in the paper about your evidence," noticed Mary.

"Umm," remarked Frances, rather uninterested in the evidence she had given.

"Here! This is the part I was looking for," said Mary, and read directly from the paper. "PC Ballard said that in the bedroom he found a large envelope on which was written, 'It is now eleven-thirty. Where are you Mary?', and in the deceased's pocket he found a diary, in which there were numerous references to Mary."

Poor Mary looked horrified. "What on earth had he written about me?"

"They never read out any of its contents in court. Look, dear, if there was anything to link you to the Mary in the diary, don't you think you would have had a visit from the police by now?"

"I suppose you're right."

"You have nothing to worry about. The doctor at the inquest said that death was due to coal gas poisoning and that Fred had received psychiatric treatment in hospital on more than one occasion. The coroner said there was evidence Fred had a drink problem and other problems in his life. He was in no doubt that Fred was not responsible for his actions when he took his life and that the balance of his mind was disturbed. You have nothing to feel guilty about."

"I know you're right, but it's the note and the diary which have quite upset me."

"I understand. I think we should just put this behind us now and move on," said Frances as she gently took the newspaper from her friend and began to fold it up.

"I'm so sorry, Frances. This is all my fault. If I hadn't asked if Fred could stay at your house, none of this would be happening."

"Let's say no more on the matter. Agreed?"

"Agreed," replied Mary.

Frances remained at her home on Potley Hill Road until her own death, aged ninety-one. She and Mary remained friends and never spoke of Fred again.

Betty

Betty confidently strode out across the shingled beach armoured with pebbles. She was heading down towards the sea, where the tide was out, revealing golden sands. Western Beach wasn't too busy today with holiday makers and the temperature was pleasant enough for a paddle.

It was August 1955, and she had travelled here by car with her friends Molly and Richard, their children and Betty's eldest son, Rupert. She had left her other three children in the capable hands of her mother, who had been a godsend since she had moved in with them two years ago. Her mother had held them all together through the most terrible of times. She had kept them strong.

The heat from the sun in its perfect blue sky was like a blanket wrapping itself around Betty's body, comforting her and making her feel safe—the safest she'd felt in a very long time.

The pain she had been forced to endure at the hands of her husband, no one should have to suffer. How had she been so weak, falling for his artificial charms and false promises? She had been so young, and he had taken advantage of this fact. She could never forgive him for the things he had done.

It pained her to remember the things her husband had been accused of doing to their daughter. It made her feel physically sick to recall what Juliet had said her father had made her do. These things should never have happened to Juliet. It all was so terrible. Betty's only way through it all was to try to obliterate it from her mind. Today, she hoped, would help her to do that.

She was briefly distracted by shrieking noises from seagulls as they fought over some food high above her head. The constant rise and fall of the waves as they gently lapped the shoreline was relaxing and calming to her. The normality of the sounds around her allowed her to function like every other average human being on the beach because in some strange way they made her feel assured.

The distant voices of the holidaymakers as they enjoyed their time away from their usual routines, and the squeals from their children as they played at the water's edge, splashing one another and building sand castles, also left Betty feeling at peace. This was a feeling she thought she might never get to experience ever again.

As her feet met the seawater and became emerged, the initial shock from its cool temperature sent a surge through her body. Recapturing her breath, she turned back to look up the beach. It took her a moment, but squinting into the sun, she could just make out her good friends Richard and Molly sitting on deckchairs watching her. They were keeping a cautious eye on her. She waved to them, and they enthusiastically waved back. Rupert hadn't noticed her. Her son was too busy playing in the sand with Richard and Molly's two children.

What would she have done without Richard and Molly? They had helped and supported her so much over the past months. She knew she could never have got through it without them. They had always seemed to know what to do and how to make things better. While her life limped from one crisis to the next, they had always managed to stay calm and help her through it.

Molly was a good friend. Someone in whom Betty knew she could confide anything and it would go no further. She seemed to understand her; although how this was possible, she found difficult to fathom. She and Molly just seemed to know what the other was thinking and feeling. You might call it a sixth sense. But Molly had never suffered at the hands of her husband. Molly had found herself a reliable partner. Someone who truly loved her. Someone who wouldn't do anything to hurt her or her children.

Richard had been a tonic. When Betty had believed that all men were like Fred, it had been Richard who had shown her that wasn't true. He was kind, reassuring, honest and trustworthy, and had proved it to her time after time. Richard was the opposite of Fred. He was someone she could rely on. Someone who never expected anything from her in return and never had a hidden agenda for his actions. She knew exactly where she stood with Richard.

When Fred had first pleaded not guilty and was given bail, it had been Molly and Richard who had supported Betty. When there had been a chance that Juliet might have to give evidence and Betty had been beside herself with worry for her daughter, it had been Molly who had been there. Molly had comforted Betty during those darkest days.

Richard and Molly had been there for her last autumn as well, when Fred had turned up on their doorstep. Taking advice from Richard, she had begged Fred to do the right thing that day. Thankfully, when they had returned to court in the November, Fred had pleaded guilty. Their solicitors had agreed to accept his guilty plea to a lesser charge of indecent assault rather than incest on the understanding that he would give Betty a divorce.

Richard had accompanied her to each court hearing, while Molly had helped with the children. In the November, she had returned to court for Fred's sentencing, which had been postponed until December, so that his medical report could be accessed. Betty had left the court distraught that day, and Richard had supported her back to the car, where she had almost collapsed under the weight of her anxiety. She had assumed that that day would have put an end to it all.

When the following year she had signed her divorce papers, it had been Richard and Molly who had spurred her on, encouraging her to embrace the next chapter of her life. Betty's mother had also been there for her. She had been strong for Betty, but the situation had taken its toll on her. Betty had noticed her mother suffering. They were very alike in their opinions and their approach to life, and by some means during this terrible time they had managed to use this to their advantage, remaining strong. But it had been a constant battle to continue to be so resilient.

Betty had witnessed her mother's health decline again more recently, and her appearance had also begun to deteriorate. Her youthful looks which she had managed to hang onto late into her sixties had suddenly begun to vanish. She had aged dramatically, and Betty realised that soon it would be she who would need to look after her mother.

Betty had no idea from where she kept finding the inner strength to deal with her problems, but it was there and she was determined to use it for as long as it lasted. She refused to allow Fred to ruin the rest of her life. She and her children at last had the opportunity to enjoy an ordinary existence, which was all she had ever wanted for them. They all deserved to be happy, as none of them had ever done anything wrong. She knew this now.

Betty shook herself mentally. She must stop thinking about all of that now and enjoy her day out. After all, that was why she was here. It was definitely not to be thinking about Fred and everything he had put her through. What an excellent idea it had been of Molly's to visit the beach today.

***

Betty had forgotten how good it was to feel the sand between her toes and to feel free from the stresses and worries of life. It had been so awful for such a long time, that she had forgotten how to relax and enjoy life. Looking down into the salty water, she could see her fat toes as they wriggled in the soft sand. They sent out clouds of dust in all directions, drifting across the seabed as she moved them gently through the water. Soon she was knee-deep in the ocean—no longer feeling the coldness of the water against her skin—experiencing a sensation of pleasure, which was something else she had forgotten still existed. She continued for some minutes, heaving her legs forward through the water and causing the sand to swirl around her feet, careful not to go in too deep. Her mind drifted along with her body in no particular direction. It was enjoying its freedom, embracing the feeling of weightlessness.

Then the dark cloud descended over her again as her thoughts flipped back to Fred. How had her situation become so terrible? Where had it all gone wrong? Why had Fred done all of those terrible things? Had it been her fault, any of it? Could she have done anything differently? Perhaps she should have listened to her sister during the war, when Fred had first become difficult. Perhaps she should have listened to her father when he had said Fred was too old for her and had too many problems which she shouldn't have to deal with. Had it been the loss of his first wife, and then his son, which had triggered Fred's undesirable and inexcusable behaviour? But then, she thought they were happy when they had first got together, so was it really that? Or was it the war which had changed Fred? Had it been all the things he had witnessed—the things that he would never discuss with her—which had damaged him? Was it the army's fault?

Why was she still making excuses for him and his behaviour? Why was she still looking for answers to try to explain something which was never going to be explained? Why did she continue to try to justify what he had done? What was the matter with her? Fred was a bad person. That's all there was to it. It was no one's fault but his own. It was Fred, and Fred alone, who had been cruel and calculating, manipulative and controlling. She didn't want to think about it any longer. She was determined to enjoy today. She had nothing to worry about any longer. Today was going to be a good day. *Take your mind off him, Betty*, she told herself. *Go for a swim.*

Betty moved further out into the water, the invigorating sea eventually coming up to her waist. She experienced another surge through her whole body as the waves splashed her costume above her waist, followed by the strong and powerful emotion of being alive. She gently lay back into the water, gasping suddenly because of its chilly temperature, and allowed the sea to carry the weight of her body. She relaxed on her back as her body grew used to the cool water and gently drifted back and forth rhythmically with the tide. Her whole body tingled. Once she had become acclimatised to the water and its temperature, she turned herself over and began to swim breaststroke slowly through the water. She felt euphoric as she effortlessly made her way through the sea. Her body felt weightless and her mind free from her worries. All of her senses came alive. She could feel every movement her body made within the water. She observed each beam of light from the sun as it bounced off the heaving sea. She could smell the sea air as it mixed with the perfume she had applied behind her ears that morning. She could hear the other bathers squeal with delight as they too experienced the pleasures of the water and she could taste its salty spray on her lips as it splashed her in her face and hair.

Betty continued to swim for a few minutes longer, checking

intermittently that she was not straying too far from the shore by touching the sand with her toe. She didn't want to get out of her depth and find herself in difficulty, as she knew she wasn't a particularly strong swimmer. In places, the current felt stronger and she had to push her body to work harder in order to stop herself being dragged further away from the shore.

Suddenly, she felt a rush of panic. What if she lost control and found she had drifted out too far? What if the water became too deep for her to stand up in and she couldn't make it back? What would she do? She couldn't call for help. No one would hear her. If she waved, everyone would think she was waving to a friend. Dear Lord! What would become of the children? She headed back towards the beach while she was still able, taking comfort in noticing that Richard was still observing her movements.

When comfortable she was close enough again to the shore, Betty stopped swimming and stood up. The water came to just below her waist. It sloshed around her, gently rocking her back and forth and causing her to feel light-headed. Betty glanced towards the beach. A man was standing on the sand, directly in her line of sight and temporarily blocking her view of her friends and children. He stood out from the crowd because of the clothes he was wearing. The other holidaymakers were dressed in beachwear, but he was wearing a three-piece dark grey suit, complete with trilby hat, and a long overcoat slung over his right arm. He looked so out of place on the beach, that she couldn't help but notice him. As she continued to watch this man, it appeared he was heading straight towards her, his pace quickening the closer he got. It was at that moment, she realised this man, although clean-shaven, looked just like Fred. But it couldn't be Fred ... Could it?

Don't be stupid, Betty told herself. *Fred is dead.* She knew that. But the closer the man got, the more familiar he looked, and she began to convince herself that it was Fred.

"It can't be. It's not possible," she spoke out load. "Fred is dead. Fred is dead!" But no one could hear her.

Unexpectedly, Betty then experienced a sharp stabbing pain in her chest which was so intense that it caused her to instantly lose consciousness. Her upper body fell forwards in slow motion, her head gradually disappearing under the water as though she had stopped to look down at something. Once submerged, her whole body twisted and turned in the water, assisted by the movement of the current, which resulted in her toes appearing on the surface of the water.

Molly was playing with Rupert and her son at this time, while her daughter entertained herself with the doll she had brought along. Thankfully, Richard was witness to these events. He could clearly see that all was not as it should be with his friend. He jumped up and ran down the beach towards the water as quickly as he could; all the time, not taking his eye from the spot where Betty floated in the water. By now it was also becoming clear to others on the beach and in the water that something was wrong.

Molly, realising that something terrible must have happened because of the way her husband had raced off without saying anything, told the children to stay where they were and quickly followed the same route her husband had just taken.

Richard was breathless. He hadn't run like this for quite some time. His trousers became soaked as he waded into the sea to rescue his friend, reaching her before anyone else did. He placed one arm under Betty's knees and the other around her back and under one arm, then he lifted. Betty's body was flaccid. It appeared she was not breathing. He headed out of the sea, kicking up and splashing water as he went.

"Fetch an ambulance, would you!" Richard shouted to a suit-wearing member of the small crowd which had started to gather on the sand.

"I'll go!" shouted another bystander, sprinting off at speed.

Just at that moment, Molly appeared at her husband's side.

"What's happened? Is she all right?" she asked.

"Not sure," replied Richard as he knelt and placed Betty gently down on the sand.

The curiously dressed man turned and walked away, the overcoat across his arm flapping back and forth in the breeze as he went.

"Betty, dear. Can you hear me?" asked Molly kindly. She was leaning in close to her friend, attempting to listen for her breathing. There was no response.

After what felt like an age, a policeman appeared at their side. "Let me through, please," he asked the now-much-larger crowd. "And would you all please move back."

The constable could instantly see that Betty had stopped breathing and began to give her artificial respiration. He checked inside her mouth to make sure she had nothing inside obstructing her breathing then began compressions to her chest. He continued to do this for several minutes while Richard and Molly looked on helplessly. Molly might have tried herself to give Betty artificial respiration if she hadn't been suffering from shock at the sight of her poor, dear, unconscious friend.

Richard

————◇————

During the Second World War Richard had been a second lieutenant in the King's Royal Rifle Corps. For a short time at the end of the war he had been held prisoner by the Japanese at Ubon, Thailand. Although his stay at the camp had not been particularly enjoyable, it had been the waiting around for a month after the war was over that had been the most frustrating. Like many others, he had suffered with various tropical diseases, and when eventually released had been transported to a hospital in England for treatment. This was where he had met Molly.

Born in Ireland and eight years his senior, Molly had trained as a nurse. After the war their paths had crossed when Molly helped nurse him back to health in a London hospital. A proposal of marriage had quickly followed. They tied the knot in early 1946, in the Hampshire village of Brambleton, where Richard's family lived. They travelled to Italy with Richard's work, and in the December of the following year Molly gave birth to a son. It was after this event, that Richard and Molly made the decision to come back to England. To begin with they had moved into the Lodge House, next to Richard's parents' more grandiose house.

In May 1949 Richard and Molly had a daughter. She was baptised at St Mary's Church in the village in July. At this time Richard was working in the textile industry, and on occasion could be away from home, working abroad. When his children were three and five years old, their grandfather had become ill and Richard had moved them all into the big house to be close to his parents. After a long illness, Richard's father died in June 1953.

Some months before this event, a new army family moved into the area. Having moved back to England from Germany, they set up home in the village at White Gates, where a fellow army officer and friend,

Dereck, and wife, Peggy, lived. Peggy's sister and her children also lived at the house, and Richard and Molly were good friends with them all. Richard and Molly were introduced to this new couple and their four children. They appeared pleasant enough, and everyone seemed to get along.

Richard and Molly were informed that Fred had recently served in Germany and his wife Betty had at one time worked as a beauty consultant. She and Molly got along well, and three of Betty's children were of a similar age to Richard and Molly's children, so they began seeing quite a lot of one another. Richard tolerated Fred. He found him to be overly self-assured. He gave everyone the impression that he knew everything there was to know about everything and everyone. This prevented Richard from wanting to spend any great length of time in his company. Fred was too sure of himself for Richard's liking.

Richard was a very private man and had never warmed to this type of character. He also disliked the amount of alcohol Fred was able to consume in one evening. Whenever Fred had a drink, he became even more obnoxious. Molly didn't appear to have a problem with Fred, as he could be very charming with the ladies, so in the beginning Richard had kept his feelings about Fred to himself.

Richard and Molly had not known the family long when Betty invited them to her children's baptisms in August 1952. They were to be held at the same village church that their own daughter had been baptised in four years earlier. It was a glorious summer's day, but they had been surprised not to see Fred attend. When Molly enquired as to his whereabouts, Betty informed her that Fred had moved out, but she had not explained why.

Speaking to Richard after the ceremony, Molly explained, "Betty didn't tell me why Fred had left, which is understandable. It's a very private matter and none of my business, but I can tell she's keeping a secret and I suspect it isn't a pleasant secret. Each time I've seen her recently, she has looked more troubled. The poor woman clearly has a great deal on her mind."

"Do you think he's been hitting her?" asked Richard.

"No. I don't think that. Whatever gave you that idea?"

"I'm not sure really. Can't say I've ever warmed to the man."

"No?"

"No. I find him rather annoying if I'm honest."

"My guess is that he's been unfaithful," suggested Molly. "He's never disguised the fact that he likes the attention of other women."

"True."

"I'm sure it will all come out eventually, when Betty is ready. In the meantime I intend to give her as much support as I can. It's not going to be easy for her on her own with four children."

"No, I dare say it's not," agreed Richard.

Richard and Molly were left to ponder this event for some time. Their friends, Dereck, Peggy and Barbara, kept any information they had about the couple to themselves. Although Richard and Molly felt a little left out, they respected everyone's privacy and did not wish to pressure any of their friends during what was clearly a difficult period.

***

The following year was difficult for everyone. Betty was to contend with going through a difficult divorce and Richard lost his father in the June, after a long illness. His father had suffered since the beginning of the year, and Richard had described the last couple of months of his father's life to Molly as a 'waiting game'. His father's behaviour had become very strange towards the end of his life, which was very out of character for the strong, independent man they all knew and loved. He repeatedly insisted that he saw a man at his window, then a man in his room. No one else ever saw this man, and when the doctor was informed, he concluded that Richard's father was suffering from delirium—a condition which was causing his father's brain to rapidly deteriorate.

They were all terribly upset about having to watch a man they all loved, who was once both strong in character and physically fit, wither away slowly and painfully. *Life can be so cruel and unjust*, thought Richard. When his father endured a fall while alone in the garden one day and it resulted in his death a week later, Richard suffered the most terrible feelings of guilt for having left his father unattended.

Before the year had passed, and with the departure of Dereck and

Peggy from the village, due to a new army posting, Betty confided more in Molly. She informed her that she and Fred were getting a divorce and the reason why. Molly was horrified by what Betty told her. Of all the different scenarios Molly had puzzled over, the real reason for Fred's departure had never come close to her thinking. Richard too was appalled and outraged by Fred's behaviour. He had always known that he disliked the man, and now he knew why.

"We must concentrate on Betty and the children now," said Molly. "Is there anything we can do to help them? What do you think, Richard?"

"I have absolutely no idea, Molly. I guess all you can do is let her know we will be here for her if ever she needs us."

"I've already told her that."

"Then just be her friend."

Richard could see a change in Betty, and he knew it would take her a great deal of time to feel anything like ordinary again. Fred's behaviour had taken a great toll on her. In an attempt to give her children a fresh start, Betty moved to a new house, a little up the road from Richard and Molly. Her mother also joined Betty and the children, and she was quickly introduced to Richard and Molly, who found Eliza very pleasant.

Richard noticed that Betty's confidence began to improve daily once her mother had arrived. They shared the household chores and the care of the children, and having her mother around enabled Betty to feel calmer. Betty and the children's lives started to improve. They began to heal and could start to feel more optimistic about life.

During this period, Molly and Betty saw more of one another and became much closer. Betty shared with Molly the few infrequent letters which Fred had written to her and she often asked Molly for advice. Molly would later share these conversations with Richard to reaffirm that she had given Betty suitable guidance. They all agreed that it was best if Betty did not answer Fred's letters, and if she chose not to even read them—destroying them instead—then that was up to her. At this time Fred had not realised that Betty had moved house and continued to address his letters to her at White Gates. Barbara kindly passed them on to Betty, but was careful never to enquire after their contents.

Betty informed Molly that she was unable to destroy any of Fred's letters and always read what he'd written. She explained how he had never once asked about how she or the children were. His letters only contained what *he* was doing, the treatment *he* was receiving, the work *he* might be getting or the places *he* was living.

Whether it was because she had never replied to his letters, or that he would have chosen to visit her anyway, Fred appeared in the village one blustery autumnal day in 1954. When he discovered that Betty was no longer living at White Gates, he turned up on Richard and Molly's doorstep in search of her. It just so happened that Betty was inside the house with Molly at the time. Richard had been out, and afterwards, when Molly had informed him of Fred's visit, he was glad he had not been at home. He was afraid he may have done something he would have regretted. Molly suggested that Betty speak to Fred inside her house, but Betty didn't want to invite Fred in and chose to keep him at arm's length on the doorstep. There was not a chance she was taking him across the road to her house, where her mother and children were. Richard was relieved to hear this.

Betty told Molly later that she was convinced Fred had been drinking. She could smell it on him. He was slurring his words and was unable to stand still. She assumed he had probably needed a drink to pluck up the courage and had spent longer than intended at the pub, building up enough strength to speak to her. He looked poorly and extremely malnourished. It was clear he was very nervous about making the visit, so Betty did everything she could, not to upset or antagonise him.

Of course, she knew why he was there. It was always the same with Fred. He claimed he had changed. He told her he'd had some treatment, he was cured, he missed her and he wanted her back. She'd heard it all before, but nothing had changed. Not for Fred anyway. "If you won't have me back, there's only one way out for me, isn't there?" he'd threatened her. But she thought it was just a threat.

When Fred had finally left, Betty told Molly some of what had been discussed. "He told me he's completed another lot of treatment at a hospital in Kent. Then he begged me to take him back."

"He just doesn't give up, does he? You did well, Betty. I'm not sure I

SARAH LYSAGHT

could have kept as calm as you did."

Betty relayed the same story to Richard when he arrived home later that afternoon. "I asked him if he was working at the moment, knowing full well he wouldn't be; not least from the look of him."

"What was his answer?" enquired Richard.

"He said he'd not got a regular job at the moment but expected to have one soon. He went on to tell me about a friend of his who'd mentioned to him that there might be some work going in a factory that makes sweets. I don't expect anything will come of it."

"Umm. Did he ask you to take him back?"

"Begged me."

"How did you get rid of him?" asked Richard.

"I just told him that if he found a proper job, I might consider it."

Richard raised his eyebrows.

"Don't worry, darling. She just said that to get rid of him," reassured Molly.

The year 1955 showed more promise for Betty, when it had begun with a wedding. She had popped over very excited one crisp January morning to inform Richard and Molly that her sister was getting married in a week's time.

"You remember Marie?"

"Of course, although we only spoke briefly at the baptism," recalled Molly. Richard and his wife had both commented later on how close the two sisters had seemed.

"But she hadn't met her husband-to-be back then," Betty informed them.

"What's he like?" enquired Molly.

Betty knew why her friend was asking and what she was wondering. "I've not met him yet, but he sounds nothing like Fred, you'll be pleased to hear."

"I'm sorry Betty. I wasn't—"

"I know," Betty smiled.

"What does he do for a living, Betty?" asked Richard in an attempt to lighten the dark mood which appeared to have descended upon them at the mere mention of Fred's name.

"He's a composer, and by all accounts a rather distinguished one—celebrated even. Marie sounds so happy and excited," smiled Betty.

"We're very happy for her, aren't we, Molly?"

"Of course. And for you, Betty. You deserve something good in your life at last."

"Mother and I would like to go to the wedding. And we'd like to take Juliet and Rupert. Marie has asked if Juliet and I will be bridesmaids."

"How wonderful," smiled Molly.

"Would you be able to look after Anne and Freddie for us?"

"Of course. They'll be just fine here with our two."

"It's a week on Saturday."

"That's perfect. Don't worry about Anne and little Freddie. They'll be quite happy with us, won't they, Richard?"

"Oh, we'll get up to no good. You can be sure of that," grinned Richard.

"Thank you. I don't know what I'd do without you two."

"Off you go then," insisted Molly with tears in her eyes. She was so happy for her friend. It was about time she had some good news. "I suspect you've got a hundred and one things to sort out before next weekend."

In March Betty and her mother were still relishing the family wedding they had recently attended, relaying to Richard and Molly the many things they had seen and done that day. They shared photographs and discussed the society people they had been introduced to. However, not long after this Betty's world came crashing down around her once more when she received a visit from the local constable informing her and her mother that Fred had taken his own life.

Once again Fred was to throw Betty's life into chaos. The poor woman was beside herself, not knowing which way to turn as she staggered across the road to Richard and Molly's house.

"He's gone and killed himself," were her first words to Richard and Molly. But they knew instantly as to whom she was referring. "They need me to identify his body and attend the inquest at Maidstone tomorrow," Betty continued as tears spilled from her eyes.

"I'll take you," offered Richard.

"It's over a hundred miles away, Richard," worried Betty.

"It would take you twice as long if you went by train," suggested Molly.

"I'm so sorry to cause you this trouble. You've both been so good to me already."

"It's absolutely no trouble. The old girl could do with a good run out," announced Richard. Molly shot Richard a look of astonishment and he quickly followed this up with, "The car! I was referring to the car."

A moment of silence ensued, then all three of them burst into laughter, which sliced through the sense of hopelessness which had previously filled the room.

"We will need to start out early tomorrow morning," announced Richard.

"Would you help Mother with the children, Molly?" Betty asked.

"Of course, dear. You don't need to worry about them." She paused. "Have you told them about their father?"

"I don't know what to say to them. It's all just too terrible. I didn't think he could do anything else to hurt us, but just as we were getting some normality back into our lives, he manages to smack us all cruelly with one final blow."

"*Coup de grâce*," said Richard. Both women turned to look at him, unaware as to the meaning of what he had just said. "Never mind," added Richard. It was not worth explaining.

The journey to Maidstone was long, and on the way home Betty had fallen asleep in Richard's car, completely drained by the day's events. Identifying Fred's body had proved too traumatic for Betty. Richard had gone in with her for support, but she had found herself unable to even briefly glance at her husband and pretended to do this. She confirmed to the coroner that it was Fred, then they exited the room as quickly as possible. "It was him, wasn't it?" she asked Richard once outside.

"Yes, Betty. It was him." Richard had made sure of it and taken a good look.

Afterwards Betty was forced to explain to the coroner the reasons for her divorce. She was asked about Fred's time in the army and about the last time she had seen him, when he had turned up at Richard's house. Betty explained that they had corresponded on occasions, and that had been how she had learned he'd been in and out of jobs. The coroner had then asked Betty if Fred had ever threatened to take his life. She had replied, saying that he had often said there was only one way out, but he had never attempted anything.

Richard had never known a woman who had had to endure so much suffering at the hands of one man. He glanced across at his friend as she slept, her head resting on the window of his car. She was one of the strongest women he had ever met. He just hoped that from today onwards she would at last be able to put her life with Fred behind her and enjoy happier times.

***

By the summer of 1955 Molly and Betty were seeing one another almost on a daily basis. Richard and Molly's children got along well with Betty's children, and this made for congenial days out and gatherings. The two families were constantly back and forth between one another's homes, and everyone was happy with this arrangement—most of all the children. They had the freedom to visit each other as often as they liked, their mothers never worrying about them at all. The boys played constantly with their wooden Tommy guns or Airfix Spitfires, while the girls enjoyed their many dolls and the swing in Richard and Molly's garden. It had been during this summer, that Betty had helped Juliet find some work over the school holidays in one of the grocery stores in the village.

The danger which had once been there was no longer around, and Richard could see that Betty was now a different person—able to enjoy life once more. Her mother, Eliza, had been a godsend, allowing Betty the freedom to rediscover herself, and Molly and Richard had also played a big part in this. Betty and Molly would occasionally use Richard's car if he were at home and take themselves off on a shopping expedition. Richard was happy with this, and also to be left with the children in the evenings, enabling the women to attend WI (Women's Institute) or church events.

Molly often spoke to Richard about the difference she now saw in her friend, but she was still unable to fathom how one man could have had such a negative impact on her friend's previous behaviour. The subject of Fred was usually avoided, but he did occasionally come up in conversation. It was usually the children who asked after him, as they were too young to understand the devastation their father had caused to his family. On these occasions the subject was swiftly and seamlessly changed, and thankfully Betty was now able to cope with these brief queries and interruptions to her family routine.

Richard had endured a particularly busy time recently at work. He was due a break, so Molly suggested they go out for the day with the children. "The weather forecast looks good for the weekend. We could take a picnic to the coast. I could ask Betty if she'd like to come along."

"That sounds lovely, dear. Some fresh sea air will do us all the world of good," agreed Richard, who had been feeling rather tired recently.

"I'll find out who wants to come along, then I'll know what to buy from the shops for a picnic."

"We might not get everyone in the car if they all want to come," interrupted Richard as his wife was in a rush to organise her plans.

"We could fit two or three more in though, couldn't we?"

"As long as people don't mind sitting on each other's laps. It's about fifteen miles away, darling. People won't want to be feeling cramped for too long."

"Leave it with me," said Molly, and she soon disappeared to see Betty.

In the end it turned out that only Betty and Rupert were joining them for the car journey to the coast. Eliza was to stay behind with Betty's two youngest children and Juliet had planned to spend the day with one of her school friends. Their journey by car to the coast that sunny August day was not uncomfortable, and there was plenty of room for the enormous amount of picnic food, rugs, towels, bathing costumes and buckets and spades which Molly had packed.

Having arrived and parked the car, the party made their way down onto the beach, struggling to carry the countless items Molly had chosen to bring with them. They hired three deckchairs and found a spot they were all happy with, then made themselves comfortable for the duration. Rupert, along with Richard's two children, immediately began to make sandcastles and dig holes. They attempted to build a moat around their structures, helped by Richard, who encouraged them to keep going back to the sea to fill up their buckets with water in order to fill in the moat.

Each time they did, the water would soak away into the sand and he'd tell them to quickly fetch some more. Each time, they disappeared at speed—returning to the water's edge—and the adults would laugh at their children's foolishness.

"Johnathan's going to realise in a minute, Richard, and then you'll be in for it," Molly laughed. Sure enough it was his son who questioned his father's motives before anyone else, but it did take him longer than his mother had thought it would. They all laughed about it when the children realised they had been getting nowhere fast, and then Johnathan suggested they all bury his father in the sand. Richard was game for this, instructing them for the next half an hour about how they would need to make their hole much bigger if he were going to be able to fit into it.

All this time Molly and Betty chatted and relaxed. Everyone was having a great time, including Richard, who by now was up to his chest in sand. When the children decided they'd had enough of burying him, they ran off to paddle in the sea.

"Don't wander too far," shouted Molly.

"And don't let the water go higher than your knees," instructed Betty.

"You can't just leave me here like this," Richard shouted after them. "Help! Help!" he pretended as the children ran off in giggles.

They all enjoyed their picnic lunch, and afterwards the children played close by while the adults had a snooze. Around an hour after lunch, Betty said she was going to brave the sea temperatures and go for a swim. "The children have said it's nice and warm," she told Richard.

"They would. They only put their toes into it."

"Oh well. I think I'll give it a go. Are you all right to watch Rupert for me?" she asked Molly.

"Of course. You go and enjoy yourself. You're braver than I am."

Richard and Molly watched as Betty made her way down the beach to the water's edge. She turned back to them and waved. They both waved back at her. Molly became distracted by the children and started playing with them, but Richard kept his eye on Betty, watching her go further into the water, yet not out of her depth. He continued to observe her as she intermittently floated on her back for a time then began to swim on her front.

After some time, Betty stood up in the water and looked towards the beach. Then in slow motion she fell forward, her head going under the water. It took Richard a couple of seconds to register that his friend was in trouble, then, jumping up, he raced down the beach towards her. When he finally reached Betty, he lifted her lifeless body out of the water and instructed an onlooker to fetch an ambulance. A few moments later Molly realised something was wrong and joined Richard at the water's edge.

"What's happened? Is she all right?" she asked.

"Not sure," replied Richard as he knelt and placed Betty gently down onto the hot sand.

"Betty, dear. Can you hear me?" asked Molly, now leaning in close to her friend. There was no response. She didn't know what to do. All of her nursing knowledge seemed to have escaped her.

A policeman was called, and he gave Betty artificial respiration. Then a doctor and an ambulance arrived at the beach, but by the time they got there, Betty was dead. Everyone had done what they could to help, but it was no use.

Richard and Molly did what they could to console Rupert, but the poor child sobbed all the way home in the car. When they informed Eliza of her daughter's unexpected death, she was completely stunned and quickly went into shock. Molly acted swiftly this time and put her nursing training into practice, lying Eliza down on the floor before she fell there.

Because Betty's death was sudden and unexpected, there had to be an inquest. Richard was asked to give evidence. He was her good friend and had been the one who had brought her out from the water. During the inquest, Richard was asked to explain how he knew the deceased.

"I've known Betty for three or four years."

Asked how the deceased had seemed that day, Richard replied, "She was quite normal and cheerful that afternoon and went in for a bathe by herself while I sat on the beach and watched. She swam about for a few minutes, never out of her depth," he stated, "and then swam back towards the beach."

He was finding it increasingly difficult to give his evidence as the memories of that terrible day played over in his mind again and again. From somewhere, Richard found the strength to continue. "She then appeared to stand up and put her face in the water, as if she had either seen something on the bottom or was wetting her hair. The next thing I noticed was that her feet were on the surface, and that was when I realised something was wrong. I ran down the beach to the sea and brought her out."

The policeman who gave Betty artificial respiration on the beach was also there to give his evidence and explain how he had applied artificial respiration to Betty for several minutes without success. "A doctor and an ambulance had been called, but the woman was already dead," he concluded.

During the inquest, Betty's sister, Marie, also gave evidence of identification and explained how she had not seen Betty for a number of months. She told the coroner that Betty suffered from a heart condition. This came as a complete surprise to Richard.

Later a pathologist stated that the immediate cause of death was drowning, "but the deceased had suffered from a heart condition, which might have been a contributory factor towards explaining her sudden loss of consciousness." Why had she never mentioned her heart condition to them? Richard wondered.

The coroner concluded, "It is clear that had it not been for her heart condition, the accident would never have happened. We shall never know what really happened. It may have been a momentary seizure."

Richard felt his eyes welling up with tears. How would he tell Molly that if they had known, they might have been able to prevent it?

A verdict of accidental death was recorded.

Richard and Molly attended Betty's funeral a couple of days later, devastated by her loss and overwhelmed by their guilt. How much tragedy was one family expected to endure in such a short space of time?

"Those poor darling children. Have they not been through enough?" Molly sobbed in Richard's arms. He held his wife close and thanked God that she and his children were all fit and well. He wouldn't know what to do if anything ever happened to any of them.

"We have to be strong and stay positive for the children now, Molly," Richard reassured his wife. "And what will become of them with no mother and no father?"

"They still have their grandmother to care for them. She's doing an excellent job. And we will continue to help. Betty would have wanted that."

"Yes, she would." Molly began sobbing once more. She would miss her friend terribly.

Marie

———◆———

Temperatures had been warmer than usual for March in 1957, but today it was raining, adding to everyone's discomfort and distress. In the graveyard of St Mary's, Marie's father stood on one side of her and her husband on the other as her mother's coffin was gently lowered. Both were attempting to support Marie—not only emotionally, but also physically. She was shaking, her legs had turned to jelly and she felt as helpless as a lamb. Her father and husband had both witnessed the effect these past years had had on her. They knew they must remain strong for her, especially today.

This is all Fred's fault, she thought. Marie still hated Fred. Really hated him. It made her feel ill to even think about him. How dare he still make her feel this way. She couldn't comprehend how she could detest another human being so vehemently. Why did she still despise him? Even now, after he'd been dead for two years, she still hated him for what he'd done, and was still doing, to her family. Because of Fred's actions, people were still suffering.

Marie was convinced that her mother's death was a direct result of all the suffering Fred had caused her family. The strain that monster had put on her sister's heart, and now her mother too had succumbed. It was all just too much for her to bear.

Marie needed to be physically supported as she stood over her mother's grave. She stared deep into the ground at her mother's coffin. If her father and husband had not been holding her up, she may well have fallen in beside her mother. Hadn't it been a mere eighteen months ago that they had all stood together in this exact spot and buried Betty? She could hardly believe she was back here again, and so soon. She suspected that Richard and Molly, who were standing opposite her on the other side of her mother's grave, were most likely having exactly the same thoughts.

The children—all but Juliet—quietly sobbed, clinging on to one another. They had loved Marie's mother immensely and had depended greatly on their granny after their mother had died. Each took a turn to throw a single flower down onto the coffin lid. They had chosen them that morning, when Marie had walked with them into the village to the florist's shop. Rupert, Freddie and Anne had all chosen white lilies, but Juliet had gone for a blue delphinium. Now, Juliet hesitated before throwing her flower into the grave. It broke Marie's heart every time she thought of the children. They didn't deserve any of this. What would become of them now?

After the funeral they all went back to the house. There were the seven of them, as well as Richard and Molly and their children. Molly had popped home for the children because they hadn't wanted them to attend the funeral, and now they were playing with Marie's nephews and nieces at the back of the house. Richard and Molly sat chatting to Marie's father Vincent and husband Raymond in the more comfortable front room.

Marie busied herself in the modest kitchen, making tea, slicing cake, arranging sandwiches on plates and then offering them around between her younger guests. It wasn't long before Molly came to find her.

"Will you join us in the front room, Marie?"

"I'd rather keep myself busy. The children have the appetites of elephants."

"It's the children we thought we ought to talk about," she whispered.

"I see. All right then. Does everyone in there have a cup of tea?"

"Yes. We're all fine, thank you, dear."

"I'll just pour myself one and be right in."

Discussing the children and their futures was something she knew she had to do and had been putting off. What in heaven's name was going to become of them now?

The discussion began in a relaxed manner, with Richard leading it, and it continued in that vein. Being impartial, he was able to keep a clear head and allow everyone their opinion. She knew he wanted the best for her sister's children. They were all given a chance to say what they thought. No one disagreed with any suggestions made by anyone else, and within half an hour they had all managed to reach an agreeable decision.

The decision had been made in the best interests of the children, but making it had not been easy. The children's lives were to change forever again, and they had done nothing to deserve this continued disruption and upheaval. They were all completely innocent in all of this but deemed too young to make their own decisions, so their family were forced to make it for them.

Vincent explained how he was desperate to help but didn't think he would be able to look after his four grandchildren. When he finally confessed that he had been secretly living with another woman for a number of years and now that he was officially a widow would have the freedom to marry her, Marie was a little taken aback. She did not blame her father, as she knew her parents' relationship had broken down many years earlier. She accepted what her father told her because he confirmed this woman made him very happy.

"We have a little money saved up. It would be unfair to ask her to take on four children. As company director I need to travel abroad on occasions. You know that," he said, looking at Marie. "The children need someone who will always be at home for them, and I'm not getting any younger. Even if I retire soon, I would probably not have the energy needed to keep up with them all. They seem to be growing so quickly."

"Father, you don't have to justify your reasons to me. Raymond and I also feel unable to care for the children. We live in a small, one-bedroom flat in the centre of London, so we don't have the space. We too have important jobs which take us away from home for long hours, and we too often travel abroad. We could not give the children all they need. It pains me to admit it, but it's true."

"The way I see it is that we need to find them a new family. Preferably one where the couple have no children of their own but would be prepared to take on four at the same time," said Richard in a low voice, so as not to be overheard. He too wanted the best for the children.

"That's a big commitment, Richard," commented Molly.

"Yes, I know, dear."

"I think it is important not to split them up; don't you, Father?" exclaimed Marie.

"In an ideal world, my darling, yes, I would agree."

Richard had a thought. "I may just know the perfect couple," he quietly interrupted. "There's a chap I know from my army days called Pete. He and his wife have never had any children, but that wasn't their choice. They have plenty of money and a big house in the country. I think they'd be perfect." Everyone nodded in agreement.

"We'd have to go through the correct channels, of course. Pete's a bit of a stickler for doing things properly. I know he would want it done legally through the courts," continued Richard. Once again everyone nodded in agreement with Richard's suggestion. "All right then. I'll contact Pete tomorrow and we'll take it from there."

***

That evening, after Marie had settled the children and then joined Raymond in bed, thoughts of the past came flooding back to her. She couldn't sleep. It was strange not being in her own bed. It was even stranger being in her sister and mother's house without them being there.

After Raymond had given her a cuddle, he quietly sang to her, hoping it would enable Marie to relax enough to get to sleep. When he'd finished, he kissed her goodnight and was soon sleeping soundly, while she was still running through past events over and over in her head.

It was no use thinking 'If only Betty had never laid eyes on Fred'. It was no use thinking 'If only her father had never employed him'. It was no use thinking 'If only Fred had been killed in the war'. Even though she really did wish all of those things.

Marie missed her sister and her mother terribly. They had all been so close. If she didn't have Raymond, she didn't know what she would have done. Marie was unable to change what had happened. It was all too late. Silent tears ran from her eyes, trickling over her cheeks before dripping onto her pillow.

Marie tried to think about the happier times she had shared with Betty. Predictably, these had been during the war, when Fred had been away. They had only themselves to consider at this time, and little Juliet of course. Marie and her parents had moved to the country at the start of the war. Having turned eighteen, she moved back to London in 1942 to be with Betty and Juliet when Fred had joined the war effort. Marie and her sister relied upon each other a great deal during this time.

Although they had lived in constant fear of a bomb being dropped on them, Marie and Betty were happy. Marie would rush home after work to care for Juliet, allowing Betty to leave in time for *her* work. She had adored her little niece. She would often take her out for long walks in her pram in order to allow Betty time to tidy up or just put her feet up for half an hour.

As Juliet had got older, Betty and Marie found time and took a picnic to the park or visited London Zoo. London Zoo had been closed multiple times during the war, due to bomb damage, but it had always been a great day out, especially when Betty had gone along as well.

Marie had played for hours on the floor in Betty's flat with Juliet and her dolls. Teddy bears and dolls of all shapes and sizes would be collected from every orifice of the flat; all carefully placed upon a checked tablecloth and given pretend tea in cups and make-believe cake on plates. Betty would often enter the flat to find Marie playing with her daughter, both giggling together, and join them on the floor in their imaginative play.

Marie recalled how Juliet had them both on their hands and knees one afternoon pretending to be horses as she took it in turns to ride on their backs and have a race. All three of them had ended up on their backs in hysterics when Betty had crashed into the table leg and sent all the tea things crashing down.

Marie was very fond of all her nieces and nephews, but she had always had a special bond with Juliet. She loved them all so very much, and it would break her heart if they could not find them a family in which they would be well cared for and loved as much as her sister and mother had loved them.

Her thoughts turned quickly to Fred again. Marie's first recollection of him had been the evening he had hammered on the door of her family's home. His behaviour had frightened her that night, and she supposed most days since. Perhaps this should have been a sign of things to come, but she had been sixteen back then and had little experience of the world. How could she have known how everything would turn out?

After that initial evening, she remembered the rest of her family becoming very serious and gloomy for a time. This must have been when Betty and her father had gone to the inquest into Fred's first wife's death. Again there was a warning sign, but none of them had spotted it. Marie dwelled on this time for a moment, trying to recall those events and the facts surrounding that woman's death. *It's all too horrid* she thought. *I can't think about that now.*

Marie turned her attention to how happy her sister was in the year before the war, when her parents had come round to the idea of Betty marrying Fred and when Fred had agreed to marry at the family's church. In the months leading up to Betty's wedding, the two sisters had discussed every minute detail of the day, so that it would be perfect.

Marie had never seen her sister as euphoric as she was on her wedding day. Betty asked Marie to be her bridesmaid, and both had looked stunning as they'd walked down the aisle of St Peter's towards Fred and Alan beside the altar. Marie had always thought her sister would marry Alan, who had grown up on the same street as they—a boy she had known since her schooldays. He had always shown a great interest in her sister. When his family later moved house and Alan was completing his training at the hospital to become a chemist, he had continued to visit her father's salon most weeks to catch a glimpse of Betty. They had even gone out a couple of times to the cinema, but Betty had always insisted they were just good friends.

Marie had been a little surprised when Betty had invited Alan to her wedding, and even more surprised when she discovered she'd asked him to be Fred's best man. Alan was still infatuated with Betty and obviously found her difficult to refuse. He was a witness and signed the marriage register in the vestry alongside Marie, much to Fred's disgust. Marie believed that Betty had thought the two of them would get along. But her sister could not have been more wrong. Although Alan made every effort to be friends with Fred, Marie was sure he only did this for Betty's sake. It was obvious to her that Fred wanted nothing to do with Alan. She suspected he was jealous of Alan, but said nothing to her sister, as she didn't wish to spoil her day.

A couple of years after her sister's marriage, Marie discovered that Fred had instructed Betty never to see Alan. It had been Alan who had told Marie this. Apparently, he had turned up at the house one day and Betty had appeared rather upset and wouldn't let him in. Alan asked Marie not to mention anything to Betty. He didn't want to cause Betty any more problems, and from then on he had stayed away from her and Fred.

In January 1941 Betty had told Marie the devastating news that Alan had been killed. It had been Fred who had broken it to Betty, and he had appeared to take pleasure in announcing Alan's death. Fred told her that Alan had been on his way home from work at the hospital when a German bomb had been dropped above the Underground station where Alan had been travelling on a train. Reports in the paper said he had died instantly. Many other people had been killed in and around the Underground that day. It had been all over the news. Alan's family were devastated. Betty and Marie had both sent flowers to Alan's mother and secretly, unbeknown to Fred, had attended Alan's funeral. They had both chosen never to mention this to Fred.

When the war had reached its conclusion and Fred had finally returned home, he had immediately started to make Marie's life difficult. The situation quickly escalated, and it was clear to Marie that Fred did not want her around. When Fred was asked to vacate the property in which they all lived, it had forced Marie into finding other accommodation as well. But this suited her by then. She didn't know how Betty could stand to be around the man. She found Fred quite repulsive most of the time.

After that it seemed to Marie that Fred was unable to stay anywhere for any great length of time. He had a knack of upsetting people and deciding on a whim that he'd had enough of somewhere, then he just moved. He thought nothing of packing in his job if he didn't like it or uprooting his family just as they had settled somewhere. She was thankful, however, that although he had moved her sister around a great deal, she had remained local enough for the two of them to continue to see each other regularly.

***

I really must try and get some sleep thought Marie. But it was no use. Thoughts of Fred would not leave her mind. She recalled the time when Fred had found himself a job with the army again and insisted Betty move with him to Germany. Marie did not know if she would ever see her sister again. Fred had been determined to split them up. In her opinion, Fred thought she and Betty had become too close while he had been away. First he'd driven Marie out of the house, and then, because the sisters had remained in regular contact, he decided to move his family away to live abroad; his goal being, Marie now realised, to isolate Betty from anyone and everyone she cared about—other than him.

Betty was too clever for Fred. She had kept in regular contact with Marie all the time she had been in Germany. Her early secret letters had always sounded positive. She rarely mentioned Fred and what he was doing in any of her correspondence. They usually discussed Juliet and Rupert: how well Juliet was getting on at school and how she had picked up the local dialect and how Rupert had started walking. She would describe the area where they lived and the local town and explain how the inhabitants were all very friendly towards the officers and their wives. On occasion Betty would mention the army complex in which she lived and how she disliked having to attend the evening functions the army organised, which Fred always insisted she accompany him to. She had usually included in her letters a picture drawn by Juliet, and Marie had treasured these drawings and kept them all safe. She still had them somewhere.

For the majority of the time her sister had been in Germany, she had been pregnant. No sooner had she arrived in the country, she discovered she was going to have another baby and had shared her news and concerns in a letter to Marie. There was little excitement between them, as they both worried about Betty's health during this time. Marie was confused as to whether she was more relieved her sister had not told Fred about her weak heart or more concerned she hadn't told him. It was a huge relief to both Marie and Betty when after the birth of Anne both mother and baby were declared healthy.

Two months after her sister's third child had been born, Betty wrote saying that she had discovered she was pregnant again. Marie knew this must have been Fred's intention, as her sister could not have wished this to have happened again so soon. The two sisters were forced to endure another nine months of worry. Marie tried to keep her letters to Betty reassuring and positive, but it was difficult. She had been hugely relieved when a couple of months after giving birth to Freddie, Betty returned to England.

While her sister had been abroad, her later letters had read very differently from the earlier ones, and it appeared to Marie that Betty was unhappy. Some of these letters had contained information that clearly concerned Marie. Betty mentioned that she was always feeling tired and having to care for her four young children was a strain, as she received no help from Fred. He had started drinking again and at times was making her life impossible.

Then Betty's letters had suddenly stopped without warning, and Marie suspected that Fred had found out about them and put a stop to them. She had later asked Betty about this, and it was true. Fred had intercepted almost all of her later letters and read them, confronting her about them. Betty had told her his drinking had become even worse after this. Marie had also asked her sister what had happened to the letters she had sent. Betty had confessed that she had burnt all of Marie's letters immediately after reading them, so that Fred wouldn't discover them. The emotional anxiety that man regularly inflicted upon her sister was unforgivable. However, her sister continued to put on a brave face, for the alternative, as Marie now knew, could be far worse.

Marie now turned her thoughts to her own husband, hoping this would improve her chances of falling asleep. She had been so lucky in finding the perfect gentleman in Raymond. Although he was much older than she, by twenty-five years, and only six years younger than her father, Marie was the happiest person in the world and knew she had made the right decision.

In 1935, when Marie was only ten, Raymond and his first wife were taking trips to Australia. His first wife was a journalist and he a publicist at this time. Raymond had also been working as an organising secretary for a village settlement in Cambridge, where a self-contained village had been built for 1,000 tuberculous patients and their families to live and work in. Six years after their marriage they had a son, but sadly he had died aged nine, ironically from an infectious disease. By this time Raymond was no longer living with his wife and they'd had their marriage dissolved. He had explained to Marie that he and his first wife had both been very work driven and because of work commitments hardly saw one another and had drifted apart. He had then moved to Knightsbridge with his work and later into a flat on Dolphin Square after the war. It had been here where they had met in 1954.

Marie had thought she was the luckiest person in the world to have secured her one-bedroom flat in Beatty House. She had at this time found herself a job in the Westminster area of London and could afford to rent a small flat for herself. Her mother had by then moved to Hampshire to be with Betty, and Marie's new flat provided the security and social inclusion she so desperately needed at this time.

Dolphin Square was comprised of thirteen blocks of self-contained flats, designed in the Art Deco style, with landscaped gardens. Each of these blocks was named after a famous seafarer—Marie's being named after David Beatty, a decorated admiral of the Royal Navy. Dolphin Square boasted a swimming pool, gymnasium, petrol station, underground car park, car wash, court gardens, children's nursery, restaurant and bar.

Her next-door neighbour just happened to be Raymond, a writer and conductor of music whose piano she could hear being played daily and whose music she joked had drawn her in like a moth to a flame. There was an instant attraction, a friendship was formed and the pair quickly spent more and more time in each other's company. Marie had never looked back. Their relationship was so very different to that of Betty and Fred's.

With Marie's feelings of contentment came feelings of guilt. It had been difficult for her to show her true emotions about Raymond whenever she was around Betty because her sister had endured such a difficult time of it. At first she had not told Betty about the new man in her life, with it being at the same time that Betty was seeking a divorce. It would have been unfair to have danced happily around in front of her sister, whose life was in pieces, shouting about the love she had for this wonderful man, which is what she had really wanted to do.

It was difficult to believe that only two years ago her mother, Betty, Juliet and Rupert had all made the trip to London for her and Raymond's wedding. 1955 had started out so well for them all. It had held such promise. Marie had wonderful memories of that Saturday in January. She had asked both Betty and Juliet to be her bridesmaids and her father had given her away. The day had been cold and snow lay on the ground, but everything had gone smoothly from start to finish.

The registry office in Westminster had been packed, mostly with Raymond's friends. His best man was his best friend, Andrew. A few years younger than Marie's husband, Andrew had made his name as a lyricist in Australia in the 1920s before moving to England where he was now well known as a scriptwriter for radio, cinema and comics. He had written the lyrics to many songs. More recently he'd written a crime series for the radio, and working alongside Raymond, they had become good friends. The pair of them had treated Marie like a princess on her wedding day.

At a small reception afterwards, their guests too had been treated like royalty—waited on hand and foot, with all of their requests met without delay. Raymond had seen to it that Marie's day had been perfect. Juliet had excelled herself, fussing over her aunt with confidence, and Betty was clearly glowing with pride for her daughter. The photographs taken on the day showed them all laughing and having fun. Guests who did not know Marie and her family could never have suspected the secrets they were keeping hidden.

Marie and Raymond had not returned from honeymoon long, or even had chance to settle into married life in Beatty House, before news of Fred's death reached them. Marie left London to be by her sister's side, but she didn't stay for long. Betty had been desperate to get on with her life once Fred was no longer around. She longed for some normality, and Marie did not overstay her welcome. It was almost as though Betty knew that her time left was going to be short and wanted to make the most of every day.

Marie knew Fred had nothing to do with her sister's death, but if he had still been alive at the time, she may have thought differently, especially as his first wife had also drowned. She couldn't help wondering about Fred's first wife. She had been very young at the time of her disappearance, but she had read all about it in the newspaper, and Betty and her father were always talking about the inquest with her mother at the dinner table.

The more she'd read about the death of Fred's first wife, the more suspicious she had become. She had kept all of the newspaper cuttings from that time, and when Fred and Betty had divorced, she had found them again and studied them. She had become quite obsessed with it all. She couldn't understand why a woman suffering with depression after having a child, who's flat was so untidy and disorganised and who was about to commit suicide, would take off her coat and gloves and leave them neatly folded beside the water's edge. Surely, if a person was in such terrible turmoil, they would either leave their coat and gloves on to enter the water or just let them drop to the floor in a heap. You wouldn't spend time folding your coat neatly, would you? And how does a grown woman drown in just three and a half feet of water anyway? She knew the woman couldn't swim, but Marie thought this must be near impossible and found it highly suspicious.

Then there was the note and the woman's handbag. Wouldn't you take your handbag with you? If the woman had gone round to her neighbour with her child in a pram to ask her to look after the baby, wouldn't she have her handbag with her? Wouldn't she then have left it with her coat and gloves at the edge of the pond? But Fred had apparently found it on a chair in their flat. There were also the words of the suicide note that didn't quite ring true for Marie. 'You have been wonderful. No blame attached to you' appeared to exemplify Fred from any blame for his wife's actions. It all seemed too convenient to Marie.

And had he anything to do with his baby's death? Could he have made the child's illness worse in some way, causing his first wife to become concerned and take it to the hospital? Knowing Fred as she did now, it certainly seemed feasible that he would not have wanted to have been lumbered with the responsibility of a young baby to bring up.

Marie had gone round and round in circles with these thoughts for months after the inquest and again after her sister's divorce. She had never said anything to Betty or either of her parents or Raymond about the matter, nor to the police. She thought they would all think she was being ridiculous. In any case, there was nothing anyone could do now, as Fred was dead.

But what if she was right? What if there was more to the story and Fred had done something terrible back then. What if she had mentioned her concerns to the police at the time and they had discovered that Fred had been involved? Would her sister still be alive today? Would her mother? None of these terrible things would ever have happened to her family because Fred would have been punished. Fred would have received the death penalty.

***

Daylight was squeezing through the bedroom curtains, and Marie had not slept a wink. How had it all come to this? Only two weeks ago she was in West Germany with Raymond and Andrew. They had been attending a song contest for which Andrew had written the lyrics and Raymond the music. The evening had been enjoyable, if not a little tense at times, but the result had been disappointing, as their song had only scored six points, coming seventh place out of the ten contenders.

Raymond had sat for many hours at the piano in their flat working on the tune, and she had been there supporting and encouraging him. The result on the night hadn't deterred her from continuing to adore his song, which now started to play in her head on a loop. She found herself humming the tune then singing the lyrics, while next to her Raymond opened his eyes slowly and smiled.

"What a delightful way to be woken in the morning." He glanced at his watch. "Even if it is only six-thirty."

Then Marie heard the children's voices. Marie's life would have to remain on hold a little longer. Her nieces and nephews had to come first. She thanked God that she knew she could rely on her husband to help her though this distressing time.

Juliet

Juliet truly hated her life. How she had appeared so happy and positive to everyone over the years, hiding her secret so well, was impossible to ascertain. She had suffered greatly, mentally and emotionally, through no fault of her own because of the cruelty imposed upon her by her father.

The one person who should have protected her was the one person who had controlled, threatened and abused her all her life. But he also loved her, in his own way, and this was what had made it all the more difficult for her when he had left. At that time, she had hated her mother with such passion it frightened her, and now she deeply regretted how she had treated her. She had never had the chance to apologise to her. She had left that too late.

From an early age Juliet had blamed herself when things had gone wrong. She had taken these feelings with her through to puberty. She had been, and remained, too young to realise that none of it was her fault and how adults could be very selfish. When she was younger it was difficult for Juliet to understand her father's actions and words. However, she quickly learnt that when she did as he asked, this was the time he was most kind to her. There had been the odd time when she had refused to do the things he'd wanted her to do. On these occasions her father had been cruel with his words, threatened to tell her mother and hurt her for her unwillingness to comply with his request. She had quickly learnt never to refuse her father's demands.

Appreciating the intricacies of adult relationships was impossible for Juliet when she was little. Juliet's father could get angry, losing his temper quickly. She had always believed it was her mother's fault. It seemed that Juliet's mother would go out of her way to antagonise her father. He would then shout and often storm out of the house, leaving her mother usually in tears and Juliet attempting to offer some

284

comfort. She resented her mother during these times because she thought her mother had brought it all upon herself.

Juliet believed that when her mother was patient with her father, he could be the best husband and father in the world. He would buy her mother flowers, and she would catch them laughing together about something silly. Juliet enjoyed the times when her father would read to her, buy her sweets or take her to the park. It was during times like these that Juliet believed they were just the same as every other family in the world. But Juliet's puerile understanding of her situation when she was younger was very different from reality.

Juliet's father had started to sexually abuse her from around the age of six. He had begun by making Juliet feel that she was special and important, allowing her to believe that he was frightened of losing her. He told her it had to remain their secret because her mother and other people would not understand how they felt about each other and would try to stop them from being together.

When Juliet was young, she did not mind her father's company in her bedroom at night. She took pleasure from his attentions and he was always gentle with her. As the abuse increased over the years, Juliet would often lie in bed at night praying her father would not come into her room. Most nights she was unable to sleep until she was sure that he was not going to pay her a visit.

Juliet suffered with nightmares and found it difficult to get to sleep. She often felt angry and would sometimes take out her frustrations on her younger siblings, especially Rupert. This was most likely because the abuse had started around the time of his birth.

As the abuse continued and escalated, Juliet had tried to stop her father on a couple of occasions, but he'd threatened her and told her that something terrible would happen to her or her mother if she told anyone. He explained that her mother would no longer love or want to look after Juliet if she ever found out what Juliet and her father had been doing.

Juliet's father would make her promises when they were alone and then never fulfil them. The one person Juliet believed loved her more than anyone else could be cruel and would often tease her when her mother wasn't around. She grew to believe she could not trust any adults, especially men. It had been her father who had taken away her childhood, yet she would not realise this until she was much older.

Juliet's situation reached crisis point shortly after her tenth birthday when her mother had confronted her about her relationship with her father. At this point Juliet's life seemed to crumble and fall away. Piece by piece, what she had thought to be true turned out to be a lie, and nothing would ever be the same again.

Juliet soon came to believe that it was her fault her father had left and her fault her mother wanted a divorce. Juliet's mother chose not to share with her daughter information about the court case she had brought against her husband. She had done everything she possibly could to protect her daughter from this discovery. She did not wish her daughter to have to suffer any more unnecessary distress, but her mother really had no idea of the magnitude of guilt which Juliet harboured surrounding her father's actions.

In an attempt to start afresh, Juliet's mother moved her family into a small, semi-detached house within the village of Brambleton. At the same time, Juliet's grandmother had also moved in with them. There were plenty of bedrooms and space for everyone. Their new home had a small garden, but her brothers and sister tended to play on the large grassy area situated opposite the house. Many a game of cricket was played there with the friends they made in the local area.

Juliet's mother seemed far happier once her grandmother was living with the family, as she was able to make more time for herself. She had remained friends with the woman from their previous home at White Gates and also with another army family. Her mother was always back and forth from Richard and Molly's home.

At last Juliet and her mother were able to start rebuilding their relationship. Juliet felt able to confide in her mother and trust her more with her thoughts, feelings and fears. She had started her periods and they'd had a conversation about growing up, which had opened up a more adult and personal relationship between the two of them, bringing them closer together. Soon her mother had been able to convince Juliet that none of what had happened had been her fault and all blame lay with her father. Both Juliet and her mother had been treated appallingly by Juliet's father, but together they were gaining in strength and her mother was convinced they would go on to have a much happier life without him.

It appeared that her mother's belief was realised when in January 1955 Juliet, Rupert, her mother and grandmother all travelled by train to London for her aunt's wedding. Her Aunt Marie was to marry a musician and composer, and her mother had told her that he was a gentleman and very well off. Juliet was excited because she and her mother had been asked to be bridesmaids. They were to wear the most beautiful silk dresses. It proved to be the most perfect day—one filled with love and laughter. A day when she could forget what had happened with her father, as most of the guests there did not know of her terrible secret.

The January day was chilly, and her aunt's new husband and his best man had seen to it that they had not stood outside the registry office for too long for photographs. Her aunt had looked beautiful, and Juliet had fussed over her, helping her with her lace veil and holding her bouquet while she signed the register. The reception afterwards was packed with her aunt's friends, and they had all—including the children—been treated like royalty and the food had been delicious.

Juliet had felt grown up that day—positive and confident. She had comforted her grandmother when she'd cried in the registry office and kept her younger brother occupied when he had become bored at the reception. Her mother had told Juliet how very proud she was of her. A couple of weeks later they were able to relive the happy occasion and share their memories when her mother received an album full of wedding photographs. Her aunt had sent them through the post. On every picture they were all smiling and enjoying themselves. Juliet wished her life could remain this happy forever more. But life often had a habit of not working out the way you would like it to.

It had been just as she and her mother were beginning to draw a line under what had happened to them that Juliet's father brought all the familiar feelings of guilt, hatred and resentment flooding back into their lives when he had taken his own life by gassing himself. Her mother had attempted to protect her siblings from their father's actions by keeping the circumstances of his death secret, but she had felt she owed it to Juliet to be more honest and shared some of the details with her.

Juliet was horrified about what her father had done and once again blamed herself. But her mother and grandmother had put an abrupt stop to these thoughts. She was quickly made to realise that what her father had done had been *his* choice, and his alone. But Juliet hated him for it. How could a man do this to his children? He obviously had no concern for the emotions of any of them. To put them through so much heartache was utterly despicable.

Her mother had been forced to attend a hearing and identify her father's body, which must have been dreadful. Juliet felt as though her father was laughing at them all, and this made her angry. She took this anger out on the ones she loved: her mother, her grandmother and her siblings.

Once again it was her mother who was there for her, picking up the pieces and gluing her back together. How was her mother still so strong after everything she had been through? Juliet wished she was more like her mother and grandmother: more resilient. How many times was one family expected to suffer then get back up, brush themselves down and get back on with life? This had to be the final hurdle. Surely.

Five months later Juliet was forced to deal with her mother's death. It came as an enormous shock to learn that her mother had drowned. The day after, she could remember running from the house, unable to see where she was running to, for the tears pouring from her eyes were so endless. She ran across farmers' fields, through hedges and between trees, trying desperately to escape the feelings of despair which were consuming her whole being.

***

Some time later she found herself three miles away in Stowerby. There she collapsed on the green outside the White Lion public house, and one of the patrons took pity on her and brought her out a cold drink.

There were people everywhere. The weather had brought them all out. She couldn't seem to escape their inquisitive glances, and all she could think about was how on earth she was going to continue without her mother. She sipped the cool drink slowly, all the while trying to regain her composure and telling herself that everything was going to be all right and she would get through this.

Juliet had almost managed to pull herself together when she spotted a man who she thought looked familiar. He headed out of the pub and was walking across the green in her direction. Her stomach did a somersault and she thought she was about to be sick. The man looked so similar to her father and he was still heading straight towards her. Juliet was frozen to the spot. She could not move. She could not stand. The man was getting closer and he was definitely heading towards her. Then he smiled at her and she panicked.

Gathering all her strength, she jumped up, dropping the glass she had been holding, and with all the speed she could muster, she ran and ran until she was almost back in Brambleton. Not once did she dare to glance back over her shoulder, but thankfully the man appeared not to have followed her. Her grandmother had sent out a search party after a couple of hours of her not returning, but by then she was already making her way back home.

When Juliet arrived home, she headed straight for her bedroom. On her bedside table she kept a treasure pot. It was a small round pot with a liftable lid, where she kept little treasures which reminded her of happier times. She would always go through the contents of this pot whenever she felt upset by something.

Juliet had a number of coins which reminded her of days out, fragments of pottery she had found in the garden at White Gates and a couple of buttons: one from an old coat she had loved as a child and another which she had been allowed to keep from her mother's sewing box many years ago. She had been drawn to this particular button because of its iridescent colours. She turned them all over individually in her hands, spending time with each one and remembering its significance.

Juliet came across a brown leather button. She had no memory of this item before today or how it had come to be in her pot, but she was sure it had belonged to him. She could remember his coat. She lifted the button to her nose and sniffed. She recognised his smell. He must have put it there, which meant her father had been in her room and inside the house. She felt sick. How could this be? He was dead. Her mind must be playing tricks on her. It was impossible. But what if it wasn't?

Juliet rummaged inside a draw for a piece of paper and pen. She ripped a small amount of paper from the notepad. Then she wrote, 'I know you've been here. I know what you did.' She folded the paper very small, and along with the rest of her treasures, she returned them all safely to the pot and replaced the lid. Surely her imagination was running away with itself, but just in case it wasn't and there was a small chance her suspicions were correct, she wanted him to know.

***

After her mother passed away, her grandmother did what she could for Juliet and her brothers and sister, but she was not their mother and they all missed their mother desperately. Juliet's younger siblings didn't understand and they clung to their grandmother for reassurance. But Juliet's grandmother was in her seventies and no longer in good health, so her care was limited.

When her grandmother's health deteriorated further during the winter of 1956, Juliet wondered what would become of them all if she too were to die. They would be orphans. Might it be left to Juliet to care for her younger siblings? She would be fourteen soon. She only had one more year left at school. But her grandmother's death came sooner than she had anticipated.

Members of her extended family descended on her family home in March 1957—the same ones who had attended her mother's funeral less than two years before. She had been relieved when her aunt had arrived, but she too was terribly upset, although she had her husband with her for support. Juliet began to feel completely alone in the world. There appeared to be no one left who could help her through this latest tragedy. What would become of her and her brothers and sister now? Who would look after them? Where would they go?

Juliet found she could not cry over her grandmother's death—not even during her funeral. She thought she must have no tears left after having to deal with the loss of her parents and what her father had put her through. She never wanted to cry again.

After the funeral everyone went back to the semi-detached house. Juliet was left to entertain all the children in the back room while the adults sat drinking tea in the front of the house. Her aunt entered intermittently with plates of sandwiches and cakes, but she was being ignored otherwise. Obviously, none of the adults felt she was old enough to join them in the front room.

Juliet became bored with looking after her charges and stood in the hallway attempting to overhear the conversation that was being had in the front room. But it was useless. The adults in there were all talking in whispers, and she could only make out the occasional word from the other side of the door.

Later the house guests began to disperse and she helped her aunt get the younger children ready for bed. Once in bed herself, her aunt came in to kiss her goodnight, explaining that she was too tired to discuss it tonight, but tomorrow they would talk about what might happen to them all. Juliet was left to wonder all night, getting very little sleep. When she did finally drift off, she dreamt of her father.

The following morning her aunt was true to her word. The younger children were sent to play outside on the green, as it was a sunny day, and their uncle was charged with keeping an eye on them. Juliet and her aunt made themselves comfortable in the front room. Juliet listened patiently to her aunt explain the many reasons why she and her siblings would not be able to live with her or their grandfather. She couldn't help feeling that her aunt was coming up with excuses.

"We think it will be best if we can find all of you a new home with a new mother and father."

"Separate us?"

"No, darling. No, that's not what I meant at all. I mean stay together in a new home."

"But whoever they are will be strangers," argued Juliet.

"At first they will, darling, but if we can get it right, they won't feel like strangers for long."

"Where will you find them? And how will you know if they are going to be a good mother and father to us?"

"I'm going to be completely honest with you now, Juliet. You've been through too much heartache already during your short life. You don't need any more uncertainty. Nevertheless, the truth is I don't know. And there are no guarantees."

Juliet was surprised by her aunt's frankness.

"We plan to do the absolute best we possibly can for you all," continued her aunt. "You like Richard, don't you?"

"Yes. He and Molly were good friends to Mum. Their children are sweet too," replied Juliet.

"Richard thinks he knows of a couple who would like to be parents to you all. A new mum and dad. It's early days, but we should know soon if they would like to meet you all."

"What happens if we don't like them?" asked Juliet.

"We will just have to wait and see. They might not like you."

Juliet had not been expecting that response from her aunt, and her aunt noticed Juliet's face dramatically change.

"If this couple does not work out for whatever reason, then we will just keep looking until everyone is happy."

"Honestly?"

"I promise," replied her aunt. "I cannot tell you how important it is to us all that all four of you are happy and that we find you the best new home and parents possible."

Juliet believed her aunt was being genuine and leaned forward to embrace her.

"Now, you're not to worry. We will try to let you know what will be happening before it does, and if you have any questions, you just come and find me. All right?"

Juliet nodded.

"I'm not going anywhere just yet. Not until I know you're happy."

"Promise?"

"I promise."

But right at that moment, Juliet remained unsure. She wanted to trust her aunt, but trusting any adult was difficult for her. The only thing she was sure of was that she still hated her life!

Lightning Source UK Ltd.
Milton Keynes UK
UKHW010628040122
396592UK00001B/33